PENGUIN BOOKS

COLLECTED STORIES: BERYL BAINBRIDGE

Beryl Bainbridge was born in Liverpool in 1934 but now lives in north London. She was an actress before she began to write. She is the author of seventeen novels, three works of non-fiction and six plays for stage and television. Her books, *The Dressmaker* and *An Awfully Big Adventure*, have been made into films. Her recent work includes *Every Man for Himself*, which was shortlisted for the Booker Prize in 1996 and won the Whitbread Novel of the Year Prize in 1997, and *Master Georgie*, which was shortlisted for the Booker Prize in 1998 and won the W. H. Smith Literary Award and the James Tait Black Memorial Prize in 1999.

Of her books Penguin publish *Another Part of the Wood*; *Harriet Said*; *The Dressmaker*; *The Bottle Factory Outing*, which won the *Guardian* Fiction Award; *Sweet William*; *A Quiet Life*; *Injury Time*, which was awarded the Whitbread Prize; *Young Adolf*; *Winter Garden*; *Watson's Apology*; *Collected Stories*; *An Awfully Big Adventure*, which was shortlisted for the Booker Prize; and *The Birthday Boys*, shortlisted for the Whitbread Award.

Beryl Bainbridge is divorced with three grown-up children and two grandchildren.

BERYL BAINBRIDGE

COLLECTED STORIES

PENGUIN BOOKS

PENGUIN BOOKS

Published by the Penguin Group
Penguin Books Ltd, 27 Wrights Lane, London w8 5tz, England
Penguin Books USA Inc., 375 Hudson Street, New York, New York 10014, USA
Penguin Books Australia Ltd, Ringwood, Victoria, Australia
Penguin Books Canada Ltd, 10 Alcorn Avenue, Toronto, Ontario, Canada m4v 3b2
Penguin Books (NZ) Ltd, 182–190 Wairau Road, Auckland 10, New Zealand

Penguin Books Ltd, Registered Offices: Harmondsworth, Middlesex, England

Mum and Mr Armitage first published by Gerald Duckworth & Co. 1985
'Eric on the Agenda' first published in *Bananas* 1975
'The Man from Wavertree' first published in the *Liverpool Daily Post* 1976
'Evensong' first published in *Unnatural Causes* by Javelin Books 1986
'Poles Apart' first published in *The Penguin Book of Modern British Short Stories* 1987
'The Beast in the Tower' first published in Penguin Books 1994
'Kiss Me, Hardy' first published in Penguin Books 1994
Filthy Lucre first published by Gerald Duckworth & Co. 1986
This collection first published in Penguin Books 1994

2

Copyright © Beryl Bainbridge, 1975, 1976, 1985, 1986, 1987, 1994
All rights reserved

The moral right of the author has been asserted

Filmset by Datix International Limited, Bungay, Suffolk
Printed in England by Clays Ltd, St Ives plc
Set in 11/13 pt Monophoto Baskerville

CONTENTS

HOW I BEGAN

My father and mother bickered a lot, which is why, there being no such thing as television to distract one, or any other room in which to escape from the raised voices, my mother encouraged my natural inclination to scribble in notebooks.

I began to write stories when I was eight years old – about an old sea-dog called Cherry Blossom Bill who kept his rum supply in his wooden leg. This was not unusual; most of my school-friends kept diaries, wrote poems or composed little playlets, though these had mainly to do with fairies living inside marigolds. Writing was more beneficial an occupation to us than attending a psychiatric clinic, should such a place have existed, and helped to get rid of anxieties nurtured by the particularly restricted sort of upbringing common to lower-class girls in wartime England. It says a lot for my mother that she was always more than ready to clear the table so that I could get down to my next chapter. If I worked for more than two hours she would say, 'Run out into the garden, pet. All authors must play.'

I began a novel when I was ten, but circumstances had forced me to destroy it before it was completed. I had bought a book on Livingstone's travels in Africa, a volume as big as a family bible, its pages tipped with gold leaf. I wrote my epic on pieces of exercise paper and glued them with flour-and-water paste to the existing pages. Apart from the sacrilege of defacing such a beautiful book, this attempt at secrecy was useless. In no time at all the flour swelled and the book refused to close. I was alarmed that my mother would find it and read the contents – it was an in-depth account of what I thought of her life with my father – and I didn't want to hurt her. I coated the book with dripping, put it in the bin on the path at the side of the house and set light to it. The back door caught fire.

For three years I contented myself with writing short stories to do with a lonely boy who roamed the seashore talking to seagulls. I repeated sentences in the manner of D. H. Lawrence and grew lyrical about the dark blood of the senses. Then I saw *The Thief of Bagdad* at the local picture house and launched into more exotic, carpet-flying tales.

It seemed to me, even then, that a short story was a waste of a good idea, and so I began *Filthy Lucre*. It owes a lot, undeniably, to Dickens and to Robert Louis Stevenson, two authors I was reading at the time. The character of the legless Robert Straffordson is obviously one up on Long John Silver.

I was dissatisfied with the result, mainly because it wasn't 'real life' and I had invented the characters and the plot. I don't think I have ever invented anything since. Reading it now I am of the opinion that writing is very like music, in the sense that if you hear a song often enough it becomes impossible not to go on humming the same tune. I also feel that I must have had a macabre sense of humour, because the best bits – personally speaking – have to do with either death or murder. I don't remember reading anything about the Chinese Opium War, although my father was always raving about the Yellow Peril, and I can't think where I got such a puritanical view of drinking. My poor father and mother hardly touched a drop except for a port-and-lemon at Christmas.

I still think short stories are a waste of a good idea, which is why some of the stories in the collection ended up as television plays or full-length novels.

B. B.

MUM AND MR ARMITAGE

For Charlie and Bertie Russell

MUM AND MR ARMITAGE

Being elderly, Miss Emmet, the thin lady from the Midlands, expected to be left out of things. And she was. Some of the younger guests – Walter Hood for instance, whose mother had recently died, and the girl who had served in the Land Army during the war and was wearing a halter-top in spite of the weather – took it badly.

'I think it's downright rude,' the girl said, when for the third evening on the trot the regular crowd went off into the library to play cards, jamming their chairs so tightly against the door that it was impossible for anyone else to join them.

'I've never even set foot in the library,' complained Walter Hood. 'They're in there every blessed minute.'

Thinking that six shelves stacked with detective novels hardly constituted a library, Miss Emmet said Goodnight and went up to her room. But for the smoke that billowed out from the hearth as she closed the door the young people would scarcely have noticed she was gone.

'Perhaps things will get better when Mum and Mr Armitage arrive,' the land-girl said. She felt brighter just mentioning their names.

The regular crowd who frequented the Herbert Arms Hotel Christmas, Easter and summer never stopped talking among themselves about Mum and Mr Armitage. What good sports they were! What fun they were to be with! Life hummed when Mum was in the vicinity. Her real name was Rosemary Mumford, but nobody ever called her that. At least, not after she became a widow. In the middle of the war she had received one of those telegrams regretting that her husband was missing, believed killed. He had last

been seen above Düsseldorf, baling out of a blazing Wellington bomber. It was thought that he and Mum had spent
their honeymoon at the hotel, in No. 4, the big room at the
front with the brass bed by the window and the stuffed
stoat on the mantelpiece. They had returned again the
following year, in summer. Mum had known the area as a
child; her uncle, it was said, had been in charge of the mine
over at Marton. When she was little Mum had gone down
the mine with a candle attached to her helmet.

The stoat had been ensconced in the front bedroom for
the last ten years, out of consideration for Mum's feelings.
It had previously stood, impaled on a stick on a bed of
withered bracken and encased in glass, on the window-sill
in the library, until, the Christmas after she had received
the telegram, Mum had knocked the case to the ground,
shattering the glass. It was assumed it was not an accident.
Bits of stuffing had come out of the stoat and Mr White
had hidden it out of sight in the front bedroom so as not to
cause Mum further aggravation. It obviously reminded her
of her husband.

There was even talk that Mum had undergone one of
those breakdowns peculiar to arty types, that she had
actually been put into hospital; although some argued that
it was more physical than mental, or rather that something
had happened, while her mind was temporarily distracted
with grief, which had resulted in an injury. What sort of
injury, no one could say. It was all very much a matter of
conjecture, and so long ago.

That she had loved Mr Mumford, to the extent that life
without him had no longer seemed worth living, went
without saying. Of course, this was simply the opinion
voiced by women members of the regular crowd. Their
menfolk, if trapped in the discussion, either looked sheepish
or instantly remembered something pressing that had to be
done.

Certain people, Annie Lambert for one, swore she remembered that week in June when Mum had stayed at the hotel with her husband, though for the life of her she couldn't describe what he had looked like, or how tall he was. Nor was she sure of his name. 'Bert', she thought – or perhaps it was 'Stanley'. It was an ordinary sort of name. And she had an inkling that he may have been an insurance agent before he was drafted into the RAF. Not a door-to-door salesman; something a bit grander than that, as one might expect.

'What sort of fellow?' people asked.

'Ordinary,' she said. 'Definitely ordinary.'

'Was he very demonstrative?' Molly Berwick had wanted to know.

'It's a blank,' Annie confessed. 'But I think he called her Rosemary.'

Most people didn't even know her proper name. She had always been Mum to the crowd at the hotel. Not that she was motherly – far from it. True, she was well built, but they all agreed that the twinkle in her coquettish eyes was neither matronly nor maternal. Her friend Mr Armitage, who had cropped up a year or so after her husband went missing, was the perfect partner for her. Not that they were partners except in the companionable sense. Mum certainly wasn't his fancy woman; she wasn't that sort of person, though it was obvious that he thought the world of her. He never addressed her as anything else than Mum, and the others followed suit because Mr Armitage was such a card. They both were. You could bowl people down with a feather, people who weren't in the know, when they heard him calling her Mum, because he looked old enough to be her father. Really, it was comical.

Guests often told the proprietor, Austin White, that he ought to give Mum and Mr Armitage a discount, on account of their entertainment value. In theory, he felt they had a point. They were indeed splendid company, and although a fortnight at the hotel, with full board, was very reasonable, the atmosphere was never quite the same without Mum and Mr Armitage. The things they got up to! The tricks they played! The land-girl had been staying at the hotel for a week now and knew most of the stories by heart. There was the Easter when Mr Armitage painted the horns of all the cows with some sort of luminous paint and then let them loose from their stalls after dark just as Captain Lewis from the Pennines, who'd had a harrowing experience at Arnhem, had come cycling back from the pictures in Welshpool. He was so surprised that he rode his bike into the ditch and cricked his neck. And another time, in the summer probably, Mum had organised a midnight bathing party down at the river and no one had worn costumes, not even the retired bank manager from Norfolk who had some sort of disfigurement and wouldn't have gone naked if Mum hadn't hidden his bathing trunks. That was the marvellous thing about Mum and Mr Armitage – everyone became part of the fun, no one was allowed to stand on the sidelines. To crown it all, there had been a full moon. The stories were endless.

Last night, at supper, someone had complimented Mr White on the floral arrangements, and Albert Ward, one of the regular crowd, had picked up a rose and held it between his teeth. He had caused a riot at the table. Apparently it reminded everybody of the year they had gone with Mum to the flower show at Powys Castle, when Mum had dressed up as a Spanish dancer and persuaded that woman from Manchester, the one with the goitre, to climb . . . but the rest of the story had been lost in uproar, and shortly afterwards the regular crowd had left the table and shut themselves up as usual in the library.

'Did you catch what happened the day of the flower show?' the land-girl asked Walter Hood.

'Someone fell,' he said.

'Who?' she asked. But he was looking down at the mourning band on his arm and his eyes were watering.

The next day, shortly before teatime, Miss Emmet was sitting in her mackintosh in the little garden at the side of the hotel, pressing wild flowers between the pages of her nature book, when she was startled to see a procession of guests trooping through the French windows on to the lawn; some of them had obviously just risen from an afternoon nap, because they were still in dressing-gowns and slippers. The man they called Albert Ward was wearing a tea-cosy on his head. From within the hotel came the boom of the dinner gong, struck with frenzy and accompanied by laughter.

'Is it a fire?' asked Miss Emmet, alarmed.

Outside the hotel a dozen people had assembled on the road. Mr and Mrs Hardwick were attempting to keep their children under control, lining them up according to height beneath the library window. One of their daughters, the tomboy child with the plaits, was stabbing a fork into the wistaria which, only yesterday, the proprietor had so carefully and protectively tethered behind a complicated cat's cradle of string. Molly Berwick, the schoolteacher from Huddersfield, and her friend Annie Lambert were standing to attention against the church wall; they had been over at the bowling green and Mrs Lambert still held the jack. As usual, her friend had a cigarette stuck to her lip.

'Eyes front, girls,' shouted Albert Ward, and he ran into the yard at the back of the hotel and returned with the mucking-out brush, carrying it over his shoulder as though it was a rifle. He began to parade backwards and forwards in front of the porch, barking out military commands like a madman. The diversion this caused gave Mr Hardwick, smiling broadly, the opportunity to snatch the fork from his daughter's hand and smack her quite brutally over the head.

'Whatever is going on?' demanded Miss Emmet, perplexed. She couldn't understand why the child with the plaits wasn't howling.

Then suddenly the two middle-aged men from Wigan – they were always referred to as 'the lads' – who habitually wore shorts, even at supper, and who had been hogging the most comfortable seats in the lounge ever since lunch, snoring, and dangling their speckled legs over the arms of the chintz sofa, rode out of the yard on their tandem bicycle. Wobbling somewhat before gathering speed, they pedalled off down the road towards the hump-backed bridge. The Hardwick children ran in pursuit, whooping like Indians. From the churchyard came a tremendous clatter as rooks lifted from the tops of the elm trees and swooped across the sky.

'Is it a race?' persisted Miss Emmet, not expecting an answer. A few moments later a faint cheer rose from beyond the bridge, and then Mr White's black car, horn tooting like the devil, appeared round the bend of the lane, flanked by the tandem and the screaming children.

'They're here,' shouted Mollie Berwick, stamping her muddy plimsolls up and down on the puddled road. It was hard to believe that she was a teacher.

'They're here,' echoed Annie Lambert, and she sent the jack hurtling like a cannonball into the hedge.

The regular crowd surged forwards. Without a second's hesitation the land-girl ran behind, clapping her hands.

Miss Emmet went back into the garden. Collecting her nature book from the bench, she let herself out by the wicket gate and set off in the direction of the village. She could hear the telegraph wires humming, high and quivering above her head. Unaccountably, after days of rain the sun came out.

When Miss Emmet returned some hours later, the gong had already sounded for supper. The din from the dining-room could be heard outside on the road. As a general rule she would have gone without food rather than sit down at the table in her walking clothes, but there was a delicious smell of casseroled rabbit above the scent of roses in the garden and her long tramp in the sunshine had increased her appetite. She didn't think she would look out of place in her tweed skirt; the majority of the guests seemed to favour casual attire of one sort or another. On the night of her arrival, when she had come downstairs in one of her two silk frocks, Albert Ward had remarked that they didn't stand on ceremony at the Herbert Arms Hotel. 'So I gather,' Miss Emmet had replied, for she had found herself seated next to the stouter of the two 'lads', and when she bent to pick up her napkin which had fallen to the floor, she inadvertently brushed his hairy leg with her arm. He had made some innuendo, and one or two people had sniggered. She had pretended to be amused.

Miss Emmet went round the front of the hotel into the yard and through the scullery door. Fortunately she had left her court shoes in the cellar when changing into her brogues that morning. The spaniel dog was nosing its tin bowl across the flagstones, ferociously lapping water. Miss Emmet kept her distance. It was not that she was afraid of dogs, simply that she disliked not being able to tell at a glance whether they be friend or foe. It was difficult, she felt, to trust anyone, man or beast, whose eyes gave nothing away. Washing the blackberry stains from her hands at the scullery sink, she went down the passage to change her shoes.

She was just stooping to undo her laces when she realised that she was not alone. There was a man in the cellar, standing on a three-legged stool among the barrels of beer, doing something to the trap door in the ceiling. She was flustered, and stared at him quite rudely.

'Sssh,' the man warned, and he tapped the side of his

nose meaningfully with his little finger. Miss Emmet was taken aback. All the same, she found herself going on tiptoe out of the cellar. She was leaning awkwardly against the larder door, one shoe off and one on, when he came after her. 'Joke time,' he whispered. 'It will be our little secret.' And he bounded off down the passage in his striped blazer.

It was difficult for Miss Emmet to get to sleep that night. The noise from the rooms below, the shouting, the gusts of laughter, continued well into the small hours, long after the public bar had closed and the last customer had relieved himself against the cowshed wall beneath her window and gone squelching away up the muddy yard.

As soon as supper had finished, Mr Armitage, assisted by Albert Ward and supervised by Mum, had shoved the long table to the far end of the dining-room before carrying the oval table through from the library.

'What game are we playing?' the regular crowd had wanted to know, bumping into each other and ferrying chairs from one corner to another. Miss Emmet hadn't waited to find out.

Whatever sort of game it was, it was obviously complicated and of long duration. At one point it necessitated the singing of a negro spiritual, at which the spaniel set up a melancholy howling. It woke the collie dog in its kennel. Though Miss Emmet stuffed her fingers into her ears she still heard the brute's strangled yelps as it hurled itself the length of its chain beyond the pig-sty. Shortly before dawn she thought there was a sound of glass breaking.

Miss Emmet breakfasted alone. Even the children had not yet come down. Mr White hardly spoke when he brought in the fried bacon. None of the windows appeared to be broken.

At midday Miss Emmet bought some buns at the village shop and ate them in a field down by the river. It was annoying to miss a meal already paid for, but she felt she couldn't face luncheon at the hotel.

Last night at supper both Mum and Mr Armitage had addressed her directly. Mr Armitage had asked her what part of the world she came from, and having been told, declared it a lovely spot, which it wasn't by any stretch of the imagination, being not far from the centre of Wolverhampton and dreadfully built up, and Mum, prompted by some absurd remark of Albert Ward's to the effect that Miss Emmet was a child of nature – always messing about with flowers – had promised to send her a box of geranium cuttings. 'And she means it, you know,' cried the schoolteacher. 'It's not one of those comments thrown out at random. Mum always keeps her word.' Miss Emmet had not doubted her. She had already observed how cleverly Mum apportioned each guest his share of the limelight, how unfailingly she hit upon the one topic that suited – and oh, how unstintingly, without ever taking her attention off the speaker or averting the gaze of those light brown eyes ringed with spiky lashes, she passed the salt, the bread, the greens. Really, she had quite ordinary eyes, but for the moment, hunched beside the river, Miss Emmet thought of them as frightening, not for what they had seen, but for what they hadn't.

Later that afternoon, when she was sitting in the garden waiting for the gong to sound for tea, Miss Emmet overheard the land-girl and Mrs Hardwick discussing the events of the night before. 'It was so unexpected,' Mrs Hardwick was saying. 'I know, I know,' the land-girl said. 'If you ask me, it was uncanny. Uncanny.' And she gave a little scream.

'But such fun,' admitted Mrs Hardwick.

'Not for him,' said the girl and, laughing, they both sat up in their deck chairs and looked guiltily across the garden to where Walter Hood lay on his back in the shade of the hedge.

When they had recovered, Mrs Hardwick called out, 'I

expect it wasn't much fun for you either. I don't suppose *you* got much sleep.'

'I always sleep very soundly,' Miss Emmet said. 'Last night was no exception.'

Mrs Hardwick expressed surprise. 'I thought we made enough racket to raise the dead,' she said.

At which the land-girl started to laugh all over again – in the circumstances it was such an apt remark – and then both she and Mrs Hardwick began to recount the story from the beginning, not so much for Miss Emmet's benefit as because neither of them could bear to let the subject drop.

First Mr Armitage had moved the table from the library into the dining-room; in the process a little bit of wallpaper had been scuffed off from under the light switch, but Mum said it was hardly noticeable. Mr Armitage said that if they wanted to get in touch with the spirit world it was always better to choose the oldest part of a house for the setting. Really they should have gone down into the cellar, but Mr Armitage said it was too difficult to transport the table, so the next best thing was to be in the room directly above. He'd done a lot of it in India apparently, when it was too wet to do anything else.

'When it rained,' interrupted the girl, 'even the books turned mouldy.'

'Not mouldy,' objected Mrs Hardwick. 'Just limp.'

They had tried to get in touch with the spirits, but the wine glass kept spelling out 'Shut up' whenever Albert Ward asked if there was anyone waiting on the other side. It was a scream. Of course some people weren't taking it seriously, and Mum said that was probably what was causing the interference.

'He took it seriously,' the land-girl said, lowering her voice and pointing discreetly at the prone figure on the grass.

'Yes,' said Mrs Hardwick, solemn for the moment, and then she was off again.

The glass had finally whizzed straight off the table and hit the window. Mr White had looked a bit put out, but there was no damage. Then Mum told an eerie story of an aunt of hers who had levitated right up to the rafters during a church service. She was in the choir at the time. So they had all stood in a circle round Molly Berwick and put their hands on top of her head, the way Mr Armitage instructed, and pressed down. They sang 'Shall we gather by the river', because Mr Armitage thought it would help, though not all of them were sure of the words. Nothing happened except that Molly complained of feeling dizzy; that, and of the havoc they were causing to her permanent wave.

'Don't forget the dog,' squealed the girl, and for a time Mrs Hardwick almost choked laughing.

Then Mr Armitage said they ought to stand in a line facing the hearth, on account of the mirror above the fireplace. Mirrors, especially oval ones, were known to be conducive to the appearance of phenomena. If they all stood in a line and really concentrated, particularly the doubting Thomases, perhaps there would be some sign. And by Golly, it worked.

'Oh, it did,' shrieked the girl. 'It did. It was uncanny.'

Mr Armitage had missed it all. He'd just that minute popped out to get himself another gin and tonic, and while he was away the carpet rose in the air. Not all in one piece like in *The Thief of Baghdad* but in the middle. They all saw it. Mr Armitage said afterwards that he could kick himself, missing it like that.

'And then *he* got a bit upset,' whispered the land-girl, winking and gesticulating in the direction of Walter Hood. 'He was moaning. When the carpet fell flat again he got down on his hands and knees to study it. And then suddenly he shouted and clutched his nose. He hadn't been drinking.'

'Something went up it,' explained Mrs Hardwick. 'He said it felt like a bit of wire.'

'He bled,' said the girl.

'Not badly,' protested Mrs Hardwick.

'He called for his mother,' the girl said, and in spite of herself she couldn't stop laughing.

At teatime, and again at supper, Mum apologised to Miss Emmet for the rowdiness of the night before. 'How we must have disturbed you,' she said. 'It was very thoughtless.'

'Please don't mention it,' Miss Emmet had replied on the first occasion, and on the second, 'I may be old, but I hope I'm not a spoil-sport.'

After supper Mum said that she could do with an early night, though it was hard to believe it. She had changed from her matador trousers into a grey costume with square shoulders. In her sling-back shoes, her silk scarf, blood-red, which she wore turban-fashion about her head, she looked ready for a night on the town – had there been one. 'We could all do with an early night,' she insisted, and everyone agreed with her. The land-girl, bitterly disappointed, nodded vehemently.

Miss Emmet was about to go out of the dining-room door when the spaniel padded across the threshold. She stepped aside to let it pass.

'You don't like dogs, do you?' said Mum.

'No, I don't,' Miss Emmet said, and could have bitten off her tongue.

The rest of the week was relatively uneventful. Albert Ward grazed his knees – it had something to do with an egg-and-spoon race organised by Mr Armitage – and one of the Hardwick daughters fell out of an apple tree while watching the bowls tournament. She had been told to stay

on the ground. Luckily Mum broke the child's fall, and one
of her own fingernails in the process. It was ironic really;
the child involved wasn't particularly in favour at the time,
having been caught dragging the stuffed stoat on a piece of
string along the corridor. The child knew perfectly well
that the stoat was anathema to Mum. Everyone did. Fortunately Mum had been out playing tennis. There was also
an incident, recounted to Miss Emmet by the land-girl, in
which someone had dressed up in a white sheet and flit-
ted about the churchyard, frightening the life out of Mrs
Lambert and another guest, who may or may not have had
a heart condition, but no harm resulted.

The land-girl had become almost one of the regular crowd,
though not all of them remembered her name. She had taken
to painting her toenails, and wore turbans, night and day, in
imitation of Mum. On the Sunday, as Miss Emmet was
coming downstairs ready for church, Mr Armitage called out
to her from the bar parlour. He and Mum were without
company for once. Reluctantly she went through to them.
Mr Armitage asked if he might be allowed to buy her a drink.

'Oh, no,' said Miss Emmet. 'I don't drink, and besides
I'm just on my way to church.'

'So are we,' he said. 'There's plenty of time.' And he
took her by the elbow and practically forced her to sit
down. It wasn't yet opening hours and Mr White was out
bell-ringing, but Mr Armitage felt so much at home that he
nipped behind the counter and poured out two gin and
tonics and a glass of lemonade. 'Drink up,' he said, setting
the glass before her. And obediently Miss Emmet sipped at
the fizzy liquid, for, although it was a long time ago, she
had once been used to doing what men told her.

Neither he nor Mum were dressed for church. He wore
his blazer, and Mum was wearing grey flannel trousers and
a jacket to match. Her white turban was printed all over
with the heads of dogs.

17

'We were wondering,' said Mum, 'if you'd care to come for a run this afternoon. Just the three of us. Mr White has offered the loan of his car.'

'Do come,' Mr Armitage urged.

'Well, now,' Miss Emmet told them, 'I was thinking of writing letters.'

'It would give us so much pleasure,' said Mum.

Miss Emmet couldn't help smiling; it was such a ridiculous statement.

Mistaking that smile, Mr Armitage cried out jubilantly, 'Jolly good,' and took the matter as settled.

During morning service Miss Emmet prayed that Mum would think of something better to do with her afternoon. She and Mr Armitage had changed their minds about coming to church, and it was not beyond the bounds of possibility that even at this moment they were driving off into the countryside. But when she came out into the sunshine the first thing she saw was the black motor-car parked against the hedge.

She hardly touched her lunch. Not for years had anyone sought her company, and the thought of two hours, one hundred and twenty minutes, in which Mum and Mr Armitage would give her their undivided attention, interrogating her, raking over all the small details of her life, took away her appetite. She considered hiding in her room. But then, how would she deal with the rest of the week?

Mr Armitage gallantly helped her into the back seat of the car. There was a smell of fertiliser and warm leather. Mum sat at the front. The land-girl hovered in the porch of the hotel, hoping to be included even at this late stage. Mum gave her a cheerful wave as they drove off. A Hardwick child ran with them as far as the corner. 'Little pest,' said Mum.

They took the Marton road towards Corndon and the heather-covered slopes of the mountain, winding uphill between fields of barley hedged with hawthorn.

'What a beautiful day,' said Mr Armitage.

'Beautiful,' murmured Mum, dangling her hand outside the window as though the breeze were the sea. Miss Emmet, with her hat on, said nothing.

They reached a plateau of moorland above Marton. Mr Armitage stopped the car and got out to stretch his legs. Mum appeared to be asleep; her turbaned head lolled against the window. Miss Emmet too fell into a doze. Presently Mr Armitage returned and they drove on.

After perhaps half an hour the car stopped again. Waking, Miss Emmet saw that they were at a crossroads. On her right, some few yards down the lane, stood ornamental gates, flanked by posts topped with stone birds, green with moss. The gates were open.

'Oh, look,' said Mum. 'Do let's go in. I love old houses.'

'We'll be trespassing,' said Mr Armitage, and looking over his shoulder asked Miss Emmet what she thought. Miss Emmet said she had no idea.

'Please,' said Mum. 'We can say we took a wrong turning.'

They drove up a dark avenue of towering rhododendrons, and emerged into the sunlight beside a kitchen garden, beyond which squatted a brick bungalow with vulgar shutters at the windows. An ugly baytree stood in a tub on the brick front step.

'Oh dear,' said Mum. 'How disappointing.'

'They're obviously away,' Mr Armitage said, and he pointed at the runner beans withering on their canes.

'I'd be away if I lived somewhere like that,' remarked Mum, quite fiercely, and Miss Emmet was surprised, for she had imagined Mum as living in just such a house, though without the grounds.

'There's a water tap,' said Mr Armitage. 'And a hose-pipe. Those plants could do with a spot of moisture.' He turned again to Miss Emmet. 'What do you think?'

'Don't be silly,' said Mum.

'It does seem a shame,' Miss Emmet said, looking at the shrunken lettuces, the parched blackcurrant bushes, and making up her mind she opened the car door and struggled out.

'Don't blame me if you're caught,' called Mum.

Miss Emmet had advanced some way down the path towards the water tap – Mr Armitage had not yet left the car – when she heard the dog. Its howl was deep-chested, threatening; it was an awful sound. Miss Emmet froze on the path, clutching her old woman's coat about her, too frightened to breathe. Joke time, she thought, knowing she had been caught.

The Alsatian that bounded round the side of the bungalow was jet-black, huge. It was followed by a smaller, emaciated red setter with a mean and bony head. The ferocity of their barking, the slither of their claws on the gravel as they rounded the fence almost drove Miss Emmet out of her mind. Both dogs stopped ten yards from her, ears flat, teeth bared.

Someone screamed, but it was not Miss Emmet. She was concentrating on the red setter; he was the leader, she was sure of it. If she transmitted her fear the brute would go for her throat. She forced herself to look into its hateful eyes. It lay down on the path, snarling.

Miss Emmet heard the click of the car door as it opened behind her. 'Don't move,' she called out, keeping her voice as steady as she could manage. 'You mustn't move.' She could smell mint in the garden, and thyme, and saw dust spiralling upwards in the sunlight as the dog's heart thumped in its chest against the path.

After minutes had elapsed, or it might have been hours, Miss Emmet began to move backwards in the direction of the car. The setter wrinkled its muzzle and half rose. Miss Emmet halted. The dog crouched again.

It took an age. Once, the dog ran forward alarmingly, but this time it stopped of its own accord, and Miss Emmet continued to move backwards, slowly, slowly, and now she had only to put out a hand and she would touch the bonnet of the car.

'Close the windows,' she said, and waited. 'Now, open the door on my side.'

But it was already open for her, and she was through it and scrabbling to slam it shut as the red setter hurled itself against the glass, the Alsatian leaping like a dolphin as high as the roof, slobbering as it snapped its jaws, flecking the windows with spittle.

Mr Armitage said it was an outrage, a disgrace; she might have been mauled to death. The village constable must be told. Only a madman would go on holiday leaving that sort of dog roaming at will. His hands shook on the wheel.

Miss Emmet sensed, rather than saw, the road stretching ahead, the fields beyond, the distant mountain, all permeated by the clear and golden light of the afternoon. There was no shade anywhere, no darkness, except in her heart.

Mum was crying. Twice, she swivelled round on her seat as though she meant to say something to Miss Emmet, but the tears just ran down her cheeks, and she turned away again. Her head in its scarf patterned with dogs wobbled as she wept. But then, thought Miss Emmet, tears were cheap.

The land-girl was disappointed when Mum failed to come down for her usual drink at six o'clock. And during supper she found Mum subdued, not quite up to par. When she attempted to tell her what had happened that afternoon at the bowling green – it was an amusing story and featured one of the 'lads' – Mum cut her short and spoke instead to Miss Emmet, who had caught the sun and whose eyes blazed in her scorched face. Mum talked to no one else during the entire meal. On the few occasions Miss

Emmet bothered to reply her tone of voice was peculiarly condescending. Everyone noticed it, or at least the members of the regular crowd, of whom the land-girl was now one.

As soon as the pudding plates had been cleared away, Mum went up to her room. Eyebrows raised, the crowd looked at Mr Armitage. 'She's a little under the weather,' he explained, and left the table.

He went upstairs to her room and did his best to comfort her. He said the ordinary things, the right things; that she mustn't punish herself, that she was not to blame.

'I know,' she said, 'I know.' But oh, how she blamed herself. If she had not insisted on their driving up to that awful house it would never have happened. Miss Emmet was such a frail woman, such a lonely woman. How she must have suffered, not only this afternoon but through all the other afternoons of her solitary life in which she had stood alone, facing fearsome beasts.

'She wouldn't let me go to her,' said Mr Armitage, distressed at the implication. 'I tried, but she told me to keep still. You heard her.'

'I know,' said Mum, and she wept afresh.

It was the land-girl's turn to make the tea and fetch the cheese and biscuits – at this time of the evening Mr White was busy in the bar – but before going through into the kitchen she went upstairs to the first floor. The Hardwick children slept in No. 4, and they, of course, were downstairs at the supper table. She was in and out in a jiffy, the stoat in her arms. It would be such a joke.

She had just closed the door of No. 1 behind her, the small room at the back overlooking the cowshed, when she heard muffled voices coming from Mum's room. No matter how hard she strained to hear the words she could make neither head nor tail of them, but Mum was upset, that much was obvious. Bursting with curiosity, the land-girl went downstairs to put on the kettle.

'Something's up,' she announced importantly as she carried in the tray, and then stopped; she had forgotten that Miss Emmet was still at the table.

Mr Armitage and Mum appeared again shortly before nine o'clock. As soon as they entered the room Miss Emmet rose from her chair by the fire. It was quite marked, the way she left just as they came in.

Some of the crowd went into the library to play cards. Molly Berwick and Mrs Lambert sat with Mum at the dining-room table. They whispered together, as though there was illness in the house. Mr Armitage sat by the fire, alone, and saw monsters in the flames.

Miss Emmet had felt ill during supper. Undressing in her tiny room, she began to shudder. Such a reaction was only to be expected, she told herself, and pulling back the sheets she climbed into her bed.

At first she thought the thing in her bed was a dead dog, and that too was to be expected. A moment before she had been feverish; now, cold with anger, she put on her dressing-gown and slippers, and holding the stoat by one leg so that its sawdust blood dripped onto the floorboards, she went in search of Mum.

Talking it over with her friends had done Mum the world of good. Molly Berwick had practically proved that Miss Emmet was almost entirely at fault. No one had asked her to get out of the car, certainly not Mum, who by her own admission had said it was a silly thing to do. And in any case, no harm had come from it, though – God knows – it sounded a close thing. Miss Emmet hadn't been scratched, let alone bitten, and if she had been going to suffer a heart attack from the experience, she would have had one there and then, on the path, or coming home in the car.

'I do feel better,' Mum said. 'Thank you.'

'What are friends for?' asked Molly, and only fleetingly did Mum wonder if she knew the answer.

It was at that precise moment that Miss Emmet thrust open the door and ran into the room. She was carrying the stuffed stoat in her arms, and wore her hair net. 'I have known all kinds of people,' said Miss Emmet, 'rich and poor, stupid and intelligent, but none of them have exhibited the degree of malice to be found in you. It is obvious that you have never known what it is to be vulnerable or unhappy.'

It was an impressive speech, and they looked at her with respect, though some had not understood what she said. Mum couldn't make out what it was she held in her arms. At first she thought it was some kind of fur tippet, stiffened with age. Lifting the stoat into the air with both hands, Miss Emmet flung it at her. The stoat skimmed above the table, raking Mum's turban from her head, and bounced on the floor behind the gramophone.

Afterwards those of the regular crowd who had been in the bar or in the library said that they were glad to have missed the excitement. They could not have borne the sight of Mum, humiliated at the table, the waxen skin of her burnt scalp shining like an egg in the lamplight. So they said.

BEGGARS WOULD RIDE

On 22 December 1605, two men on horseback, cloaks billowing, hoofs striking sparks from the frozen ground, rode ferociously from the Guildhall to a hill near the village of Hampstead. Dismounting some yards from the summit and a little to the east, they kicked a shallow depression in the earth. Several villagers, knowing in advance the precise and evil properties of the talisman they carried, gawped from a safe distance. Dropping to their knees, the horsemen buried a small round object wrapped in a piece of cloth. Upon rising, the taller of the two men was heard to observe that he wished he was in front of a warm hearth; at which moment the earth erupted and belched fire. For an instant the men stood transfixed and then, cloaks peeled by dancing flame, they whirled upwards, two lumps of burning rag spinning in a blazing arc against the sky.

On the Friday before Christmas, Ben Lewis and Frobisher met as usual in the car park behind the post office. Ben Lewis arrived a quarter of an hour late and, grimacing through the windscreen of his estate car, proceeded to take off his shoes. It annoyed Frobisher, still left waiting in the cold. When the wind stirred the dead leaves on the concrete ground, there was a sound like rats scampering.

'Bloody parky,' shouted Frobisher, but the man in the car was now out of sight, slumped between seat and clutch as he struggled to remove his trousers.

Frobisher, chilled to the bone, jogged to the boundaries of the car park and back again, passing two women seated inside a green Mini, one reading a newspaper, the other noticeably crying.

Ben Lewis emerged wearing shorts and a pair of white sneakers with blue toecaps.

'There's two women back there,' Frobisher told him. 'By the wire netting. One's blubbing into a handkerchief.'

'Really,' said Ben Lewis.

'The other's reading,' said Frobisher. He looked down at Ben Lewis's sneakers and smiled insincerely.

'They're new,' he said. Privately he thought them ridiculous; his own plimsolls, though stained and short on laces, were otherwise all that they should be.

Ben Lewis unlocked the boot of his car and took out a long canvas bag. 'Let's go into the bushes,' he shouted, and ducking through a gap in the fence shouldered his way into a dense undergrowth of alder and old privet.

The ground was liberally strewn with broken glass and beer cans. 'Funny,' remarked Ben Lewis, 'how few whatsits one sees these days.'

'Don't follow you,' said Frobisher.

'Contraceptives,' said Ben Lewis, whose mind was often on such things.

Labouring over the rusted frame of a child's pushchair, Frobisher stubbed his toe on a small, round object half buried beneath decaying leaves. 'I wish,' he panted, 'we could get the hang of the game. Just for an hour or so.'

Twice a week, during the lunch hour, they played tennis together. Frobisher worked just across the road in the National Westminster Bank, and Ben Lewis drove from Hampstead where he was a partner in a firm of estate agents.

'Whose turn is it to pay?' asked Frobisher, when, out of breath, they reached the entrance to the tennis courts.

He always asked that. He knew perfectly well that he had paid on Wednesday. He had a horror of being thought mean.

'Yours,' said Ben Lewis, who had no such fears.

The attendant marked them down for Court 14, which was listing slowly and surrounded on three sides by trees.

Though the court itself was full of pot-holes and the net invariably wound too high, it did have the advantage of privacy. Neither Frobisher nor Ben Lewis cared to be watched. When they had first started to play together, having chummed up in a pub in Belsize Park and mutually complained of being unfit, they had imagined it would be a matter of weeks before their game improved. Both had last played, slackly, at school. A year had passed and improvement had not come. Ben Lewis's service was quite good but he gained little advantage from it because it was too good for Frobisher to return. Frobisher had a nice forehand of a sort, the sort that lobbed the ball high into the air. Ben Lewis couldn't see the ball unless it came low over the net. They comforted themselves with the thought of the benefit they obviously derived from bending down and trotting about in the open air.

Of the two, Ben Lewis was the more outwardly narcissistic. He used aftershave and he hinted that he'd once had a sauna. He worried about his hair, which was now sparse, and the way his cheeks were falling in. He felt it was all right for Frobisher to sport a weathered crown – his particular height and porky-boy belly put him into a defined category – but he himself was on the short side and slender. He didn't want to degenerate into an elderly whippet with emaciated flanks, running like hell after the rabbit in the Waterloo Cup, and balding into the bargain.

'People are awfully callous these days, aren't they?' said Frobisher.

'What?' said Ben Lewis.

'The way they read while other people cry.'

'I shouldn't care for it,' said Ben Lewis. 'Not outdoors. Not in this weather.' He pushed open the rusted gate to Court 14 and began to unzip his bag.

'How's Margaret?' asked Frobisher.

'Fine, fine,' said Ben Lewis. He didn't inquire after

Frobisher's wife. Not any more. Frobisher's wife was called Beth, and Ben Lewis, who some years ago had directed *Little Women* for his local Amateur Dramatic Society, had once referred to her, jokingly of course, as 'Keep Death Off the Road'. Frobisher, not having seen the play, hadn't seen the joke. Far from it. He'd made some pretty silly remarks about it sounding disrespectful to his wife. Ben Lewis thought it was hypocritical of him, seeing that Frobisher had admitted to having a woman on the side. The previous summer, when excessive heat had forced Frobisher to remove his shirt, he had positively boasted about the two scratch marks Ben Lewis had noticed on his back. At the time, Ben Lewis had thought of rubbing his own back against a rose bush in his front garden, only he forgot.

Frobisher removed his overcoat and scarf and was discovered to be wearing a dark-blue tracksuit with white stripes on each shoulder.

'That's new,' said Ben Lewis, smiling insincerely. He had the strangest notion, when he strolled into position on the court, that his new shoes had springs in the heel.

Without warning, Frobisher hit a very good ball down the line. Ben Lewis returned it, though he was dazzled as usual by the horizontal of the grimy net and the glittering rectangles of the tower block built lower down the hill. For perhaps half a remarkable minute they successfully kept the ball in play until Ben Lewis, misjudging his own strength, sent it flying into the wire netting with such force that it lodged there like some unlikely fruit. 'You won't believe it,' he told Frobisher. 'But I thought the net was higher or you were lower.'

'Optical illusion,' said Frobisher kindly, scrambling up the grass bank to pluck the ball from the wire. 'It's that jetstream.' And he indicated with his racket two white and wobbling lines stretched across the sky. He felt unusually light on his feet and remarked confidently that it was all a question of rhythm. He could feel, he asserted, a definite sense of rhythm creeping into his stroke. They were both exhilarated at this sudden improvement in form. Secretly, Ben Lewis thought it had something to do with his shoes. Frobisher openly expressed the belief that his tracksuit had contributed to his new-found skill.

'A fellow in the office,' said Ben Lewis, 'started to get into trendy trousers last summer. His wife egged him on. He pulled off a fairly complicated land deal in South Woodford.'

'Direct result, you mean?' said Frobisher.

'Nothing was ever proved,' replied Ben Lewis, and he bounced on his toes and served with quite extraordinary speed and verve.

After a quarter of an hour an awed Ben Lewis said that in his opinion they were Wimbledon standard and possibly better than that bad-tempered fellow on the box who was always arguing with the man up the ladder. 'And you're right about the rhythm,' he said. He kept to himself the fanciful idea that they were dancing a slow foxtrot, championship standard, not a foot wrong, every move correctly timed, sweeping backwards and forwards across the court to the beat of an invisible orchestra.

Frobisher would have given anything for his wife Beth to have been watching him. She was always telling the children that he had no sense of co-ordination. It struck him as absurd that only last week he and Ben Lewis, trailing towards the bushes to return to the car park, had openly sneered at the dedicated players on Court 12. The tall man with the sweat-band round his head, who was generally there on Wednesday and Friday, had caused them particular amusement – 'that ass with the hair ribbon', as Ben had called him. Frobisher wondered if it would be going too far to have a band round his own forehead.

It came to Ben Lewis, fleetingly, sadly, as he arched his

back in preparation for a particularly deadly service, how different things might have been if he had always played like this. Only once in his life had he experienced applause, at the curtain call of *Little Women* in East Finchley. In imagination he multiplied the volume of that first, last and giddy applause, and flinging his racket to the linesman leaped, gazelle-like, over the net.

After a further twenty inspired minutes, Frobisher suggested that perhaps they should rest. Though perspiring, neither of them was the least tired.

'I do feel,' said Ben Lewis, with a touch of hysteria, 'that we might be hospital cases tomorrow.' Weak with laughter they flopped down on the sodden bench at the side of the court and lolled against each other.

'Doing anything for Christmas?' asked Frobisher at last. It was better to behave as if everything was normal.

'Usual thing,' said Ben Lewis. 'Margaret's mother, Margaret's mother's sister . . . that sort of thing. What about you?'

'Nothing special,' said Frobisher. 'Just me and Death.' From beyond the trees came the fragmented screams of children running in the playground of the Catholic school.

'Do you think,' said Frobisher, unable to contain himself, 'that it's the same thing as riding a bike?'

'A knack, you mean,' said Ben Lewis. 'Once learnt, never lost?'

'Yes,' said Frobisher.

'Maybe,' said Ben Lewis. But he didn't think it was. They both fell silent, reliving the last three-quarters of an hour, until Frobisher remarked generously that Ben Lewis might have won the last set if the ground hadn't been so full of pot-holes. 'Not your fault,' he added. 'It was jolly bad luck.'

Ben Lewis found that he was gripping the edge of the bench so tightly that a splinter of wood pierced his finger.

He knew that if he relaxed his hold he would spring upward and in one bound rip from the rusted fence a length of wire to tie round Frobisher's neck. He said as calmly as he was able, 'I don't believe in luck, bad or otherwise.'

From the playground came the blast of a whistle. The chattering voices receded as the children flocked indoors. Frobisher stood up, and, adjusting the top half of his tracksuit, strode purposefully back to his previous position on the court. 'My service,' he called curtly.

His first ball bounced low on the ground. Ben Lewis, gripping his racket in both hands as if running in an egg-and-spoon race, stumbled forward and scooped it skywards. It flew over his head, over the wire, and vanished into the trees.

'My God,' said Frobisher. He stood with one hand on his hip and gazed irritably at Ben Lewis. 'You'd better retrieve it,' he ordered, as though Ben Lewis were a dog. He watched his opponent lumber through the gate and heard him squelch down the muddy path in the direction of the attendant's hut. Frobisher took a running jump at the net and hurdled it with ease.

Ben Lewis, passing Court 12, saw that the man with the sweat-band round his head had a new opponent. A woman. She was crouching down, racket held in both hands, head swinging from side to side like a bull about to charge.

Having skirted the attendant's hut and entered the bushes, Ben Lewis tried to visualise the flight path of the erratic ball. He was probably not far enough back. He tried to clamber up the bank to see if Court 14 was visible, but the bushes grew too thickly. He scuffed with his shoes at the broken glass and refuse, thinking his search was hopeless, and almost at once uncovered the missing ball. He bent down and picked it up. He was now sweating and the muscles in his legs were trembling. He found he held not only the ball but something round and small clinging to a scrap of rotting cloth. Shivering with revulsion, he flung both ball and rag away from him and wiped his hands on his shorts.

He wished he was in a nice hot bath . . .

Frobisher, fretting on Court 14, was startled by the noise of steam escaping from some large funnel. He supposed it came from the ventilation system of the tower block further down the hill. When he looked in the direction of the car park he observed a large white cloud drifting above the trees. He went in pursuit of his opponent. Struggling through the bushes calling Ben Lewis's name, he was astonished to see that the ground had been swept clear of rubbish. Ben Lewis's car was still parked near the fence. The woman at the steering-wheel of the green Mini said she hadn't seen anybody, she'd been too busy reading.

'Didn't you hear that noise?' asked Frobisher severely. 'Like a train stopping. A puffer train.'

The woman stared at him. 'Perhaps he's just gone home,' she suggested.

'He's not wearing trousers,' said Frobisher. He retraced his steps to Court 14 and found it deserted.

Frobisher told his colleagues in the bank that his friend Ben Lewis had in some mysterious way disappeared. They weren't interested. Most of them thought Frobisher a bit of a slouch.

Before it grew dark, Frobisher slipped over the road to see if Ben Lewis's car was still near the gap in the fence. It was. Frobisher went into the bushes again and this time found the tennis ball and a smooth round object lying side by side on the ground.

He wished he knew where Ben Lewis had gone . . .

THE LONGSTOP

Words and cricket seem to go together. Whenever I watch the game, by mistake, on television, I think it's not true that you can't get blood from a stone.

I only ever played the game once myself, in the park with some evacuees from Bootle. I was allowed to join in because I held a biscuit tin filled with shortbread that my mother had baked. They said I could have a turn if I gave them a biscuit afterwards. I didn't make any runs because I never hit the ball, and when I kept my promise and began to open the tin the evacuees knocked me over and took every piece of shortbread. They threw the tin over the wall into the gentlemen's lavatory. I had to tell my mother a six-foot-high naughty man with a Hitler moustache had chased me; she would have slapped me for playing with evacuees.

Mr Baines, who was my maternal grandfather, was a lover of cricket. Mr Jones, my father, didn't care for the game. He cared even less for my grandfather. In his humble estimation Mr Baines was a mean old bugger, a fifth columnist, and, following his self-confessed denouncing of a neighbour in Norris Green for failing to draw his curtains against the black-out, a Gauleiter into the bargain. He was also a lounge lizard, a term never satisfactorily explained, though it was true that my grandfather fell asleep between meals.

Apart from words, my father was keen on sailing ships. He subscribed to a monthly magazine on the subject. If he was to be believed, he had, when no more than a child, sailed as a cabin boy to America. In middle age, his occupation a commercial traveller, he prowled the deserted shore beyond the railway line, peering of an evening through the barbed wire entanglements at the oil tankers and the black destroyers that crawled along the bleak edge of the Irish Sea; it was a gloomy mystery to him where that fearless lad before the mast had gone.

Every week Mr Baines came for Sunday dinner. There had been a moment at the outbreak of the war when he had contemplated coming to live with us, but after three days he returned home. He said he preferred to take his chances with the Luftwaffe. His conversation during the meal was always about cricket, and mostly to do with a man called Briggs. Briggs, he said, had just missed greatness by a lack of seriousness. If only Briggs had taken batting more seriously he would have been, make no bones about it, the best all-round cricketer in England since W. G. Grace. Briggs, he informed us, took bowling and fielding in deadly earnest, but as a batsman he was a disaster; he seemed far more anxious to amuse the crowd than to improve his average.

Nobody listened to my grandfather, certainly not my father who was often heard to remark quite loudly that, had he been in control, he wouldn't give the old skinflint the time of day, let alone Sunday dinner, world without end.

However, one particular Sunday in the summer of 1944, Mr Baines, without warning, excelled himself when describing a cricketer called Ranjitsinhji.

'Just to set eyes on him,' said Mr Baines, 'was a picture in motion. The way his shirt ballooned –'

'A black chappie,' my father exclaimed, taken aback at my grandfather speaking civilly of a foreigner.

'An Indian Prince,' said Mr Baines. He was equally taken aback at being addressed in the middle of his monologue. He was used to conversing uninterrupted throughout the devouring of the black-market roast pork.

'They're two a penny,' my father said.

'More potatoes?' asked my mother, worriedly.

'Even when it wasn't windy,' continued Mr Baines, 'his shirt ballooned. Whether half a gale was blowing on the Hove ground or there wasn't enough breeze to shift the flag at Lord's, the fellow's shirt flapped like the mainsail of a six-tonner on the Solent.'

'Blithering rubbish,' said my father. He stabbed at a sprout on his plate as though it was alive.

My mother told Mr Baines that they played cricket in the park every Sunday afternoon. Not a proper team, just old men and young lads. Not what he was used to, of course. 'But,' she said, eyeing my father contemptuously, 'it will do us good to get out into the pure air.'

She didn't mean my father to come. We were never a family who went anywhere together. My father's opinion, had he voiced it, would have been that the family who stood together fell out together. Often we would attempt an outing, but between the closing of the back door and the opening of the front gate, misunderstandings occurred and plans were abruptly abandoned. She was astonished when, having washed up and taken off her pinny, she found my father in the hall putting on his trilby hat. She didn't like it, you could tell. Her mouth went all funny and the lipstick ran down at one corner. Shoulder to shoulder, more or less, we set off for the park.

I wanted to nip over the garden fence and through the blackberry bushes into Brows Lane, but my mother said my grandfather wasn't about to nip anywhere, not at his age. We trotted him down the road past the roundabout and the Council offices. The brass band was practising in the hut behind the fire station. When he heard the music, Mr Baines began to walk with his arms held stiffly at his sides, only the band kept stopping and starting and the tune came in bits, and after a little while he gave up playing at soldiers and shuffled instead. My father looked at the ground all the time; there was a grey splodge on the brim of his hat where a pigeon had done its business.

The park was quite grand, even though it had lost its ornamental gates at the entrance. My mother said they'd been removed to make into tanks. My father swore they were mouldering away in a brick field down by the Docks, along with his mother's copper kettle and a hundred thousand front railings. The park had a pavilion, a sort of hunting lodge with mullioned windows and a thatched roof. People were worried about incendiary bombs. The park keeper kept his grass roller inside and buckets of water. In front of the pavilion was a sunken bowling green, and beyond that a miniature clock-golf course. We used to ride our bikes up and down the bumps. Behind the pavilion, within a roped enclosure, was a German Messerschmitt. It had been there for two years. It hadn't crash-landed anywhere near our village; it was on loan. The park keeper was always telling the Council to tell someone to come back for it. At first we had all run round it and shuddered, but after a few weeks we hardly noticed it any more. It just perched there, propped on blocks, one wing tipped up to the sky, the cockpit half burned away, its melted hood glittering beetle-black in the sunlight.

When he saw the aeroplane, my father cried out, 'Good Lord, look at that!' He flung his arms out theatrically and demanded, 'Why wasn't I told?'

No one took any notice of him; he was always showing off. He stared up at the plane with an expression both fearful and excited, as though the monster was still flying through the air and he might yet be machine-gunned where he stood.

My mother and Mr Baines sat on wooden chairs pressed against the privet hedge. My mother was worried in case we were too near the wicket. She was for ever ducking and flinching, mistaking the white clouds that bowled across the sky for an oncoming ball. It wasn't an exciting game as far as I could tell but my grandfather sat on the edge of his chair and didn't fall asleep once. There was a man fielding who was almost as old as Mr Baines, and when the bowler was rubbing the ball up and down the front of his trousers preparing to run, the old man rested in a deck-chair on the pitch. The butcher's boy from the village shop was crouching down behind the wicket wearing a tin hat and smoking a cigarette.

'That fellow,' said Mr Baines, pointing at the elderly batsman in Home Guard uniform, 'is taking a risk. If he misses the ball he'll be out leg before or he'll get his skull stove in.'

'Heavens,' cried my mother, cringing backwards on her chair.

'Briggs used to play that sort of stroke,' said Mr Baines. 'Of course, he knew what he was doing.'

My father came and sat down beside him. He said: 'I never knew it was there. I never knew.' He still looked excited. He'd taken his hat off and there was a mark all round his forehead.

'As soon as he saw what ball it was,' Mr Baines said, 'he'd stand straight in front of the wicket and wait until it looked as if it would go straight through his body —'

'I never knew,' repeated my father. 'I never even guessed.' He was very unobservant. He'd been morosely loping to and from the railway station night and morning for twenty years and never bothered to look through the trees.

'Be quiet,' said my mother. 'We're concentrating.'

'At the last moment,' Mr Baines said, 'Briggs would hook it. Glorious stroke. Poetry in motion.'

'If I could have served,' remarked my father, 'I would have chosen the Merchant Navy.'

'Mind you,' Mr Baines said. 'It had to be a fast ball.'

'Failing that, I think I'd have fancied the Air Force,' said my father.

There wasn't anything one could reply to that piece of poppy-cock. If my father had been healthy enough to join up, he wouldn't have been any use. When Wilfred Pickles said on the wireless, 'And how old are you, luv? Ninety-seven!', my father had to blow his nose from emotion. If he happened to hear 'When the lights go on again all over the world' on Forces' Favourites, he had to go out into the scullery to take a grip on himself. According to my mother, Auntie Doris had turned him into a sissy. He was a terrible cry-baby. He cried one time when the cat went missing. My mother said that most of the time his carrying on like that was misplaced. Once he went all over Southport pressing shilling pieces into the hands of what he called 'our gallant boys in blue'. They were soldiers from the new hospital down by the Promenade. My father told them he was proud of them, that they were the walking wounded; he had a field day with his handkerchief. Afterwards it turned out there was nothing wrong with them, nothing wounded that is, it wasn't that sort of hospital. They were soldiers all right, my mother said, but they'd all caught a nasty disease from just being in the army, not from fighting or anything gallant like that, and it was certainly nothing to be proud of.

'I'm not criticising,' said Mr Baines, looking at the fielder resting in his deck-chair, 'but these fellows lack self-discipline. The true sportsman is a trained athlete. He dedicates himself to the game. Only way to succeed. Same with anything in all walks of life — cotton, fishing, banking, shipping —'

'Doesn't he ever get tired of his own voice?' said my father savagely.

I sat on the grass with my back propped against my

mother's knees. I could feel her trembling from indignation. My grandfather began to clap, slapping the palms of his hands together above my head as the elderly batsman left the crease and began to trail towards the pavilion. Mr Baines was the only one applauding; there were few spectators and most of those had swivelled round the other way to look at the bowling green. The new batsman was younger and he had a gammy leg. When he heard Mr Baines clapping he glared at him, thinking he was being made fun of.

'One time,' said Mr Baines, 'Briggs got stale. The Lancashire committee suggested that he should take a week's holiday. He went to a remote village in Wiltshire —'

'Don't think I don't know what the old beggar's getting at,' said my father. 'Talking about cotton like that. Did he think I wanted to come a cropper in cotton —'

'Word got round as it will,' Mr Baines said. 'Second day there a fellow came up to Briggs and asked him how much he'd take for playing in a local match. Ten pound, said Briggs, thinking that would be prohibitive —'

The park was shimmering in sunshine. You couldn't see the boundary by the poplar trees; all the leaves were reflecting like bits of glass. The man with the gammy leg was out almost at once. I didn't know why, the bails were still standing. I couldn't follow the rules. A fat man came out in a little peaked cap. I could hear the dull clop of the ball against the bat and the click of the bowls on the green as they knocked against each other. Behind me the voices went on and on, another game in progress, more dangerous than either cricket or bowls, and the rules were always changing.

'Briggs's side lost the toss,' said Mr Baines, 'and he had to begin the bowling. His first ball was hit out of the ground for six —'

'If I'd had any appreciation all these years,' my father

said, 'things might have been different. When I think how I tramp from door to door in all weathers while you and your blasted Dad put your feet up —'

'Finally he had two wickets for a hundred and fifty runs. The crowd was looking quite nasty,' Mr Baines said. 'But what finished them off was that when he went into bat he was bowled second ball.'

'All I needed was a few bob at the right moment,' said my father. 'Just a few measly quid and the old skinflint wouldn't put his hand in his pocket —'

'Don't speak about him like that,' cried my mother. 'I won't have him called names.'

'Only a stalwart policeman and the train to London saved him from a jolly good hiding,' said Mr Baines. 'He never tried village cricket again.'

'If you'd been any proper sort of woman,' groaned my father, 'you'd have been a help-mate.'

'Be quiet,' my mother cried. 'Shut your mouth.'

'You've only been a bloody hindrance,' my father shouted. He jumped up and knocked over his chair. He walked away in the direction of the aeroplane, leaving his hat on the grass.

'What's up?' I asked. Though I knew. 'Is he off home, then?'

'Ssh,' said my mother. 'He's gone for a widdle.' Her voice was all choked.

'Don't upset yourself,' said Mr Baines. 'It's not worth it.'

'He sickens me,' my mother said. 'Sickens me. Whimpering over the least thing when inside he's like a piece of rock. He's hard. He's got no pity for man nor beast.'

'Don't waste your tears,' said Mr Baines. 'You can't get blood from a stone.'

At that moment the ball flew past the wicket and striking the ground rolled to my grandfather's feet. He leapt up and striding to the side of the pitch chucked the ball at the batsman. He didn't exactly bowl it; he sort of dipped one shoulder and flung the ball like a boy skimming a stone on water. The batsman, taken by surprise at such an accurate throw, swung his bat. The scarlet ball shot over Mr Baines's shoulder and went like a bullet from a gun after my father.

When we ran up to him he was stood there in the shadow of the Messerschmitt with his hand clutched to the side of his head. The ball hadn't hit him full on, merely grazed the side of his temple. But he was bleeding like a pig.

'That's a turn-up for the book,' said Mr Baines.

PEOPLE FOR LUNCH

'We simply must,' said Margaret.

'Do we have to?' asked Richard.

'No,' said Margaret, 'but we will. We've been to them eight weekends on the trot. It looks awful.'

Thinking about it, Richard supposed she was right. Every Sunday throughout May and June they had motored down to Tunbridge Wells, arriving in time for lunch. They had left again at six o'clock, after Dora and Charles had made them a cup of Earl Grey tea. Apart from an obligatory inspection of the kiddies' new bicycles or skate-boards, or being forced to listen to some long feeble jokes told by young Sarah, the hours spent in Dora's well-appointed house had been pleasant and restful. 'I don't think they expect to be asked back,' said Richard. 'They're not like that.'

'Not *expect*,' agreed Margaret. 'But I think we should.'

Dora and Charles were asked for the following Sunday. Richard and Charles had gone to university together, been articled together, and now worked for the same firm of lawyers, in the litigation department. 'Jolly nice of you,' said Charles, when he heard. 'We're looking forward to it.'

It had been a little tricky suggesting to Dora that she leave the children behind. 'They'll be so bored here,' explained Margaret, when speaking to her on the phone. 'As you know we've only a backyard. There's no sun after eleven o'clock in the morning. And Malcolm won't be here.' She didn't feel too awkward about it because after all Dora had a marvellous woman who lived in, and Dora herself was frightfully keen once the penny had dropped.

'How did you put it?' asked Richard worriedly. 'I hope you didn't imply we . . .'

'Don't be silly,' said Margaret crossly. 'You know me. I was the soul of tact.'

Two unfortunate events occurred on the morning of the luncheon party. The sky, which earlier had been clear and blue, filled with clouds, and Malcolm, who had promised faithfully he was going out, changed his mind. He said there was a programme he wanted to watch on TV at one o'clock.

'You can't,' wailed Margaret. 'We'll be sitting down for lunch.'

'I'm watching,' said Malcolm. He switched on the set and lay full-length on the wicker couch from Thailand, flicking cigarette ash on to the pine floor.

'Can't watch the telly, old chap,' said Richard bravely. ''Fraid not. We've people coming.'

'Piss off,' said Malcolm.

At midday Richard suggested Malcolm come with him to the pub to buy the beer. 'I'm not shifting,' said Malcolm. 'I don't want to miss my programme.'

While Richard was away, the clouds lifted and the sun shone. Margaret looked out of the window at the square of paving stones set with shrubs and bordered by a neat privet hedge. Although only seventeen, Malcolm was extremely tenacious of purpose. He would spend the entire lunch hour jumping up and switching on the telly after Richard had turned it off. The only slight chance of stopping him lay in hitting him over the head, and then there'd be a punch-up and it would undoubtedly spoil the atmosphere. She began to carry chairs through to the front door; if it were not for the privet hedge, they would be sitting practically on the pavement, but it couldn't be helped.

'What the hell are you doing?' asked Richard, when he returned with the drink.

'It's your fault,' cried Margaret shrilly. 'You shouldn't have boxed the television in. I'm not entertaining guests with the damn thing blazing away.' After several harsh words Richard strode into the house and began to man-handle the table into the hall.

'I will not ask you to help,' he called to Malcolm. 'I will not point out that your unreasonable behaviour is the cause of all this upheaval.' He swore as the table, wedged in the narrow passage, crushed his fingers against the jamb of the door.

'Stop muttering,' shouted Malcolm. 'If you've got any-thing to say, say it to my face.'

The table, once settled on flagstones, sloped only partially at one end. Covered with a tablecloth, a vase of roses placed in the centre, the effect was charming. 'I think it's better than indoors,' said Margaret. 'I really do.'

'I could have a heart attack,' said Richard. 'We both could – and that boy would trample over us to change channels.'

'Sssh!' said Margaret. 'Don't upset yourself.'

Dora and Charles arrived promptly at twelve-thirty. The moment they stepped out of the car the sun went behind a cloud.

'It's a little informal,' called Margaret gaily, 'but we thought you'd prefer to sit outside.'

'Rather,' said Charles, gazing at the row of bins behind the upright chairs. Richard kissed Dora and Margaret kissed Charles; the merest brush of lips against stubble and powder. 'I'm afraid I haven't shaved,' said Richard.

'Good God,' cried Charles, who had performed this ritual at seven-thirty. 'Who the hell shaves on Sunday?'

They went into the front room and had a drop of sherry, standing in a group at the window and eyeing the table outside as if it were a new car that had just been delivered.

'Lovely roses,' said Charles.

'Home-grown?' asked Dora. They had to shout to be heard above the noise of the television.

'No,' said Margaret. 'We do have roses in the backyard, but the slightest hint of wind and they fall apart.'

'I know the feeling,' said Dora, who could be very dry on occasion.

They all laughed, particularly Dora.

'Belt up,' said Malcolm.

They trooped in and out, carrying the salad bowl and the condiments, the glasses for the wine.

'This is fun,' said Charles, stumbling over a geranium pot and kicking a milk bottle down the steps. He insisted on fetching the dustpan and brush. Malcolm was eating an orange and spitting pips at the skirting board.

'You're doing "O" levels, I suppose,' said Charles. 'Or is it "A"s?'

'You what?' said Malcolm.

'Any idea what you want to do?' asked Charles, leaning on the handle of the brush.

'Nope,' said Malcolm.

'Plenty of time,' said Charles. He went outside and confided to Richard. 'Nice boy you've got there. Quiet but deep.'

'Possibly,' said Richard uneasily.

It was an enjoyable lunch. Margaret was a good cook and Richard refilled the glasses even before they were empty. It was quite secluded behind the hedge, until closing time. Then a stream of satisfied customers from the pub round the corner began to straggle past the house.

'What's so good about this area of London,' said Richard, after hastily dispatching a caught-short Irishman who had lurched through the privet unbuttoning his flies, 'is that it's not sickeningly middle-class.'

'Absolutely,' agreed Charles, listening to the splattering of water on the pavement behind his chair.

Margaret was lacking spoons for the pudding. 'Please, Charles,' she appealed, touching him briefly on the shoulder.

He ran inside the house glad to be of service. He looked in the drawers and on the draining board.

After a moment Margaret too came indoors. There was no sign of Malcolm. 'Have you found them?' she shouted.

'Stop it,' said Charles.

'They're right in front of your eyes,' she bellowed.

'For God's sake,' he whispered. 'They'll see us.'

He backed away down the room. It was infuriating, he thought, the knack women had of behaving wantonly at the wrong moments. Had they been alone in some private place, depend upon it, Margaret would have been full of excuses and evasions. In all the twelve years he had known her, there had never been a private place. He had wanted there to be, but he hadn't liked to plan it. God knows, life was sordid enough as it was. He didn't know how old Richard stood it – his wife giving off signals the way she did. The amount of lipstick Margaret wore, the tints in her hair, the way everything wobbled when she moved. Dora was utterly different. You could tell just by looking at her that she wasn't continually thinking about men.

'Where's Malcolm?' asked Margaret.

'I've no idea,' he said. He found he was being man-oeuvred between a wall cupboard and the cooker. He had never known her so determined. He glanced desperately at the window. All he could see was the back of his wife's head. 'All right, you little bitch,' he said hoarsely. The word excited him dreadfully. It was so offensive. He never called Dora a bitch, not unless they were arguing. 'You've asked for it,' he said. Eyes closed and breathing heavily, he held out his arms. Margaret, looking over her shoulder, was in time to see Richard rising from his chair. He waved. She fled soundlessly from the room.

Dora quite enjoyed being in the front yard. It was handy being so near the dustbins. When the weather was good they often lunched on the lawn in Tunbridge Wells, but

there the grass was like a carpet to Charles and he grew
livid if so much as a crumb fell to the ground.

'Where's Malcolm gone?' asked Margaret. Richard told
her he was in the basement, probably listening to records.
Actually he had seen Malcolm sloping off down the street a
quarter of an hour before, but he didn't want to worry her.
Lately, Malcolm had taken to going out for hours at a
stretch and coming home in an elated condition. They both
knew it was due to pot-smoking, or worse. In a sense it was
a relief to them that he had at last found something which
interested him.

'Do you know,' said Charles. 'I do wonder if we're doing
the right thing, burying the children down in the country.'

'Oh, come on,' scoffed Margaret. 'All that space and
fresh air . . . not to mention their ponies.'

'I know exactly what he means,' said Dora. 'They're
very protected. When I think of Malcolm at Sarah's age,
he was streets ahead of her.'

'Was he?' said Richard.

'Well, he was so assured,' Dora explained. 'Handing
round the wine, joining in the conversation. I always remember that time we came for dinner with Bernard and Elsa,
and Malcolm hid under the table.'

'I remember that,' said Charles thoughtfully. 'He
crapped.' There was a moment's startled silence. 'It was
your word,' Charles said hastily, looking at Richard. 'I
remember clearly. I said to you, I think Malcolm's had a
little accident, and you said to me, Oh dear, he's done a
crap. I thought it was marvellous of you. I really did.'

'Really he did,' said Dora.

'I wonder what happened to Elsa,' said Margaret. When
they had finished their coffee, Richard fetched a tray and
began to gather the dishes together. It had grown chilly.

'Leave those,' said Margaret, shivering.

Dora put on her old cardigan. It hung shapelessly from

her neck to her thigh. Peering through the hedge she caught sight of the camellia in next door's garden. 'Isn't it a beauty,' she enthused, waving her woolly arms in excitement.

'I'll show it to you,' offered Richard. 'They won't mind you taking a dekko. They're a nice couple. He's something of a character. He wears Osh-Coshes.'

'Charles,' said Dora. 'Please ring Mrs Antrim. Just to check if the kiddies are all right.'

Obediently Charles went into the house. He was followed by Margaret.

The telephone was on a shelf outside the bathroom door. He couldn't remember the code number. 'Doesn't he remember his little codey-wodey number?' said Margaret, who had been drinking quite heavily.

'Be careful,' he protested. 'The front door's open.'

'They've gone next door to look at the flowers,' she said.

'They might pop back at any moment.'

'Well, come in here then.' And with brute force she pushed him from the phone towards the bathroom.

It was quite flattering in a way, the urgent manner in which she propelled him through the door. He wished her teeth would stop chattering; she was making the devil of a noise. Feeling a bit of an ass, he sat on the edge of the bath while she stood over him and rumpled his hair.

'Steady on,' he said. 'I haven't a comb on me.'

'Kiss me,' she urged. 'Kiss me.'

'Look here,' he said, wrenching her fingers out of his ears. 'This is neither the time nor the place. I can't relax in this kind of situation.'

'Oh, shut up,' she said, and shoved him quite viciously so that he lost his balance and lay half in and half out of the bath. At that instant she thought she heard someone coming up the hall.

'Christ,' she moaned, dropping to one knee and peering

48

through the keyhole. There was no one there. 'Listen,' she told Charles, who was struggling to get out of the bath. 'If they come back, I'll go and you stay here. You can come out later.'

'What if Richard wants to use the lavatory?' he asked worriedly. Margaret said if that happened, he must nip down the steps into the yard and hide in the basement until the coast was clear.

'But what about Malcolm?' asked Charles. 'Malcolm's down there.' Margaret assured him Malcolm would be in the front room of the basement. Even if he did see Charles it wouldn't make much difference – Malcolm hardly said one articulate word from one week to the next.

'If you're sure,' breathed Charles. Half-heartedly he embraced her. He didn't quite know how far he should go. He felt a bit out of his depth. 'Are we . . . is it . . . should we?' he murmured.

'Play it by ear,' Margaret said mysteriously.

Charles was just unbuttoning his blazer when they both heard footsteps outside. In a flash Margaret was through the bathroom door and closing it behind her. He heard her calling. 'Cooee, I'm here.' Panic-stricken, he undid the bolt of the back door and crept on to the small veranda. Beneath him lay the yard, overgrown with weeds and littered with rose petals. A rambler, diseased and moulting, clung ferociously to the brick wall. Trembling, he descended the steps and inched his way towards the basement door. He stepped into Richard's study, gloomy as the black hole of Calcutta and bare of furniture save for a desk and a chair. Margaret had been right. Malcolm was in the front room playing records. Charles recognised some of the tunes from *Chorus Line*. He wasn't over-fond of modern music but he couldn't help being impressed by the kind of enjoyment Malcolm seemed to be experiencing. There were distinct sighs and moans coming from beyond the wall. He eased himself into Richard's chair and waited for Margaret to send some sort of signal. The amount of paperwork Richard brought home was staggering. No wonder poor old Margaret behaved badly. Of course she didn't have any hobbies or attend evening classes. She wasn't like Dora, who was out several nights a week at French circles and history groups. He supposed things were different in the country. For some reason he felt terribly sleepy – probably nerves at being in such an absurd situation. He began to shake with weak and silent laughter and, when it was over, fell into a peaceful doze.

He was awakened by a shower of spoons clattering on to the flagstones outside the window. The record in the next room had been turned off. Cautiously he advanced into the yard and peered upwards. Someone was standing at the kitchen window. Adopting what he hoped was a casual stride, he walked to the back wall and inspected the rambling rose. 'Green-fly,' he shouted knowledgeably, looking up at the window. 'Riddled with green-fly.' It was Margaret's face at the window. She beckoned him to come upstairs.

When he came down the hall, Richard was standing at the front door with Dora. He turned and looked at Charles with disgust.

'I've been pottering about in the garden,' stammered Charles. He thought he might faint.

'Isn't it sickening,' said Richard. 'Someone's pinched the table.'

Charles stood on the top step and looked distressed. 'Where are the dishes?' he said, at last. 'And the glasses?'

'Gone,' cried Margaret shrilly. 'Every damn thing.' She put the kettle on to boil while Richard phoned the police. When Richard came back, Charles offered to jump in the car and drive in all directions. 'They can't have got far,' he said.

'He's already driven round the block umpteen times,' snapped Margaret.

Just as the tea was being poured out Malcolm strolled in and helped himself to the cup intended for Dora. He leaned against the draining board, stirring his tea with the end of a biro.

'Where have you been?' asked Margaret. 'You've been out for hours.'

'The park,' said Malcolm.

'Use a spoon,' ordered Richard. Shrugging his shoulders, Malcolm ferreted in the kitchen drawer. 'There ain't no spoons,' he said. His father ran up and down stairs, looking to see if his camera had gone or his cufflinks, or the silver snuff box left him by his uncle.

Charles and Dora couldn't stay for the arrival of the police. Charles said he hoped they'd understand but he didn't want to risk running into heavy traffic. Driving home to Tunbridge Wells, he told Dora he thought it had been a bit silly of Margaret to put the table in the front yard. 'I'm the last person in the world,' he said, 'to laugh at other people's misfortunes, particularly Richard's, but it struck me as affected, you know. Damned affected. I was right up against a dust-bin. Come to think of it, it was bloody insulting.'

'Why?' asked Dora.

'Well, I think she was probably poking fun at us. You know, lunch on the lawn . . . that sort of thing.'

'Rubbish,' said Dora. 'She's just starved of sunshine.'

Charles felt awful. It was sheer worry that made him speak so spitefully of his friends. As soon as Malcolm had mentioned he had spent the afternoon in the park, he had realised how mistaken he himself had been about the noises in the basement. While he had sat at Richard's desk, the thieves had obviously been in the next room. He felt almost an accomplice. And those damned spoons lying in the yard

– the police would think the thieves had dropped them. He could never tell Richard about it. Richard would be bound to ask what the hell he'd been doing in the basement. Even if it didn't occur to him for one moment that he'd been after old Margaret, he'd still think it odd of him to have been snooping around his desk. Nor, thought Charles sadly, could he confide in old Dora.

She was leaning trustingly against his shoulder, tired after her pleasant day, humming the theme song from *Chorus Line.*

PERHAPS YOU SHOULD TALK TO SOMEONE

We don't talk much in my family, according to my mother. We did when I was younger, she said, but after a bit it sort of died out. Evolution, I suppose. It's one of my mother's things, talking. She never stops going on about the importance of being articulate and communicating, but when you listen to her, it's just words. I mean, she's articulate all right but what she communicates isn't especially mind-blowing. Mostly it's pretty feeble, like being reminded to hang up clothes or put things away. When it's not like that she's pointing out how it's socially immoral to buy magazines with the money she gives me for tube fares. I might mention she uses the family allowance to buy cigarettes. Also, being progressive, my mother and father pretend to have this creepy belief in trust and privacy. Sad really. There's not much to discuss if they're not prepared to spy on you. Everyone I know with parents like mine, they all have to do the same. Keep quiet, I mean. What else can they do? 'I trust you ... I respect your privacy ... I would never dream of reading your diary.' They just allow you to get on with what you intended to do in the first place, but you tend to get this dreary guilt problem building up over nothing at all. It isn't as if many of us have got anything to be private about.

Actually my mother does read my diary, otherwise how did she find out I was having sex with William Hornby? As a matter of fact I'm not bothered about her violating my privacy. I mean, my mother doesn't have a thing to do after she's done the cooking and finished stuffing the clothes into the washing machine. I don't mind her having an interest. Anyway, I don't write the truth in my diary; most of it's made up. If you ask me, it's her that can't communicate. She's so screwed up about this trust thing that she's been rendered practically speechless except for muttering about tidiness and such like. She'd like to tell me to work harder at school but she knows it's a losing battle. After all, it was she who insisted that I should be educated by the State. She realises now that it was a crummy idea but she can't go back on her principles. My father says the same, but really it's because they can't afford it, and even if they could I'm so thick now that they couldn't get me in anywhere else. It's too late. It's not such a serious problem. I'm not alone. None of my friends have been taught anything either.

My mother really worries about not being able to talk to me. This summer she sent me away for a week to stay with an Aunt, just to get me away from William Hornby. She didn't say so, of course, but I knew that was the reason. Also, she's got a friend living in London called Moona who's divorced with one child by her ex-husband and another one by nobody in particular. That's probably a little too progressive for my mother, but she's known Moona for years and she's got this totally erroneous idea that I get on well with her. Actually, I don't mind Moona. She's pretty harmless. She sends postcards at Christmas of male statues without figleaves, and those ones of fat ladies in bathing costumes when she goes on holiday. She always writes a message about foreign parts. I've collected them all and put them in a box somewhere. Anyway, my mother said she'd write to Moona and I could go and see her when I was staying with my Aunt. 'You've always liked Moona,' she said. 'Perhaps you could talk to Moona.' I didn't mind either way. Everywhere's a bit deadly. You have to take yourself with you wherever you go. I suppose I could have told her that I thought William Hornby was a bit of a creep after all, and saved her the train fare, but what was the use? I couldn't summon up the energy.

I went to London and after a day or two Moona rang up my Aunt and asked to speak to me.

'Hallo, flower,' she said. She calls everyone that. I expect she thinks it's friendly. 'Why don't you come round and talk to me. I've got a letter from your Ma and there's a few things she wants me to ask you about.' Moona's got an odd voice, slightly clipped and a bit hoarse. She sounds as if she's heading for cancer.

I went round to see her. She lives in a big house in a terrace. The front door has two knockers on it, a plain black one and an ornate tarnished thing made out of brass. It's one of Moona's jokes. She always asks if you like her knockers.

'I'm in a bit of a crisis,' she said, as soon as she saw me. She showed me into the sitting room which has a sofa as old as the hills. When I sat down lots of dust went up to the ceiling. Moona's all right, really. Every time I've ever met her she's been in a bit of a crisis.

'There's this man,' she said. 'He's terribly odd. I can't fathom him at all. First he says he loves me, then he says he doesn't. He swore he'd come and see me today, but he won't.'

I didn't have to say anything; she wasn't really talking to me. She kept rubbing the side of her neck with her hand, the one holding her cigarette, as though there was something tied too tightly round her throat. I thought it was probable she might set fire to her hair.

Suddenly she asked, 'Have you got a boy-friend? A real one? You can tell me, flower. I won't breathe a word to your mother.' I knew she would; she wouldn't be able to help herself.

'Sort of,' I told her. I couldn't figure out what she meant by real.

'Are you in love with him?'

I stared at her and said nothing.

After a bit, she asked, 'Do you like him?'

'Not a lot,' I said.

She seemed bothered about something. I helped myself to one of her cigarettes.

'Do you smoke already?' she wanted to know.

'Sort of,' I said.

'When I was your age,' she babbled, 'I was in love quite badly. He worked for an insurance company. I can even remember his name.' She couldn't, not right away. 'It was Gerald . . . no, Gerard – Gerard Carr. He was quite old. There was something odd about him. How old is your boy-friend?'

I said he was nineteen. Actually, that creep William Hornby is only sixteen. He doesn't even shave.

'I never liked young boys,' said Moona. 'It was always some friend of my father's that I got a crush on. They used to pinch my bottom.' She laughed quite loudly. 'What do you talk about?' she asked.

'Nothing much,' I said. I rested my head against the back of the sofa and closed my eyes. I felt sleepy. She was saying, 'I suppose it must seem strange to you that someone like your mother should have a friend like me.'

I didn't find it strange. I don't imagine my mother is the person she presents to me. I wasn't very interested. It's nothing to do with me.

Someone came into the room and I heard Moona say, 'Oh, Bernard, you must meet Katie.'

I opened my eyes and this large man with brown hair was standing there. I think he wore glasses. Moona told me he was her lodger. She told him that I was the daughter of Agnes, her oldest and dearest friend. 'Agnes is a wee bit worried about her daughter growing up and all that,' she said. 'I do think it's sad the way the young can't communicate with their parents. They always turn to those outside the family circle.' She did look dreary about it; it really seemed to bug her.

Just then there was a knock at the front door and Moona ran to the mirror and fiddled with her hair and threw her cigarette into the hearth. She suddenly looked stoned out of her mind. 'Oh, Christ,' she moaned. 'It's *him*.' She sort of sank into a heap onto the carpet.

'Steady up,' said Bernard. He sounded like one of those instructors at a riding school.

'Dear God,' wailed Moona. She was grinding her teeth and looking up at me. 'Don't ever wish,' she implored, 'for something very badly when you're young, because you just might get it when you're middle-aged.' I hadn't a clue what she was going on about.

Then she clutched Bernard around the ankles and begged him to take me down into the basement. 'Please talk to Katie,' she pleaded. 'I must be alone with *him*.'

'Right-ho,' Bernard said, and I followed him downstairs.

You could hear Moona greeting someone in the hall. Her voice was all breathless as if she'd been running for miles. I supposed it was her odd man calling after all.

Bernard was pretty odd too. He cooked some food and I lay on his bed and read magazines. Most of them had pictures in them of women without clothes. There was a lot of music and thumping about going on upstairs.

Two days later Moona telephoned and suggested that I come over for lunch. We had chops and a salad and some bread that Moona said was Greek. 'How did you get on with Bernard?' she wanted to know.

'All right.'

'He's sweet, really. He pays forty-five pound a week for that basement and he's lovely with it. He was married once, you know, but something went wrong. We're very close but we've never had an affair . . . isn't that odd? He's my best friend.'

I had thought my mother was her best friend. Possibly Moona has lots of best friends. It's no skin off my nose.

'Do you know what I did the other day?' she asked.

'No,' I said.

'Me and this odd man I'm mad about put on records and we danced. Did you hear us jogging about?'

'No,' I said.

'I'm sorry I left you alone with Bernard but I have been a bit unhappy lately and I did want to talk to this man and tell him one or two things.' She lit herself a cigarette but she didn't offer me one. 'I always feel better after I've talked things out . . . don't you?' She looked at me and her eyes glittered. Maybe she was feeling weepy. 'You won't understand yet,' she said. 'You wait until you have children and fall in love.'

I thought at the time it was a weird thing to say. The children coming first, I mean. Actually, I never think of Moona as having children. They're always out at discos or gone hop-picking.

'Look here,' said Moona. 'Your Ma is a bit worried about you. She doesn't know how far you've gone.'

I helped myself to one of her cigarettes. She fidgeted and plucked at the skin on her neck. 'I mean,' she said, 'have you or haven't you?'

I kept quiet.

'You do know what I'm getting at, don't you?' she asked.

I shrugged.

'I can't think why she didn't ask you herself,' said Moona.

'She tried,' I said.

'And did you tell her the truth?'

'Maybe,' I said.

I don't see what it's got to do with Moona or my mother. I don't ask them what they do with men. I doubt my mother does anything, seeing she's got my Dad. Actually, me and William Hornby haven't done anything either. Nothing to write home about, that is. We used to spend hours in his bedroom listening to records, just sitting there. His hands used to shake when he changed the record. Once he put his hand on my jumper and I punched him. I don't fancy him any more. He's shaved his head and he's got a tattoo on his arm.

When Moona was washing the dishes she talked a bit more about her man. I didn't really listen. He'd bought her a book of poems or something. She'd bought a new dress to go out with him later that afternoon. She showed me the dress. I said it was all right. She complained again that she couldn't fathom her man.

I lay on her bed while she busied herself getting ready to go out. *He* was sending a taxi for her. She had a bath and came back wrapped in a blue towel. She looked a hundred years old. The skin at the tops of her arms was all loose. When she was ready she didn't know what to do with me. 'I could give you a lift part-way in a taxi,' she offered.

'It's all right,' I told her. 'I'll go and talk to Bernard.'

When she had gone I looked about for cigarettes but there weren't any. I read a letter in a drawer from some man who wanted to tweak her nipples. It wasn't very well written; it was about the same standard as a letter from that creep William Hornby. I went down to the basement.

'Oh, it's you again,' said Bernard.

I lay on his bed and after a time he lay down too. He didn't touch me; he just lay there with his arms at his sides and his eyes wide open staring at the ceiling. It was raining somewhere. You could hear water trickling down a gutter. There were no traffic noises, no cups rattling, no clocks ticking. It was like being in a cave and as if there were no other people anywhere in the world; as if Bernard wasn't there either. Just me.

I didn't like it. I didn't like him being so quiet. I asked him to give me a cigarette but he shook his head. I don't know whether he meant he didn't smoke or that I couldn't have one. After a while he kissed me. I expected he would. You can generally tell. He was covered in after-shave lotion. William Hornby says that only creeps use after-shave. I thought that maybe, in between kissing me, Bernard might say something. But he didn't. It spoilt it really. There was a man I met in a cinema once, and another man last Christmas at a party. They asked me questions. They made noises. They wanted to know how old I was and all sorts of different things about me. I never answered them, but at least they asked.

I didn't want to stay in the basement with Bernard, not without cigarettes and nobody talking. I said I had to go now.

'Righty-ho,' he said.

I didn't see Moona again. When I went home my mother didn't have much to say for herself. 'Moona phoned me,' she said. 'I must say I was a bit ashamed. She mentioned you helped yourself to her cigarettes.'

Fancy Moona noticing that. I don't suppose Bernard told her anything about me. I feel sorry for both of them. Probably they should talk to someone.

THROUGH A GLASS BRIGHTLY

Norman Pearson went to the meeting because his neighbour's wife, Alison Freely, told him he ought to mix more. He was afraid that Alison's reference to the meeting was a roundabout way of telling him that he was taking up too much of her time, and instantly said that he had every intention of going, that indeed he had already made inquiries about it long before she had brought up the subject.

Two years before, his wife had left him for a career woman with a villa in Spain. He had never met the woman, but his wife had cruelly left a photograph of her in the suitcase on top of the wardrobe. He often took down the photograph and studied that unknown face, those eyes that had winked at his wife across a crowded room and spirited her out of his life. In spite of every effort, he had not yet adjusted to being on his own. He had read that single men were in demand at dinner parties and things, but though he had casually let drop, in conversations with colleagues at the office, that he was on the loose, in a manner of speaking, no one had ever taken him up on it, not even to the extent of asking him round for a cup of tea. Last February he had become quite pally with a divorcee in Mount Street – patting her dog, passing the time of day – until she sent him a note complaining about the dilapidation of the party wall at the back of his house. It wasn't that he objected to sharing the cost of doing something about it, rather that he dreaded some cowboy builder mutilating the rambler rose that he had planted against the wall in happier times. Actually, his wife had planted it; lately, he couldn't rid himself of the superstitious thought that if the rose didn't thrive, neither would he. The divorcee was still sending him solicitors' letters, because of course they were no longer on speaking terms and even the dog ignored him. He had come to the conclusion that if there was a demand for deserted men, men on the loose, then it existed somewhere else, in exotic Islington perhaps, or Hampstead, and had not yet reached East Croydon.

The meeting was called to discuss arrangements for the Mary Street Carnival, and was held upstairs in the Hare and Hounds. The accountant from No. 111, who owned a typist and a photocopying machine, had sent out the notices. It went without saying that his close friend J. J. Roberts, who was something controversial in the television world, took the chair. Not that people were fighting for the privilege of being that involved; not any more. Mary Street had organised a carnival, in summer, for the past eight years, and those serving on the Committee usually ended up out of pocket. It was a headache trying to recuperate expenses once the Steel Bands and the Inter-Action Groups had muscled in on the occasion. Nor had anyone forgotten the year the Committee, accused of being too middle-class in its attitude, had been persuaded to join forces with the Youth Centre at the end of the street. The youth leader, who was called Sunday and was an ethnic minority, had talked the landlord of the Hare and Hounds into applying for an extended licence. Afterwards, a majority of the residents, particularly those who had suffered broken windows, had protested that it was meant to be a day for the children. There was no denying that the Carnival itself had been a great success, at least until eight o'clock when the Committee were counting the day's takings in the Church Hall. Then someone shouted out the word 'Fire!', and naturally they had all run to see what was up. They only went as far as the door. Even so, when they turned round the cash boxes had simply vanished into thin air. There were the usual reasoned arguments along the lines of shooting being too good for 'them', and, send 'them' back on the next banana boat, but nothing came of it. The accountant had gone so far as to have notices printed, which were wired to the lamp posts, promising forgiveness all round and pleading for the money to be returned anonymously. Needless to say, he never heard a dicky bird. Since then, the accountant and J. J. Roberts, accompanied by a minder from the Leisure Centre, had gone round the stalls every half hour collecting whatever had accumulated in the cash boxes.

Carnival Day had evolved out of a desire to beautify the street. The proceeds of that first event had gone towards buying, and subsequently planting, trees along the edges of the pavement. This idea of environmental improvement was abandoned shortly after it was discovered that no one had taken into account the camber of the road. In no time at all the roots of the trees had begun to interfere with the drains, and the Council had to come round and uproot them – it came out of the rates, of course – and stick them back into huge concrete tubs that were an eyesore. Alison Freely had a tub right outside her house, which meant she couldn't park her car properly. She put poison in the soil and killed off her tree, but the Council said they hadn't the manpower to remove the tub. Now nobody really knew what the Carnival was in aid of, or indeed what happened to the proceeds. For many it was just an excuse to get rid of worn-out clothing and broken furniture.

At the meeting, when suggestions were called for, Mrs Riley the architect said what about a competition for a model of the street as it might be in fifty years time.

'Marvellous,' said J. J. Roberts. 'Bloody marvellous.'

Nobody else came up with anything quite as complicated, though the graphic designer from No. 89 attempted to persuade people that it would be a fun thing to paint their balconies in different colours. He said it wouldn't cost much and urged them to think of those sticks of rock one used to buy at seaside resorts: such colours – such luminous pinks and greens.

Betty Taylor, whom J. J. Roberts always referred to as Elizabeth Taylor, and who lived in compulsorily purchased property, said that it wasn't fair on people who didn't have balconies. A senior citizen, she had recently attended a talk given in the Church Hall by a member of the Women's Workshop and was becoming increasingly aware of the divisions caused by privilege. She said that if sticks of rock were only going to be distributed to balcony owners, then she would vote against it. The accountant told her that in his opinion balconies gave easy access to thieves, and she should thank her lucky stars she was without one.

It was then that Norman Pearson remarked that his mother had once been burgled in Streatham. The swine had taken her television set and the transistor radio but ignored her crystal ball on the mantelpiece. He was astonished at the reaction resulting from this routine, though undoubtedly sad, little tale.

'Fortune telling,' hissed Mrs Riley. 'Fortune telling.' The accountant beat at his thigh with his fist and laughed uncontrollably. 'Christ,' exploded J. J. Roberts. 'How bloody marvellous.'

The next morning, when they were both emptying rubbish into their respective bins, Alison asked Norman how he had got on at the meeting. He said he had found it stimulating. 'That show-off Roberts was in charge.'

'Of course,' Alison said. 'Many others turn up?'

'One or two,' he said, and as she was going back into the house, called out, 'I'm going to tell fortunes.' But his words were lost in the slamming of her door and he was glad that she hadn't heard, because he had promised not to tell anybody, so as to be more mysterious on the day.

He collected the crystal ball from his mother's a week before the Carnival. She didn't want to part with it; she said it was valuable. In the end he almost snatched it from her, and was surprised at its weight. Though he looked into it for hours, even after he had drunk three-quarters of a bottle of retsina, he could see nothing within its depths but a milk-white cloud. Irritated, he shook it, as though it was one of those children's snow-flake scenes encased in glass, but still he saw nothing beyond that impenetrable mist. His own life, he thought, staring gloomily out at the bunting already strung across the street, was becoming equally opaque. Deep down, he blamed his wife, for if she had not been so flighty he would never have been in such a predicament.

Preparations for the Carnival began at eight o'clock in the morning. They were lucky with the weather, in that it wasn't actually raining. J. J. Roberts strode up and down in a pair of shorts, chalking lines and circles on the surface of the road, and pointing at the sky. 'Lots of blue,' he shouted optimistically, whenever anybody appeared on the balconies. When he saw Norman, he cried out, 'Looking forward to it, Pearson?'

'Rather,' said Norman, wishing he had the courage to go to a main-line station and take a train in any direction.

At one o'clock the merry-go-round, the slide, the racks of second-hand clothing were in their allotted spaces. The home-made cakes, the bags of fudge and toffee, the rag dolls and the tea-cosies lay spread along the trestle tables. From behind each privet hedge wafted a smell of frying sausages and hamburgers, of kebabs roasting above charcoal. A man on stilts, thin arms held wide, stood like a pylon in the middle of the road. Hordes of little children, pursued by parents, ran between his legs, screaming.

The Lady Mayoress opened the proceedings, standing on J. J. Roberts's balcony and shouting through a loudspeaker. Norman was crouched at a rickety table inside a wigwam anchored precariously in the gutter. He wore a

flouncy dress loaned to him by the accountant's wife, dark
glasses and a Davy Crockett hat. No one had recognised
him when he appeared in the street. He was straining to
hear the Mayoress's words when some children pushed
against the wigwam. The table collapsed, sending the crystal ball flying into the gutter. When he picked it up there
were tiny hair-line cracks upon its surface. It made all the
difference.

His first customers were a man and a woman, neither of
whom had he ever seen before, and he was able to tell them
that they were going on a long journey, somewhere hot,
without vegetation.

'Good heavens,' breathed the woman.

Encouraged, Norman studied the scratches carefully
and, screwing up his eyes, fancied he saw the marks of tyre
tracks.

'It's not going to be all plain sailing,' he said. 'I foresee
trouble.' He charged the couple ten pence and realised, too
late, that he could have asked for fifty. He heard them
outside the tent, informing someone that the crystal gazer
was incredible, absolutely incredible. She had told them all
about that documentary they had made for 'War on Want',
when the crank shaft went and David, but for the cham-
pagne, would almost certainly have died of dehydration.

A queue began to form outside the wigwam. The noise,
the jostling, was tremendous.

'Stop it,' Norman protested, as a youth with a plug of
cotton-wool in his ear insisted on entering with two of his
friends.

'There's no room,' he warned, hanging on to his Davy
Crockett hat as the tent lurched sideways.

'Get on with it,' ordered the youth belligerently.

'Well,' said Norman. 'You've been ill recently, with
headaches.'

'Rubbish,' sneered the youth.

'Earache, then,' said Norman. 'I see a tall man with very long legs. He's waving his arms.'

'Bugger me,' said the youth, all the cockiness gone from him.

'You were mugged,' said Norman confidently, staring at a wavy line that looked not unlike the handle of a teacup. 'Attacked in some way.'

'Gerroff,' cried the youth, recovering. 'I weren't attacked, you stupid bag. Me Dad hit me with a poker.'

When Betty Taylor came into the wigwam, Norman found himself telling her that she had not had much of a life.

'You're right,' she said. 'You're right.'

'You've never had it easy, right from a child.'

'No,' she sniffed. 'I haven't.'

'And I can't see anything better in the future,' Norman said. 'You're not one of Nature's darlings. I wish I could pretend otherwise, but the crystal ball never lies.'

Betty Taylor left the wigwam in tears. Norman felt dreadful the moment she had gone, and wondered what had made him so peculiarly truthful. After all, she had done nothing to him.

Nevertheless he enjoyed himself; it was simple once he'd got the hang of it. Nicotine stains on the fingers pointed to a death-wish, blood-shot eyes denoted too much dependence on the bottle, nervous laughter was a sure sign of inferiority. It was all a matter of observation.

Half way through the afternoon a woman in a white dress squeezed into the wigwam. She was coughing. 'You're supposed to be frightfully good,' she said huskily. 'Do tell what's in store for me.'

Norman looked at her face, at her eyes, and then peered into the crystal ball. 'Sometimes,' he told her, 'I find it's not altogether wise to pass on the information. It might upset people – some people – if the exact picture were given.'

'Oh, come now,' she said. 'You can tell me. I've paid my ten pence.'

'I see a house,' he said. 'It's painted white. It's not here . . . it's somewhere abroad.' He glanced at her sunburnt arms and went on, 'You've only recently returned. You weren't alone.'

'Go on,' said the woman. 'You're awfully good so far.'

'This other person,' he said, 'is unhappy. It's a woman. Her surname begins with P, I think. Yes, it's definitely P.'

'What does this P person do?' asked the woman. She was holding a little fold of skin at the base of her neck, twisting it between thumb and forefinger.

'Nothing at the moment,' said Norman, 'that's the trouble. She used to look after someone, but then she walked out.'

The woman stared at Norman.

'I think it was her mother,' he said. 'Someone close, anyway. At any rate they took it badly. I see a station platform and a figure standing very near the rails. There's a train coming.'

'Oh, God!' said the woman.

'There's something else,' Norman said, 'something else coming through. I've got it. I've a picture of a woman lying down and someone bending over her, someone in a white coat. Is she at the dentist's, I wonder?' He took his time; he was sweating and his dark glasses kept sliding on the bridge of his nose. At last he said, 'The woman has a sore . . . no, not a sore, more like a small lump just beneath her adam's apple. It's serious.'

After a moment the woman asked, 'Which one is it? The woman at the station or the one with the name beginning with P?'

'Ah, well,' said Norman, 'I'm only the projector, not the identifier. I leave it to those who consult me to work out whose life is in danger.'

68

The woman put a pound note on the table and ducked out into the street. Norman could hear her coughing above the noise of the Steel Band on the corner.

When it was all over and he'd been congratulated on his success – more than one member of the Committee asked if he was free next week for drinks, for supper – Norman went home, and removing the suitcase from the wardrobe took out the photograph and tore it in half across the throat.

Then he sat at the table and wrote a note to the divorcee, telling her that she could pull down his wall whenever she felt like it. If necessary he would pay for the whole caboodle.

Life wasn't all roses.

BREAD AND BUTTER SMITH

Whenever the Christmas season approaches I always think of the good times we had, my wife and I, at the Adelphi Hotel just after the war. When I say 'times' I wouldn't like to give the impression that we were regular visitors to the hostelry at the foot of Mount Pleasant – that would be misleading. As a matter of fact we only stayed there twice. Before and in between those occasions we put up at the Exchange Hotel in Stanley Street, next door to the station.

Though born and brought up in Liverpool, I had crossed the water and gone to live on the Wirral at the earliest opportunity – you did if you came from Anfield – but I was in the habit of popping over on the ferry each Christmas to carve the turkey, on Boxing Day, for my sister Constance. She was, apart from my wife, my only surviving relative. Leaving aside the matter of Mr Brownlow, Constance's house in Belmont Road wasn't a suitable place to stay – to be accurate, it was one up and one down with the WC in the backyard – and as the wife and I found it more convenient to occupy separate bedrooms I always booked into an hotel. I could afford it. I was in scrap metal, which was a good line of business to be in if you didn't mind being called a racketeer, which I didn't. The wife minded, but as I often tell her, where would she be today if I hadn't been. She'd soon buck up her ideas if she found herself languishing in the public ward of a National Health hospital.

If it hadn't been for Smith, we'd have stuck with the Exchange and not gone on switching hotels the way we did. Not that it achieved anything; he always ferreted us out. I fully believe that if we had changed venues altogether and given Blackpool or Hastings a whirl he'd have turned up in the grill room on the night before Christmas Eve, wearing that same crumpled blue suit, as though drawn by a magnet. I don't want to malign the poor devil, and don't think I'm being wise after the event, but I always found him a bit of a strain, not to mention an aggravation, right from the moment we met him, which was that first year we stayed at the Exchange.

We'd had our dinner, thank God, main course, pudding and so forth, and the waiter had just brought us a bowl of fruit. No bananas or tangerines, of course – too soon after the end of hostilities – but there was half a peach and a few damsons and some apples nicely polished.

'Shall I have the peach?' my wife said.

'Have what you like,' I told her. I've never been enamoured of fruit.

It was then that this fellow at the next table, who seemed to have nothing in front of him but a plate of bread and butter, leaned forward and said to me: 'The waiter is doing what King Alcinous may have done to the storm-beaten Greeks.'

That's exactly what he said, give or take a few words. You meet a lot of loopy individuals among the educated classes, and at the time I mistook him for one of those. Loopy, that is.

I ignored him, but the wife said: 'It's a thought, isn't it?' She was nervy that far back. Once she'd been foolish enough to respond, we couldn't get shot of him. I'm an abrupt sort of person. I don't do things I don't want to do – never have – whereas the wife, long before her present unfortunate state manifested itself, is the sort of person who apologises when some uncouth lout sends her reeling into the gutter. Don't get me wrong, Smith was never a scrounger. He paid his whack at the bar, and if he ever ate with us it was hardly an imposition because he never seemed to order anything but bread and butter. Even on

Christmas Day all he had was a few cuts of the breast and his regular four slices. He wasn't thin either. He had more of a belly on him than me, and he looked well into his fifties, which I put down to his war experiences. He was in the desert, or so he told the wife, and once saw Rommel through field glasses.

All along, I made no bones about my feelings for Smith. That first night, when he intruded over the fruit, I turned my face away. Later on, whenever he began pestering us about the Maginot line, or the Wife of Andros, or his daft theory that the unknown soldier was very probably a woman who had been scurrying along the hedgerows looking for hens' eggs when a shell had blown her to pieces at Ypres, I just got to my feet and walked away. My wife brought it on herself. She shouldn't have sat like patience on a monument, listening to the fool, her left eyelid twitching the way it does when she's out of her depth. His conversation was right over her head.

Not that he seemed to notice; he couldn't get enough of us. When we said we wouldn't be available on Boxing Day, he even hinted that we might take him along to Belmont Road. I was almost tempted to take him up on it. Mr Brownlow was argumentative and had a weak bladder. Constance had picked him up outside the Co-op in 1931. It would have served Smith right to have had to sit for six hours in Constance's front parlour, two lumps of coal in the grate, one glass of port and lemon to last the night, and nothing by way of entertainment beyond escorting Mr Brownlow down the freezing backyard to the WC.

The following year, to avoid the possibility of bumping into Smith, we went to the Adelphi. And damn me, he was there. There was a dance on Christmas Eve in the main lounge, and I'll never forget how he and the wife began in a melancholy and abstracted manner to circle the floor, her black dress rustling as she moved, and he almost on tiptoe because he was shorter than her. Every time he fox-trotted the wife in my direction he gave an exaggerated little start of surprise, as though I was the last person he expected to see. When he fetched her back to the table, he said, 'I do hope you have no objection to my dancing with your lady wife. I wouldn't like to give offence.'

'No offence taken,' I said. I've never seen the point of dancing. 'Do as you please.'

'We shall, we shall,' the wife said, laughing in that way she has.

We had to play cards with the blighter on Christmas Day. On Boxing Day it was almost a relief, which was saying something, to travel out on the tram to Anfield for the festivities with Constance and Mr Brownlow.

The next year we tried the Exchange again, never thinking that lightning would strike twice, or three times for that matter but, blow me, it did. Smith turned up an hour after we arrived. I did briefly begin to wonder who was avoiding who, but it was obvious that he was as pleased as punch to see us.

'My word,' he cried out. 'This is nice. My word, it is.'

I sensed he was different. There was nothing I could put my finger on; his suit was the same and he still blinked a lot, but something had changed in him. I mentioned as much to the wife. 'He's different, don't you think?' I said.

'Different?' she said.

'Cocky,' I said. 'If you know what I mean?'

'I don't,' she said.

'Something in the eye,' I insisted.

But she wouldn't have it.

All the same, I was right. Why, he even had the blithering nerve to give me a present, wrapped up in coloured paper with one of those damn soft bows on the top. It was a book on golf, which was a lucky choice, inspired almost, as I'd only taken up the game a few months before. I didn't run amok showing my gratitude, nor did I scamper upstairs and parcel up one of the handkerchiefs the wife had given to me. To be frank, I didn't even say thank you.

I didn't need acquaintances, then. As long as I had the wife sitting there, reading a library book and smoking one of her Craven A cigarettes, I didn't have to go to the bother of being pleasant. Not that Smith noticed my lack of enthusiasm for his company. It appeared to me that no matter where I was, whether in the corridor minding my own business, or coming out of the lift, or having a quiet drink in the Steve Donoghue Bar, he was forever bobbing up alongside me, or behind me – and always a mine of useful information. 'Are you aware,' he'd ask, eyeing the beer pitching in my glass as a train rumbled out of the station below, 'that the first locomotive was so heavy that it broke the track beneath it?'

He didn't seem to know anybody in the city, but a couple of times I saw him going down in the lift very late at night with his hat and coat on. God knows where he was off to. Once, I saw him in the deserted booking-hall of the station. I was on the fourth floor of the hotel, in the small hours, looking out of the back windows at the arched roof beneath, estimating what price, per ton, the cast-iron ribs would fetch on the scrap market. It was raining and Smith was perambulating up and down, hatless, holding an umbrella in a cock-eyed way, followed by a flock of pigeons. While I was watching, Smith suddenly spun round and flourished his brolly at the pigeons. I took it that he was drunk. The birds flapped upwards in alarm. There wasn't a pane of glass left intact in the roof – it had all been blasted to smithereens during the blitz. One of the pigeons in attempting to escape through the ribs must have severed a wing on the shards of glass. It sort of staggered in mid-air and then dropped like a lump of mud to the granite floor of the booking-hall. I couldn't hear the noise it made, flopping down like that, but it obviously gave Smith quite a turn. He froze, his gamp held out to one side like some railway guard waiting to lower his flag for a train to depart. I couldn't see his face because I was looking down on him, but I could tell by the stance of the man, one foot turned inwards, one arm stuck outwards, that he was frightened. Then he took a running kick at the thing on the ground and sent it skidding against the base of the tobacco kiosk. After a moment he went over to the kiosk and squatted down. He stayed like that for some time, rocking backwards and forwards on his haunches. Then he took out his handkerchief, laid it over the pigeon, and walked away. He was definitely drunk.

That final year, 1949, I switched back to the Adelphi. You've never clapped eyes on anything like that hotel. It's built like a Cunarder. Whenever I lurched through the revolving doors into the lobby, I never thought I'd disembark until I'd crossed the Atlantic. The lounge is the size of a dry dock; there are little balconettes running the entire length of it, fronted by ornamental grilles. Sometimes, if the staff dropped a nickel-plated teapot in the small kitchen behind the rostrum, I imagined we'd struck an iceberg. I never used to think like that until Smith put his oar in. It was he who said that all big hotels were designed to resemble ocean liners. On another occasion – because he was a contrary beggar – he said that the balconettes were modelled after confessionals in churches. I never sat in them after that.

We arrived at four o'clock on the 23rd December and went immediately into the lounge for tea and cakes. I had just told the wife to sit up straight – there's nothing worse than a slouching woman, particularly if she's got a silver fox fur slung round her shoulders – when I thought I saw, reflected in the mirrors behind the balconettes, the unmistakable figure of Smith. I slopped tea into my saucer.

'What's up?' asked my wife.

'I could swear I just saw that blighter Smith,' I said. 'Could I have been mistaken, do you think?'

'What?' she said. 'You? Surely not.' She was lifting up her veil and tucking it back over the brim of her hat, and you could tell how put out she was; both her cheeks were red with annoyance.

The odd thing was that he never came into the grill room that night. 'Perhaps it wasn't him,' I said. 'Perhaps it was a trick of the light.'

'Some trick,' she said.

'If he has the effrontery to present me with another little seasonal offering,' I warned her, 'I'll throw it back in his face.'

After we had finished our pudding my wife said she was off to her bed.

'You can't go up now,' I said. 'I've paid good money to be here.'

'If I'm to live through the excitement of visiting Constance and Mr Brownlow,' she said, 'I'll need all the rest I can get.' She fairly ran out of the grill room; she never had any staying power.

I had a drink in the bar and asked the fellow behind the counter if he'd seen Smith, but he didn't seem to know who I was talking about. That's the trouble with shifting from one hotel to another – none of the staff know you from Adam. I looked into the smoking-room about ten o'clock and he wasn't there either. I could have done with Smith. The hotel was crowded with guests, some in uniform, full of the Christmas spirit and anxious that everyone should join in. Several times I was almost drawn into one of those conversations about what branch of the services I'd been in during the hostilities. I'll say that much for Smith; he never asked me what I'd done in the war. At a quarter past ten I went into the lounge and ordered myself another drink.

There weren't too many people in there. A dance was in progress in the French room; I could hear the band playing some number made popular by Carmen Miranda. The waiter had just set my glass down in front of me when the doors burst open at the side and a line of revellers spilled into the lounge and began doing the conga down the length of the pink carpet towards the Christmas tree at the far end. They wound in and out of the sofas and the tables, clasping each other at the waist and kicking up the devil of a noise. Mercifully, having snaked once round the tree, showering the carpet with pine-needles, they headed back for the dance floor. And suddenly, for a split second, before he disappeared behind the tree, I thought I saw Smith near the end of the line, clutching hold of a stout individual who was wearing a paper hat. The fat man appeared again, but I was mistaken about Smith. Oddly enough, he must have been on my mind because for the rest of the evening I fancied I caught glimpses of him – coming out of the gents, going into the lift, standing at the top of the stairs looking down into the lounge – but it was never him.

Shortly after midnight I went upstairs to unpack my belongings. My room was on the first floor and overlooked Lewis's department store. I'd changed into my pyjamas – such as they were – and was putting my Sunday suit on a hanger when I realised that my wife had forgotten to include my grey spotted tie among the rest of my things. It wasn't that I gave a tinker's cuss about that particular tie, it was just that Mr Brownlow had bought it for me the previous Christmas and my not wearing it on Boxing Day would undoubtedly cause an uproar.

I went out into the corridor, determined to ask the wife what she meant by it. It wasn't as if she had a lot on her mind. Unfortunately, I forgot that the door was self-locking and it shut behind me. I rapped on my wife's door for what seemed like hours. I've never seen the point of chucking money away on pyjamas; the draw-string had gone from the trousers and there wasn't one button left on the jacket. When my wife finally deigned to open up, she too stepped over the threshold, and in an instant her door had slammed shut as well. I admit I lost my head. I ran up and down, swearing, trying to find a broom cupboard to hide in; any moment those blighters from the French room could have come prancing along the corridor.

'Fetch a porter,' advised my wife.

'Not like this,' I shouted. 'I'm not fit.'

'Here,' she said, and she took off her dressing-gown – it had white fur round the sleeves – and handed it to me.

I had crept half way down the stairs when I heard carol singing one floor below. I just couldn't face anyone, not wearing that damn-fool dressing-gown and my trousers at half mast. I hopped back upstairs and at that moment the wife called out to me from the doorway of her room; apparently her door hadn't been locked after all.

I spent an uncomfortable night in the wife's bed – I don't sleep well – and when I switched on the light to see if I could find anything to read, there was only the Bible. The room was a pig-sty; she hadn't emptied her suitcase or hung anything up, and there was a slice of buttered bread on top of her fox fur. I woke her and asked if she had a library book handy.

'For God's sake,' she said. 'I'm worn out.'

I was having afternoon tea the following day, on my own – the wife had gone window-shopping in Bold Street – when Smith arrived at the hotel. He said a relative had been taken ill and he'd had to visit them in hospital. Being Smith, he couldn't leave it at that. He had to give me a lecture on some damn-fool theory of his that we thought ourselves into illnesses. Our minds, he said, controlled our bodies. Some blasted Greek or other had known it centuries ago.

Faced with him, and realising that he'd be dogging my footsteps for the next forty-eight hours, I grew irritated. Don't forget, I hadn't had much sleep, and there was some sort of expression on his face, some sort of light in his eyes that annoyed me. I don't know how to explain it; he looked foolish, almost happy and it rubbed me up the wrong way. I wanted to get rid of him once and for all. It was no use insulting the man; I had done that often enough and it was like water off a duck's back. Then an idea came to me. I had recognised right from the beginning that he was a prudish sort of fellow. I knew that he had never married, and I had never seen him strike up a conversation with an unescorted woman, apart from the wife. He preferred the company of married couples, providing they were respectable.

'Blow me down,' I said. 'I've been getting pains in my legs for the past eight years. Now I know why.'

'Why?' he asked.

'On account of the wife,' I said.

'Your wife?' he said, tugging at his little ginger moustache.

I implied that the wife had led me something of a dance. She was under the doctor for it, of course. It had gone on for years. She couldn't be blamed, not exactly. That's why I was forced to keep changing hotels . . . there had been various incidents of a somewhat scandalous nature with various men. As I spoke I stumbled over the words – I knew he wasn't a complete fool. I expressed the hope that he wouldn't betray my confidences. I didn't feel bad telling lies about my wife. It wouldn't get back. There was no danger of Smith repeating it to somebody he knew, who might repeat it to somebody we knew, because none of us knew anybody. It shut him up all right. The light went out of his eyes.

At seven o'clock that evening, according to the waiter on

duty, Smith came into the smoking-room and ordered a pot of tea. The waiter noticed that he kept clattering the ash-tray up and down on the table. When the tea was brought to him, he said, 'Oh, and I'll need some bread and butter if it's all the same to you.' While the waiter was gone Smith took out his service revolver and shot himself in the head. He died almost at once. He must have been more upset about his relative being ill than he let on.

We never went back to the Adelphi, or to the Exchange for that matter. Not because of anything to do with Smith, but because less than a year later the wife began to show signs of instability; in any case the following August Constance passed on and there was certainly no call to clap eyes on Mr Brownlow ever again.

One could say that my wife has passed on too, only in her case it's more that she's wandered out of reach. As Bread and Butter Smith might have put it: 'All the world's against her, so that Crete (alias Rainhill Mental Institution) is her only refuge.'

CLAP HANDS, HERE COMES CHARLIE

Two weeks before Christmas, Angela Bisson gave Mrs Henderson six tickets for the theatre. Mrs Henderson was Angela Bisson's cleaning lady.

'I wanted to avoid giving you money,' Angela Bisson told her. 'Anybody can give money. Somehow the whole process is so degrading . . . taking it . . . giving it. They're reopening the Empire Theatre for a limited season. I wanted to give you a treat. Something you'll always remember.'

Mrs Henderson said, 'Thank you very much.' She had never, when accepting money, felt degraded.

Her husband, Charles Henderson, asked her how much Angela Bisson had tipped her for Christmas.

Mrs Henderson said not much. 'In fact,' she admitted, 'nothing at all. Not in your actual pounds, shillings and pence. We've got tickets for the theatre instead.'

'What a discerning woman,' cried Charles Henderson. 'It's just what we've always needed.'

'The kiddies will like it,' protested Mrs Henderson. 'It's a pantomime. They've never been to a pantomime.'

Mrs Henderson's son, Alec, said *Peter Pan* wasn't a pantomime. At least not what his mother understood by the word. Of course, there was a fairy-tale element to the story, dealing as it did with Never-Never land and lost boys, but there was more to it than that. 'It's written on several levels,' he informed her.

'I've been a lost boy all my life,' muttered Charles Henderson, but nobody heard him.

'And I doubt,' said Alec, 'if our Moira's kiddies will make head nor tail of it. It's full of nannies and coal fires burning in the nursery.'

'Don't talk rot,' fumed Charles Henderson. 'They've seen coal fires on television.'

'Shut up, Charlie,' said Alec. His father hated being called Charlie.

'Does it have a principal boy?' asked Mrs Henderson, hopefully.

'Yes and no,' said Alec. 'Not in the sense you mean. Don't expect any singing or any smutty jokes. It's allegorical.'

'God Almighty,' said Charles Henderson.

When Alec had gone out to attend a Union meeting, Mrs Henderson told her husband he needn't bother to come to the theatre. She wasn't putting up with him and Alec having a pantomime of their own during the course of the evening and spoiling it for everyone else. She'd ask Mrs Rafferty from the floor above to go in his place.

'By heck,' shouted Charles Henderson, striking his forehead with the back of his hand, 'why didn't I think of that? Perish the thought that our Alec should be the one to be excluded. I'm only the blasted bread-winner.' He knew his wife was just mouthing words.

Mrs Rafferty's answer to such an outlandish invitation was a foregone conclusion. She wouldn't give it houseroom. Mrs Rafferty hadn't been out of the building for five years, not since she was bashed over the head coming home from Bingo.

All the same, Charles Henderson was irritated. His wife's attitude, and the caustic remarks addressed to him earlier by Alec brought on another attack of indigestion. It was no use going to his bed and lying flat. He knew from experience that it wouldn't help. In the old days, when they had lived in a proper house, he could have stepped out of the back door and perambulated up and down the yard for a few minutes. Had there been anything so exalted as a back door in this hell-hole, going out of it certainly wouldn't improve his health. Not without a parachute. He couldn't even open the window for a breath of air. This high up there was generally a howling gale blowing in from the river — it would suck the Christmas cards clean off the sideboard. It wasn't normal, he thought, to be perpetually on a par with the clouds. People weren't meant to look out of windows and see nothing but sky, particularly if they weren't looking upwards. God knows how Moira's kiddies managed. They were stuck up in the air over Kirby. When Moira and Alec had been little they'd played in the street — Moira on the front step fiddling with her dolly, Alec on one roller-skate scooting in and out of the lamp-posts. Of course there was no denying that it had been nice at first to own a decent bathroom and have hot water coming out of the tap. After only a few weeks it had become unnecessary to scrub young Alec's neck with his toothbrush; the dirt just floated off on the towel. But there was surely more to life than a clean neck. Their whole existence, once work was over for the day, was lived as though inside the cabin of an aeroplane. And they weren't going anywhere — there wasn't a landing field in sight. Just stars. Thousands of the things, on clear nights, winking away outside the double glazing. It occurred to Charles Henderson that there were too many of them for comfort or for grandeur. It was quality that counted, not quantity.

At the end of the yard of the terraced house in which he had once lived, there had been an outside toilet. Sitting within the evil-smelling little shed, its door swinging on broken hinges, he had sometimes glimpsed one solitary star hung motionless above the city. It had, he felt, given perspective to his situation, his situation in the wider sense — beyond his temporary perch. He was earthbound, mortal, and a million light-years separated him from that pale diamond burning in the sky. One star was all a man needed.

On the night of the outing to the theatre, a bit of a

rumpus took place in the lift. It was occasioned by Moira's lad, Wayne, jabbing at all the control buttons and giving his grandmother a turn.

Alec thumped Wayne across the ear and Charles Henderson flared up. 'There was no cause to do that,' he shouted, though indeed there had been. Wayne was a shocking kiddie for fiddling with things.

'Belt up, Charlie,' ordered Alec.

Alec drove them to the Empire Theatre in his car. It wasn't a satisfactory arrangement as far as Charles Henderson was concerned but he had no alternative. The buses came and went as they pleased. He was forced to sit next to Alec because he couldn't stand being parked in the back with the children and neither Moira nor Mrs Henderson felt it was safe in the passenger seat. Not with Alec at the wheel. Every time Alec accelerated going round a corner, Charles Henderson was swung against his son's shoulder.

'Get over, can't you?' cried Alec. 'Stop leaning on me, Charlie.'

When they passed the end of the street in which they had lived a decade ago, Mrs Henderson swivelled in her seat and remarked how changed it was, oh how changed. All those houses knocked down, and for what? Alec said that in his opinion it was good riddance to bad rubbish. The whole area had never been anything but a slum.

'Perhaps you're right, son,' said Mrs Henderson. But she was pandering to him.

Charles Henderson was unwise enough to mention times gone by. He was talking to his wife. 'Do you remember all the men playing football in the street after work?'

'I do,' she said.

'And using the doorway of the Lune Laundry for a goal-post? It was like living in a village, wasn't it?'

'A village,' hooted Alec. 'With a tobacco warehouse and a brewery in the middle of it? Some village.'

'We hunted foxes in the field behind the public house,' reminisced Charles Henderson. 'And we went fishing in the canal.'

'You did. You were never at home,' said Mrs Henderson, without rancour.

'What field?' scoffed Alec. 'What canal?'

'There was a time,' said Charles Henderson, 'when we snared rabbits every Saturday and had them for Sunday dinner. I tell no lies. You might almost say we lived off the land.'

'Never-Never land, more like,' sneered Alec, and he drove, viciously, the wrong way down a one-way street.

When they got to the town centre he made them all get out and stand about in the cold while he manoeuvred the Mini backwards and forwards in the underground car park. He cursed and gesticulated.

'Behave yourself,' shouted Charles Henderson, and he strode in front of the bonnet and made a series of authoritative signals. Alec deliberately drove the car straight at him.

'Did you see what that madman did?' Charles Henderson asked his wife. 'He ran over my foot.'

'You're imagining things,' said Mrs Henderson, but when he looked down he saw quite clearly the tread of the tyre imprinted upon the Cherry Blossom shine of his Sunday left shoe.

When the curtain went up, he was beginning to feel the first twinges of his indigestion coming on again. It wasn't to be wondered at, all that swopping of seats because Moira had a tall bloke sitting in front of her, and the kiddies tramping back and forth to the toilet, not to mention the carry-on over parking the car. At least he hadn't got Alec sitting next to him. He found the first act of *Peter Pan* a bit of a mystery. It was very old-fashioned and cosy. He supposed they couldn't get a real dog to play the part.

Some of the scenery could do with a lick of paint. He didn't actually laugh out loud when Mr Darling complained that nobody coddled him – oh no, why should they, seeing he was only the bread-winner – but he did grunt sardonically; Mrs Henderson nudged him sharply with her elbow. He couldn't for the life of him make out who or what Tinkerbell was, beyond being a sort of glow-worm bobbing up and down on the nursery wall, until Wendy had her hair pulled for wanting Peter to kiss her, and then he more or less guessed Tinkerbell was a female. It was a bit suggestive, all that. And at the end of the first scene when they all flew out of the window, something must have gone wrong with the wires because one of the children never got off the ground. They brought the curtain down fast. Wayne was yawning his head off.

During Acts Two and Three, Charles Henderson dozed. He was aware of loud noises and children screaming in a bloodthirsty fashion. He hoped Wayne wasn't having one of his tantrums. It was confusing for him. He was dreaming he was fishing in the canal for tiddlers and a damn big crocodile crawled up the bank with a clock ticking inside it. Then he heard a drum beating and a voice cried out 'To die will be an awfully big adventure.' He woke up then with a start. He had a pain in his arm.

In the interval they retired to the bar, Moira and himself and Alec. Mrs Henderson stayed with the kiddies, to give Moira a break. Alec paid for a round of drinks. 'Are you enjoying it then, Charlie?' he asked.

'It's a bit loud for me,' said Charles Henderson. 'But I see what you mean about it being written on different levels.'

'You do surprise me,' said Alec. 'I could have sworn you slept through most of it.'

Moira said little Tracy was terrified of the crocodile but she loved the doggie.

'Some doggie,' muttered Charles Henderson. 'I could smell the moth balls.'

'But Wayne thinks it's lovely,' said Moira. 'He's really engrossed.'

'I could tell,' Charles Henderson said. 'They must have heard him yawning in Birkenhead.'

'It's one of his signs,' defended Moira. 'Yawning. He always yawns when he's engrossed.' She herself was enjoying it very much, though she hadn't understood at first what Mr Darling was doing dressed up as Captain Hook.

'It's traditional,' Alec told her.

'What are you on about?' asked Charles Henderson. 'That pirate chappie was never Mr Darling.'

'Yes it was, Dad,' said Moira. 'I didn't cotton on myself at first, but it was the same man.'

'I suppose it saves on wages,' Charles Henderson said. Alec explained it was symbolic. The kindly Mr Darling and the brutal Captain Hook were two halves of the same man.

'There wasn't more than a quarter of Mr Darling,' cried Charles Henderson, heatedly. 'That pirate was waving his cutlass about every time I opened my eyes. I can't see the point of it, can you, Moira?'

Moira said nothing, but her mouth drooped at the corners. She was probably thinking about her husband who had run off and left her with two kiddies and a gas bill for twenty-seven quid.

'The point,' said Alec, 'is obvious. Mr Darling longs to murder his offspring.' He was shouting quite loudly. 'Like fathers in real life. They're always out to destroy their children.'

'What's up with you?' asked Mrs Henderson, when her husband had returned to his seat.

'That Alec,' hissed Charles Henderson. 'He talks a load of codswallop. I'd like to throttle him.'

During Act Four Charles Henderson asked his wife for a

peppermint. His indigestion was fearsome. Mrs Henderson told him to shush. She too seemed engrossed in the pantomime. Wayne was sitting bolt upright. Charles Henderson tried to concentrate. He heard some words but not others. The lost boys were going back to their Mums, that much he gathered. Somebody called Tiger Lily had come into it. And Indians were beating tom-toms. His heart was beating so loudly that it was a wonder Alec didn't fly off the handle and order him to keep quiet. Wendy had flown off with the boys, jerkily, and Peter was asleep. It was odd how it was all to do with flying. That Tinkerbell person was flashing about among the cloth trees. He had the curious delusion that if he stood up on his seat, he too might soar up into the gallery. It was a daft notion because when he tried to shift his legs they were as heavy as lead. Mrs Darling would be pleased to see the kiddies again. She must have gone through hell. He remembered the time Alec had come home half an hour late from the Cubs – the length of those minutes, the depth of that fear. It didn't matter what his feelings had been towards Alec for the last ten years. He didn't think you were supposed to feel much for grown-up children. He had loved little Alec, now a lost boy, and that was enough.

Something dramatic was happening on stage. Peter had woken up and was having a disjointed conversation with Tinkerbell, something to do with cough mixture and poison. *Tink, you have drunk my medicine . . . it was poisoned and you drank it to save my life . . . Tink dear, are you dying? . . .* The tiny star that was Tinkerbell began to flicker. Charles Henderson could hear somebody sobbing. He craned sideways to look down the row and was astonished to see that his grandson was wiping at his eyes with the back of his sleeve. Fancy Wayne, a lad who last year had been caught dangling a hamster on a piece of string from a window on the fourteenth floor of the flats, crying about a light going out. Peter Pan was advancing towards the audience, his arms flung wide. *Her voice is so low I can hardly hear what she is saying. She says . . . she says she thinks she could get well again if children believed in fairies. Say quick that you believe. If you believe, clap your hands. Clap your hands and Tinkerbell will live.*

At first the clapping was muted, apologetic. Tinkerbell was reduced to a dying spark quivering on the dusty floorboards of the stage. Charles Henderson's own hands were clasped to his chest. There was a pain inside him as though somebody had slung a hook through his heart. The clapping increased in volume. The feeble Tinkerbell began to glow. She sailed triumphantly up the trunk of a painted tree. She grew so dazzling that Charles Henderson was blinded. She blazed above him in the skies of Never-Never land.

'Help me,' he said, using his last breath.

'Shut up, Charlie,' shouted Mrs Henderson, and she clapped and clapped until the palms of her hands were stinging.

SOMEWHERE MORE CENTRAL

I never took all that much notice of Grandma when she was alive. She was just there. I mean, I saw her at Christmas and things – I played cards with her to keep her occupied, and sometimes I let her take me out to tea in a cafe. She had a certain style, but the trouble was that she didn't look old enough to be downright eccentric. She wore fur coats mostly and a lot of jewelry, and hats with flowers flopping over the brim; she even painted her fingernails red. I was surprised that she'd died and even more surprised to hear that she was over seventy. I didn't cry or anything. My mother made enough fuss for both of us, moaning and pulling weird faces. I hadn't realised she was all that attached to her either. Whenever that advert came on the telly, the one about 'Make someone happy this weekend – give them a telephone call', Mother rolled her eyes and said 'My God!' When she rang Grandma, Grandma picked up the receiver and said 'Hallo, stranger.'

The night before the funeral there were the usual threats about how I needn't think I was going to wear my jeans and duffle coat. I didn't argue. My Mum knew perfectly well that I was going to wear them. I don't know why she wastes her breath. In the morning we had to get up at six o'clock, because we were travelling on the early train from Euston. It was February and mild, but just as we were sitting down to breakfast Mother said 'Oh, look Alice,' and outside the window snow was falling on the privet hedge.

When we set off for the station, the pavements were covered over. Mother had to cling onto the railings in case she slipped going down the steps. The bottoms of my jeans were all slushy in no time, so it was just as well she hadn't succeeded in making me wear those ghastly tights and high-heeled shoes. I thought maybe the trains would be delayed by the snow, but almost before we reached the station it was melting, and when we left London and the suburbs behind the snow had gone, even from the hedges and the trees. The sky turned blue. I was sorry on Mother's behalf. You can't really have a sad funeral with the sun shining. She looked terrible. She looked like that poster for 'Keep death off the roads'. She'd borrowed a black coat with a fur collar from the woman next door. She had black stockings and shoes to match. She doesn't wear make-up, and her mouth seemed to have been cut out of white paper. She never said much either. She didn't keep pointing things out as if I was still at primary school, like she usually does – 'Oh look, Alice, cows . . . Oh, Alice, look at the baa lambs.' She just stared out at the flying fields with a forlorn droop to her mouth.

Just as I'm a disappointment to Mother, she'd been a disappointment to Grandma. Only difference is, I couldn't care less. Whenever I have what they call 'problems' at school, I'm sent to the clinic to be understood by some psychologist with a nervous twitch, and he tells me it's perfectly natural to steal from the cloakroom and to cheat at French, and anyway it's all my mother's fault. They didn't have a clinic in Mother's day, so she's riddled with guilt. Apparently Grandma was very hurt when Mother got married and even more hurt when she got divorced. First Grandma had to go round pretending I was a premature baby and then later she had to keep her mouth shut about my father running off with another woman. She didn't tell anyone about the divorce for three years, not until everybody started doing the same thing, even the people in Grandma's road. Actually I don't think Grandma minded, not deep down; it was more likely that she just didn't care for the sound of it. There were a lot of things

Grandma didn't like the sound of: my record player for one, and the mattress in the spare room for another. If we went down town for tea, she used to peer at the menu outside the cafe for ages before making up her mind. It drove Mother wild. 'I don't think we'll stop,' Grandma would say, and Mother would ask irritably, 'Why ever not, Grandma?' and Grandma would toss her head and say firmly, 'I don't like the sound of it.' And off she'd trot down the road, swaying a little under the weight of her fur coat, the rain pattering on the cloth roses on her hat, with me and Mother trailing behind.

Once I went on my own with Grandma to a restaurant on the top floor of a large shopping store. We were going to have a proper meal with chips and bread and butter. The manager came forward to show us where to sit and we began to walk across this huge room to the far side, towards a table half-hidden behind a pillar. My mother always moves as if she's anxious to catch a bus, but Grandma took her time. She walked as if she was coming down a flight of stairs in one of those old movies. She looked to right and left, one hand raised slightly and arched at the wrist, as though she dangled a fan. I always felt she was waiting to be recognised by somebody or expecting to be asked to dance. She went slowly past all these tables, and then suddenly she stopped and said quite loudly, 'I don't like the sound of it.' She turned and looked at me; her mouth wobbled the way it did when she'd run out of peppermints or I'd beaten her at cards. I was sure everybody was looking at us, but I wasn't too embarrassed, not the way I am when Mother shows herself up – after all Grandma had nothing to do with me. The manager stopped too and came back to ask what was wrong. 'You're never putting me there?' said Grandma, as though he'd intended sending her to Siberia. She got her own way of course, 'somewhere more central', as she put it. Before we had tea she smoked a cigarette. When she flipped her lighter it played a little tune. 'I don't like being shoved into a corner,' she said. 'There's no point my light being hid under a bushel.'

I wasn't really looking forward to the funeral. I'd been in a church once before and I didn't think much of it. I couldn't have been the only one either, because the next time I passed it they'd turned it into a Bingo hall.

When we were nearly at Liverpool my mother said if I behaved myself I could go to the graveside. 'You mustn't ask damn fool questions,' she warned. 'And you mustn't laugh at the vicar.'

'Are they going to put Grandma in with Grandpa?' I asked. I knew Grandma hadn't liked him when he was alive. They hadn't slept in the same bed.

My mother said, Yes, they were. They had to – there was a shortage of space.

'Do you know,' she said, 'your Grandma was madly in love with a man called Walter. He played tennis on the Isle of Wight. He married somebody else.'

I wanted to know more about Walter, but the train was coming into Lime Street Station and Mother was doing her usual business of jumping round like a ferret in a box and telling me to comb my hair and pull myself together. She led me at a run up the platform because she said we had to be first in the queue for a taxi. We had a connection to catch at another station.

It turned out that there was a new one-way system for traffic that Mother hadn't known about. If we'd walked, all we'd have had to do, she said, was to sprint past Blacklers and through Williamson Square, and then up Stanley Street and we'd have been there. As it was we went on a sort of flyover and then a motorway and it took twenty minutes to reach Exchange Station. She was breathless with anxiety when she paid the cab driver. We hadn't bought tickets for the next train and the man at the barrier wouldn't let us through without them.

'But they're burying my flesh and blood,' shouted Mother, 'at this very moment,' as though she could hear in her head the sound of spades digging into the earth.

'Can't help that, luv,' said the porter, waving her aside.

Then Mother did a frantic little tap-dance on the spot and screamed out, 'God damn you, may you roast in hell', and on the platform, echoing Mother's thin blast of malice, the guard blew a shrill note on his whistle, and the train went. I kept well out of it. The only good it did, Mother making such a spectacle of herself, was to bring some colour back to her cheeks. When the next train came we had to slink through the barrier without looking at the porter. On the journey Mother never opened her mouth, not even to tell me to sit up straight.

We weren't really late. My Uncle George was waiting for us at the other end, in his new Rover, and he said the cars weren't due for another half hour. 'Mildred's done all the sandwiches for after,' he said, 'and the sausage rolls are ready to pop into the oven.'

'That's nice,' said Mother, in a subdued tone of voice, and she leaned against me in the back of the car and held on to my arm, as if she was desperately ill. I couldn't very well shake her off, but it made me feel a bit stupid.

My Uncle George is an idiot. He said I was a bonny girl and hadn't I grown. The last time he'd seen me I was only six so you can tell he isn't exactly Brain of Britain.

It was funny being in Grandma's house without her there. She was very house-proud and usually she made you take your shoes off in the hall so as not to mess the carpet. My Auntie Mildred was dropping crumbs all over the place and she'd put a milk bottle on the dining-room table. There was dust on the face of the grandfather clock. Grandma was a great one for dusting and polishing. She wore a turban to do it, and an old satin slip with a cardigan over. She never wore her good clothes when she was in the house. My mother and her used to have arguments about it. Mother said it wasn't right to look slovenly just because one was indoors, and Grandma said Mother was a fine one to talk. She said Mother looked a mess whether she was indoors or out.

I wasn't sure where Grandma was, and I didn't like to ask. When the cars came I was amazed to find that Grandma had come in one of them and was waiting outside. There were only two bunches of flowers on the coffin lid.

'Why aren't there more flowers?' asked my mother. 'Surely everyone sent flowers?'

'I thought it best,' explained my Uncle George, 'to request no flowers but donations instead to the Heart Diseases Foundation. Mother would have preferred that, I think. She always said flowers at a funeral were a waste of good money.'

Mother didn't say anything, but her lips tightened. She knew that Grandma would be livid at so few flowers in the hearse. Grandma *did* say that flowers were a waste of money, but she'd been talking about other people's funerals, not her own.

I don't remember much about the service, except that there were a lot of people in the church. I thought only old ladies went to church, but there were a dozen men as well. At the back of the pews there was an odd-looking bloke with a grey beard, holding a spotted handkerchief in his hand. He seemed quite upset and emotional. He kept trying to sing the hymns and swallowing and going quiet. I know because I turned round several times to stare at him. I kept wondering if it was Walter from the Isle of Wight.

For some reason they weren't burying Grandma at that church. There wasn't the soil. Instead we followed her to another place at the other end of the village. The vicar had to get there first to meet Grandma, so we went a longer route round by the coal yards and the Council offices.

It was a big graveyard. There were trees, black ones without leaves, and holly bushes, and marble angels set on plinths overgrown with ivy. Four men carried Grandma to her resting place. Ahead of her went some little choirboys in knee-socks and white frilly smocks. They sang a very sad song about fast falls the eventide. It wasn't even late afternoon, but the sky was grey now and nothing moved, not a branch, not a fold of material, not a leaf on the holly bushes.

The vicar followed directly behind Grandma, and after him came my Uncle George, supporting Mother at the elbow, and lastly me and my Auntie Mildred. We went up the path from the gate and round the side of the church and up another path through a great field of grey stones and tablets and those angels with marble wings. But we didn't stop. The small boys went on singing and the men went on carrying Grandma and we reached a hedge and turned right and then left, until we came to a new plot of ground, so out of the way and unimportant that they'd left bricks and rubble lying on the path. And still we kept on walking. I don't know why someone didn't cry out 'Wait', why some great voice from out of the pale sky didn't tell us to stop. I thought of Grandma in the restaurant, standing her ground, refusing to budge from her central position.

After she was put in the earth, before they hid her light under a bushel, we threw bits of soil on top of the coffin.

I didn't like the sound of it.

THE WORST POLICY

Sarah made up her mind during Sunday lunch, after watching John help himself to his sixth roast potato. 'You shouldn't do that,' she said, as he poured yet more salt onto his plate.

'Hang it all, woman,' he complained. 'I've a big frame.'

As soon as he had gone out into the garden she telephoned her best friend, Penny. 'I've decided to go ahead,' she said. 'I thought you'd like to know.'

'Oh, Sarah,' said Penny. 'Are you sure?'

'Yes,' she said, 'we could all drop dead at any time.'

'*You* won't,' objected Penny. 'It's only John that's at risk.'

'My mind's made up,' said Sarah, and she replaced the receiver.

After tea she telephoned Penny again. John had gone into the living room to watch television with the children. 'What if *he* drops dead,' she asked, 'while we're in the middle of it?'

'It would be a bit awkward,' Penny agreed.

'If he actually went,' said Sarah, 'I mean actually in the middle I'd pull him off the bed and roll him under it until it got dark.'

'How would you be sure?' asked Penny. 'I mean, what would I do if he came to in the night and started moaning? How would I explain it to Roy?'

'I've read about it,' Sarah said. 'There are certain signs. It's not just a question of holding a mirror to the lips.'

'I can't talk now,' whispered Penny. 'Paul's just come in.'

'Oh, *him*,' said Sarah crossly, and she hung up.

97

Paul was Penny and Roy's son. It wasn't a nice thing to admit, even to herself, but Sarah didn't like him. She had never taken to him, not even when he was a baby. As a toddler he had been a pest, and he didn't greatly improve as he grew older. Once he had torn all the heads off the carnations in her front garden – John was furious – and another time he told Roy's mother that Sarah and John had gone away for the weekend leaving the children all alone in the house. Roy's mother had actually rung up to check. Only two years ago he had used a pair of wire cutters on Sarah's bicycle chain. Of course she couldn't prove it, but she knew it had been him. His parents, if one was unlucky enough to run into him as he morosely entered or left the house, referred to his behaviour as absent-minded, vague. He never answered when spoken to and was quite capable of pushing aside anybody who happened to be in his path. 'He's a bit of a dreamer,' Roy often remarked. Both Sarah and John felt there were other words that might more accurately describe him, such as bloody-minded, self-engrossed and plain rude. Paul was now four-teen, large for his age and half way to growing a moustache. Irritatingly, Sarah's own son, Jason, admired him intensely, and, to her way of thinking, saw far too much of him. She was afraid that Paul was a bad influence; she knew for a fact that he smoked, and he still told lies. Penny called them 'fibs', but then she was his mother. Sarah herself was a stickler for the truth – as far as her children were concerned. 'Don't ever lie to me,' she would say. 'It's just not worth it. The truth never harmed anybody.'

It was fortunate that her opinion of Paul had not affected her friendship with Penny, for after twelve years of marriage Sarah had more or less embarked on an affair with Tony Wentworth.

Tony Wentworth was in the wine-importing business. He and Sarah had met at evening classes at the local primary school. Right from the beginning, when they both could tell that it was going to go further than it should, they had agreed not to bring their private lives into the conversation. Naturally, Sarah had slipped up once or twice, such as the time she couldn't help mentioning that Jason had just passed his cello exam, Grade II.

'Don't tell me,' Tony Wentworth had said. 'I don't want to know.' And quickly Sarah had added that Jason was away at boarding school, in the country somewhere, and had been for years; she implied that she hardly knew him. It was a lie, of course, but then it sounded better, less adulterous, Jason being away from home and out of reach, instead of around the corner at the local comprehensive school and very much part of her life. 'I don't want to know about your past,' Tony Wentworth had said. 'The past has nothing to do with us.' It was a frightfully romantic thing to say.

Penny had met him too; she went to a different evening class but she'd seen him in the canteen. She'd spoken to him once and, though she couldn't remember in what context, she was sure he'd given the impression that he wasn't married. Talking it over, neither she nor Sarah particularly believed him. Recently, Penny hadn't been able to look him in the eye, not since she'd known about the affair. Every time she saw him in the corridor she turned bright pink, as though she'd spent most of her life in a convent. Not that it was actually an affair, not in the true sense, not as yet. Sarah telephoned her, sometimes twice a day, to talk about him. Penny didn't disapprove. She thought John took Sarah far too much for granted, and in a sense listening to the details of Sarah's love life was almost as much fun as having a love life of one's own. More fun in fact, because in time Sarah was bound to be caught out and, knowing old John, possibly dragged through the divorce courts, whereas she herself would remain happily married. Well, married at any rate.

'Have you seen him?' she would ask, whenever Sarah rang, and Sarah would usually reply that she hadn't or, if she had, that it was only for a few snatched moments outside Woolworths or the Savings Bank. 'So it's not getting very far, is it?' Penny would say, and Sarah would have to admit that it wasn't. But then, as she rightly said, they had nowhere to go. Surely she was too old for thrashing about in the back of a car? 'You could come here,' Penny often told her – she was quite sure that Sarah would never dream of it – and then Sarah would go on again about what would happen if Tony Wentworth dropped dead of a heart attack while they were in the middle of it. Inwardly, Penny wondered whether Sarah gained some sort of perverse excitement from the thought of lying under a corpse. Or on top of one. After all Tony Wentworth was at least six years younger than Sarah, and looked as fit as a fiddle.

On Monday morning, as soon as the children had left for school, Sarah telephoned Penny. 'Well,' she said, speaking in a defiant tone of voice, 'what day will be convenient?'

'Oh dear,' Penny said.

'You did offer,' Sarah reminded her.

'I know I did,' said Penny.

'Well, then?'

'I don't know what I'm doing this week.'

'Yes, you do. You always go to the hairdresser's on a Thursday.'

'So I do,' said Penny.

'And Paul has football practice.'

'So he does,' said Penny.

'Then it'd better be Thursday,' Sarah said severely, as though it was Penny and not she who was asking for the loan of a house for an illicit meeting that might end in tears.

They discussed what time Sarah should come round, and whether it would be better to have another key cut or to use Paul's key which was always kept under the plant-pot on the front step.

'Another one cut?' asked Penny, alarmed. 'Surely that's not necessary.' It was going to be difficult enough sitting under the dryer thinking of Sarah and Tony Wentworth bouncing about in her bed on Thursday afternoon without contemplating it on a regular basis.

'Paul *will* go to football?' asked Sarah. 'He won't bunk off?'

'He only bunks off school,' said Penny. 'Never football practice.'

She brought up the subject of Sarah's own children. Was it at all likely that they would come home early and finding her not there call round at Penny's house? Sarah said they had their own keys and, besides, Jennifer had ballet on Thursday and Jason his cello lesson.

'Well, that takes care of that then,' Penny said, and rather fiercely she slammed down the phone. In the afternoon she rang to find out whether Sarah had had second thoughts. Sarah hadn't.

On the Tuesday Penny nearly didn't go to her evening class; she didn't feel she could face Sarah, let alone Tony Wentworth. She felt she had been cast into the role of a procuress, a madame, though of course she wasn't going to take money at the door.

During the coffee break Tony Wentworth sat at a table in the far corner of the canteen with the fat girl who taught car maintenance.

'Have you asked him?' hissed Penny, shielding her face with her hand and speaking through clenched teeth.

Sarah nodded.

'And is he coming?'

'Yes,' said Sarah. She looked far from happy. Her face was pale and her hair, which was curly, seemed to have lost its bounce.

'It's not too late to change your mind,' whispered Penny. 'You could say one of the children was ill.'

'You forget,' said Sarah, 'I'm only supposed to have one child, and he's away at boarding school.'

'Tell him your husband's ill then.'

'I've hinted I'm a widow,' Sarah said, 'so he's already dead.'

'Well, tell him it's against your religion,' said Penny, and she began to giggle quite loudly.

'It's no use,' said Sarah, 'I've got to go through with it.' She looked gloomily down at her foot in its open sandal and jiggled her toes, as though they were gangrenous and amputation was the only answer.

When the bell went at the end of the evening Penny ran into the toilets and hid until she was sure Tony Wentworth had gone. She felt if she bumped into him she might make some suggestive remark, some obscene gesture; after all it was her bed he would be using.

She telephoned Sarah on the Wednesday. 'Sorry I rushed off,' she said. 'I remembered I'd promised to help Paul with his French.'

'I didn't notice,' Sarah said. 'Isn't it a dreadful day? I hate wet weather.'

'It's good for the flowers,' said Penny.

They fell silent, looking out of their windows at the roses bending under the beneficial rain.

'How do you know Paul actually goes to his football practice?' asked Sarah abruptly.

'How do you know Jason goes to his cello lesson?' countered Penny.

'Jason's not a liar,' said Sarah and, stung, Penny put down the phone.

During the afternoon Sarah rang to apologise for being so tetchy. 'You know how it is,' she said. 'I'm so on edge.'

'I don't know how it is,' Penny said heatedly. 'I'm not in your situation.'

'Am I fat?' asked Sarah.

'You mean without clothes?' said Penny. 'How should I know?' And again she hung up without saying good-bye.

Sarah called round at Penny's house a quarter of an hour later. She was tearful and talked about the picnics she and Penny had gone on in the past, when the children were so little that they'd had to wear sun hats. And did Penny remember that time on Clapham Common when a dog had run up to little Jennifer and little Paul in his romper suit had toddled between her and the doggie, waving his chubby little fists and shouting, 'Go 'way, bad bow-wow.'

'I remember the time Paul ate all the chocky bickies,' Penny said, 'and you said one of them must own up, that the truth never harmed anybody, and Paul said it was him and your Jennifer went and bit him.'

'Oh,' whimpered Sarah, 'weren't they little darlings! What lovely days those were.'

Penny poured her out a glass of sherry and told her not to be such a fool. If she didn't want to go through with it, all she had to do was to say so. She, for one, would be relieved. What if John ever came to hear of it? What if Roy ever found out? Why, he'd probably insist on fumigating the house.

'Of course I'll bring my own sheets,' said Sarah, offended, and Penny gave her another glass of sherry because she was weepy again.

On Thursday morning Sarah telephoned to say that she would come round before lunch. Penny said, no, she wouldn't, that she didn't want her there until she herself had gone to the hairdresser's. The whole thing was somehow so deceitful, so calculating; she couldn't think how she'd been talked into it in the first place. She must have been mad. Roy didn't like people using his lawn mower, never mind his bedroom. The key would be under the plant-pot, and would Sarah please vacate the premises by five o'clock at the latest. Then she laughed; she was close to hysteria.

The Worst Policy

It was strange being in the house without Penny there. And even odder stripping the bed and changing the sheets; Roy's pyjamas were still under the pillow. Sarah had told Tony Wentworth to come at two o'clock, not a moment earlier and not a moment later. He believed he was coming to *her* house, and she'd invented a cleaner who left at a quarter to two in order to pick up a child from nursery school and returned on the dot of four o'clock. That way Tony Wentworth wouldn't run into Penny going out, or stay too long and catch her coming in. If the worst came to the worst, she told herself, she could always pass Penny off as the cleaning lady.

At ten to two Sarah was upstairs at the bedroom window, peering through the net curtains at the dusty little garden and the deserted road beyond the hedge. She had decided she would bring Tony Wentworth straight up the stairs. She didn't want him to see the living room; there was one of those Spanish dolls on the settee. It was disloyal of her but she wouldn't like Tony Wentworth to think she was capable of choosing quite such a cheerful carpet.

He was on time and he brought her flowers. She had hoped that he might have thought of bringing a bottle of wine. He was wearing a green sports jacket that she hadn't seen before.

'It's a fair-sized house,' he remarked, 'for one person.'

'I prefer it that way,' said Sarah. 'It's nice living on one's own. We'll go straight up, shall we?' And she led the way as though she'd been doing this sort of thing all her life. Which in a sense she had, only with her husband.

Now that Tony Wentworth was actually in Penny and Roy's bedroom, standing there with that bunch of chrysanthemums crushed against the lapels of his unfamiliar jacket, Sarah felt let down, tired. She longed to put her feet up and watch television. While she was undressing she thought of all the untruths she would tell if John asked her what sort of a day she'd had. It was wicked to tell lies.

She was lying awkwardly in Tony Wentworth's arms – they hadn't done anything yet; his skin didn't feel right and his feet were icy – when they both heard a scrabbling sound outside the window. It's a cat clawing at the drainpipe, she thought, and then there was a thump. Looking over Tony Wentworth's pimply shoulder she watched the window swing inwards and Paul clambering over the sill.

'Hang on,' he called out to someone on the path below, 'I'll let you in.' He crossed the room and went out of the door.

Tony Wentworth jumped out of bed and struggling into his trousers hopped in pursuit. 'Come back,' he shouted, 'come back, you rotten crook.'

Sarah sat there for a moment with the covers pulled up to her chin. Paul had seen her of course, or rather he had looked straight at her, as though she was part of the furniture. Surely he couldn't be that self-obsessed. She went to the window and looked down into the garden. There was a young girl in a mini-skirt staring up at the house. Then Paul ran down the path and out through the gate. The girl followed him to the bend of the road, until one of her shoes came off.

Penny telephoned that evening and complained that Sarah hadn't tidied up the bedroom. 'You left your sheets on the bed,' she said. 'And where are Roy's pyjamas?'

'In the dirty clothes basket in the bathroom,' said Sarah. She waited.

'Everything go all right?' asked Penny. Her voice was perfectly normal.

'I decided not to go through with it,' said Sarah. 'I'll tell you about it another time. I've got something else on my mind. Jason's not been going to his cello classes. He's been telling lies.'

'Oh, dear,' Penny said, 'never mind. They all do it. Are you going to let him see Paul tonight? He's expecting him.'

'I don't know how I can stop him,' said Sarah. 'It's bound to get out some time!'

'What are you talking about?' asked Penny. 'Are you all right? You sound terrible. Is it the lies? Is it Tony Wentworth that's depressed you? Is it the weather?'

'It's the truth,' said Sarah, and she hung up.

The truth, as she now realised, always harmed somebody.

THE MAN WHO BLEW AWAY

From the moment he arrived at Gatwick, Pinkerton began to be bothered by God, or rather by signs and portents of a religious nature. It was unexpected, and quite out of character, and he imagined it had something to do with suppressed guilt.

For instance, he was standing in the queue at the bookstall, waiting to pay for a newspaper, when the man in front of him turned abruptly round and uttered the words 'Go back'. The man wore a chain round his neck from which dangled a crucifix; it was easy to spot because his shirt was unbuttoned to the waist. And then, later, standing in line ready to check in his baggage, Pinkerton realised that he was encircled by nuns. They were not those counterfeit sisters in short modern skirts but proper nuns clad in black from head to foot, moon faces caught in starched wimples. Pinkerton was not a Catholic – if anything, he was a quarter Jewish, though he often kept that to himself – but he immediately felt unworthy at being in such sanctified company and stood aside, losing his place in the queue. It was then that one of the nuns distinctly said, 'It's too late, you have been chosen', and Pinkerton replied, 'You're right, you're absolutely right.' Then he shivered, because she had spoken in a foreign language and he had answered in one, though he had always been hopeless as a linguist and until that moment had never been vouchsafed the gift of tongues. At least, that is how it struck him at the time.

Thinking it over on the aeroplane, he wondered if there wasn't a simple explanation. The man with the crucifix had obviously not been urging him to return to Crawley but merely requesting that he should step back a few paces.

107

Perhaps his heels had been trodden on. As for the nun, far from alluding either to life in general or to *his* life in particular, she had referred only to the passing of the hour. Possibly she had meant that there was no time to go to the Duty Free and buy *crème de menthe* for the Mother Superior. The business of his sudden comprehension of Dutch or German, or whatever guttural language it had been, was a little more tricky to explain. But then, hadn't he muddled it up a little and got the words in the wrong order? What she must have said, to a nun behind him, was *You were chosen* and then added the bit about it being too late, not the other way round. It made far more sense.

He had just decided that he had been the victim of one of those flashes of intuition which women seemed to be afflicted with most of the time, when he happened to glance out of the window. In the fraction of the second before he blinked, he saw a dazzling monster swimming through the blue sky, half fish, half bird, with scales of gold and wings of silver. He turned his head away instantly, and ordered a Scotch and soda. Afterwards he fell asleep and dreamed he was having a liaison, of a dangerous kind, with a woman who had been convent-educated.

At Athens there was some hitch in the operational schedule and he learnt that his flight to Corfu would be delayed for several hours. There was nowhere for him to sit down and the place was crowded. After two hours he gave in and, spreading his newspaper on the floor, sat hunched against a concrete ash-tray. Miserably hot, he was afraid to remove his sports jacket in case his passport was stolen. It would be all up with him if he had to turn to the British Consulate for help. They would very probably telex home and ask Gloria to describe him, and she, believing him to be elsewhere, would almost certainly say that it couldn't be him; disowned, he would be flung into jail. He had heard about foreign jails. A youngster in the office had been involved in some minor infringement of the traffic regulations in Spain and it had cost his widowed mother three hundred pounds to have him released. It was obviously a racket. To add insult to injury, he had been stabbed in the ankle by a demented Swiss who happened to be sharing his cell.

When at last Pinkerton's flight was called it was fearfully late. He arrived on Corfu in the middle of the night and was persuaded to share a cab with a large woman who wore white trousers and an immense quantity of costume jewellery. She was booked into the Chandros Hotel, which, she assured him, was in the general direction of Nisaki, and it would be a saving for both of them. It was pitch dark inside the car save for a red bulb above the dashboard illuminating a small cardboard grotto containing a plastic saint with horribly black eyebrows. The woman sat excessively close to Pinkerton, though in all fairness he thought that at the pace they were travelling, and bearing in mind the villainous turns in the road, she had little choice. He himself clung to the side of the window and tried not to think of death. Now and then, in response to something he said, his companion slapped him playfully on the knee.

At first, when she enquired his name and what part of London he hailed from, he answered cagily; after all, he was supposed to be in Ireland, coarse-fishing with Pitt Rivers. But then, well-nigh drunk with fatigue, and dreadfully anxious as to what he was doing driving through foreign parts in the small hours, he found himself confiding in her. Talking to a stranger, he told himself, as long as it was in darkness, was almost as private as praying and hardly counted. With any luck he would never set eyes on his confessor again. 'I'm meeting a lady friend,' he said. 'She gave me a sort of ultimatum. I'm married, of course, though I'm not proud of it.'

'Of course you're not,' the woman said.

'Either I came out and joined her for a few days, or it was all off between us.'

'Oh, dear,' said the woman.

'Half of me rather wants it to be all off.'

'But not your other half,' said the woman. 'Your worst half,' and they both laughed.

'I shouldn't be here,' he said. 'I should be sitting in the damp grass at the side of a river.'

'Of course you should,' she said. 'You've been chosen.' And she slapped him again, and he heard her bracelets tinkling as they slid on her wrist.

She was quite inventive. When he admitted that he was worried about being out in the sun – it always rained in Ireland in July – she said why didn't he come up with some allergy. One that brought him out in bumps.

He agreed it was a jolly good idea. 'I tan very easily,' he explained. 'On account of Spanish blood some way back.'

'You'd be best under an umbrella,' advised the woman. 'You can hire them by the day for a couple of roubles. Failing that, if you want to economise you can always hide in your room.'

They both laughed louder than ever because it was very droll, her confusing the currency like that. He would have told her about the allegorical creature outside the aeroplane window but he didn't want her to find him too memorable.

Upon arrival at the hotel it became evident that the woman was a bit of an expert on economy. She kept her handbag firmly tucked under her arm and appeared to have altogether forgotten her suggestion that she should contribute to the cost of the journey. He carried her luggage into the lobby, hoping that the sight of his perspiring face would remind her, but it didn't. She merely thanked him for his gallantry and urged him to get in touch should he and his lady friend fall out before the end of the week.

Pinkerton didn't think much of the hotel. The fellow

behind the reception desk had a mouth full of gold teeth, and there was a display of dying geraniums in a concrete tub set in front of the lifts. If he had not been so exhausted he would have insisted on their being watered immediately.

'I really must be off,' he said, and he and the woman pecked each other on the cheek. It was natural, he felt, seeing they were abroad.

'Don't forget,' she said. 'You know where I am. We don't want you coming up in bumps all on your own, do we?' And winked, and this time, his knee being out of reach, slapped his hand.

All the same, he was sorry to lose her. The moment he was again seated behind the silent driver his worries returned. What if there was an emergency at home and Gloria was compelled to telephone Ireland? Supposing one of the children had an accident and he was required at a moment's notice to donate a kidney? And what if Pitt Rivers's wife ran into Gloria in town and was asked a direct question? Pitt Rivers had boasted that though he himself, if called upon, would lie until hell froze over, he couldn't possibly speak for his wife, not with her Methodist background. How absurd in this day and age, thought Pinkerton, to be troubled with religious scruples, and he peered anxiously out of the window into the impenetrable blackness and watched, in his mind's eye, the roof of his half-timbered house outside Crawley engulfed in forty-foot flames. In the squeal of the tyres on the road he heard the cracking of glass in his new greenhouse as the structure buckled in the heat and his pampered tomatoes bubbled on their stems. It was so warm in the car that he struggled out of his jacket and rolled up his shirt-sleeves.

He had fallen into a doze when the car stopped outside a taverna set in a clearing of olive trees at the side of the road. For the moment he feared that he had arrived at the hotel, and was shocked at its dilapidated appearance. Not even Agnes, who was capable of much deception, would have described it as three-star accommodation.

A young woman sat at a rickety table, holding an infant on her lap. The driver left the car and approached her; Pinkerton imagined that she was his wife and that he was explaining why he was so late home.

In any event the young woman was dissatisfied. An argument ensued.

Pinkerton grimaced and smiled through the window, conveying what he hoped was the right mixture of apologetic sympathy. 'The plane was delayed,' he called. 'It was quite beyond our control.'

The young woman rose to her feet and she and the driver, both shouting equally violently, began to stalk one another round the tables.

'Look here,' called Pinkerton. 'I'm terribly tired.'

They took no notice of him.

Presently, he got out of the car and joined them under the canopy of tattered plastic. Yawning exaggeratedly, pointing first at his watch and then at the road, he attempted to communicate with the driver. For all the notice that was taken of him he might not have been there. Wandering away, he inspected with disgust various petrol tins planted with withered begonias.

He was just thinking that it bordered on the criminal, this wanton and widespread neglect of anything that grew, when the young woman broke off her perambulation of the tables and darting towards him thrust the child into his arms.

Taken by surprise he held it awkwardly against his shoulder and felt its tiny fingers plucking at the skin of his arm. 'Look here,' he said again, and clumsily jogged up and down, for the child had begun a thin wailing. 'There, there,' he crooned, and guided by some memory in the past he tucked its head under his chin, as though he held a violin, and swayed on his feet.

He was looking up, ready to receive smiles of approbation from the parents – after all, he was coping frightfully well considering he had been on the go for almost a day and a half – when to his consternation he saw that the man was walking back to the car. As gently as was possible in the circumstances he dumped the child on the ground, propping it against a petrol drum, and ran in pursuit.

The driver handled the car as if it had done him a personal injury. He beat at the driving wheel with his fists and drove erratically, continuing to shout for several miles. At last his voice fell to an irritated muttering, and then, just as Pinkerton had leant back in his seat and settled into a more relaxed position, the car veered sickeningly to the right, almost jerking him to the floor, and stopped.

Pinkerton tried to reason with the driver, but it was no use. The domestic crisis had evidently unsettled him; he refused adamantly to go any further. Jumping out of the car he opened the side door and dragged Pinkerton on to the road.

'I'll pay you anything you want,' cried Pinkerton, foolishly.

Three thousand drachmas were extorted from him before his suitcase was flung out into the darkness, and the driver, taking advantage of his stumbling search for it on the stony verge, leapt back into the car, reversed, swung round and drove off at speed in the direction from which they had just come. Pinkerton was left alone, stranded in the middle of nowhere.

It was another hour, perhaps two, before he reached his destination. If he had understood the driver correctly, the track leading to the hotel was unsuitable for vehicles and dangerous for pedestrians to walk down at night, being nothing more substantial than a treacherous path between two chasms cut by the Ionian Sea. Remembering his days as a Boy Scout he had sat for a while on his suitcase, which he had retrieved from a clump of bushes so densely studded with thorns as to resemble a bundle of barbed wire, and waited for his eyes to adjust to the darkness. In time he saw the sky threaded with stars, but the earth remained hidden. He had wasted precious matches lighting his pipe and, puffing on it furiously, held the bowl out in front of him like a torch; to no avail. He had jumped to his feet and bellowed unashamedly, 'Help, help, I am Inglesi', and fallen over a boulder, bruising his shin. Finally he had sat on his bottom and dragging his suitcase behind him, begun laboriously to descend. Now and then, as the breeze shifted the branches of the olive trees below him, he caught a glimpse of a glittering ship on the horizon, and heard a roll of thunder as an unseen plane approached the airstrip of the distant town.

He was perhaps half way down the mountain when a curious light appeared above his left shoulder, illuminating the path ahead. Startled, he looked round and saw nothing. As he later tried to explain to a sceptical Agnes, it was as though someone was following him, someone rather tall, carrying a lantern. He was too relieved to have found what he took to be the means of his salvation to be frightened at such a phenomenon.

Soon the darkness melted altogether and he stood bathed in the electric lights of the car park of the Nisaki Beach Hotel. He climbed the shallow steps up to the reception area and only then did he look back. In the instant before the hotel was plunged into darkness he thought he saw a man dressed all in white, whose shadowy brow was flecked with blood.

The woman at the reception desk mercifully spoke English. She assured Pinkerton that the power cut was temporary and that it was not an unusual occurrence. She also said that it wasn't allowed for him to enter Mrs Lowther's room. It had nothing to do with the hour. Mrs Lowther was a package holiday and he wasn't included. She would rent him a room on the same floor, with twin beds, shower and use of cot. The latter convenience would be two thousand drachmas extra. Too tired to argue, and aware that the seat of his trousers was threadbare and his jacket torn at the elbow, he paid what was asked and, the lifts being out of order, borrowed a torch and toiled up the eight flights of stairs to his room on the fourth floor.

He was awakened during the night by a severe tingling in his arm. Finding that he was still in his clothes, he sat wearily on the edge of the bed and began to undress. The sensation in his arm had now become one of irritation; he scratched himself vigorously, imagining that he had been attacked on the mountainside by mosquitoes. Looking down, he was astonished to see a patch of skin on his forearm fan-shaped and topped by a pattern of dots so pale in contrast to the rest of his skin as to appear luminous. He tried to find the light switch so that he could examine his arm more closely. It was not inconceivable that he had been bitten by a snake, or even by a series of snakes, for he counted six puncture marks, though his flesh was perfectly smooth to the touch. Unable to locate the bedside lamp and not suffering from either pain or nausea, he fell back on to the pillow and slept.

Agnes telephoned his room the next morning. 'So you've turned up,' she said. She made it sound like an accusation, as if he was pestering her rather than that he was here at her insistence.

'I've had a terrible time,' he told her. 'You wouldn't believe it. First of all there was the plane journey, travelling all that way alone.'

'You mean you flew in an empty aeroplane?' she asked.

'You know perfectly well what I mean,' he said crossly. 'And there was a five-hour delay at Athens.'

'Stop moaning,' she said. 'I'll see you at breakfast.'

He shaved and showered and put on a clean shirt and the only other pair of trousers he had brought with him. He hid the woollen socks and jumpers, packed by his wife, inside the wardrobe and bundled his wellington boots under the bed. He hoped Agnes wouldn't spot them.

In spite of his experiences of the night before he felt amazingly fit, almost a new man. True, his hands were covered in cuts and scratches and his shin somewhat grazed and tender, but in every other respect he had never felt so healthy, so carefree. The view from his balcony – the green lawns, the flowering shrubs, the gravel paths leading to bowers roofed with straw and overhung with bougainvillaea, the glimpse of swimming pool – delighted him. Beyond the pool he could see striped umbrellas on a pebbled beach beside a stretch of water that sparkled to a horizon edged with purple mountains. It was all so pretty, so picturesque. The whole world was drenched in sunshine. A tiny figure, suspended beneath a scarlet parachute, drifted between the blue heavens and the bright blue sea.

Even Agnes sensed the change in him. 'I thought you said you'd had an awful time.'

'I did,' he replied cheerfully. 'Absolutely dreadful.' And he helped himself to yoghurt and slices of peach and didn't once grumble at the absence of bacon and eggs.

He wasn't quite sure how much he dare tell her: and yet he longed to confide in someone. Agnes could be very cruel on occasions. Omitting only the words *You've been chosen*, he told her about the nun at the airport at Gatwick.

Agnes listened earnestly, and when he had finished remarked that she herself had often understood foreign languages, even when she didn't know any of the words. She'd met a Russian once at a party and she'd known, really known, exactly what he was saying. She thought it had probably something to do with telepathy. 'Mind you,' she admitted, 'the vodka was coming out of my ears.'

'Yes,' he said doubtfully, 'but I answered her. In Dutch as far as I know.'

Agnes agreed that it was odd; she looked at him with interest. She was frowning and he was pleased because he recognised her expression of intense concentration as one of sexual arousal. As far as he remembered she had never been excited by nuns before. Encouraged, he recounted the episode on the mountainside and his terrible descent.

'There's a perfectly good road higher up,' she said. 'It's sign-posted. It's only a hundred yards further along from that track.'

'How was I to know,' he said. 'It seems to me that I had no choice.' He described the guide dressed in white.

'No,' said Agnes. 'I can't buy that. It's almost blasphemous.'

'I'm only telling you what I saw,' he protested.

'But a crown of thorns,' she cried. 'How can you say such a thing? It's far more likely that you saw a fisherman in his nightshirt and one of those straw hats they all wear.'

'I know a hat when I see one,' he argued. 'I'm not blind.'

'It had probably been chewed by a goat,' she said. 'Or a donkey. You just saw the chewed bits, damn it.'

He attempted to change the subject and tell her about the baby at the taverna. Agnes was still aroused, though no longer in a way that would be beneficial to him. If he didn't watch his step she would lock him out of her room for days. 'It was a dear little soul,' he said. 'Quite enchanting, if a little pale.'

'Why the hell,' interrupted Agnes, 'would Jesus want to guide *you* to the Nisaki Beach Hotel? You're an adulterer.'

'An unwilling one,' he snapped, and fell into an offended silence.

He apologised to her that afternoon. She forgave him and consented to come to his room. When he closed the shutters the bars of the cot lay in striped shadows across her thighs. Her body was so dark after a week in the sun that it was like making advances to a stranger. He wasn't sure that the experience was enjoyable.

'Why have you kept your shirt on?' she asked him later, and he explained that he was perspiring so copiously with the heat that he was afraid she'd find him unpleasant.

'You are a bit sweaty,' she said, and wrapped the sheet round her like a shroud.

After three days he decided that he ought to go home. Agnes was behaving badly. He had run out of excuses for keeping out of reach of the sun and was tired of being insulted. When he lay in the shade of the olive trees Agnes snatched the newspaper from his face and complained that he could be mistaken for an old dosser. 'For God's sake,' she ordered, 'take off those woollen socks', and for his own sake he fought her off as she clawed at the laces of his shoes. All the same, he couldn't make up his mind when to leave, and lingered, dozing in his room or in one of those fragrant bowers in the pleasant garden. He still felt well, he still felt that absence of care which he now realised he had last known as a child. At night he put his pillow at the foot of the bed and fell asleep with his hand clutching the bars of the cot.

Towards the end of the week they went on an excursion into Corfu Town. Pinkerton said he wanted to buy Agnes a piece of jewellery. They both knew that it was his farewell gift to her. She pretended that it was kind of him. When she returned to England he would telephone her once or twice to ask how she was, perhaps even take her out to lunch, and then the relationship would be over. Something had changed in him; he no longer needed her to berate him, and she was too old to change her ways. He could tell that she was uneasy with him, and wondered if his wife would feel the same.

Agnes chose an inexpensive bracelet and stuffed it carelessly into her handbag. She said she was off to buy postcards. He offered to go with her but she wouldn't hear of it. 'You hate shopping,' she said.

He arranged to wait for her at a café in the square. She didn't look back, which was a bad sign. He wasn't at all sure that she hadn't gone straight off to hire a cab to take her back to the hotel.

Half an hour passed. He was sitting at a table at the edge of the cricket pitch, smoking his pipe, when a woman in a red dress sat down opposite him and slapped his wrist.

'Good heavens,' he cried, recognising the gesture if not the face.

'I owe you some money,' she said. 'My share of the cab fare', and though he protested, she insisted. She had also bought him a little present, because she had known she would bump into him sooner or later. She took an envelope from her handbag and gave it to him. Inside was a cardboard bookmark with a picture on it.

'How very kind of you, ' Pinkerton said, and began to tremble.

'It's St John of Hiding,' said the woman. 'The saint of all those who carry a secret burden of hidden sin.'

Before they parted she asked him how he was getting on with his lady friend. He admitted that it was pretty well all over between them.

'I'm glad to hear it,' the woman said. 'I'm sure you're destined for higher things.'

Agnes saw the bookmark by mistake. When they got back to the hotel and Pinkerton was looking for money to pay the cab fare, he inadvertently pulled it out of his pocket. 'Why did you buy that?' she asked.

'It's a picture of a saint,' he said. 'A Greek one.'

'It's not very well drawn,' she said. 'One of the hands has got six fingers.'

Alone in his room he took off his jacket and laid it on the bed beside the bookmark. Rubbing his arm he went out onto the balcony and watched the scarlet parachute blow across the sky.

The next morning he told Agnes that he was leaving. He thought she looked relieved. He said that before he went he was determined to have one of those parachute rides.

'Good God,' she said. 'I mustn't miss this.'

She went to the jetty with him and watched, grinning, while he was strapped into his harness. 'Wonders will never cease,' she called out, as he took off his shirt.

He was instructed to hold on to the bar and break into a run when he felt the tug of the rope. When he was in the air he must hold on to the bar even though the harness would support him. He said he understood.

The speedboat chugged in a half circle beyond the jetty, waiting for the signal to be given; then, accelerating, it roared out to sea. Pinkerton was jerked forward, and gasping he ran and jumped and was swung upwards, his mouth wide open and his heart thudding fit to burst. Then he was riding through the air, not floating as he had hoped, for he was still tethered to the boat. He felt cheated.

The sudden and furious gust of wind that seized the rope in its giant fist and tore it, steel hook and all, from the funnel of the boat, was spent in an instant. Then Pinkerton, free as a bird, soared into the blue under the red umbrella of his parachute.

Everything else that had happened to him, he thought, had a logical explanation; the nuns, the man who had come to his aid on the dark mountain, the woman and her choice of bookmark. Even the creature outside the aeroplane window had been nothing more than a reflection of the sunlight on the fuselage. Everything but that –

And before he blew away he looked up at that luminous imprint of a six fingered hand which was stamped on the flesh of his arm.

HELPFUL O'MALLEY

O'Malley let the girl into the house and showed her the room on the second floor. He had put the card in the tobacconist's window only that morning and already he had interviewed three people. Two had been career women and the third a young man who had laughed and joked all the way up the stairs. Neither the women nor the laughing boy had been right for the room. Of that O'Malley was sure.

Mrs Darnley, who owned the property and had returned to Dublin because the taxes were killing her, trusted O'Malley implicitly in the matter of tenants. He had a flair for picking the right people – solvent people who could be relied upon to pay the rent into the bank every month regular as clockwork. People, what is more, who when they moved on left the place as they found it, or, more often than not, in an improved condition. Not that any of them had wanted to move on – at any rate none of those occupying the ground, first or upper floors. They all said that they had been very happy in the house, that they would never forget their time in it. But for getting married, taking a new job in another part of the country, or having an addition to the family, wild horses wouldn't have dragged them from the place. It wasn't an especially interesting-looking house: the plumbing needed overhauling, and keeping warm in the winter was always a problem. All the same, tenants grew attached to it, and many came back over the years, just to visit for half an hour or so, and sometimes they would spend the last five minutes standing in the front garden staring up at the windows, smiling at memories. There was still coloured glass in the fanlight above the door.

The letting of the second floor, however, had always posed a problem. Finding the right person was a constant source of worry to O'Malley. No tenant ever stayed for very long on the second floor; several had moved on in the space of a few weeks, and certainly none of those was ever likely to come back.

O'Malley had had the room redecorated three times in as many years, hoping to break some sort of pattern. He'd also taken it upon himself to choose a new bed, charging it to Mrs Darnley, and he had wanted to replace the old gas fire with an electric heater. Mrs Darnley had opposed the idea; she thought it would interfere with the character of the house. Besides, it would mean new meters. Perhaps he should lop off a few branches from the tree in the back garden, she had suggested, to make the room a little lighter, less gloomy in winter; but O'Malley had refused adamantly. He had spoken on the telephone to Mrs Darnley and told her he wouldn't hear of it.

'I'm only talking about one branch,' she had reasoned. 'Two at the most. Never the whole tree.'

'Over my dead body,' he said, and in the circumstances she had let the matter drop. O'Malley wasn't in Mrs Darnley's employ. He was a tenant, not a caretaker. He looked after the house and Mrs Darnley's interests because she no longer lived on the premises and he liked to be of use. He was helpful by nature.

O'Malley wasn't altogether sure that the girl was right for the room. Wasn't she a little too self-possessed, a shade off-hand in the way she eyed the furniture, the new bed, the brand-new rug in front of the hearth? Didn't that sort often feel the world owed them a living and in the end do a flit with the cutlery and the bed linen stuffed into a haversack? Of course, she could be putting it on. Usually he could tell by their eyes whether they were suitable or not, but this one was wearing dark glasses. He couldn't tell a thing from her clothes. There were patches on her trousers and her shirt could have done with a wash. One of her shoes had a bit of string for a lace. But then, young Mrs Temple on the first floor wore jumpers with holes in them and she was the daughter of a baronet.

'Will you have it?' he asked, taking a gamble.

'I might as well,' the girl said. 'I suppose you want a month in advance.'

'That I do,' he said, and she wrote him a cheque, signing it 'Edith Carp'.

'Why is it so cheap?' she asked, standing beside the cooker and looking out at the tree. She reached up to pull down the window.

'It's nailed up,' he told her. 'It's an old house and the frames don't fit. We're not out to make a fortune, simply to cover costs. You won't find it easy to keep warm. There's a meter in the cupboard under the sink. It fairly gobbles up the money.'

'Is there anything else I should know?' the girl asked. Her tone of voice sounded insolent, but then he couldn't be sure, not without seeing her eyes.

'We shouldn't like you to bring anyone back,' he said. 'Not for longer than the odd night or so. It's not the morals we're on about. The bathroom's shared and it won't run to a crowd.'

'I won't be bringing anyone back,' said the girl. 'Not even for an hour.'

Then O'Malley knew that his instinct hadn't failed him. Edith Carp was perfectly right for the room.

He left her alone for the first week, as was his policy. People didn't like being interrupted when they were busy changing the room to fit their personality. The girl before last had pulled down the curtains and hidden the engraving of the Death of Nelson under the bed, but he hadn't known that until her departure. And the girl before her had tried to put up shelves, bringing down a quantity of plaster; even though he had heard the hammering he hadn't knocked on her door until the week was out.

Not that Edith Carp made any noise at all. She evidently didn't own such a thing as a radio, and he was certain she hadn't bothered to rent a television set. She couldn't have brought with her more than two or three books at the most and he was at a loss to think how she spent her time, for though he couldn't swear to it he didn't believe she had been out of the house for more than a couple of hours since her arrival. Possibly she was sleeping. He didn't like to dwell on the possibility that she might be on drugs. That sort of problem was beyond him and he wouldn't be able to help her. Worse, she wouldn't need his help.

Edith Carp was so quiet that on the Thursday young Mrs Temple met O'Malley on the stairs and inquired whether he had managed to let the room.

'That I have,' he said.

'To whom? What sort of person?'

'A female,' he replied. 'Young and unemployed but with a bank balance. Her cheque has gone through.'

'And is she – all right?'

'I hope so,' he said, and crossed himself.

'Does she know? Did you tell her?'

'That I didn't,' he admitted. 'It would hardly have been an inducement.'

'Keep an eye on her,' begged Mrs Temple.

He assured her that he had every intention of doing so, and went on down the stairs to fetch the milk.

Still, it was easier said than done, seeing that Edith Carp remained so much in her room. She didn't pop out to borrow tea or sugar or the use of a bottle-opener, and though he waited she didn't come to him for instruction on how to light the antiquated geyser in the bathroom.

Twice he stood listening on the landing outside her room

in the middle of the night. On neither occasion did he hear anything of significance, nothing that couldn't be traced to the tapping of the tree against her window.

Shortly after lunch on the Monday he knocked on her door. She was sitting on the rug in front of the gas fire. The fire was unlit and the room was freezing. She was wearing a coat over her dressing-gown, and had left off her glasses.

'I just wanted to make sure,' he said, 'that you have two of everything – cups, plates – the requisite amount of forks.'

'There's only one of me,' she said listlessly.

The room was untouched. There wasn't a photograph on the mantelpiece or a poster on the wall. The bed hardly looked as though it had been slept in.

'I'm giving myself a party on Friday,' he said. 'The other tenants have accepted. Would you consider coming yourself? Just for the odd ten minutes.'

'No,' she said. 'I wouldn't.'

'I see,' he said. 'You don't like the look of me.' Raising his coat collar about his chin in an attempt to hide the livid birthmark which covered his face like a wrinkled rag, he left the room, closing the door meekly behind him.

He didn't doubt she would change her mind. Such a remark usually had an effect on women. First they experienced guilt, then pity; and later they felt resentful, which made them talkative. He couldn't help them unless he could persuade them to talk. That girl two years ago, the one whose young man had thrown her over after he'd found out she'd had an abortion, had been even more unapproachable than Edith Carp, and yet she had come to his party. It was different with men, of course. If the subject was raised, they generally skipped pity and guilt and jumped immediately into resentment. With men who needed help he never alluded to his disfigurement.

Edith Carp came to his room the following day. He was surprised at the quickness of her response. She wondered if she could ask him a favour? She wanted to move the wardrobe to the other side of the room and didn't feel she could manage it on her own. He said he was always more than ready to lend a helping hand.

Afterwards she insisted on making him a cup of instant coffee. He took his flask from his pocket and asked if she would like a small drop of whisky with her drink. She said she would. Neither of them imbibed all that much.

She told him that she had rented the room to get away from her mother who was dying of cancer.

He wasn't sure it was the truth, but then he'd been wrong before and so kept an open mind.

It was wrong of her, she said, but she hadn't been able to stand it. 'I can't bear the way she looks any more,' she complained, and turned red. He said he understood. All his life, when looked at, he had seen revulsion in people's eyes.

'I don't want to go on living,' she said. 'I want to die now, not wait for something like cancer to catch up with me.'

He said that was understandable too, though he himself wouldn't have the courage. He had read only recently, he said, in some magazine or other, that cancer was probably a virus and could be caught as easily as the common cold. If one had been in contact, that is.

'If you did have the courage,' she asked. 'How would you do it?'

'It's not something I've put my mind to,' he told her. 'Though I remember the time I had a tooth out with gas. It was a wonderful feeling, like falling from one mattress to another and every one of them filled with duck feathers. I didn't want it to stop. The dentist had to slap my face to bring me back.'

Edith Carp began to cry. He noticed that her eyes were small and carried the suggestion of a squint.

Before he went back to his own room he showed her

where the key to the gas meter was hidden. 'It's always kept under the strip of lino in the cupboard,' he said. 'Most people get out their money and use it all over again. I doubt if the box has been more than half full since the thing was put in. You don't need to suffer from the cold. Mrs Darnley doesn't need the money. She's as rich as Croesus.'

He thought probably she wouldn't take advantage of the key for several days, possibly weeks. Not until her mother, if she still possessed one, had died and the room grew as cold as the grave. By then the excitement of the party would have been forgotten, the hopes of friendship dashed. All of the tenants lived very full lives and, beyond saying good morning to her as they passed her in the hall, would hardly be aware of her existence. He himself would lie low; he had done what he could.

Young Mrs Temple smelt the gas on the landing less than a week later. Edith Carp had departed some time during the night. Mrs Temple took it badly.

'We're all to blame,' she sobbed. After all, Miss Carp's was the fifth death on the second floor, not the first. They could all have done so much more, tried that bit harder to put themselves in her place, alone in London without a job, without a friend in the world.

'With the exception of you, Mr O'Malley,' Mrs Temple amended, drying her eyes. 'You were always very good to her.'

'I did my best,' he agreed modestly. 'I don't feel I could have helped her much further.' And going into his room he put on his black tie and went out to order his usual flowers.

UNCOLLECTED STORIES

ERIC ON THE AGENDA

My childhood friend rang at twelve o'clock. She said she was very well and that she had met such a nice man on the train up to Scotland and she had given him my address. She hoped it was all right. I hadn't seen my friend for at least ten years so I couldn't tell her she was rotten for giving my name to a perfect stranger.

'Of course it's all right, Anthea,' I said. 'And how are all the children?'

'He's a bit fat,' said my friend. 'But you were never superficial.'

'What's his name?'

'Eric. He wears a trilby hat . . . I thought at the time you and he had a lot in common.'

At two o'clock the taxi arrived with my Mum. She stood on the pavement, nylon wig motionless, fox fur quivering in the sunlight. She laughed shrilly like some animal caught in a trap when I embraced her. I touched her frozen curls and buried my mouth in the soft fur at her neck. How we hugged each other, how we began sentences and never finished them, what a noise she made; how she teetered between the cracks in the flagstones of the tiny garden. She had painted her nails scarlet and she wore her serpent brooch and her pearls and her second-best watch. I carried her two suitcases inside and left them in the hall alongside the hat box in which she kept her Joyce Grenfell wig.

'Don't leave my cases there, dear,' she said. 'If you don't mind.'

She was still laughing on that high prolonged note of joy, waving her plump little hands about, and I dragged her luggage into the front room where she could keep an eye on it. I knew what was in the cases. Three or four cocktail dresses and a ball gown or two. Shoes to match. Also bunches of cloth flowers, roses, and purple pansies with limp stitched leaves, a little gold safety pin at the back, ready to adorn her waist or breast or shoulder strap. The dresses – the midnight blue silk, the green satin with diamante bodice – would hang reproachfully from the picture rail in my living room, until it was time to pack them again. The sight of them filled me with despair, flaring out from the wall whenever I opened the door too quickly; the rustle of taffeta, the whisper of silk. When I switched on the electric light the glory of the bodice blinded me.

She never asked if we were going to any Balls. She just hoped. She never asked if I minded her taking my bed. She just assumed. She hid her teeth and her diamond rings under the pillow at night. She put her wig over my statue of a lady patting a dog. Once, a long time ago, Alice, my youngest, had gone in to see her early in the morning. She had tugged at the bedclothes and asked, 'Are you the cleaning lady?' I don't know where she got the idea from. We had never had a cleaning lady, certainly not one that slept on the premises, and my Mum said Alice took after me. During that same visit she offered to buy me a wig. She said I would look a blooming sight better without those rattails falling about my ears. I said I couldn't bear it – what happened if somebody stroked your head and it all slipped sideways? – and she said, you mean *men* . . . you're no better than a prostitute, and I said I never got any money for it. But that was some years past and I treated her better now, more like a parent to a child.

'Anything on the agenda for this evening?' she asked, sitting down at the table.

I pretended I hadn't heard. Instead I said, 'I've got those choccy biccies you like.'

She said, 'Goody, goody.'

Whilst I was pouring the tea the phone rang and I answered it without thinking. It was Eric. He said he was in London for twenty-four hours and he would call round quite soon if I had no objection. I knew my Mum was listening so I couldn't say no, you can't, my Mother is here, because she would think it was someone vital and interesting asking me to a Ball and I was putting them off on account of being ashamed of her who had given me birth. So I said, 'Yes do, thank you.'

'I'll bring a drop of the you-know-what,' he said.

'Who was that?' asked my Mum.

'A friend of Anthea's.'

'Anthea who?' She was looking at me hungrily, searching my mouth as if she was deaf and needed to lipread. Just at the edge of her powdered chin was a smear of chocolate.

'Anthea Wilson . . . you know . . . down the lane.'

'Anthea Wilson. My word! Her grandmother is still alive, you know . . . still popping up and down in the lift at the Bon Marché.'

'Is she?' I said. 'What about Uncle Teddy?'

'Uncle who?'

'The one with the boating blazer.'

'What boating blazer?'

'You've got choccy on your chin.'

She took out a handkerchief and rubbed her mouth. I stared at her. The light went out of her eyes. 'There never was an Uncle Teddy,' she said.

She never noticed the new curtains or the fact that the floor had been polished. She stared out of the window at the newly planted fox-gloves by the bins and said the weeds were getting out of hand. She didn't comment on the clean tablecloth. She did spot immediately that the stairs looked bare. She was like a trained athlete when the starting flag begins to dip – she was off in a flash, mouth drooping in disappointment, head a little to one side as she contemplated the naked wood.

133

'What happened to your stair carpet?'

'I lent it to Edith. I'm getting it back.'

'I see.' She pulled herself up by the banister rail, a little bundle of fur and false curls, shrunken now the reunion was over, and as always, not up to expectation.

The man in the trilby hat came at four o'clock. He was awful. He was shaped like a pear drop and his coat wouldn't fasten and he wore spectacles and woolly gloves. He was holding a big cardboard box in his arms.

'I've brought the you-know-what,' he said. I don't think he liked me either. He was a bit like my Mum, the way his glance slid away from my face – you could almost see the dream of fair women fading from the dull green glass of his eyes. He was more her age than mine, the same vulnerable generation, quite incapable of disguising disappointment. You'd have thought with all that experience of hunger marches and depression and inhibition, they'd be twice as good at not showing their feelings; but there he stood, face quivering like a neglected baby, eyelids trembling as if to stop tears, just like my Mother over me lending the stair-carpet to Edith. I couldn't think what Anthea had told him. When we were little she had been the pretty one, sort of Shirley Temple whilst I was sort of Margaret O'Brien. Then later on I thought I got better looking and she went on wearing ankle socks and her high-heeled shoes with her slacks. But that was ten years ago – and standards are different in London. My Mother thinks I look awful, too.

'Oh hallow,' she cried, perking up as Eric came into the kitchen with his cardboard box. She gave one of her social laughs and tossed her curls about. You could tell Eric was surprised to find a Mother in the house.

'I can see,' he said, 'that it's not convenient at the moment. I'll call back later.'

'Oh, you'll call again, will you?' she trilled. He put down on the table his box full of the you-know-what. He said he would return at nine o'clock when things were settled and I was more myself.

'He seemed rather nice,' said my Mother. She felt inside the carton with inquisitive fingers. 'What's he returning for?'

'It's business,' I told her. 'Something to do with Anthea.'

She was lifting out a bottle of whisky. 'Is he a traveller,' she asked, 'for Johnny Walker?'

'I think he's Anthea's accountant.'

There were three bottles of whisky, three of gin, and what my Mum called the equipment − dry gingers and bitter lemon.

'Rum sort of accountant,' she said, 'bringing all drink.'

'What's he mean about me being more myself?' I worried. 'I'm me now.'

'He probably meant when things were tidier,' she reasoned, but she was smiling as if the evening promised well for us all. It made me very sad. Sad that Eric on the agenda gave her cause for excitement, sad for Eric that I hadn't been what he expected, and resentful at both of them for being dependent on me.

'Things,' I cried, 'are very tidy. And I'm not asking Edith for the stair carpet back just for that silly old turd in a trilby hat.' I don't think she knew what the word meant. She said he had raised his hat to her when he came in. In the end I went round to see Edith and told her to pop in about nine for a drink.

'It's desperate,' I said. 'This awful man thinks there's going to be an orgy.' Edith offered to phone Lily. She said Lily was jolly useful at that sort of thing.

My Mother got dressed up at about eight o'clock. Not exactly a cocktail gown, but practically − off the shoulder brocade and shoes to match. She played several rounds of gin rummy with the children. She couldn't bear to lose at cards. She added up her score triumphantly and squirmed on her chair with satisfaction, writing down the total with her gold pencil with the tassel. 'I've won, I've won,' she cried, radiant with laughter. The children said nothing.

I put on a clean jumper and really tried with my hair, back combing it and spraying it to stay in place. 'Do make yourself presentable,' said my Mother when I had finished.

Edith behaved beautifully to her. Gentle and complimentary – almost flirtatious – fingering her earrings and saying how pretty they were and admiring the winkle-picker shoes. 'You look younger than ever,' she cried, and my Mum never mentioned the missing stair carpet. They both wanted to start on the drink at once but I wouldn't let them. I went to the pub and bought a half bottle of whisky to keep them cheerful. They thought I was mad not touching Eric's cardboard box.

'If he wants to bloody well waste your time coming here, he ought to provide the booze,' said Edith, looking at me with contempt. My Mother never noticed if other people swore.

'I don't want to be beholden to the bloody man,' I protested.

'Wash your mouth out,' said my Mum.

I couldn't sit still, I was so bothered about what Eric expected. I kept thinking of him in his woolly gloves sitting opposite Anthea on the train up to Scotland. She'd probably told him she had an arty friend in London who was divorced and very friendly and who loved a drop of the you-know-what. It was all based on her knowledge of me when I was fourteen, when she and I had gone to the cinema to see Stewart Granger in *Caravan* and I had got off with a soldier from Harrington Barracks. 'Rita Moody,' Anthea had whined, corkscrew ringlets quivering with agitation, 'just you dare go off with that soldier.' And I said it was none of her business and she'd followed me to the Park and seen me go into the bowls pavilion with the soldier and a bottle of sparkling Vimto. She confessed she had listened to the noises we made – she even wrote it down in her diary and put my name in it. I never spoke to her again until we were grown up.

When Eric came he was smelling of after-shave and he had changed his tie.

'Good God,' said Edith. 'So you're Eric.'

He was terribly nonplussed at seeing the two women at the table. He huffed up and down the kitchen with his feet splayed out and he gave them a whole bottle of whisky to add to the half-bottle, and some of the 'equipment'. My Mum kept digging Edith in the ribs, and Edith kept rolling her eyes.

'We'll just go upstairs,' I said, 'and talk a bit of business.' It was a foolish thing to say but I couldn't spend the whole evening in the kitchen and not explain that there had been some mistake.

He did notice the lack of stair carpet. 'Spot of decorating?' he said. He thought my living room, once it had been reorganised and decorated, would be very nice. I had spent two years getting my living room as I wanted it, though the ball gowns hanging from the rail obscured the pictures and the photographs. We sat on my green sofa. It was worth an awful lot of money though the springs were lax and he wasn't doing them any good. We talked about him meeting Anthea on the train.

'Lovely girl,' he said.

'Look,' I began, 'I think there's been some mistake.'

'I found her very simpatico . . . if you follow me.'

'Her grandmother,' I said, 'is still alive. And her Uncle Teddy.'

He said, 'May I make a bold suggestion?' and I thought how I would write Anthea a very cool letter just as soon as I had a moment. He said if I would turn the light off it would make him feel more peaceful, so I did, because I thought it would be easier to tell him where to get off, if I couldn't see his face. I had my legs crossed under my long black skirt and a pair of tights and some Greek sandals. I couldn't really keep the sandals on with stockings, but I tried, and suddenly he caught hold of my ankle.

'May I,' he said, 'ask you something personal?'

'There may have been,' I said, 'a misunderstanding.'

'I just want to hold your big toe.'

I didn't know what to do. 'I'm not taking my sock off,' I said weakly. So we sat there in the darkness and he stroked my big toe.

After a while he confided. 'I'm very much in favour of going into Europe, though I'm not in favour of a Labour government.' He sounded very peaceful, almost sleepy.

'I must pop down and see if my Mum is all right,' I said. She and Edith had almost finished the large bottle of whisky. My Mum looked pretty and gay and unresentful. Had she been alone and without a drink she would have long since created a scene and called me a loose woman.

'Do you know,' I said, 'he's been fiddling with my big toe.' And we all clutched our stomachs and bellowed with mirth.

'Darling,' said Edith, 'it can be very enjoyable . . . no, don't laugh' . . . and I looked from her to my little Mum and back again and my mouth stretched wide open and for some reason I thought about the chocolate-covered coon man, singing about his silvery moon in the sky, and how once when I was small my Mum had wheeled me on a bicycle when I had been fetched home from school with a stomach ache.

'Do you remember,' I said, 'how you held me on that bicycle' – but she didn't, she had no recollection. She started saying – 'what bicycle, what coon, what are you on about?' – and I went back upstairs to Eric. He wanted to know when they were going home.

'They're not,' I said. 'They live here.' I sat on a chair on the other side of the room.

'Do you know,' he said, out of the darkness, 'I could guarantee that if we lay down anywhere I would not be capable of doing you know what.'

'Well,' I said, 'now you mention it, I can guarantee I wouldn't lie down.' And we both sat silent, listening to the dresses whispering on the wall.

'Rita . . . Rita . . .' called my Mother. He said he better be going back to his hotel. It had been very nice meeting me.

'I don't approve of the Common Market,' I told him, as he went noisily downstairs. 'And you shouldn't mess about with people's feet.'

He shook hands with my Mother and with Edith. Though she was hostile, you could tell he wished Anthea had given him her address instead of mine. We all watched to see if he would take his cardboard box with him. He moved towards it but Edith looked at him so brutally that he faltered and said he would call for it another time. I wouldn't go to the door with him. I pretended I felt sick.

My Mum and Edith talked for hours. Edith fetched a bottle of gin from Eric's box and they began on that. I couldn't go to sleep because my Mother had my bed and I was supposed to sleep on the sofa. I didn't have any extra blankets and I didn't want her to know how uncomfortable I was when she came to stay. I put on my old fur coat and lay down. She was telling Edith how strange I was. How I'd always been awkward, even as a child.

'That business about the bicycle,' she said. 'I don't know what she's on about. We never had a bicycle. My husband –'

'– my Dad,' I said.

'– never had a bicycle. My son never had –'

'– my brother,' I told her, but she wasn't listening.

The room was turning round. I could hear the music. There was Edith with her dark head circling above the tablecloth, and my little Mum, shoulders dipping and her pearls like a string of stars as she flew with outstretched arms, skirts whirling, in a great circle about the ballroom.

THE MAN FROM WAVERTREE

Rose had a lodger called Purdy living in the upstairs attic. In the beginning, when he had come to inquire about the vacant accommodation, she had interviewed him in her sitting room. He was a man of taste, she could tell at once. It was the way he looked at the furniture, the wallpaper. His eyes were full of admiration. It was winter and there was a nice fire burning in the grate. She started to tell him the rules of the house; he must keep his crumbs off the floor – she lived in mortal fear of mice – he was not to leave smelly milk bottles on the landing. While she was talking he advanced closer, neck stuck out like a tortoise above his wing collar, till they were standing nose to nose on the rug, squinting at each other. Ho, ho, she thought, this is a right one all right, and on the thought was spun round with two hands low on her hips, and then held with one hand while Purdy beat at her bottom with his flat check cap. Her skirt had begun to smoulder. After he came to live in the house, he said he couldn't believe his luck, her catching fire like that, and Rose said it was no wonder seeing he had to talk to one so intensely. He explained that he had wax in his ears and relied on lipreading. She did once persuade him to have his ears cleaned out, but he suffered terribly for weeks from all the cups rattling in the Kardomah, and she was forced to buy him earplugs till the wax re-formed. It was the least she could do. They now understood each other, though he had never taken any further liberties with her since that first warm and audacious introduction.

One evening Purdy asked Rose if she wouldn't mind answering the telephone on his behalf. He was going to the bagwash. 'I don't expect anyone will ring,' he said. 'But if you wouldn't mind taking a few particulars, I'd be grateful.' He didn't have a high opinion of her business capabilities, but he couldn't see what actual harm she could do in the space of an hour.

'I'll be glad to,' she said. 'You run along and attend to your smalls. Leave it to me.'

She followed him down the hall, inquiring, 'What will they be ringing about, dear? Anything special?'

'My bike,' he said. 'I'm selling my bike. Just give them the address and say I'll be back in an hour.'

Rose didn't like it; she dithered reproachfully on the front step, looking at his motorbike chained to the black railings. 'Poor little bike,' she said. 'How would you like to be sold to strangers?'

'Just say I won't be long,' he persisted callously, walking off down Huskinson Street with his washing slung over his back in a pillow slip.

When he had gone, Rose went upstairs to see if he'd messed the bathroom; he had a habit of spattering the wall above the basin with toothpaste. As she was coming downstairs, the phone rang. It was a gentleman saying he'd seen the advertisement in the *Echo* and could he know the make of the vehicle in question? No, he couldn't, she told him. 'But it's very nice and it's got a nice red seat.' There was a pause. Someone began to knock loudly at the front door.

'How much?' asked the man on the telephone. He was well spoken – by the sound of him he came from Wavertree. 'Just a seccy,' said Rose, 'I've a client clamouring to get in.'

She ran to the front door and let her next door neighbour into the hall. 'Hang on,' she told her. 'I'm needed on the telephone.'

She gave her address to the Wavertree gentleman and told him he was very welcome to call. 'I'm awfully friendly,' she said, by way of reassuring him. She mentioned he couldn't miss the house because there was a Union Jack draped upon the balcony, left over from the Festival of Britain. 'It's a bit bedraggled but you can't avoid it.'

'Is it all above board?' asked the man. He sounded dubious – possibly he didn't care for the district. Of course it had gone down since the war, but there were still some beautiful houses, and if he was that lah-di-dah, why wasn't he buying a nice new shiny motor car instead of a worn-out old bike?

She asked her neighbour if she wanted her hair washed and set, as well as cut. 'The lot,' said Mrs Mallison, who was going to a masonic do with her husband on the Saturday.

Rose put on her overall. She'd bought it in a jumble sale. It was made of pink satin and the word Mother was embroidered across the left breast pocket. It wasn't quite the ticket, more like a long bed jacket than anything else, but Rose liked it. With her red hair, her thin legs bare of stockings, she stalked flamingo fashion about the sitting room. Mrs Mallison removed her jumper and skirt in the warmth, and then climbed the stairs to the bathroom. Rose had already arranged the dryer and a comfortable armchair. It wasn't entirely a convenient arrangement – the electric cable stretched like a trip wire from the bathroom to the socket on the landing – the door had to be left open. Still, there was a small table with a bowl of plastic flowers, and a heap of magazines that Rose had borrowed, some years before, from a dentist's surgery.

Mrs Mallison was set and under the dryer when the man from Wavertree knocked at the door. He had a boy with him who had dark eyes and an adolescent stoop. 'My boy, Ronald,' the man said. 'We're interested in the motorbike. My name's Wilson.' It seemed to Rose that he was a very cautious individual – he moved extremely slowly along the hall ahead of her. Maybe he was scared of bumping into something. He had a curious way of holding one hand behind his back, fingers fluttering like a shirt tail, as though he was signalling to someone. The hall wasn't really dark — cosy was how Rose would have described it. Indeed the red bulb, hanging above the door, lent a certain mysterious charm to the narrow passageway.

'Sit down,' said Rose. 'Make yourself comfortable. Take something off if you like.' She stood smiling at the boy, gesturing toward the chairs grouped around the table. Even the back kitchen was warm and intimate, owing to her flair for interior decoration. The scarlet lamp-shade, fringed with silken tassels, spun in the draught; shadows raced across the walls.

'Don't move,' ordered the man from Wavertree. The boy, about to sit down, froze. 'Keep on your feet,' said his father. 'I don't like the look of this at all.'

The blessed nerve, thought Rose, who had been contemplating offering him some refreshment. She slammed the cupboard door and folded her arms. 'It takes all sorts,' she said. 'I daresay someone like you prefers pastel tones . . . strip lighting and chintz, that sort of caper. My front room was once in the papers.'

'The owner,' said the man, 'of the bike . . . where the devil is he?'

'You come with me,' snapped Rose. 'This moment.' She was incensed at his previous scathing reference to her decor. No one, not ever, not once, had ever said they didn't like it. The man was completely lacking in style.

She flung open the door of the sitting room. It had a large brass bed, an upright piano with panels painted with nymphs, and several brass tables set with various lamps, each with a poppy-coloured shade. The whole room glittered and leapt in the firelight.

'Where is he?' asked the Wavertree man, dazzled by golden reflections.

'Who?' she said.

'The advertisement. I came about the motorbike.'

'In the bagwash,' she said, taking a fearful dislike to him. She pushed him out of the room and slammed the door shut. The boy smiled in wonder.

'I've never seen a piano in a bedroom,' he told her.

'Or put it another way,' said Rose kindly. 'Have you ever seen a bed in a music room?' She was always sorry for people with preconceived notions, particularly the young.

At that moment Mrs Mallison switched off the hair dryer. She called out peevishly – 'Rose . . . I've had enough . . . I'm properly done.'

She came out of the bathroom and careless of the wire stretched across the landing, took a pace forward. She didn't fall – she gave a kind of hop and a stumble, which brought her to the top of the stairs and sent her, accelerating at every step, down the last flight into the hall; unable to stop, she continued to run in her pink slip, as if the race wasn't yet won, headlong towards the front door.

The man from Wavertree thrust his son behind him and held out his arms protectively.

'We're leaving,' he cried. 'It can't go on.'

'Is he from the social security?' asked Mrs Mallison, breathing heavily and sinking onto the hall chair.

The boy came back into the hall, leaving his father hovering on the dark pavement. 'My gloves,' he said loudly. 'I've left me gloves.' He whispered into Rose's ear. 'Can I come back on my own?'

'Get off with you,' cried Rose, dimpling with delight, and she bundled him down the steps to his waiting Daddy and shut the door.

When Purdy returned from the bagwash, Rose was sitting by the fire drinking tea. 'Anyone ring?' he asked, standing there with his check cap at an angle.

'Nobody nice,' said Rose. 'Only a man from Wavertree with no sense of style.'

EVENSONG

Louise swore several times, mildly, as she pulled up weeds, raked out stones. There was no fear of being overheard, not on a weekday. The row of dismal little gardens was deserted, everyone out at work or watching films on video. 'Come on up, damn you,' she urged, tugging at a piece of concrete lodged in the wet soil. She supposed that builders found it more economical to dump their rubble in the earth rather than transport it to some tip.

She carried the offending lump to the bins at the back door and then realised that the bin men would almost certainly refuse to dispose of it. She took it into the garage instead. She'd have to get Keith to take it for a walk somewhere; possibly he could drop it over the railings by the council offices, on top of all those bedsprings and rusty cookers flung among the daffodils.

'Naughty, naughty,' she reproved herself and, picking up the cricket bat, returned to the garden. She'd forgotten to put on her wellingtons and her shoes were saturated. Still, there were other things more important than physical health.

'Blast you,' she muttered, as she knelt by the border and unearthed a length of piping and a crumbling brick.

It wasn't as if she was a country person at heart, or even that she was particularly interested in growing things, simply that it was necessary to spend as much time as possible out of doors. She didn't put it into words, any more than Graham did, but the house was hateful. It was too small, too ugly. She could feel its presence behind her, a box made of red brick with the second lid of the grey sky clamped above its chimneyless roof.

When she woke in the mornings from bad dreams, opened her eyes to the coffin-like dimensions of the cream-painted bedroom dark with furniture, she felt she was still asleep, still caught in nightmares. The wardrobe inlaid with mother-of-pearl which had illuminated the landing of her parents' home, flashing silver in the sun on summer afternoons, now blotted out the light. Year by year, the tables and the chairs, the bookcase and the sideboard which had furnished her childhood, grew more oppressive, more threatening.

Graham had suggested that they put it all into store. 'Though I don't expect we shall be here very long,' he had said, ten years ago. She had pretended that she couldn't live without the Chippendale desk, the George III library stairs, her parents' bed with its cluster of wooden grapes on the headboard.

'I know they look out of place here,' she had told him, 'but unless you feel strongly about it I should like to keep them. I need them.' And of course he hadn't felt strongly about it. How could he? It would have been her money, that small and dwindling inheritance left to her by her father, which would have paid the storage costs.

They couldn't afford such costs, any more than they could have afforded to buy new furniture to put in place of the old. It was Graham who always referred to it as her money; she herself would gladly have given it to him, had tried to, but he wouldn't hear of it. 'I couldn't touch a penny,' he often said. 'John meant it for you.' It was only one of a number of small deceptions they practised, this pretence that the money was for her use alone.

Remembering that the rambler rose needed staking against the wind, she went on hands and knees further down the garden to attend to it.

Beyond the house the long corridor of the road was deserted

too, save for a few cars parked at intervals along the kerb and the dust-cart abandoned under the lamp-post. A child's swing creaked above a patch of scuffed lawn. It was half past three in the afternoon. And then an ordinary young man came round the corner from the direction of the High Street and began to walk down the road, nudging the privet hedges with his shoulder as he passed, for earlier it had rained and he took pleasure in the way the leaves sprang back, spattering the pavement with drops.

When he drew level with the church he stopped and looked across at the house, at the board nailed to a post beside the gate. On it was written in Gothic lettering 'Vicarage'. Underneath, daubed in white paint, were the words 'God is out. Call again'.

He walked up the side path to the church and entered by the vestry, leaving the door on the latch behind him. The oval door into the church was ajar; someone was playing the harmonium. On tiptoe he moved cautiously round the cheap wooden table with its dusty water jug and its pile of parish magazines, and peered through. He had a clear view of the two of them, the man seated at the harmonium, the girl standing beside him, her hand resting on his neck. The music stopped.

He dodged back instantly, flattening himself against the damp raincoat hanging on the wall behind him. He heard the girl say in a complaining voice, 'But we're not doing any harm,' and then the Sunday school hymn began again. He ran out of the vestry and down the path and, looking neither to right nor left, crossed the road to the vicarage.

When he pushed open the door the chimes rang out. Even before they had finished striking he was down the hall and into the living room. He noticed nothing but the handbag on the table. He was taking a £5 note out of the leather purse when he heard a dull clopping sound. Beyond the French windows, in the square of garden, he saw a woman wielding a cricket bat in both hands, stomping a stake into the earth beside a rose bush.

The young man put the note into his pocket, the one in which he kept his knife. He watched as the woman flung down the bat and began to take off her gardening gloves. He took out the knife and flicked it open as the woman turned, one hand rubbing the small of her back, and approached the house.

She came in through the French windows. She looked first at the table and then at the young man. 'How much have you taken?' she asked.

'I never touched your bloody bag,' he protested.

'It's no good lying, Keith,' she said. 'I know exactly how much I had.' She left the room and he heard her moving about in the kitchen, running water into the kettle. He stuffed the £5 note into the handbag, not bothering to replace it in the purse and, sitting down at the table, began to jab with his knife at the papers covering it.

Louise returned carrying a tray with two cups and set it down in front of him. She said, 'Do stop that. They're Graham's notes for his sermon.' Her tone was matter of fact, without emphasis.

'You've left his cricket bat out,' he told her.

'Damn,' she said.

'He'll do his nut,' he warned her.

'He won't be back for another hour. He's gone to visit old Mr Syme at the Cottage Hospital.' She bent down to switch on the electric fire.

'That's good of him,' said Keith evenly.

'I'll put it away after I've had a cuppa,' she said, and went out into the kitchen to make the tea.

He called through to her, asking where her cousin was, but Louise didn't reply. He knew she had heard him. He stared at the photograph in its ornate frame on the wall behind the door, frowning. 'Where's your cousin?' he repeated, when Louise came back with the teapot.

Louise said that Pamela was at the hairdresser's. She didn't look at him. She took her cup to the armchair by the fire and sat down, positioning herself sideways so that she was facing the photograph. As always when gazing at the image of her father her expression softened. He was standing in a garden holding a cricket bat over his shoulder, smiling at the camera. The photograph had been taken before she was born, when he was a young curate in Surrey.

'How long is Pamela going to go on staying here?' Keith asked.

'Until she's ready to leave, I suppose,' said Louise, and she made a little gesture with her hand, signalling that he should keep quiet.

Sullenly he drank his tea. He knew he should offer to go out into the garden and finish whatever job it was that Louise had begun. It was what he was here for − to help out, to make himself useful. He had promised yesterday that he would clean the windows, but he hadn't got round to it. He didn't expect he'd get round to it today either.

He said loudly, 'I never knew my Dad. He scarpered before I was born.'

'Rubbish,' said Louise. 'Graham met him when he went to see your probation officer.'

'Well, we've never got on. He's a bad-tempered bastard. It wasn't like you and him. I never got no attention.'

'I'm not deaf,' she said, and she leaned back in her chair and closed her eyes. Defeated, he flounced out into the garden, slamming the doors behind him.

Louise felt guilty, but only for a moment. God knows, these days she seemed to spend more time with Keith than anyone else. She thought how dangerous it was, this craving for attention which everyone had, herself included, as though it was some drug which once given could never be withdrawn. She supposed it all began in infancy. 'I never got none,' she said out loud, mimicking Keith and speaking to the photograph.

Of course it had been a disappointment for him, having a daughter when he had wanted a son. Not that he'd really shown it, just that she had always known deep down that she was second-best. When she had met Graham, her father had been almost pathetically pleased at her choice. She suspected that he was also baffled that someone like Graham should find her interesting. She had overheard him telling her mother that he was a catch, though Graham had only recently come down from Cambridge and had neither money nor prospects.

Her father had done his best to ensure that Graham was subjected to the full range and intensity of his friendship, lending him books, employing him as a temporary secretary when he went to the ecumenical conference at St George's Chapel in Windsor, introducing him as his prospective son-in-law to the Bishop of Chichester. He was doing it for her, of course, just as taking Graham to the Test Match at Lords on her birthday had been mostly for her benefit.

He had married them and paid for the honeymoon and telephoned Graham every morning at the hotel in Broadstairs. Once he had asked to speak to her, but there must have been some electrical fault because when she picked up the telephone the line had been disconnected. He had hung on for three years waiting for a grandson to be born, and when she hadn't obliged he had died. The local papers had written briefly about his work in the parish, and at length about his days as a county cricketer. He had left a letter for Graham in his desk. Graham hadn't told her what was in it, and she didn't suppose she would ever know, for the letter had since been lost, if not destroyed, and besides, it had all happened twenty years ago and no longer mattered.

She got up and put the cups on to the tray. She could

hear Keith outside in the garden, whistling 'There's a friend for little children above the bright blue sky'. It was almost dark and the rain was falling again, streaking the windows.

When Pamela came in her hair was flattened to her head. She said she'd had to walk back from the hairdresser's, and she hadn't taken an umbrella. 'What a waste,' said Louise.

At a quarter past five Hilda arrived. She was already crying as she came through the door. Pamela, who was typing at the table, gave her an insincere smile. Ten minutes later Mr Mahmood called at the house. He was wearing his best suit, his only suit. He said he had an appointment with Graham. He was clearly appalled by Hilda, and nervously paced about the room, tugging at the points of his striped waistcoat with plump fingers encircled with thin gold rings.

'My father also was a cricketer,' he said, standing on tiptoe to examine the photograph. 'He learnt the batting in the British Army. Is the vicar playing the game also?'

'No,' said Louise. 'He used to, but not any more.'

'Ah, well,' observed Mr Mahmood. 'He is a very busy man. He is helping everyone.'

'In what way is he helping you, Mr Mahmood?' Louise asked. She was twisting the strap of her watch round and round on her wrist.

'He is getting me rehoused.'

'Really,' Louise said, and added, 'How nice.' She took a Kleenex tissue from the box on the table and handed it to Hilda.

'I am living on the Bayham council estate and it is not a nice place,' Mahmood confided. 'My neighbours are posting me shit through the letterbox. Mr Sinclair is talking to the council and getting me a little house of my own . . . possibly with a garden.'

'I see,' said Louise. She was aware that Pamela was watching her.

Mahmood began a detailed description of the sort of house he had in mind. Four bedrooms would be enough, though probably later he could do some extending, as he was handy with the nails and the hammers. If it had a porch he would hang a name plate from it on chains. His uncle was a sign-maker in Bermondsey and would make him one cheap. There must also be a shed for his bicycle. At the moment his bicycle was living in the bedroom and it was catching at his trousers whenever he moved.

'I am a very lucky man,' he enthused, 'meeting so good a vicar. He is a very kind man.'

'He is certainly a well-intentioned one,' said Louise, and managed a smile.

Shortly afterwards Graham came home. He apologised to Mr Mahmood for keeping him waiting and said he had been unavoidably detained. Depressed as he was, he was still charming.

Mahmood was overcome. He protested that it was not a question of Mr Sinclair being late, rather that he himself had presented too early. Wearily Graham told him to come through into the front room. He had given up calling it the study. For a time he had referred to it as the Surgery – Louise had advised against it – until that woman with the dyed red hair had insisted that he examine her for gallstones.

'How was Mr Syme?' asked Louise. 'Is he any better?'

He was disconcerted, and showed it. What a fool I am, he thought, jeopardising my peace of mind, my happiness. And then it occurred to him that he had not been happy for years.

He was saved from an outright lie by Hilda, who at that precise moment began to utter thin little screams. It was only an effort of will which prevented him from covering his ears to blot out the dreadful noise of her misery.

'I am anxious to finalise things,' said Mr Mahmood,

unexpectedly pushy, the skin under his hopeful eyes the colour of plums.

'There, there,' Graham murmured, patting Hilda awkwardly on the shoulder. He took Mahmood by the elbow and escorted him from the room.

After a cup of tea and a biscuit Hilda recovered sufficiently to remember the children waiting for her at home. When she had gone Pamela said she didn't know how Graham stood it.

'Graham,' cried Louise, exasperated.

'I'm not at all sure that it doesn't make her worse, pandering to her, letting her sit here and wail like a soul in torment.'

'She is in torment,' said Louise. She prowled about the room, arms crossed, hugging herself. At last she said, 'I wish he wouldn't do it. It's so unfair. He shouldn't promise people like Mahmood that he'll help them. It's damaging. It's almost cruel.'

'You're unfair,' Pamela accused her. 'You can't resist knocking him, can you?' She knew she shouldn't say such things aloud. Louise wasn't a complete fool. All the same, she couldn't bear Graham to be criticised. 'It's part of his job,' she said, 'helping people. Just as it's your job to encourage him.'

'Who does Graham know on the council?' asked Louise. 'He has no authority, no influence.'

'He needs your support,' Pamela shouted.

'Dear God,' said Louise, and fearing she might strike the girl she left the living room and marched in the dark about the tiny kitchen. It was unjust of Pamela to suggest that she wasn't supportive. Who had succeeded in getting Syme into the Cottage Hospital when the social services had told Graham that the old man wasn't a priority case? Who supervised Keith, made his lunch, thought up jobs for him to do, listened to his whining complaints about his parents, his excuses? And in the end it would be her who would be left to cope with Mahmood.

She knew exactly what would happen, because it had happened before. First, Mahmood would give up his rent book; then the phone calls would begin, calls which Graham would avoid. And then one afternoon, depend upon it, the poor deluded Mahmood would trot up the path, homeless, dispossessed, followed by a wife and numerous children.

Picturing the scene with frightful clarity, tears welled up in her eyes. She leaned against the sink and stared into the darkness. She saw Keith's face pressed to the window, his nose grotesquely squashed against the glass. 'Go home,' she mouthed, and ran back into the living room and drew the curtains. Pamela was still sitting at the table.

'Keith's out there,' Louise said. 'Spying on us. He never leaves me alone.'

'He doesn't like anybody but you,' said Pamela. 'You can't blame that on Graham. He did try to get him a job.'

It was true, thought Louise. He had tried. But then, who but Graham would think it was possible to find employment for a boy like Keith.

'What did Keith do?' asked Pamela.

Louise proceeded to tell her, though she omitted certain details, such as the blood on the floor, the smashed spectacles which had become embedded in the bridge of the nose. The man behind the counter of the corner shop had almost died. Not from the blow on the head but from the vomit in his windpipe. He had been drinking all day. And it was all for a packet of cigarettes.

'Poor Keith,' murmured Pamela. Her blue eyes were tender with misplaced sympathy.

'Don't be ridiculous,' Louise said. 'You're as bad as Graham. There are thousands of people with backgrounds every bit as deprived as his and yet they manage to live perfectly ordinary, decent lives. They're the ones you should be sorry for.'

'I wish I understood about violence,' said Pamela. 'I often feel angry, but never murderous. I wonder what stops most of us from harming each other?'

Louise didn't reply. Nothing stops us, she thought. Nothing at all.

The following morning the hospital telephoned to say that Mr Syme had died in the night. When Pamela went through into the front room to see if Graham needed her to type letters, she was shocked at his appearance. He looked terrible, as if he had suffered a personal loss. He sat there, drawing little squiggles on the blotter on his desk. He told her to leave him alone.

Louise told Pamela not to worry, that he would be all right in a day or two. 'He hardly knew him,' protested Pamela.

'What has that got to do with it?' said Louise, and she smiled and went upstairs to make the beds.

Pamela waited until lunchtime. She knew that Graham had an appointment with the social services department, and she hid in the garage. When he saw her his expression altered. Before, he had looked sad, now he was irritated.

'I must talk to you,' she said. 'There's something I want to discuss.' He said that he was too depressed, that the last thing he needed was a discussion. She had thought it all out, rehearsed the words of comfort, and now it was her turn to be annoyed. 'I want to help you, dammit.'

'I don't need your help,' he said, fitting the key into the lock of the car. She came towards him and he backed away down the garage, putting distance between them, as though she was contaminated with some virus.

'I don't mean any harm,' she said. 'We're friends.'

'We're not friends, Pamela, and you know it.'

'You're always preaching about love,' she accused.

'Not this sort I'm not,' he said.

'Are you frightened of Louise? Is that what's depressing you?'

'I refuse to discuss Louise,' he said. 'You know nothing about it.'

She stood there, close to tears, and watched as he opened the car door and struggled inside. He wouldn't look at her. On other occasions he had said that she mustn't cry, that he couldn't bear to see her unhappy. She was such a little scrap, he had said. Such a dear little scrap, why, his heart melted just hearing her voice.

She turned away from the car and walked down the garden, devising schemes, thinking up ways of gaining his attention. Perhaps she could draw a picture of that old man who had died, and leave it on Graham's desk. She had once done a pencil sketch of the view from the back window and he had praised it. He had said that talent was a gift from God. But then, she didn't know what the old man had looked like, and in any case she was no good at faces.

She went miserably indoors and found Keith in the living room with a plate of sandwiches on his knee. The television was on.

She watched as he pulled the cheese from the bread and gobbled at it. He wasn't all that much younger than she was, thought Pamela. They were of the same generation. She could probably understand him far better than Louise. If she got to know him, gained his confidence, he might come to rely on her. Graham would be pleased.

She leaned forward and switched off the television.

'What's the bloody game?' Keith said.

'I thought we might have a chat.'

He was looking at her legs and hurriedly she smoothed her skirt down over her knees. 'It's silly,' she said, 'seeing

hunted by larger ones. There was a distant shot of a dusty horizon and a herd of cow-like beasts. The commentary was promising. It is only a matter of time, the voice said, before the weakest member of the herd will fall behind the rest of the pack.

He was still watching television at seven o'clock that evening, though earlier he had hosed out the garage and disposed of a lump of concrete. Louise and he were watching Channel Four news when Graham came home. Louise said she would make him an omelette, but he told her not to bother. He wasn't hungry, and he had a headache. Besides, there wouldn't be time. Mrs Crombie was coming.

Keith got up and made for the door. It was obvious old Graham was in a bad mood.

'Turn the television off, will you,' Graham said.

Keith returned and did as he was told. He was just going out of the door when Graham shouted, 'Pick up the tray, please. Louise isn't your servant.'

Humiliated, Keith picked up the tray and dropped it on to the table. 'No,' he said, 'she isn't, you bastard. But don't you get a kick out of thinking she's yours.'

He slammed the door behind him with such violence that the photograph on the wall slipped sideways on its cord. Louise righted it, and stepped back to see if it was straight.

'Shall I tell him not to come here any more?' Graham said. She didn't reply. 'I don't appear to exert much influence on him, do I?'

Still she remained silent. He stood beside the table and fiddled aimlessly with the papers. Suddenly he hit the surface with his fist, scattering the cutlery on the tray. A fork bounced to the carpet. 'What do I ever achieve?' he said. 'I might be invisible for all the effect I have.'

Louise bent and picked up the fork. Graham turned and

clung to her. 'I don't influence anyone, do I? All I have is good intentions.' He moaned. 'I couldn't even manage to say goodbye to old Syme before he died.'

Louise stood passively in his arms, her hands at her sides. 'You meant to, dear,' she said. 'You meant to.' She let him ramble on. It was always better to let him wallow in his self-pity.

'When I think of the ideas I had,' he was saying, 'the plans. Do you remember John telling me I'd be a bishop before I was thirty?' She didn't remember, although she had heard it from him often enough. It was time to put her arms round him, to pat his back as though comforting a child. She was looking over his shoulder at the picture on the wall. 'Oh, God,' he said, 'this ugly house, that ugly church, these wretched people.' And he let out a groan of terrible, indulgent despair.

'That's enough,' said Louise. She disengaged herself from his arms and busied herself with the knives and forks. 'I detest self-pity,' she told him. 'And so did John.'

He said she was quite right, as always. He wiped his eyes with his sleeve and murmured that he didn't know what he would do without her. She must tell him what to do about Keith. There had been a moment back there, God forgive him, when he had wanted to strike him.

Louise said it was all a question of time, of having confidence. Keith would never amount to much but they must be patient. She took the tray to the door. Graham was already humming to himself, his self-esteem restored. 'Perhaps you should have struck him,' she said. 'It's one of the few gestures he understands.' Graham looked shocked. Taking pity on him, she said, 'No, of course you shouldn't. The remorse would have outweighed the satisfaction.'

An unusually large number of parishioners arrived that evening to ask Graham for his advice. Sidney came, and Mrs Crombie brought a friend. There was even a young boy, the sort with a punk haircut, who said he was thinking of getting married. Mercifully, Hilda was absent. Louise was glad for Graham: it would make him feel worthwhile, having so many people who depended on him.

She was going into the kitchen to put the kettle on for the third time when she noticed Pamela crouching on the stairs. 'Can't you find anywhere else to sit?' she asked.

'I prefer it here,' said Pamela. 'Any objections?'

Graham was showing Sidney out when Louise came back into the hall with the teapot. She heard Pamela say, 'If you don't let me talk to you I just might smash a few windows.' She pretended not to have heard and called out from the living room that Mrs Crombie was next if Graham was ready.

'Keith saw us in the church,' said Pamela.

'For God's sake,' hissed Graham. 'Lower your voice.' He called out, 'I'm ready when you are, Mrs Crombie.'

'He made me give him ten pounds,' shouted Pamela. Louise was helping Mrs Crombie up the hall. The old woman was leaning on her, breathing like a horse. 'How nice to see you,' said Graham, and taking her arm he almost pushed her into the front room and closed the door behind them.

Pamela was shaking. She wasn't sure how much Louise had overheard. She couldn't think which was worse, Keith knowing, or Louise. Trying not to whimper, she went into the living room. Louise smiled at her. She was talking to a young boy with pink hair. He was fingering the silver snuff box that stood on the mantelpiece.

'It's pretty, isn't it?' said Louise. 'It belonged to my father. Mr Sinclair keeps his stamps in it.' She took it from him and slipped it into the pocket of her cardigan. Then she poured Pamela a cup of tea, still smiling. She didn't hear, thought Pamela. All the same, her hands continued to shake, and her cup rattled in its saucer.

Later, when Mrs Crombie and her friend had gone, and the punk boy was in the front room with Graham, Louise began to talk about Hilda. She said that she was relieved that she hadn't come, but also worried. It wasn't like her to miss her tea and biscuits and the opportunity of a weep in public. She hoped she was safe.

'Is she a battered wife?' asked Pamela. Sometimes the woman's arms had been covered in bruises.

'Not in the way you mean,' said Louise. 'Her husband walked off with a younger woman. She's just very depressed.'

This is a dangerous conversation, thought Pamela, and in spite of it she said, 'I don't see the point of people hanging on to each other against their will.'

'No,' said Louise. 'I don't expect you do.'

'I mean if someone falls in love with someone else, then it's useless trying to pretend that nothing's happened. I mean, once love has gone, it's absurd to think that it can be resurrected. I think people should be more honest with each other. It's better for everyone in the end.' Suddenly Pamela was weeping, and shouting through her tears. 'Oh, I know you don't agree, Louise. You're all for duty and self-control.'

'You're right,' Louise said gently. 'I do believe in duty. I was brought up that way. I can't claim any credit for it.'

'Well, it's bloody hard on other people I can tell you,' Pamela said wildly. 'It's stifling. We all have to creep round feeling inferior. Your disapproval is killing . . . killing –' In the hall the chimes rang as Graham showed the punk boy out of the door. 'You've ruined bloody Graham,' Pamela shouted. She waited for Graham to come into the room. She wanted it over and done with, everything out in the open. And then he was standing there, his face bleak, his frightened eyes staring at her. 'Is anything wrong?' he asked inadequately.

'Oh, Christ,' said Pamela. 'He can't even think for himself any more. He's just all twisted up about whether you'll approve.' Then she was running for the open door, pushing Graham aside with her arm. He staggered and fell against the wall, jerking the picture from its nail.

The next morning Pamela apologised to Graham. 'I don't know what came over me,' she said, when Louise had gone out shopping. 'I must have been mad. It was just that I was so worried about Keith seeing us in the church together like that.'

'There was nothing to see,' he said dismissively. 'I shall ask him to give you the money back.'

'I may have been mistaken,' she admitted. 'I think he only borrowed it. Please don't mention it to him. I shall feel terrible.'

She was nothing but a trouble-maker, he thought. He told her about the picture falling off the wall and said that he would take it into town to have the frame mended and the glass replaced as soon as he had the time. She begged him to let her see to it. And pay for it. After all, it had been her fault, pushing him like that. But first she would type his letters ready for the post.

Keith turned up early for once, though he spent over an hour in the kitchen making himself rounds of toast. Louise was in the garden, building a rockery. He rapped on the window and waved at her, but she turned away instantly, as if she was sick of the sight of him.

When he had eaten he filled a bucket with warm water and went round to the front of the house to clean the windows. Graham was rummaging in the drawers of his desk, a frown on his face. There was a neat pile of addressed envelopes on the window-sill. Presently he snatched them up and left the room.

He couldn't understand what had happened to the snuff

box. He needed some stamps. Surely he had seen it on the mantelpiece only yesterday. He, too, banged his fist on the window to attract Louise's attention, but she immediately moved further down the garden, her back resolutely turned on him. He remembered that he had left his raincoat in the vestry. Perhaps he had absentmindedly slipped the snuff box into one of the pockets. He left the house by the front door, ignoring Keith, and crossed the road to the church.

Pamela was unlocking the boot of the car when Keith came up the path carrying his bucket. He stood in the entrance of the garage and looked down at the picture propped against the wall.

'Were you going to clean the car?' asked Pamela. She tried not to sound nervous.

'How did this happen?' he asked, squatting down and examining the photograph.

'It fell,' she said. 'Graham knocked it down. I'm taking it to be reframed.'

'You get in,' he said. 'I'll put it in the boot.'

Pamela got into the front seat and felt the car rock slightly as the boot slammed shut. In the mirror she saw Keith going down the path and into the house. She reversed expertly out of the garage and felt a bump as she backed on to the path by the bins. He must have left his bucket in the way, she thought, and then beyond the bonnet of the car saw the picture lying face down in a slick of oil.

The photograph was damaged beyond repair. The face of the man had been shredded by the broken glass.

Louise heard Pamela's cry of rage, of hatred. 'Damn you,' she was screaming. 'Damn you.' Sometime soon, thought Louise, I shall have to ask her to leave. She watched as Pamela ran into the house like a madwoman. Perplexed, she looked at the car parked outside on the path.

When she went into the garage she thought at first it was a rag lying there on the oil-stained concrete, and then she noticed the shards of glass. She turned the buckled piece of card over with her foot and stared down at the photograph. The face of her father had gone. All that remained was the handle of the cricket bat clenched in a blackened fist.

The snuff box wasn't in the raincoat pocket. Graham tried thinking back to the last time he had seen it, the last time he had needed stamps, but he couldn't remember. He went out into the empty church and stared hopelessly at the cross above the altar, at the flowers withering in the vases. He thought of Louise and then of Pamela. Thank God he had resisted the temptation to do more than kiss her. But then, the sad truth was that he hadn't been tempted. Even that small fall from grace had been denied him.

Suddenly he heard a noise coming somewhere from the left of the church, a soft footfall. He knew who it was. He ran across the aisle as if he was running for the crease, his face contorted, and hurled himself into the vestry. Keith was half way to the door. Graham jumped on him from behind, seizing a clump of his black hair in his fist, forcing him to his knees. He was calling the boy names, dreadful names. He was tugging his head back on his neck as if he would tear it from his shoulders. 'You rotten lump of shit,' he was slobbering. 'Give me back my snuff box. Give it to me.' Gathering saliva in his mouth and gobbling like a turkey, he spat full into Keith's upturned, terrified face.

Louise was standing facing the house when Graham came stumbling up the garden towards her. She stood quite still, her eyes blank. 'Louise, help me,' he pleaded. He was holding out his hands to her as if he was drowning.

She stepped back from him in disgust. 'Get out of my sight,' she said. 'I shall never speak to you again,' and she, too, held up her hands, fending him off, her fingers smeared with oil.

*

She kept her word. The house was as silent as the grave. After almost a week Pamela could stand it no longer. There was something wrong, she felt, something beyond the matter of the picture. It had something to do with Keith. She had seen him that morning, lounging against the fence as Graham went down the path. Graham had spoken to him, though she couldn't hear what he said. And Keith had laughed. And then Graham had come back into the house and he was crying. He had gone into the front room and locked the door behind him. It was Keith that was poisoning their world. She would write to him and tell him what he must do.

She sat down at the table in the living room and began to write. She felt inspired.

Dear Keith (she wrote),
I cannot stand by and see a family destroyed. You must know that it would be better if you stopped coming here. Graham believes that he is doing you more harm than good, and it is dreadful for him.

You must tell Louise that it was you who put the photograph for me to drive over. In some way, she holds Graham responsible.

Try to be brave. You must tell Louise the truth. We can't go on like this. You must tell her you're leaving. If you don't tell her, I will. Believe me, it's for the best.

Pamela

When she had read it over to herself she thought it wasn't long enough. A little too abrupt. She began it again and covered both sides of the notepaper, and had to use another piece for the last part, which she left unchanged.

When it was finished she put it in her handbag and tidied up the table. She found the silver snuff box under a pile of bills and replaced it on the mantelpiece. The telephone rang in the hall.

Keith had been outside the French windows, watching her. When she left the room he entered and listened for a moment to the murmur of her voice. He opened her hand-bag and taking out the folded letter thrust it into his pocket. He heard the click as Pamela replaced the receiver and slipped out again into the garden.

Pamela knocked on Graham's door. There was no reply. 'That was Mrs Crombie,' she said. 'She says you promised to run her and Mrs Haley to the OAPs' Bingo night.'

He unlocked the door and stared at her. 'That was Mrs Crombie,' she said again.

'I heard you the first time,' he said. 'I don't have to leave for another half hour.'

'You rest,' she said. 'Things will be all right now. I'll call you when it's time to go.'

She sat on the stairs, gazing at the locked door, rocking backwards and forwards.

Keith took the letter to show Louise. He told her it was important. She said she wasn't interested, either in a letter or in him. She was tying the rambler rose to the fence with a length of wire. The cricket bat lay on the grass at her feet.

He walked away from her to the other side of the garden, the letter still in his hand, and crouched down behind the privet hedge.

Sitting on the stairs, guarding Graham's sleep, Pamela indulged in fantasies. She would tell Louise that it was she who had destroyed the picture. Graham would overhear and be moved by her selflessness. You dear one, he would say, or something like that. And then she'd tell him that she was going away, so that he and Louise could grow close again. He would beg her to change her mind, or better still, offer to come with her. And of course she'd say he couldn't.

She felt sad but also relieved. I will go away, she thought. I don't really want him to leave Louise. It would be nice if before she went she could patch things up between them. Perhaps she should talk to Louise now, tell her about the letter she had written to Keith. Louise would be pleased with her, and then when she went to wake up Graham she could tell him that everything was truly all right.

'Louise,' she called excitedly, as she opened the back door into the garden.

Louise was trying to hammer the rose stake deeper into the ground. The bat was heavy and she didn't seem able to hit the wood squarely. There came to her a memory of a holiday in Hastings just after the war when her father and she had played cricket together on the sands. It was a child's bat she held, and her father was shouting at her to swing it from the shoulder. She shut her eyes because she was frightened of the ball. 'Loosen up, Louise', he told her. She could hear his voice quite clearly now, and she turned as he called her name again and swung the bat with all her strength.

When she opened her eyes, Pamela was lying face downwards on the grass. One of her shoes had come off.

'Drop it,' said Keith. She stared at him blankly. 'Drop the bloody bat,' he repeated. She let go of it. 'Take off your gloves,' he ordered, and when she made no move he tugged them from her hands. 'Walk away,' he said. 'Walk away. Don't look round.' He had to take her by the shoulders and set her off down the garden like a clockwork toy. 'Stay there till I tell you,' he called. 'Don't look back.'

First he took the bat and the shoe to the garage, and then he returned and gripped Pamela under the armpits, dragging her across the grass. He had to leave her beside the car while he went into the house to fetch the keys from Graham's raincoat in the hall. He opened the door of the car, bundled the body on to the back seat and laid the shoe beside it. He ran into the house again and took the raincoat to cover her over. He shut the car door, and carefully balanced the cricket bat against it. The letter, he thought, the last page of the letter, and taking it from his pocket he unlocked the car again and thrust the single sheet of paper into the glove compartment beneath the dashboard. Then he slipped into the house for the last time and left the keys on the window-sill in the hall.

Graham woke five minutes before he was due to pick up Mrs Haley. He had another headache. He picked up the cricket bat by its handle and placed it carefully outside the garage, propped against the fence. As he reversed the car down the path he saw in the glare of the headlights two figures standing in the dark garden, facing away from the house.

'It will be all right,' Keith told her. 'It wasn't your fault. I expect she said something to annoy you.'

'I'm frightened,' said Louise.

'That old bloke in the shop,' he said, 'the one I bashed . . . when I asked him for fags he said hadn't I heard the word please. He looked at me as if I was dirt.'

'I'm frightened,' she repeated.

'It wears off,' Keith said. 'It isn't our fault. We was driven.'

As he was approaching the corner, Graham passed Mr Mahmood and his family. He waved at them and drove on.

Mr Mahmood was wheeling his bike. From the handle-bars hung various carrier bags and a frying pan. Behind him, in single file, walked his wife and four children, each carrying a suitcase.

POLES APART

Mrs Evans had just got back from the library with her friend Miriam Fortesque when Avril Scott telephoned to ask her for Christmas.

'How very kind,' murmured Mrs Evans. 'But I really think that this year the journey might be a little too much for me.'

'Nonsense,' Avril said. 'It's Sussex, not the Outer Hebrides. You can take a taxi to the station and either Jim or I will meet you this end. It will be lovely. I'll give you a tinkle nearer the time to arrange things.'

'Oh hell,' Mrs Evans said, replacing the phone.

'Another invitation?' asked Miriam Fortesque, knowing it was a foregone conclusion. Her friend was always in demand at Christmas, was never short of invitations to parties during the run-up to the big day, to lunches the week before, to mulled wine dos on Christmas Eve, to festive dinners with all the trimmings, to elegant suppers on Boxing Night. Nor was she stuck in a corner with some child who had been bribed to keep her company. On the contrary, she was always in the forefront, on the captain's table, so to speak, and people vied to sit next to her.

'How can I get out of it?' demanded Mrs Evans, prowling irritably round the sitting-room and kicking Miriam Fortesque's stick to the carpet. 'I shall freeze to death in Sussex. They only turn the central heating on after the *Six O'Clock News*.' In her spring-chicken fifties and her autumnal broiler sixties she had appreciated the attention paid to her. Now, five years short of her eightieth birthday, she was less enthusiastic. Really, all she craved was to be left alone by her own fireside, a bottle of gin at her elbow and *The Towering Inferno* on the television.

'You're a fool to yourself,' certain friends said to her – certain geriatric acquaintances, who, though deaf, half-blind and often incontinent, sensed perfectly well the difference between sufferance and welcome – when Mrs Evans complained that this person or that had only a moment ago telephoned to ask her here, there and everywhere; to Sussex, Majorca, or worse, Edinburgh. 'If you can't do what you want at your age,' they told her bitterly, 'when will you?' 'Don't rub it in,' she would reply. 'I know I'm an egotist. I can't help feeling a refusal would offend. All my life I have walked backward into the limelight.'

Mrs Evans wasn't a distinguished woman. She had never done anything special; she hadn't discovered something, or written anything, or excelled in any given field. She had never been notorious in her own right. All the same, throughout her life – her early days, that is – she had managed to be connected with someone who had. For instance, she had just happened to be in Italian East Africa, in the station square at Diredaua in 1937 when the Duce had been present at the unveiling of some monument or other. She had caught his eye – God knows what she had been doing – and she had been asked to join his party for drinks afterwards. She swore that she had refused, but one could never tell. She described the memorial plinth as unmistakably phallic, as thrusting upwards to the heavens. 'It seemed to pierce the clouds,' she elaborated. And then she had unaccountably been sitting in some restaurant in Saragossa – of all places – with the infamous Bunny Doble, when Kim Philby, head bandaged after being blown up in a shell attack by Franco's troops, had burst in wearing a woman's fur coat. 'His hands trembled so much,' Mrs Evans recounted, 'that the food fell off his fork. And the fur was bloodied into little spikes, sharp as the nib of a mapping pen.'

Her recollections were so banal, so trivial, that it was obvious she was telling the truth. Why, she had shared a taxi with Moss Hart, the night his first play had opened on Broadway, and all she could remember was the boil on his brother's neck. And the afternoon Fatty Arbuckle had ground – for want of a better word – the life out of that young lady from Minnesota, Mrs Evans had been a guest in the house next door, and remembered how, no more than ten minutes later, Fatty had run along the gravelled drive, clad only in the loin cloth of a monogrammed towel – screaming, so she said.

'You could wait a few days,' Miriam Fortesque said, 'and then I could ring up and say you'd broken your hip.'

'I daren't risk it,' said Mrs Evans, gloomily. 'It would be just my luck.'

Even as a child she had suffered from her imagination. She still remembered the occasion, sixty years before, when unable to produce her arithmetic homework she had told her teacher that her father had suffered a brainstorm and run berserk through the greenhouse. 'My mother was cut by flying glass,' she had said. 'The blood dripped on to the page of my exercise book and I was forced to tear it out.' A year later a man in Wimbledon High Street, crazed by drink and carrying a sheet of plate glass, stumbled into her uncle Henry and severed the artery of his right leg. Another time, anxious to avoid the proposed visit of a school friend, Monica Formby, she had made the excuse that her brother Reg was at death's door with rabies. 'He froths at the mouth,' she had lied. 'We are forced to wear protective clothing.' Two days later, Monica Formby's cousin George was bitten by a monkey at the pet shop on Park Way and his arm blew up like a balloon.

'I shall say that it had slipped my mind that someone was coming to stay,' Mrs Evans told Miriam Fortesque. 'At our age we're expected to forget things.' She dialled Avril Scott's number immediately. 'That's perfectly all right, darling,' said Avril. 'Any friend of yours is more than welcome. Bring her with you. There's plenty of room.'

'It's a he,' Mrs Evans said. 'And he's very queer. I don't think he'd mix.'

'Really,' Avril said. 'What's his name? What does he do? Is he one of your theatrical friends?' Mrs Evans's mind became blank. She glanced desperately at Miriam Fortesque, who was pretending to be engrossed in her library book. 'Oates,' Mrs Evans said. 'Lawrence Oates. He's ex-army and very keen on horses. He's rather insufferable . . . very right-wing. He wouldn't go down well with Jim.'

'Rubbish,' cried Avril Scott. 'He can muck out Jason's pony.'

A week later after a snifter of gin, Mrs Evans rang Avril again. Avril listened patiently, and when Mrs Evans had finished, said, 'The Russian boy is no problem. Don't give it another thought. He can bunk up with Jason. As for the special diet, Mrs Creswell is jolly good at coping. I can't say I'm familiar with pelican hootch, but it's bound to be in Mrs Beeton. And we can certainly rustle up the Huntley and Palmer biscuits. All I have to do is ring up Harrods.'

'Help me,' appealed Mrs Evans, telephoning Miriam Fortesque twenty-four hours before she boarded the train for Sussex-by-the-Sea. Mrs Fortesque was unsympathetic. She herself had enough to do preparing for Christmas Eve, when she would be plucked from her cosy flat in South Kensington and transported to the depths of Esher where her son, his suicidal third wife, and at least one grandchild addicted to heroin were said to be longing to receive her. 'Just go blank,' she advised Mrs Evans. 'Pretend you're in your dotage.'

'God Almighty,' cried Mrs Evans, flinging down the phone.

Jim Scott met her at the station. When she inquired politely as to the state of his health, he replied, as always, that he was a bit under par. 'Nothing that I can put a finger on,' he said. 'I'm just not 100 per cent.'

'Join the club,' she said merrily, and drew her coat more closely round her. Outside the car window there was not one tree in leaf. The ploughed fields on either side of the road were rimmed with frost. Several cows, frozen in their tracks, stood in a stolid circle about a frozen pond. Even fifty miles from Camden Town the temperature seemed to have dropped appreciably.

She was surprised that Jim hadn't inquired where her 'friend' had got to. Only last night Avril had rung to say that they had moved two camp-beds into the stables to accommodate Lawrence Oates and his Russian boy. 'It's bloody parky in there,' she had said. 'Any normal human being would turn into an icicle.'

'About my friend,' began Mrs Evans. 'I'm afraid he's –'

'He's odd,' said Jim. 'I'll give you that. He gave us quite a turn, arriving on skis with that fellow Dimitrie slithering along behind. But I rather like him. He insisted on taking an inventory of the larder. He made Avril sharpen her pencil. He implied that she was a bit slack. But he's bloody willing, I'll say that for him. He's given the pony a bath.'

Mrs Evans was at a loss for words. Jim Scott had two houses, a kindly disposition, a job in the Foreign Office, inherited wealth and a valuable stamp collection. The one thing he didn't have was a sense of humour.

Avril was at the window of the sitting room when the car came up the drive. She waved frantically and mouthed greetings. The house was Victorian and had been a vicarage. But for the fourteen bedrooms Avril would have called it a cottage. As it was, she referred to it as 'our little retreat'. Almost immediately Mrs Evans was run all over the house, up stairs and down, and asked to give an opinion on the paintwork. 'It's a better colour, don't you think?' urged Avril. 'The cream was too cold, don't you think?'

'It was, it was,' agreed Mrs Evans, for whom one colour was very like another, and clutching her coat about her she hurried in the direction of the kitchen, to the blessed warmth of the Aga.

From the cobblestoned yard beyond the back door came the seasonal sound of wood being chopped.

'I must say Lawrence is frightfully useful,' said Avril. 'I didn't expect him to be so young. He's cleaned out the barn, oiled all those old saddles, wormed the dog, and tomorrow he says he's going to whitewash the stables.'

'Young,' said Mrs Evans, shocked.

'Well, youngish,' Avril said, and going to the window she rapped on the glass and shouted, 'Lawrence . . . she's arrived.'

They had tea together, the three of them. 'Where did you two meet?' asked Avril. 'Was it abroad?'

'Was it?' said Lawrence, looking at Mrs Evans. His eyes were very blue, very sad in expression. He was wearing mittens, tapping the edge of the table with the tips of his blackened nails.

'No,' said Mrs Evans. 'Surely you remember. It was at a party given by the Bells . . . in Hampshire. Kitty Bell sprained her ankle and you dipped your scarf in the lake and made a compress.'

'That's right,' he said. 'Poor old Kitty. How she blubbed. I never got the scarf back, you know.'

This is absurd, thought Mrs Evans, and as soon as she had drunk her tea she went up to her room. She had never known anybody called Kitty Bell, not in all her long life.

Supper was an ordeal. As it was not yet Christmas Eve there were just the four of them. Jim's sister was not arriving until tomorrow, or the Carter family, or Teddy and Jane Gordon. The Russian boy, Dimitrie, who spoke no English, had wolfed down a bowl of soup and retired to the stables. Even Jason, not normally one of Mrs Evans's favourite people, would have been acceptable, but he had gone out to some youth club. As it was, she was forced into taking part in the most peculiar conversations with Lawrence Oates, peculiar in that no matter where she said she had been, or to whom she had been talking, he implied that he had been there as well. She said she had gone to the theatre to see the new musical and that she had enjoyed it, and he said, yes, the first act was not bad but the second half hadn't matched up to it. Then she said George Isaacs was in hospital again, being dried out for the umpteenth time, and how awful he looked, obviously not long for this world, and Lawrence shook his head sorrowfully from side to side, echoing her words and murmuring over and over, not long for this world. Cruelly, she asked him how many years he had known George, and he looked at her out of those blue and baffled eyes and repeated helplessly, 'How many years is it, my dear?'

Shortly after supper the lights went out. 'Damn,' said Jim Scott, and he blundered about searching for candles. Avril said power failures were rather frequent in this neck of the woods. The Aga was electric too, so thank goodness they had already eaten. It was just as well there was a nice fire in the sitting room. 'And a vast supply of logs,' she said. 'Thanks to Lawrence.'

They all agreed it was very cosy, very Christmassy, sitting in candlelight beside a blazing hearth, the curtains drawn against the dark night. Only Avril and Jim Scott were telling the truth.

After a few minutes Lawrence moved from the sofa and went and sat on the hard-backed chair in front of the curtain. Avril said he must surely be in a draught. 'There's an old door behind there,' she explained. 'We can't use it because the wistaria outside has grown all over it. Jim's always talking of having it bricked in, but we never got round to it.' 'I'm not used to the warmth,' Lawrence said. 'I prefer to be away from the fire.'

*

Mrs Evans stared into the flames, and presently fell into a doze. She dreamt that she was on a walking tour in the Lake District with her dead father. It must have been winter, for she heard the low moan of the wind as it swept down from the hills. Her father kept striding on ahead and urging her to walk faster. But she couldn't, she was so tired that she could hardly drag one foot after the other. Soon her father was a blurred figure in the distance, and when next she looked up he had vanished altogether. She whimpered with fright, and woke. Opening her eyes she saw that the fire had settled and dimmed. Jim and Avril had evidently gone to bed. There were fresh candles burning on saucers on the mantelpiece. Then she heard the moaning again, and now there was a rattling sound, like canvas flapping in the wind. She knew that there was something she must do, something she must finish. One had to be cruel to be kind.

Struggling upright on the sofa she looked behind her to where Lawrence Oates stood, his mittened hands covering his face. The curtain over the door billowed outwards.

'Can you not go on?' she asked him, and he shook his head.

'You have nothing to be ashamed of,' she told him. 'You are the bravest of men. Rest assured, you have done your very best.' He uncovered his face and worked the ragged slit of his mouth. The tip of his nose had turned black, and his lips were so cracked and torn that it was agony for him to shape the words. 'I slept a little,' he whispered.

'And hoped not to wake,' she prompted. 'Now you are just going outside.'

'Yes,' he said. 'And may be some time.'

When he pulled aside the curtain the door opened easily enough. He stepped out and a flurry of snow whirled into the room. The candles blew out.

I hope I am dreaming, thought Mrs Evans; but oh how cold it was.

THE BEAST IN THE TOWER

When Rita's mother, Mrs Mountjoy, invited me to Scotland for a week's holiday, she plunged my mother into a dilemma. Thing was, Mrs Mountjoy was considered both fast and loose, on top of which she was living in sin. On the other hand, her fancy man was a Laird and the sinning was being conducted in a castle. There was also the question of my fascination with matches; could I or could I not be trusted? I'd only been ten at the time, but it was a bit embarrassing my having set fire to the shed that housed the school sports equipment. It was an accident, of course, and it was only a few old hockey sticks that got consumed; all the same . . .

After wrestling with her conscience for several minutes, my mother accepted on my behalf. I travelled up to Edinburgh with Dodie, Rita's grandmother, who sucked peppermints. My mother had always held that Mrs Mountjoy inherited her gadding ways from Dodie, who'd been seen winking at men on more than one occasion while going up in the lift to the restaurant on the fifth floor of the Bon Marché. Dodie was sixty if she was a day, but in spite of this we arrived at Edinburgh with a commercial traveller and a foreign gentleman in tow. They laughed a lot, and we sat on a bench in the booking hall while the commercial traveller went backwards and forwards to the bar to fetch measures of what he called 'the cup that cheers'.

I drank pints of tea and had to go to the Ladies Room, where I was bothered by those notices that said the Seaman's Mission would be glad to help me if I felt I had contracted something called venereal disease. There was a drawing of a boy who looked as though he had measles.

Pimples came into it, especially round the mouth, and I had plenty of those.

We missed two connections and arrived at the castle in the small moonlit hours, driven by a taxi-driver who stopped twice to go behind a hedge. The first time the car slowed down, Dodie clutched my arm and said I was to stare straight ahead. The second time, she said that if he opened the door I was to run like hell into the countryside.

Rita wasn't my best friend; we didn't even go to the same school. She'd been thrust upon me by Mrs Mountjoy, who had once, on one of her flying maternal visits, stopped me in the street and urged me to look after her daughter.

'You're an intelligent girl,' she said, 'and you know the score. I'd feel easier in my mind if you took her under your wing.'

As it happened, I didn't know the score, but it was pretty heady being called intelligent by a grown-up who wore a fox fur, even if she was considered flighty. From then on I went out of my way to let Rita buy me comics and spent every Saturday evening sitting with her in Dodie's kitchen listening to 'Bandwaggon' on the wireless.

The castle was a bit small and a bit ruined. I gathered it was being renovated, only the Laird had run out of money and work had long since been abandoned. The back door was missing and the windows on the side had fallen out. There was a ladder propped up against the north wall under Mrs Mountjoy's window. I thought it was part of the builder's left-over equipment, until Hamish, the butler, told me the Laird had put it there so he could get into Mrs M's room whenever she locked him out. Hamish hinted she locked him out fairly often.

To this day I don't really know what the Laird looked like. He swayed on his feet a lot and besides, my mother had told me to avoid his gaze. She didn't put it into so many words, but I understood it'd be best all round, he being a man of the world. Hamish said that Mrs Mountjoy and the Laird enjoyed a stormy relationship and that the ladder was a necessity.

They didn't see eye to eye over St George.

St George was a statue bought by the Laird's English mother, and consigned to a window-sill in one of the empty rooms in the tower. I went up to look at it the morning after I arrived. George was sitting on a horse brandishing a sword in the jaws of a dragon whose nostrils snorted gusts of painted fire. Actually, most of the dragon was missing; there was just his head left. Years before, owing to some argument, the hindquarters had been smashed to bits. Hamish didn't elaborate, but I took it that stormy relationships ran in the family.

Mrs Mountjoy wanted the statue brought downstairs, and the Laird said he'd rather die than have an English saint featured in the dining hall. Hamish said in his opinion, he wouldn't be at all surprised if Mrs M didn't take the Laird at his word and saw through the rungs of the ladder.

'Mark what I say, lassie,' he prophesied. 'It'll end in tears.'

I'd never heard of St George, but according to Hamish he was a refugee on the run from foreign parts, and a mercenary into the bargain. He was always galloping about righting injustices, until somebody or other hung him upside down and cut off his head. The dragon was a mythical beast. It didn't exist. Rita said George couldn't be a saint if he was a mercenary, because that involved money and he was obviously venal. I wasn't sure whether she meant he had venereal disease, so I kept quiet.

On the second day of the holiday the grounds of the castle were thrown open to what Mrs Mountjoy referred to as 'the children of the peasants'. I was a bit confused because the term before we'd studied wildlife in Sussex and I thought she meant those birds with blue caps on. I'd expected a fly-over of fluffy chicks, and all we got was a honking contingent of children, sired by Jamie Gow, the Laird's gamekeeper. There were twelve of them, seven boys and five girls, and whenever the Laird turned his back the boys pelted us with pebbles and pulled rude faces.

At the last moment Mrs Mountjoy invited the vicar, and somebody totally daft persuaded him to judge a competition for the best bunch of wild flowers garnered from the surrounding fields. Neither Rita nor I completed the course. We began, but half way through, Stuart Gow, an adolescent built like a bus, sprang up from behind a bush and fiddled with his trousers. We ran home breathless and swore a bull had chased us.

Later that evening, the sun already drowning in the loch, Mrs M said that she and the Laird and Dodie were off to a cocktail party in Kinross. We were to brush our teeth and go straight to bed. Hamish had the night off.

'Lock the front door and don't let anyone in,' she warned. 'There are some con-men pretending to be antique dealers working the neighbourhood.'

Seeing the back door had been removed, this was a pretty silly thing to say, but as she thought I was intelligent I nodded vigorously.

Rita and I had baked beans on toast for supper, and afterwards we sat on the front steps in the gloaming, watching the bats swoop from the tower. I was lighting matches and flicking them on to the gravel stones.

Twenty minutes later, we heard the car scrunch up the drive.

Rita was mithering on about whether Stuart Gow would make a good husband or not. She thought he would; she said her stomach had looped the loop when the sun touched the beginnings of his moustache. I said she was potty, that the moment he slipped the ring on her finger he'd object to her reading *The Mill on the Floss*.

'I don't care,' she said, just as the wheels of the car spat gravel.

I knew the men were suspect the moment they faced us. For one thing the tall chap wore a trilby hat with a feather in the band, and for another his companion was sporting suede shoes. My mother had alerted me to such signs of danger, along with the inadvisability of ever purchasing shop-made pork pies or sitting down on strange toilet seats.

'We were just passing through, girls,' the tall man said. 'We're into buying artefacts. Perhaps your parents are in the vicinity.'

'They've gone to a cocktail party,' Rita said, daft as a brush.

'Ah,' breathed the chappie in the suede shoes.

'They're due back any moment,' I said, 'along with Mr MacLeish from the local constabulary. Meanwhile there's a man called George from Armenia hiding in the tower.'

'A lodger?' inquired suede shoes.

'Sort of, leastways he's on the run and stations a wild beast outside his door.'

All the same, the men marched up the steps into the castle.

I whispered to Rita that she should ring for the fire brigade. Then I ran ahead to the room in the tower. St George was perched on his horse on the window-sill. In spite of his brandished sword, he looked very ineffectual. The tip of his nose was missing.

'Please God,' I said, fingering the chipped plaster where the dragon's body had once writhed, 'come to our aid.'

When I went downstairs, the man with the feather in his hat was carrying a Chinese vase out of the door. He laid it in the boot of the car and then returned to help his companion shift the Laird's writing desk across the hall.

'The man from Armenia won't like it,' I said. 'He hates things being disturbed.'

At that moment a strange whooshing sound filled the night, something like a gust of wind blowing through an empty space. We were out into the drive by now, in moonlight, the men lumbering towards the car, Rita and I skittering on the little stones, mouths trembling.

There was a tinkle of glass hitting the gravel, and we looked upwards and saw a belch of flame billowing from the top window. A sword licked by fire flashed in the moonlight against the blackened stones of the tower.

'It's St George,' I cried, 'fighting a dragon.'

At that precise, fiery moment we heard the bell of the fire brigade.

Nobody ever worked out who had started the blaze. The insurance company tried to prove the wiring was faulty, but in the end they paid out on the damage done both to the top room and to the statue of St George, which turned out to be valuable. There were thousands of such statues in the world, but only a very few with flames coming out of their nostrils. The Laird claimed the dragon had been in one piece until the fire started, and nobody dared call him a liar.

As Hamish said, 'It's an ill wind that blows somebody some good.'

My mother was a bit agitated when she heard what had happened, but she couldn't really say anything because the Laird wrote her a letter telling how resourceful I had been in urging Rita to ring the fire brigade, thus apprehending the robbers. He enclosed five pounds for my piggy bank. Besides, when she met me and Dodie and Rita at the station, Rita kept babbling on about how she had seen a dragon belching flame.

'There's no such thing as dragons,' my mother said.

'I saw it,' Rita said. 'St George was trying to slash its head off.'

I stopped being friendly with Rita quite soon afterwards.

There wasn't anything special that came between us, not unless you count the letter she got from Stuart Gow saying she had nice eyebrows. I said I expected he mentioned those because he couldn't think of anything else to praise, and she took offence.

I telephone her every St George's Day. She says, 'Who's that, who's speaking?' and I sort of pant, like I'm blowing fire down her ear. I think I'm doing her a favour. Sooner or later, we all need to slay dragons.

KISS ME, HARDY

Hardy Roget and his friend had been booked on to the cruise two months before; it seemed foolish to abandon the whole idea just because one of them had died in the meantime. There was also a penalty clause, although Roget's agent said the shipping company would never hold him to it. Not in the circumstances; it wouldn't be good publicity. Besides, now that the funeral was six weeks into the past, Damien Cartwright had stopped asking him along to the BBC club for a drink and Barbie Cartwright no longer phoned up to see if he needed a spot of shopping. And he was sick to death of eating alone.

The ship sailed from Southampton. No sooner had he entered the embarkation lounge than a tall woman in a hat waved at him. He fluttered his hand in response; it was a reflex action. Since appearing twice a week for four months, two years before, in a popular television series he had become used to people thinking they knew him. Usually, unless drunk or young, they darted towards him, realised in mid-stride he was merely a character on the box, and turned heel. The woman in the hat kept on course. She was middle-aged and her eyes were bold. 'Hardy Roget,' she said. 'Such a pleasure. I've been so looking forward to meeting you.'

'How kind,' murmured Roget. He didn't meet many people who actually knew his name, and certainly none who pronounced it as though he had compiled the Thesaurus.

'I booked immediately I read you were giving a lecture,' she said.

'It's not a lecture,' he corrected. 'There's some sort of

script-writing course for beginners . . . I'm merely on hand
to act out the finished results.'

'I wouldn't miss it for worlds,' she said. 'Why don't you
buy me a drink?'

Her name, she said, was Sheila Drummond. This was her
third cruise, only this time she was travelling with Fiona,
her tennis club friend of twenty years. For all of ten minutes
he enjoyed her company, felt flattered she had sought him
out. They sat on stools at the bar and her crossed knee
shone. She was very confident, very amusing. Nor did she
pester him with inane questions about the fictional goings
on of Bev and Ron and Didi; she didn't say she'd last seen
him enclosed in black bin liners on the floor of the extension
in that house in Newcastle. Instead, she spoke about the
recession and how her husband, John, distrusted the notion
of the so-called 'green shoots' of recovery. John wasn't
accompanying her because it wouldn't look good, he nip-
ping off to enjoy himself while business forecasts were so
dreadfully bleak. Then she said, 'You know how it is with
some men . . . they grow old before their time . . . any
excuse will do,' and she pressed the palm of her hand
against the breast of Roget's suit.

Immediately, he felt uncomfortable; he nodded and
smiled but his mouth tightened. Quite apart from other
things, if he wasn't careful she'd be expecting him to buy
her drinks for the duration of the voyage. Struggling up the
gangplank he managed to give her the slip. He found
himself ahead of two girls, one of whom cried out, 'I don't
believe this. Pinch me. Is it really happening?'

His cabin steward was called Gary. 'I'm at your beck and
call,' he assured Roget. 'Should you need anything, just
press the button by the bed and I'll whizz in like a bumble-
bee.' He placed Roget's suitcase on the bed and stroked its
top. Roget handed him a tenner. He could scarcely afford
it, but theatrical gestures were second nature to him.

'Glad to see you escaped your plastic bags,' Gary quipped.

That evening there was the usual round of cocktail parties given by the Captain, the first held at five o'clock and the most prestigious one at seven-thirty. Roget was depressed that he had been asked for the six o'clock 'do', along with thirty-five members of a wine-tasting club, a group of senior managers from Sainsbury's and a young honeymoon couple who had won some sort of competition. 'It was ever so easy,' the bride told the senior managers. 'You just had to tick what was the most important thing, money, love, or a sense of humour.'

'She put love,' said the bridegroom, at which everyone listening roared with laughter.

At dinner, Roget was placed at a round table with the tutor of the script-writing course, a man and a woman who only opened their mouths to eat, and two young girls, one from the Midlands and one from Cardiff. During the meal, Roget gathered that they had both entered a writing competition and come joint first out of five hundred entries. Their prize was a week's cruise and free tutoring on the script-writing course.

'I still can't believe it,' squealed the girl from the Midlands. 'I have to keep pinching myself.' The tutor stirred his soup round and round and emptied a bottle of red wine in under five minutes.

When the girls had gone – they'd heard there was a disco on a lower deck – he said, 'I hate this sort of thing. I'm a poet, for God's sake.' Lighting a cigarette he blew smoke across the table. The woman opposite began to cough.

'Christ,' said the tutor, glaring at the couple. When they, too, had left he confided gloomily to Roget, 'Tomorrow morning, half a dozen matrons from the Home Counties will sign up, wear us out for two hours asking damn fool questions about writing for *Emmerdale Farm* and then never be seen again.'

'Surely I won't be needed right at the beginning,' said

Roget. He had no intention of putting in an appearance a moment before it was absolutely necessary; he had been employed to speak lines, not hang around watching them being written.

He pencilled his cabin number on the back of the menu and suggested the tutor should give him a tinkle in a day or two.

'But I'll see you at meals,' protested the tutor. 'They've allotted us the same table.'

'Possibly,' said Roget, 'but I wouldn't count on it,' and added, 'I have a wasting disease, you see, and don't feel frightfully gregarious.'

'Well, sod you,' said the tutor, pouring himself another glass of wine.

Roget went up on deck and sat on a bench, staring out into the darkness. From the deck below he could hear music; in his mind he saw a glittering saxophone. He was cross with himself for inventing something so debilitating. Once the tutor had sobered up he was bound, out of remorse, to pass the information on to the entire script-writing course. I shall be forced to elaborate, thought Roget. I shall either have to cough a lot or be seen biting my lip against spasms of pain. He was just wondering if secondary lesions in the spine precluded a healthy appetite, when a voice said, 'There you are,' and Sheila Drummond plonked herself down beside him. He shifted sideways and hoped she thought he was just making room.

'It's not like being on a boat, is it?' she asked. 'It doesn't go up and down, and you can't open the portholes.'

'Ship,' he corrected her. 'Not boat.'

They had quite a pleasant conversation. At one point he almost wondered whether she wasn't cleverer than she appeared. He had explained to her, on her insistence, how you could build up character when acting out a part, add little mannerisms, inflections of speech, and she said,

'Wouldn't you get closer to the real person if you cut all that out?'

Then she asked him if he lived alone. 'Recently, yes,' he admitted. 'I have just buried my friend.' In the last few weeks, having uttered the same sentence many times, he had grown used to faces suddenly expressing assumed concern. Of course, he couldn't see her face, but there was no mistaking the tone of her voice. She said, 'I hope nobody saw you,' and he laughed in spite of himself.

He told her that Francis had played the saxophone. They hadn't been lovers for five years. Health problems, mostly. He said, 'It was difficult adapting to being just friends.'

'Who wants men and women to be friends?' she said. 'One might as well buy a dog.'

She had obviously misunderstood him and he wasn't liberated enough to say outright that his friend's name was spelt with an 'i' rather than an 'e'. It was then, to protect himself from her possible advances and as a preparation for the outcome of the script-writing course, that he told her there was someone waiting for him in Gibraltar; someone he'd corresponded with for two years.

'What does she do?' Sheila Drummond asked. He thought he detected disappointment in her voice.

'She doesn't do anything,' he said. 'She has private means.'

After a pause, Sheila Drummond asked, 'What does she look like?'

'Small,' he replied, 'with auburn hair. And she has a slight limp. Nothing really wrong, just a war injury in her childhood. Her father was in command of a battery and during a naval battle a shell fell on the barracks and she received a piece of shrapnel in the ball of her foot.'

'How dreadful,' said Sheila Drummond. 'I didn't know soldiers were allowed to have their wives and children living with them. Not in wartime.'

'Their family has been living on the Rock for generations,' he said hastily. 'An ancestor served under Nelson and is buried in Trafalgar cemetery, just outside Gibraltar's Southport Gates.'

They talked about Nelson for several minutes, whether it was likely that he had actually cried out 'Kiss me, Hardy' before expiring, and then Sheila Drummond complained of feeling chilly. Before returning to his cabin, Roget went to B deck to see if he could find a booklet on the history of Gibraltar, but the library was closed.

For the following two days he managed to avoid both the tutor and Sheila Drummond. He took breakfast in his cabin and ate lunch and dinner in the Club Lido. He read a book on the six wives of Henry VIII from cover to cover and then started it again. It was quite safe to lurk about aft of the upper deck; sea breezes played havoc with a woman's hair. It was not until Wednesday night, as he was returning from the synagogue on Three deck, that he saw her again. She was with her friend Fiona. 'You've been hiding,' she said. He was forced to escort both of them to the Grand Lounge and buy them a drink. It was quite obvious it wasn't their first one of the evening.

'It's the great day, tomorrow, isn't it?' said Sheila Drummond. He was puzzled. 'You'll be seeing your friend, won't you? Barbara, wasn't it?'

'No,' he said. 'Anne . . . Anne Cleaves.'

Sheila Drummond told Fiona that it was a real love story. There might even be wedding bells. Fiona suggested he bring Anne back on board for supper. There was nowhere decent to eat in Gibraltar. He insisted it was out of the question. Anne wasn't very well. 'Actually,' he said, 'she has leukaemia. It's only a matter of time.'

'I thought she just had a bit of cannon ball in her foot,' said Sheila Drummond.

The next morning the ship docked at Gibraltar. He was

on desk as early as possible. Even so, Sheila Drummond waylaid him. 'I'm so sorry,' she said. 'I'm afraid Fiona and I behaved very badly last night. It was the drink, you know,' and she pressed his hand and gave a sad, apologetic smile.

He spent the entire day sightseeing. Walking up Engineer's Road to the Upper Rock he was choked by the exhaust fumes of cars and coaches stuttering their way to St Michael's Cave. He climbed even higher, until he reached the observation platform on the lip of the North Face. It was raining and the view of Catalan Bay was lost in drizzle. Retracing his steps down Queen's Road he saw three apes pelting another smaller one with stones. All four animals were hideously ugly, with callused feet and armpits denuded of hair. Their victim was gnashing its teeth and leaping frantically up and down the slope. I know how it feels, thought Roget, and, depressed, he walked back down to the harbour.

At seven o'clock that evening, as he was going towards the Club Lido, Sheila Drummond leapt out at him from the bookshop.

'Anne's awfully nice,' she cried.

He stared at her.

'And she looks the picture of health. She's in the Grand Lounge with Fiona.'

He wasn't at all surprised, though his heart was still hammering, to find Fiona sitting on her own. He was damned if he was going to let them think he couldn't take a joke. The band was playing an old time waltz. Numerous couples of advanced years were gliding stiffly about the dance floor.

'Hello,' he shouted. 'Had a good day?'

'So, so,' she replied. 'Anne's gone to the loo. She won't be long.'

Roget ordered a double scotch. He hadn't eaten all day

and immediately felt amused and uplifted. 'I saw those God-forsaken apes,' he said, and gave a mock shudder.

The waltz over, the band struck up a brisk foxtrot. Several ladies approached Roget and demanded a dance. It was Ladies Night and perfectly acceptable. He explained he was already spoken for, that he was waiting for someone.

It was while he was trying to catch the waiter's eye to order another drink that he saw a small, rotund woman threading her way between the tables. She had very rosy cheeks, wore a blue bow in her red curls and was well into middle age.

'Hardy,' she said. 'Please dance with me. It's our tune, remember?'

She wouldn't let him go. She slipped one hand from his shoulder to his neck and caressed his hair; she pressed her stout body to his. She said she was sorry about Francis but that she would look after him and he was to put the past behind him. And he could give up his silly acting career. After all, she had enough money for both of them.

As they sped round the floor he caught glimpses of Sheila Drummond's face. She was openly laughing.

'I do think we ought to sit down,' he said. 'The doctor warned any exertion might prove fatal.'

'Did he?' she said, and clung the closer to him.

The body was taken ashore with almost indecent haste. Roget explained to the police that he had never set eyes on Anne Cleaves until she button-holed him at the Ladies Night. She had said something to him when she lay dying in his arms, and used his name, but he hadn't caught anything else.

Sheila Drummond told Fiona it was possibly 'Kiss me, Hardy', and felt ashamed.

FILTHY LUCRE

OR

THE TRAGEDY OF ERNEST LEDWHISTLE
AND RICHARD SOLEWAY

A STORY BY

BERYL BAINBRIDGE

WRITTEN JUNE TO AUGUST 1946

Dedication
To the auther of Dismal
England, who gave me a
chance to clothe my bitter
feelings against the unjust
london of the 1800's in a
story

I hope this book will useful be
And when you read it remember
me.
B. Bainbridge. August 18th. 1946.

the Family

Andrew Ledwhistle m Ruby (deceased)

(A spinster) Jane   Ernest •'···   Fanny   Francis (A drunkard)
                m   m
              Anna   Charles Coney

James   (No one important)   (A girl)   Charles
Ernest   Colin

the Eirin

Richard Andromitey   partnered   Francis Ledwhistle
Peter   "   Andrew
Martin (alias   Ernest
Richard Soloway)

CHAPTER 1

A small coal fire burnt in the wide horse-and-cart grate. It was a murky evening in 1851. The old man bent over his books. His head, lit by three candles, was a grizzled white. His coat was black and dusty, his neckcloth an uninspired blue. Now and then his lips would move frettishly and he would pull his beard worriedly. Once he sighed. Then he looked round the little office at the high stool, the bundles of envelopes, the red-backed books on the shelf high above the picture of the founder of the firm of Andromikey & Ledwhistle. His eyes wandered lovingly over the brass coal-scuttle that shone like a buttercup, the threadbare carpet, the nail on the door on which his top hat rested, the files on the junior clerk's desk, the quill pens in the ginger jar. He sighed again and resumed his work. The clock on the church in Pentworth Street struck the hour.

'Ten,' he muttered. 'Ten.' He straightened, swept a bundle of papers into his pocket, blew the candles out and reached for his hat. 'I should have brought me overcoat,' he mumbled. 'Serve me right if it don't.'

The door shut and he walked slowly down the stairs. He opened the big door and went out into the street and beckoned a cab, and as he drove off cast one misty glance at the brass plate on the door. It was Andrew Ledwhistle's last day at the firm he had administered and nursed for 62 years of his life. There was a lump of emotion in the old man's throat as he stared out into the November night.

'Demented old fool,' he admonished himself. 'Still, I'll miss the old job and shouting at old Steinhouse.' But at least he had the satisfaction of knowing it was not passing right out of his hands. Ernest will do his job well, he thought; he was a likely lad. But there was this Andromikey boy. He was brought back to earth with a jolt.

The coachman blew on his fingers vigorously and a mound of hot air drifted into the November night mist.

Old Ledwhistle paid him a penny and stood for a moment in contemplation as the cab wound down the road, the feet of the rangey horses striking keenly to his ears.

'You are getting old, Andrew,' he scolded, 'you're nothing but a sentimental old codger.'

He climbed the steps and twisted the key in the lock. It opened more quickly than he was used to and he stumbled a little as he entered the hall. The family were in the parlour. Usually at this hour his daughters were in their beds, but they were up tonight to hear the situation of the firm when Andrew Ledwhistle retired.

He pulled back the red-plush curtain and opened the door. His wife, who was about 65 but still able, was seated in a chair busy with some sewing. Francis, the youngest boy, was resting his head on his knee looking at a large book of lions. He was a white-faced little fellow of 6 or thereabouts, and he already showed an aptitude for figures. His thick black hair fell in a stain over his calm brow. His sister Charlotte was on her stool next to Fanny, a plump plain girl of some 16 years. Jane, the oldest in the family, was a shy musical girl of five-and-twenty. Engaged at a small table with curvy legs sat Ernest, on which burnt an oil lamp.

The scene was so peaceful and homely that old Ledwhistle halted for an instant on the threshold. His wife, a cheerful woman, rose to her feet and meekly laid her soft cheek against his weathered one. Little Francis jumped around him in delight and pulled his side-whiskers. Ernest hurried forward and dragged off his boots. Andrew Ledwhistle looked old and frail, and his loving family fussed and petted him until he was comfortable.

'Well, my loves,' he said, 'it is settled, is it not? Ernest shall go into the firm to be in my place.'

'But, Mr Ledwhistle,' interposed his wife, 'what of Richard Andromikey's grandson? He is to go with Ernest?'

'Yes my dear.' Old Ledwhistle looked at a paper he had drawn from his pocket. It was a letter. 'This,' he said, 'is from Martin Andromikey, who wishes to partner with Ernest and build up the firm.'

Ernest leaned forward. 'What is he like, Papa?'

'I've never met him,' protested his father, 'but he is coming to the office tomorrow morning.' He turned to his wife and daughters and youngest son. 'And now, my dears, to bed. I wish to talk to Ernest. We will surely meet on the morrow with God's help.'

They kissed each other soundly and retired. Ernest and his father talked well into the night.

CHAPTER 2

We will leave now, dear readers, the bright Ledwhistle
parlour and, like a bird, pass out into the November night.
We will journey down to a wharf where the slimy Thames
moves like some loathsome adder, and the houses huddle
together in squalid patterns. Here the lamplight falls on
wasted limbs and shaking hands. It lights up sin and filth
while, all aware, the cruel river twists its reptile course.

In one miserable hovel we will linger. The lamplight
shines into the broken panes and struggles manfully to press
yellowly into the gloomy interior. On the narrow bed is a
young man. The room is in a state. Shoes, socks and
trousers lie on the bare floor. A few blankets are flung over
the thin form. Over him stands another young fellow,
who has a bright red-check coat, green breeches and a top-
hat full of dust on his head. Observe, reader, what now
takes place. Read more slowly, because this is the plot
of the whole story of the Tragedy of Ernest Ledwhistle and
Richard Soleway . . .

The boy on the bed groaned. His skin was like wax
flowers in a Victorian vase. The eyes, instead of being
warm and kindling, as was their wont, were infused with a
metallic glitter. At a glance one could see he was struggling
with the fever.

The man in the check coat sat down on the bed. His
teeth bit fiercely into his lip, and his eyes had stormy clouds
swirling round their vision.

'And this,' he muttered, 'is what that damned doctor
called unimportant.'

While stout aldermen swill their ale and talk of the
ingratitude of the poor, while their gross wives whom

nobody loves laden with costly jewels, pick with lecherous fingers their dainty food, this is allowed to exist, dear reader! And, mark you, people of England and Wales, this does happen in these Satanic years, when justice is sat upon by the strong body of Gold.

The man picked up a spoon and poured a little water down the waxy throat. The hot hands grasped convulsively with weakening fingers and sweating palms at the sordid coverlet.

'Richard,' the boy said faintly, 'dear Richard, I wish to ask you something.'

The man sank to his knees and supported the palpitating head.

'Richard,' the gasping breath came again, 'dear Richard, promise me, promise me you'll go to Andrew Ledwhistle's in the morning. You see, Richard, Ledwhistle's father was the partner of my grandfather. Grandfather entrusted into Richard Ledwhistle's care a certain amount of money for me. He, when he died' – here the boy seized Richard Soleway's hand in a fierce grip – 'entrusted it to his son Andrew. Andrew Ledwhistle cheated me. I know he did, I know.' He lay back panting on the pillowcase bed. 'He cheated me of something like £35,000. Do you hear, Dick? Do you hear?'

The boy's voice rose like a plume of smoke. Richard never took his eyes off his friend. 'Yes,' he whispered urgently. 'Yes.'

'By the merest fluke,' Martin Andromikey went on, 'by the merest fluke I got to know that he was leaving and that his son Ernest was to carry on. I wrote to him telling him who I was. He doesn't know that I know he cheated me. I suppose his conscience made him give me the partnership. I was going to do such a lot, Dick.' The boy's eyes gazed with black intensity. 'Dick, I was going to make him suffer as he made me. But, Richard, listen. I want you to go and see him tomorrow. Do you hear, do you understand? . . .' The boy's words trailed off. 'What was I saying,' he muttered. 'Oh, tell me, Dick, quick – before it's too late, Dick.'

'You were saying I was to see this Ledwhistle tomorrow, Mart,' his friend answered soothingly.

'Yes, yes, of course,' cried Martin Andromikey. 'Go and see him, Dick. Say you are Martin Andromikey . . . Make him suffer, Dick . . . make him suffer.'

Richard's eyes dilated. 'You want me to impersonate you?' he asked incredulously.

'Dick, Dick.' His arm was seized in a crushing grip. 'Promise me you will make him suffer. Promise me that, promise me.' The veins in his forehead swelled and filled, while his eyes started from their sockets.

'All right, Martin, all right,' soothed Richard.

The boy forced his hand away with dreadful strength. 'Promise me, dear Dick, promise me.'

Richard Soleway stood up. 'Before God,' he said with direful quietness, 'before God, I, Richard Howard Soleway, swear by all I hold true to make Andrew Ledwhistle suffer, if suffering be his due.'

Martin fell back. 'Dick,' he whispered, 'dear Dick.' That was all.

There was silence for a while. Then the body on the bed stirred. 'Pray for me, Dick,' he said. 'Pray for me.'

Richard knelt beside the fever-racked boy and prayed with all the simple fervour of his soul. The boy smiled and shut his eyes.

When the first ribbon of the sun threaded between the hovel window and trailed lacklustrely on the floor, Richard eyed its transfusing glow with distrust. Though it was yet early, that same sun had no doubt pried into scenes of dismal horror and human degradation. It would be better if there was eternal night, he thought. He gazed down at his friend with pity and with envy, and gently crossed the two poor hands on the weary breast. For Martin Andromikey was dead.

CHAPTER 3

Ernest waited impatiently in the little office. His father was in the outer room talking to Jacob Steinhouse. The young man paced up and down. There was a quill pen on the desk and he picked it up and scrawled the words 'Ernest Ledwhistle and Martin Andromikey'. It sounded important and he flushed with pride as he thought that all this was to be his and Martin Andromikey's.

There was a sudden commotion on the stairs. A voice was raised in anger, and a young man shot into the room.

Ernest got to his polished feet. Facing him was a ballistic young man in a brilliant red-check coat and tails. His brown hair lay flatly on his head and curled sleekly onto his neckcloth. His long legs were wrapped in green breeches, and he held in his hand a top-hat of doubtful age.

Old Ledwhistle came into the room. He turned to Westbury, the junior clerk, in alarm. 'Who is this?' he asked, his very beard quivering like wheat in wind.

'My name is Andromikey,' said Richard quietly.

Ernest gasped.

Old Ledwhistle started forward. 'My dear young friend,' he amended, 'I had no idea.' He went on, 'Pray, pardon me for my incivility, but for a moment I was at a loss.'

Richard said nothing as he mentally sized up the cause of Martin's death. He hardly looks like a man who would cheat his dearest friend's grandson, he mused.

He became aware that Ernest was endeavouring to shake his hand. He bowed and sat down at length.

Old Ledwhistle took up his favourite stance, his back to the grate, hands clenched behind his coat-tails. Richard crossed his legs and hung his hat nonchalantly on his protruding foot.

203

Ernest stood very straight and grave at his side, his clean young face flushed and nervous. As his father talked to them he could not help but let his eyes wander constantly to the person in the chair. He could not avoid admiring the gay coat and the careless way in which Richard looked about him.

Old Ledwhistle was thinking too. 'Damned self-assured,' he muttered inside. 'Still, that's what the firm needs. Ernest's got plenty of backbone, but he needs leading.'

At the end of the morning he had explained to them every slightest intricacy and deed. He took them both home to lunch and introduced them to his family.

As he bowed over the hand of Jane, Richard Soleway's heart gave an uneasy lurch. Was Martin in his true senses when he had accused Andrew Ledwhistle of his debt? Or had the boy been labouring under misapprehensions brought on by his burning fever? Yet, when he thought of the boy's black eyes, and felt again the desperate grasp on his arm, he felt sure this was not so. If Andrew Ledwhistle had cheated him he certainly did not show it. His manner was calm and friendly, and it was with a feeling of regret that Richard left the pleasant household for his own.

As he walked home down the dingy streets where men, whose very clothes were foul with the stink of beer, slouched, he thought of his own life in contrast with Ernest's. His thoughts wandered back to ten years before when a boy of 12 had gazed in horror at the prone figure of his dead mother. He had no recollection of a father, and it was 13 years since he had glimpsed his step-brother, a greasy man of 37 or so. The yellow lamplight, as shallow and artificial as the inmates of the wharf, found no responsive glow in the surly Thames. As he passed a broken shop, a figure came out of the shadow.

'Hallo, Mr Richard,' a voice said.

Richard faltered, and then walked on. At the door of his hut he turned and found the stranger behind.

Richard lighted a candle and set it on the broken table.

'What do you want?' he said hoarsely, as he shut the door.

The man sat down quickly on the bed on which a short time before the bitter body of Martin Andromikey had lain. In the glaring candlelight Richard saw the face of the man he was going to hate for eternity. The eyes were the grey of sleet, not the grey of a sparrow's wing, the lips were thick and rich red blood coursed through them. His chin had a deep cleft down it. His face was crossed with furrows like a ploughed field, and the cracks were filled with dirt. He wore a brown coat with tails and breeches, no shirt, and a blue spotted neck-cloth.

'What would I be wanting now?' leered he.

Richard gritted his teeth. 'Get out,' he said slowly and clearly.

The man backed. 'All right, Mr Richard,' he whined.

When he had gone, Richard shuddered. That evil waterman knew who he was! He would interfere with his plan! He fell once more to wondering if Martin had been wrong, but dismissed the idea. He felt hungry. The lunch he had eaten earlier had stimulated his appetite. When he did not eat he did not feel hungry, but the thought of that mutton and sponge-pudding tormented his stomach.

He did not take his clothes off, but lay far into the night thinking of the years to come. As he mused so, the water lapping by the bank sucked him down into darkness.

If, readers, you had journeyed into Richard's soul that dark night you would have passed down two channels: one bitter and twisted, filled with an all-enveloping swamp of hatred against the man who had caused Martin Andromikey's death. The other one would have been bitter too, but in the spaces there would be pictures of the effect the firm's ruin would have on Ernest, his musical sister, his small brother and his pretty young mother.

Finally, Richard fell into a sleep, in which evil forces dragged him down with hypnotic eyes into the ever-waiting Thames.

CHAPTER 4

Gasper Liverwick slouched down the back streets. He made his way through the many alleys, and finally reached Thames Street. Here the lamps were yellower, the public houses more frequent and the people more degraded.

If, dear readers, when you come to the words 'public houses' and see in your mind's eye the bleary eyes and wasted limbs of the men and women staggering from such places, their yellow-skulled babies mewling in the gutters, do not call a curse on the wretched mortals who so displease your thoughts! Rather, call a fervent curse on the nobles and bishops of our London, for not giving the poor support and, what is more, self-respect − for regarding the silken coats of their many horses with delight, and for ignoring the parchment skins of their fellow-humans breeding and dying and neither eating or living, from one end of the town to another. When a heart is sick, and a mind stunted without education or enlightenment, when bodies curve unhealthily and carry disease in a warped line from head to toe, it is surprising how a glass of ale or spirits fills the guts and brain-matter with explosive feelings of relief, temporary well-being and a kind of gaiety. That is why the poor drink. To them the public houses, with warm fires kept burning to tempt the passer-by, serve as vast communal homes. Little matter that even their small coins go once more to furnish the rich brewery-owners with finer clothes and bedding, with more silken horses to pull their ladies' carriages, with more power to extract rents, taxes and tolls.

In such a home Gasper Liverwick sought refreshment. Sitting on one of the stools, sipping bad brandy, he waited for a friend. Round about on the benches ugly-looking sailors from the waterfront sprawled, and filled the air with brutal jests. Gasper smiled at the rude remarks and jeered in approval when one big brute swung the woman at his side out of the door by her hair. Blue-smoked air filled the room, and Gasper leaned back and waited and picked his teeth, which were very bad. Half an hour passed and the door swung back and a man slapped his shoulder, and called loudly for a jug of beer.

Rupert Bigarstaff was a man of about 36 years. His eyes were blue and twinkling, his features regular and pleasant, the cloth on his back of good quality. He was an odd fellow, known the length of the waterfront as the cruellest of men. He would not hesitate in doing the foulest murder, or torturing a reeling drunkard, but at the sight of a dog in pain, or a bird with a broken wing, his eyes would fill, and his hands grow as healing as the Apostles'. Many a person swore that he had the gift of healing, but he was feared for this the length of the water world. Some of his more personal acquaintances said he held the rich spellbound outside St Paul's of a Sunday. True, Rupert Bigarstaff was a strange man.

The two of them talked in low voices.

'It's getting hotter,' hissed Gasper Liverwick. 'I went to his place tonight and told him I knew, more or less.'

'He's out for Andromikey's money,' said Bigarstaff, and his face grew contorted. 'But he won't keep it long, will he, Gasper?'

His friend laughed, and such was the nature of it that the sailors on the benches stopped jesting, arms hung lifelessly round the narrow shoulders of their wenches. One man, with a big nose and a beautiful cloud of sunny hair that made him look lost beneath it, slapped his thigh and swore.

Rupert shot him a flashing glance and whispered in Gasper's ear, 'He overheard something, Gasper, me friend. Observe the way his fingers twitch.'

As Gasper could not fathom how twitching fingers denoted a person overhearing things that were not desirous to both parties, he did not trouble himself, but answered in an undertone, 'What do we do then, matey?'

'Leave it to me,' said Rupert, getting to his feet.

The yellow-locked waterman had gone out a moment before. They strode out into the night. A slight drizzle met them, and they watched their quarry turn the collar of his pea-jacket up about his ears. They followed him through the main streets and mean ones until, coming out of an alley, they saw him descend the steps of the wharf bank. He stood before turning onto his barge, maybe looking up through the drizzle and the fog, to where he dimly thought, as a child, stars had been. Then Rupert moved. There was a soft noise and down went the yellow head into the abyss of the deep. He came up and struck out for the bank. As his fingers grasped at the parapet Rupert brought his shoe down sharply on the bones. There was a screech from the man and he sank, the head now dark with water. Again, and for the last time, the clinging hands were stamped to pulp, and the body slid relentlessly away.

'Must we use violence?' asked Gasper, as they made their way homeward.

The friend at his side spoke in a soft crooning voice, the voice of a fanatic. 'That was not violence, Gasper Liverwick, that was tidiness. No man is worth human kindness. They're all soft relenting flesh, spineless. But in the next world there'll be a special kind of hell. Their bones will stretch the skin and be like iron. They'll scream for all eternity.' He laughed, and it was a nice laugh – the laugh of a schoolboy.

Gasper withdrew into himself and did not speak.

'We have one more call,' said Rupert finally. 'My very good friend Richard Soleway will be very glad to see us, and no doubt make us welcome.'

They came to the place where the said Richard lived, and Gasper peered through the window.

'There's no candle burning,' he said softly, 'but the lamp's shining on his bed. He's asleep – but fitfully, I should think, by the tossing of his body.'

Rupert flung open the door and shut it carefully behind them.

Richard sat up with a cry. His hands fumbled with the candle, and he bit his lip when he saw his unwelcome visitor again. He could not help but start at the face of the man next to him. It was lit with a bright light from within, and it glowed through the skin and teeth of Rupert Bigarstaff.

'What do you want?' he asked faintly.

'Nothing, nothing,' soothed Rupert, and such was his badness that Richard did feel soothed for the second.

'We want you to be our friend,' continued Rupert gravely. 'But I think it would not be in the nature of friendship to keep you from your rest, so I will say goodnight.' The glowing eyes lingered on his face. 'Sleep well, my dear young friend, and dream sweetly.'

When they had gone Richard lay shivering on his crumpled bed. He stumbled up at last and poured himself a glass of cheap whisky. He swilled it down and felt better, but he could not sleep. A thousand fears assailed him, fiery demons with sharp-pointed darts of hate attacked as he lay, his hand a-shaking on the coverlet.

At last, worn out with fear and wrestling inwardly with a foe that would not be suppressed, his head sank onto his breast, and he slept the sleep of the uneasy.

CHAPTER 5

Old Andrew Ledwhistle settled himself comfortably in his chair and brought out his diary. Old Andrew's diary was a kind of spiritual ritual with him; it was to him as water is to ducks. He opened it at March 9th, Saturday, the year 1851. His quill pen scrawled rapidly into the margin.

Met Father's partner's grandson today. He looks an intelligent youngster.

Here the pen pawed the empty air. Old Andrew leaned back and turned the pages slowly. November 11, 1783. He read slowly, as if savouring every word.

Father told me today that I was to be his successor in the firm. Am delighted. Am to partner with Peter Andromikey, whom I like greatly already. He is 13.

Old Andrew smiled and turned the pages rapidly.

April 4th, 1811. Father gave his blessing to Ruby and me.

His finger stopped at one page and, as he read the first lines, his head lifted and his eyes grew dreamy. 'Owing to Peter's death,' he heard his father saying, 'I am going to tell you the secret he entrusted to me. Richard Andromikey left to his grandson the sum of £45,000 in his will. He made one condition, however. Peter was not to give it to Martin unless he entered into the firm with your son and made good.' Andrew frowned. His father had sounded very solemn; it was just after the death of Ruby, he remembered. He turned over. One page read:

Father died tonight. Received a letter from Martin Andromikey asking me once more to lend him money.

He turned nearer to the back of the book.

Am to be married next week.

Then he returned to the 1851 entry again. 'Martin seems very embittered but he is a good lad or seemingly is,' he wrote firmly. He then closed his big diary, shut it in his desk and shut his eyes.

Little did Old Andrew know that Martin Andromikey had found out about his money and that he was ignorant of the conditions. Little did he know that Martin was really dead, and had died with a curse on his lips which was directed against him. Little did he know that Richard Soleway was to be the instrument that was to break his heart. Little did he know that Francis was to end his days as a petty thief and that Ernest was to be ruined.

At that moment Ernest came into the room and, on seeing his father so preoccupied, tiptoed cautiously up to him and kissed the withered old forehead so marked by time. Old Andrew started. He laid his hand on his son's head and seated him on the stool on which his younger sisters often did their sewing.

'Well, Ernest,' he said softly. 'Are you happy?'

Ernest flushed. 'Papa,' he said painfully, 'I have something I would wish you to help me about. That is, the fact of the matter is, sir, I have been strongly attracted to the daughter of your friend Rubin Mansall.'

The father smiled.

'Go on, Ernest,' he bade.

'Well, Papa, that's all I have to say – except that I venture to guess Anna loves me too.' On the word 'loves' the young man coloured hotly and swept his hair from his forehead with a 'now it's over' gesture.

Old Andrew could not suppress a smile. 'But Ernest, you are but a little over 20.'

'I have a good job now, sir, and can well keep Anna in the comfort she is used to,' protested his son.

Andrew leaned forward. 'Let us wait till you are both older and more wise,' he said carefully. 'Anna is little more than a girl and you no more than a boy. Let me talk to your mother about it.'

'I am sure it must be love, Papa,' he said plaintively, 'for it hurts here,' and he laid his hand upon his heart.

This time Old Andrew laughed, without restraint. When his son had left him he lay with his feet on the fender and closed his eyes. The fire's ruddy colour made his eyeballs burn. He had not betrayed his displeasure when Ernest had told him of his love for Anna Mansall. He had nothing against Anna herself: she was a sweet girl, and a pretty one. But her father was another matter. Rubin had, at the death of Peter Andromikey, gone into the business with him. All had gone well for a matter of 18 years, till quite by chance Andrew had discovered he was systematically robbing his firm every year. On the pretence of retiring – for Old Ledwhistle liked and respected Mansall's wife – Rubin had been dismissed and the partnership dissolved. If indeed Ernest did have any real affection for the girl and one day wished to make her his wife, things would grow very awkward. No, Old Ledwhistle told himself, Anna shall never marry my boy. It will only bring unhappiness to both of them. Then he thought of Ruby Clacy whom he had married in 1811, and of the age he had been at the time. 'Yes,' he thought chuckling, 'I've been very lucky in marriage. Ruby was a good woman, and so is Mary.'

He rose to his feet, took the candles from the mantelpiece and pulled up the blind. Down Terence Street a cab moved, the cabby sitting like a sentinel on top. Below, in the house opposite, he could see Rachel Molson and her husband sitting before their fire, with the grey cat on the latter's knee.

'Jonathan Molson was always a fool about cats,' he mumbled, as he pulled the blind into place again.

CHAPTER 6

Richard sat on his high chair, his partner Ernest opposite him. The latter was diligently working. Jacob Steinhouse and Westbury were poring over a bundle of dry-looking deeds. The three looked so solemn and owl-like, especially Jacob Steinhouse, with his big eyes and quivering side-whiskers, that Richard wondered if he dared cough. He cleared his throat loudly. Three heads and three pairs of eyes were raised. Ernest's showed veiled approval, Westbury's irritated alarm, and Jacob Steinhouse's plainly told Richard what they thought of him. Immediately the heads were lowered. Richard wondered what would happen if he started whistling. He did so, and the scandalised eyes of Steinhouse leapt to meet him.

Richard got to his feet, yawned and said loudly, 'Coming for a drink, Ernest?'

Westbury gasped audibly.

Before the horror-stricken eyes of the two clerks, Richard walked out, his hand on Ernest's arm.

'I say,' said Ernest breathlessly, 'I've forgotten my hat.'

'You don't need one,' replied his friend.

'But I do, Martin, I do,' gasped Ernest, in distress as he was hurried along Talcorth Road. 'Where are we going?' he added, a note of interest creeping into his voice.

'To Comrades Street,' answered Richard with impatience.

'But Martin,' said Ernest in a whisper, 'that road consists mostly of gin-shops and opium palaces.'

'My dear Ernest,' said Richard, highly amused, 'it's plain to me you've led a very sheltered life. When one goes out for a drink, the right place to go is Comrades Street.'

In silence they entered one such shop. The young were absent, working their backs off them, for a paltry pittance. But the old were there – men and women whose very age made them indecent. Life held no more for them but gin and gin. The eyes were lifeless, their skin purple, their brains senile.

The two young partners made a queer contrast. Richard with his gay clothes looked more at home, but Ernest in his sombre black suit and high collar, his very face pink with embarrassment, looked strange, like a daffodil against a warehouse building.

Ernest shuddered. 'Why are these people allowed to mix with others?' he whispered in Richard's ear.

Any other time his friend would have grown heated and violent, but now he answered without passion. 'Because there are no graves for them to lie in.'

Ernest was silent for a space, but when an old man with looped and yellow-flecked eyes mouthed horribly and spat at him, he grasped Richard's arm and said, 'For God's sake, Martin, let's go back to the office. I can't stand this.'

So they went.

When they were once more seated at their desks, Richard began thinking over the plan that was to ruin the firm of Andromikey and Ledwhistle. Ledwhistle, he had found out, invested money on the Stock Exchange. He was a good and shrewd investor, and held many shares. Richard meant to bankrupt the firm, but he must have money to do it. He did not know how long it would take him to do what he planned, but on his solemn oath he knew he had given his promise to a dying man.

As the day finished and the time came to leave the books and manuscripts for another day, Richard's heart grew heavy. He was unwittingly beginning to enjoy life for the first time. He said goodbye to Ernest and travelled into Billingsgate market. It had not yet closed and the scene was glaring and humorous. A man was sitting on a tub by a stall drawing. He alternately told the crowd of the excellence of his fish, and then drew them to the delight of the people, swimming in their natural element. Farther away another woman in a bright fringed shawl sold haddock while blessing all and sundry. Over everything hung the smell of fish. A salty, cold, icy smell one minute and a fierce, sickly one the next. There were all kinds of fish to be had. Big ones, little ones, round ones, flat ones, fish with spots on, fish with stripes, some fish with rings, and just fish. The laughter of humour was everywhere. Here was the lighter side of life; here at least men were equal.

The night was early and Richard did not feel disposed to go to his bed. So he wandered round. At London Street, he stopped suddenly. Two men were fighting. One was tall and lithe, one thin and short. Richard would have passed if the desperate face of the short one had not been raised in earnest pleading towards him. The tall man was a rough-looking fellow, with ugly eyes and large hands. They were very out of proportion with his body, which was trim and wiry. He hit out harshly with one flabby fist, and the white-faced victim had his chin jerked back with a crack.

Richard stepped forward quickly. 'Heh,' he said impetuously, 'stop this.' He turned to the big-handed fighter. 'Your opponent's hungry, he's starving.'

The man grinned stupidly. 'I'm not exactly overfed meself.'

The white-faced youngster hung onto his arm. Richard pulled a couple of shillings out of his pocket and handed it to the man who had last spoken. He moved away, his hand on the other lad's elbow.

'Give us a few bob, mate, please,' the boy whispered.

'You need a meal first,' answered Richard, piloting his acquaintance into a bar.

Silently the youth followed him to the parlour at the

back. Richard ordered a tureen of thick soup and a plate of chipped potatoes and beef. To add to its completion, a mug of warm ale was set down.

The boy ate ravenously, never looking at his benefactor once.

Richard watched him cautiously. His eyes noted the sunken cheeks, the bright eyes and the threadbare clothes. Afterwards as the boy leaned back in the oaken bench, he ventured to ask him his name.

'It's Robert,' was the reply that came in faint accents, 'Robert Straffordson.'

Richard forbore to ask him any more questions. He took him that night to his hut and gave him a few blankets.

The boy did not thank him, but several times he saw the glittering eyes rest on his countenance.

When the morning came, Robert Straffordson had gone. With him had gone the first £5 note Richard had ever received. Richard did not feel vexed: he felt as if life was hopeless. Everything was so bitter and twisted. Little did he know what part Robert Straffordson was to play in the drama of his life.

CHAPTER 7

Sir Phillip Hobart, Chairman of the London Stock Exchange, was a thin, prominently-nosed man of about 58 or so. He had risen to the top of his ladder by sheer hard work, but not a little dishonesty. He was a man who was well pleased with life, but he was known to keep very much to himself. Not even his greatest friends knew of the old background of Phillip Hobart. He had no relatives, or seemingly not: if he did, he never visited them. As he walked briskly down Piccadilly and passed the Strand, many people stopped and bowed to him. Many a young society lad would gaze enviously after the prosperous knight.

Richard, it so happened, was walking in the opposite direction of that gentleman. He turned a corner. There was an angry shout and Richard saw Hobart sprawled on the ground, his hand to his head. A drab-coated youth was running in the direction he had just come from.

Richard raced in pursuit. He soon outran his quarry and grasped him by the collar. As his prisoner turned, he came face to face with Robert Straffordson. Richard felt himself go limp. By this time Phillip Hobart had reached them and quite a crowd had gathered. A withered constable came up to them in haste. Hobart stated his case and a charge was drawn up against the youth. Richard refrained from making any statement: he felt only pity for the degenerate boy beside him. He became aware that the group of people had been dispelled and found his hand being shaken by Hobart.

'I can never thank you enough, young sir,' he was told, while a pair of glowing grey eyes searched his countenance. 'If you are ever in need of help, come to me.' A card was thrust into his hand, and the knight walked off.

Richard looked at the card blankly. 'Sir Phillip Hobart, Knight. 'The Garrat', Bayswater, London.' Sir Phillip Hobart? Richard's mind revolved round and round. Surely – yes, it must be. He was the present Chairman of the Stock Exchange. Fate had introduced him to the very man he wished to know. He could have laughed, if not that the eddying mass of people were moving by. A horse-drawn bus passed him, and he saw his partner, Ernest. Ernest glimpsed him and waved his hand. He clambered aboard and climbed the stairs to the open roof.

As he was talking to the young Ledwhistle, Richard dropped the card that Hobart had presented him.

'I say,' said Ernest eagerly, 'do you know Sir Phillip?'

'Well, I had the honour of doing him some slight service a minute ago,' replied Richard. 'Do you?'

'Well, I don't myself,' volunteered Ernest, 'but he and Papa hate each other, I know. Father accused him of being dishonest one time when he had just been appointed, and they never speak nowadays.'

Ah, thought Richard. So Phillip and Old Andrew dislike each other, do they? Nothing could be better. I must further my acquaintance with Sir Phillip. Richard Soleway was one step on his way on the tragedy staircase of Andrew Ledwhistle and, though he did not know it, one step further to his own ruin.

CHAPTER 8

Anna Mansall sat demurely in the sitting-room awaiting the arrival of her lover, Ernest Ledwhistle. She was a striking girl of some 18 years of age, with thick black hair which rested in a loose coil on the nape of her neck. Her eyes were grey and set wide apart, her nose long and straight, her mouth large and generous. She was not beautiful in the accepted sense of the word, but she was arresting and pretty. She wore a gown of soft blue, and it was becomingly edged with lace.

The door opened and Eliza, the maid, entered bearing a tray. 'Master Ernest is here, Miss Anna,' she told her mistress. 'Shall I show him in?'

Anna nodded her assent, as she busied herself setting the cups out.

A moment later Ernest hurried into the room. 'Anna, my dearest,' he said as he touched her hand with his lips. He would have drawn her into his arms if Anna had not put her fingers to his mouth in urgency.

'No, Ernest, not now. Listen. I hear Mama on the stairs.'

Ernest sat down quickly in the chair opposite his love, and began making polite conversation.

He was rewarded for his prudence, for the door opened and Mrs Mansall entered the room. She was a stout woman in her late fifties. She was arrayed in an elaborate silk cap and a large quantity of petticoats. Her eyes were all but lost in a swelling of very red flesh, and what was glimpsed of them was unremarkable. Her mouth was thin and bloodless, her nose short and squat, wide and flared at the nostrils.

'My dear Ernest,' she fluttered, as she held out her hand.

The flesh here too bulged round the rings and Ernest nerved himself as he bent over it. 'I hope you will be present at the ball I am giving for dear Anna's 19th birthday,' she said coyly. 'And I hear that your partner Martin Andromikey is in town.'

'Yes, Ma'm,' answered Ernest dutifully.

'Then we shall be delighted to invite him as well, shan't we, Anna dear?'

'Oh yes, Mama,' answered Anna. She tried to convey to Ernest that she would try and get her mother out of the room for an instant.

'Mama,' she said a minute later, 'will you entertain Ernest while I lie down? I don't feel well.' Before her mother could reply she darted out of the room.

'Oh dear, oh dear,' cried Mrs Mansall. 'Excuse me, won't you, Ernest. I must look after the dear child.' And, still calling out 'Oh dear, oh dear,' she closed the door.

Hardly had Ernest sat down than the door opened and Anna darted in.

'She's chasing my ghost right to the top of the house,' she laughed merrily.

This time there was no staying Ernest. He seized her, and his lips found hers.

They were thus occupied – and a very good occupation I say – when Mrs Mansall came upon them.

'Oh, dearie me,' she wailed. 'Anna, my only child.' She sat down quickly and turned to the scarlet-complexioned Ernest. 'You, you scoundrel, Ernest Ledwhistle, putting this shock to me.'

Both Anna and Ernest looked in concentration at each other. 'You don't mind, Mama?' said Anna at length.

'Mind, my loves?' cried her mother. 'Love will find a way, you know. When will you be married? Of course, I shall have to get Papa to talk to Ernest's.' She gabbled on, almost incoherently.

Filthy Lucre

Ernest could have jumped with joy. He turned to Anna. 'Come back with me now, dearest, and see Mama. I know she'll love you.'

'And I shall come too,' fussed Mrs Mansall. 'I'll just get my bonnet. Oh, but my only daughter, my darling little girl. But I must remember, I have not lost her, I have gained a son.' She could be heard reasoning in the hall outside.

Anna squeezed Ernest's arm. 'Dear Mama,' she said softly, 'and dear Ernest.'

This gave dear Ernest a chance to prove how dear he was and they were only brought to earth by a discreet and forced cough by Mrs Mansall, who looked more ludicrous than ever in an enormous flowered bonnet.

A cab drove them all to Andrew Ledwhistle's and as they climbed out, the first realisation of what he had really done swept over Ernest. He remembered how his father had looked upon it rather lightly and seemed to consider him but a boy. As he led them to his mother he felt braver. They can't help liking her though, he reasoned. And besides it was his life.

The family were having afternoon tea.

'My dear Claire,' cried Mrs Ledwhistle affectionately as she kissed her old friend on the cheek, 'I haven't seen you for years. How are you? And, my dear, how Anna has grown!'

Andrew looked up from his old partner's wife's hand, and caught his son's eye.

Ernest slipped forward. 'Papa,' he said, and stopped.

'Yes, Ernest,' replied his father. 'Go on.'

Ernest began to flounder.

'The dear boy's shy,' cried Mrs Mansall in ecstasy. 'You see, Andrew, he loves my daughter as much as Anna loves him.'

Mary Ledwhistle gave an exclamation. 'Ernest,' she cried, 'I never knew! You never told me!'

'I didn't know myself till but a week ago, Mama,' her son proffered. 'I told Papa and he said you and he would talk it over. But I do love her, Father,' he faltered lamely.

Old Ledwhistle's heart was heavy. 'Don't you think you're all a trifle hasty?' he said calmly.

Mrs Mansall's cup was suspended in the air. 'Andrew, don't you approve of the match?'

'Excellent, excellent, Claire,' responded Old Ledwhistle, 'but we must remember they're but children and not of age. They've got years ahead of them. Why, Ernest may think he's in love. I do not wish to hurt you, Anna my dear —' this in an aside — 'but it may be an infatuation you have for each other.'

'Papa, it isn't,' reproached Ernest. 'It is not, truly. I love Anna as truly as ever I'll love anyone.'

'There, you see,' cried his mother. 'It's all settled.'

Mrs Mansall could not restrain her delight.

'It is not all settled, Mary,' cried Andrew. 'Ernest is not going to marry Anna — or at least, not yet.'

Mrs Mansall was not daunted. 'Rubin will be calling on you shortly, Andrew,' she said, 'and everything will be settled up quite simply, with satisfaction to both parties.'

She bestowed a warm kiss on Mrs Ledwhistle and her daughters, nearly smothered little Francis in her voluminous petticoats, and swept out, Anna trailing dejectedly behind.

When they had gone, Ernest turned to his father in real anger.

'Papa,' he cried, 'I'm not a child. I love Anna, do you hear?'

'Yes, my boy, I do and I'm very distressed,' answered Old Ledwhistle sorrowfully. He turned to his daughter Jane. He addressed his eldest, 'Take your brother to the nursery, and Fanny and Charlotte go too.'

When they had gone, he bade his wife and Ernest be seated. 'Now,' he said worriedly, 'I will tell you a story.

Many years ago, just after I made Ruby my first wife, Peter died. Then Rubin Mansall became my partner. 18 years later I learned he was robbing the firm. The partnership was dissolved. His wife and child are ignorant of his shame. And they must never know.'

'But what difference does that make?' cried Ernest impetuously. 'They won't know because I marry Anna.'

His mother, however, thought differently. 'You mean, Andrew, that Rubin has never forgiven you and never will?'

'Yes, my dear,' answered Andrew heavily. 'He would never consent to your marriage. It would make us all miserable.'

'But, Father,' cried Ernest wretchedly, 'it'll ruin my life. She's everything to me.'

'In that case, my boy – you cherish her happiness do you not?'

'Oh yes, Father, yes,' answered his distressed son.

'Well then,' reasoned his father. 'Do you love me, Ernest?'

'Papa,' cried Ernest, 'of course I do.'

'All right,' was the reply. 'Anna loves her father too, no doubt, and if she was ever to learn of his shame it would break her heart. Rubin would never agree to her marriage. And if you did get married without his consent, he would never forgive either you or her. Rubin is a determined man.'

'I see,' said Ernest blankly.

But he didn't. And Andrew knew that, but what he did not know was that Ernest loved Anna in a way which his father did not believe man could love woman. He did not know that the breaking off from Anna would bring about Ernest's downfall.

CHAPTER 9

Rupert Bigarstaff strolled up Ludgate Hill. His eyes stared straight ahead, but he saw nothing. 'I must do something about young Soleway,' his brain said. St Paul's glowed at the sky, its mighty dome a challenge to the unlovely things of the world.

'God was a fool to make a thing like that for the wretches,' he muttered.

He climbed the many steps and leaned against a pillar. He'd make 'em sit up tonight. He'd watch 'em writhe as they tried to stop their ears and couldn't. As a boy Rupert had been a queer little chap. He had a great memory for faces and astonished his wealthy parents by, at the age of 5, healing a dog who had been crushed under a carriage wheel. The family physicians had said it had been a miracle and he had been told to lay his hand on his dying father's poisoned hand. He did, but he didn't heal him. He had told his mother that his father wasn't fit for living. His mother had been frightened, he remembered. He'd been sent away to a home for abnormal boys.

A small group was already gathering round him. He had that gift. He instinctively attracted attention. They listened till the evening sun went that white red that warns the world his time has come. The trees waved dully, and still they listened. Finally, Rupert was silent. There was no clapping. There never was, for they one and all hated him and feared him.

Rupert descended the steps and made his way homeward. He crossed London Bridge and rested for a moment on the rail. The sky was barred with red and gold. The eddying streams of colour raced over the water and were immersed in the shadows. It was very quiet, and when a footstep was heard on the cobbles he felt irritated. A young girl came towards him. Her face was streaked and dirty, her hair lank and black. Her eyes were large and without feeling, but the hand that clutched the fringed shawl was trembling. The girl said nothing. Her eyes rested hypnotically on the water. She stretched out her hand. She turned her head slowly to his.

'Do you think it'll be very cold and painful?' she asked, and her voice came from far away.

'Oh no,' answered Rupert. 'It won't. Shall I push you?'

'Oh no, no. I want to have the satisfaction of having felt courageous when I'm falling,' she replied, her eyes once more turned to the water.

She leaned over, and Rupert gave a sharp jerk.

She fell with hardly a splash. The water rippled and circled. Then all was still again.

Rupert felt pleased he had cheated her at the very end. Maybe, dear readers, you feel only horror at the thought of a young girl wishing to drown herself. But many a girl and many a boy have crept to find rest in the secretive waters of the Thames these many years.

Rupert turned and found Gasper Liverwick at his elbow. 'Hallo,' he said. 'Where are you going?'

'Wherever *you* are,' answered his crony, and arm in arm they journeyed to the waterfront.

Rupert entered his hovel and lit his lamp. It flickered strangely, not unlike the gleam in its owner's eye.

'Are we going to revisit Soleway tonight?' asked Gasper.

'No, I think not.' Rupert was final. 'We are to talk about him, though. Here, my friend, sit down.'

They sat down, and Rupert placed a bottle of stout on the table.

'Listen hard, Gasper,' he said, 'Richard Soleway today met Sir Phillip Hobart, Chairman of the Stock Exchange.

Don't ask me how I know — I just do. About what he talked about I don't know, but I can guess. Andrew Ledwhistle, as we know, invests in the Stock Exchange. Probably our young friend wishes to get to know Sir Hobart for his own ends. That will mean success for the firm, and Richard Soleway will doubtless receive his money. Then we'll take a hand, Gasper, me friend.'

Gasper nodded his head in agreement. He wondered to himself what foul death Rupert would devise for Richard Soleway. Where would it all end?

CHAPTER 10

The streets of London were festooned with flags and bunting. The children, scrubbed and shining with soap and excitement and dressed in their patchy best, waited in a fever of impatience. The grown-ups too were giving sheepish smiles, for today was to be the day that Victor Radenstone – the name which conjured passionate acclaim from many men – was going to the reception at the Town Hall in honour of his great work in the Chinese Opium War. It was to be a public holiday as well, and there was to be beer and buns for the poor, presented by the charity of the Great Man himself.

There was a sound of horses' hoofs, and the crowds lining the narrow streets gave a lusty cheer – perhaps it was aided by the thought of free ale. A shining black carriage came into view led by a team of high-mettled horses, their nostrils dilated, their magnificent shoulders rippling under their satiny coats.

As the carriage swept by, Robert Straffordson gave a grim smile. He wondered what his prosperous step-father would say when he presented himself. In short steps, his shoulders bent, he made his way to the hall. Round at a rear entrance he was accosted by an officious individual. He was forcefully ejected and, his eyes smouldering, he skulked round the back. Here he was fortunate. A window, partly shuttered, afforded him entry. As he landed with a slight noise on the floor below him, he saw he was in a cloakroom. His hand stole into the nearest pocket, and out came a pair of satin gloves, a slightly soiled handkerchief and a knife. Robert stuffed them in his coat and opened the door a space.

The hall was full to the maximum. By a table sat a row of important, stomached aldermen. Opposite them sat their wives, and standing by the table was his step-father. The face was turned sideways and Robert saw the great Victor Radenstone's profile. No, he had not altered with the years. His body was large and muscular, and his hands strong and brown. But his face was the face of a city clerk. The nose was thin and wavery, the lips fine and sensual. The eyes were a watery blue, and they held the old familiar hunted look. Robert had inherited that expression. It was as if he was a timid dog hauling, rather doubtful of the consequences, on his leash.

Radenstone turned round slowly and for an instant his eyes met those of his step-son. There was no flame of recognition. He merely fixed his eyes on the people in the front rows. Victor, as he spoke in hackneyed phrases, was puzzled. The white and haunted face of the youth by the door had startled him not a little. Besides, had he not seen the same look in the mirror himself? Yes, those eyes were rather familiar.

He was brought back to earth by the sound of clapping. He gazed vaguely at the door again, but the boy had disappeared. He became aware that he was being led from the hall, and curious eyes feasted on him. There were the eyes – brown, green, grey-black eyes – but they all held the pinched, hunted look of the youth he had seen a minute ago.

Meanwhile Robert, after helping himself to a few pockets, wandered down the streets of the city. He loved his father with a love that was as fierce and heated as any. Years ago as a little boy he remembered how he used to get a feeling of warm contentment when he felt his small hand engulfed in that big one. He had not liked his mother, and until her second marriage had stored his childish love up. When she had married Radenstone, he had showered all his affections on the big, weak-faced man. A film passed over his eyes. He had broken his father's heart 8 years ago when he had broken loose and left home. Gradually, year by year, he had fallen more and more deeply into the slough of thieving. He was nearing the water's edge, and as his eyes lighted on the dull grey of the water that moved sluggishly along he knew that he himself was growing like that year by year. Then Robert Straffordson laughed and was himself again.

CHAPTER 11

The spacious ballroom was glittering and mellow. The polished floor was an invitation to your feet, and made them want to slide, to ruffle the calm smugness of its surface. The orchestra, screened by tall ferns at one end of the room, wafted forth a whirling melody. Here was colour, happiness and breathless beauty. The ladies' skirts and petticoats, brightly sequined, swished softly round their dainty feet. The many fans fluttered and revealed flushed and bright-eyed gaiety, while the men bowed over their partners' white fingers and dabbed hastily in their snuff boxes. Round the end of the floor on gilt-backed chairs, as stiff and upright as their occupants, rested the fond mamas who gossiped rapturously as they told each other 'how well dear Bertha and that young William Darcy looked together'.

Richard looked down at his pretty young partner, a vivacious girl with bewitching dimples in the velvet smoothness of her cheeks. By the door talking to Claire Mansall, was Rubin, her husband. He was a faded edition of his daughter, with black eyes and curved eyebrows. Rubin was looking angrily in the direction of Ernest, and his wife looked tearful and distressed.

As soon as the dance ended, Rubin strode up to Anna. He took her roughly by the arm. 'Is this how you repay me for my goodness, Anna? Where are your manners? As the hostess you must pay attention to your guests. Victor Radenstone wishes to have this next waltz.' But before the astonished girl could respond she was led off.

Ernest flushed furiously. Where had he heard that name before? Of course, he was *the* Victor Radenstone. He walked sulkily to a corner where his sister Fanny sat, her foolish face one bright beam.

'Come on, Fanny,' said Ernest crossly, hauling her roughly to her feet, 'I wish you to dance this gavotte with me.'

Puffing, Fanny got to her feet. She was a silly girl with no beauty, and little brains. She irritated Ernest beyond measure by her empty expression and simpering ways.

Ernest looked moodily at Anna. She was pivoting lightly, her black eyes sparkling in the arms of a watery-eyed man. He felt he hated Victor Radenstone. Then he saw the kindly gaze in the man's eyes, and felt reassured.

He wished the dance would finish. The palms of Fanny's hands were wet, and short bursts of breath came from her clenched teeth. He tried to loosen her stubby fingers from his sleeve. He felt sure she would mark his new suit.

There was a final chord from the orchestra, and Richard walked over to him. He bowed briefly over Fanny's hand and escorted her gallantly to her wall-flower seat. With a guilty pretence of an excuse he left her, and went his way to his partner.

'I say, Martin,' cried Ernest, 'this is awful. Look at Anna. It's scandalous.'

Richard smiled. 'She's just as upset as you,' he reassured.

Ernest kicked the door angrily. A moment later Anna swept over to them. Ernest hurried forward and took both her hands in his.

'Anna,' he said peevishly, 'how could you?'

Anna glanced reproachfully at him, under lowered lids. 'Papa does not approve of you, I feel sure. When will you approach him about our love for each other?' she asked him earnestly.

Ernest's eyes clouded. 'I shall ask him tonight, dearest,' he resolved.

Anna turned to Richard. 'I hope the dancing is to your liking, Mr Andromikey,' she smiled.

'It would be much more enjoyable to me if you would honour me with the next dance,' replied Richard. He turned to Ernest. 'You do not object, partner?' he teased.

Ernest assented gaily this time. As he watched the two walk away, he became aware that a man was speaking.

'Excuse me, my dear young sir, but my name is Victor Radenstone.'

Ernest started. 'Not really?' he said. 'Indeed, this is a great honour, Sir.'

'The honour is entirely mine,' confessed Radenstone, bowing. 'I do hope you will not think me impertinent if I ask you when you and Miss Anna are to be betrothed. You see, during the dance the young lady was so flattering as to confide all to me. And my chivalry, though I blush to say it, has been aroused.'

Ernest looked downcast. 'Mr Mansall does not, I feel sure, approve of me, Sir.'

Victor Radenstone looked dreamy. 'That must be altered,' he said slowly. 'Tonight after the ball I will go with you and Miss Anna to his study. There we will persuade Mr Mansall that you are the best of fellows.' Ernest's eyes began to regain their sparkle.

'I can never thank you enough, Sir,' he stammered.

Radenstone cut him short. 'I have a son too,' he said. 'By marriage, but I have not seen him for years.'

Ernest hurried away to convey the good tidings to Anna. They both could hardly restrain themselves and were heartily glad when the guests began to disperse.

Finally, only two young men remained, besides the other three: Michael Standing, and a young nobleman named Lionel Dante. These, with great difficulty and not a little tact on behalf of Anna, were coaxed to go home. Then Anna, Radenstone and Ernest made their way to Rubin Mansall.

Rubin Mansall was just reclining in his armchair, his

glass of brandy beside him. Rubin was rather partial to a glass of warm spirits.

'Impudent young puppy,' he muttered savagely, as he crossed his feet on the fender. He was so sitting when his daughter and her two friends came softly into the room. Rubin was hardly civil to Ernest, and only barely polite to Radenstone.

Ernest began to fidget with his fingers. Radenstone broached the subject boldly. 'I have formed some affection for these two young people,' he said, 'and am well interested in their welfare.'

'Damned good of you,' barked Rubin, and Radenstone flushed darkly. 'Furthermore, Sir,' he continued, 'they wish to marry.'

As he spoke these last words Anna clutched her father's hands.

He threw her off roughly and turned on Ernest. 'Who do you think you are?' he said in a low voice. 'Why you, you little puppy, you are a partner in a firm that is as poor as it is dishonest.'

Ernest started forward, but Radenstone stayed him.

'I don't think that's quite fair, Mr Mansall,' he said grimly.

'As for you, you yellow-skinned, yellow-natured drug-curer, why don't you return to your heathland, and tame your crooning friends,' Mansall cried.

Radenstone kept his temper with difficulty. But Ernest could not. He sprang forward, his eyes glowing.

'If Father's firm is poor,' he stormed, 'it's because you stole all the money we ever got, and if we're dishonest it's because you ruined our name, and couldn't keep your hands to yourself.'

Rubin clenched his fists and grew purple in the face.

'What if I did steal your blasted money?' he screeched. 'The salary would never have kept me, or Anna or Claire, decent.'

Radenstone gripped Ernest's arm in alarm. 'Be quiet, Ernest,' he cried. 'This is a great shock to Anna.' He was just in time to catch the young girl.

Ernest carried her over to the couch. 'Anna, my love,' he cried brokenly, 'forgive me, oh forgive me.'

Rubin towered above him. 'Get out,' he thundered, 'get out.'

Radenstone pulled Ernest to his feet as the door opened and Claire Mansall hurried in.

'Oh,' she cried hysterically. 'Anna, my love, what is it? Ernest, what do you wish here? Rubin, help me quick. Oh Anna, Anna.'

She bent down and, helped by her husband, carried their daughter out of the room.

Ernest almost ran after them but Rubin had taken his precaution. Cadenlike, his manservant, politely showed them the door.

There was nothing for it but to go. As Radenstone pushed his young charge into a cab, he heartily cursed himself for his own clumsiness.

Ernest was beside himself with grief. 'Father told me to be prudent,' he cried. 'Oh, what have I done to her? She will hate me.'

Radenstone tried to soothe him. At the door of the Ledwhistle house he paid the cabbie and helped the young man up the steps.

As soon as Ernest was over the threshold, helped by old Wishlock, he turned and disappeared down the street. 'Fool that I am,' he groaned. 'Oh Robert, Robert, where are you?'

CHAPTER 12

Richard faced old Steinhouse with a cold smile.

'I know that I am young and foolhardy,' he said, 'but I also know that you are old and behind the times. These sums you invest in the Stock Exchange are too small to be of any profit to us. All I have done is to invest £700 in shares. When the shares go up, you will see whether I am prudent or not.'

Old Steinhouse was silent. He knew it was no use arguing with this young devil. He was too go-ahead, too reckless. If anything were to happen – he shuddered at the thought.

Back in the office which he shared with his partner, Richard took Ernest by the shoulder. Ernest's raised face was completely devoid of colour.

'Ernest,' said Richard gently, 'you can't go on like this. You'll be ill.'

'I've not seen Anna since that day last week,' replied the young man in distress. 'I've written, but I received no reply. Oh Martin, I must see her, I must know.'

'All right,' said Richard, 'you shall know. I shall make a point of seeing Miss Anna and arranging for her to see you. If need be I shall bring her here.' He swung on his heel.

'Where are you going, Martin?' cried Ernest.

'To visit Miss Mansall,' replied his partner. 'I shan't be long.' He gave Ernest a reassuring smile. 'Don't worry. She loves you as much as ever, I'm sure.' And with this Ernest was well content.

Richard walked briskly down the street. He liked Ernest, and was sorry for him. He could afford to be good to the young man, he thought. For yesterday, much to Jacob Steinhouse's disturbance, he had invested a considerable amount of money in the ship *Pirate's Fancy*, which was bound for the West Indies. He was confident that the money would be trebled, and step by step he would invest more and more, till the crash came.

He rang the bell of Anna Mansall's house, and was admitted into the hall. Soon Anna joined him, and led him into the sitting-room.

'How is Ernest?' she begged him, as soon as they were out of earshot of the maidservant.

'He is very stricken,' replied Richard, 'for he thinks by revealing the truth about your father's — "retirement", shall we call it? — that you will never forgive him.'

'Oh, tell him I do, I do with all my heart,' cried Anna. 'I know he has written, but Papa took all the letters and burnt them privately.'

'When can you see him?' asked Richard. 'He is beside himself with remorse.'

'It is I that is beside myself with shame,' said Anna in a whisper. 'To think that Papa should rob dear Mr Ledwhistle and nearly ruin him.'

Richard patted her hand in sympathy. 'Does your mother know?'

'I fear she does,' Anna answered. 'She has never left her room for 3 days. I do believe Papa is being sorely punished.'

'Well, I must leave you now,' said Richard at length.

'When can I see Ernest?' cried his hostess wildly.

'You shall see him tomorrow,' resolved Richard. 'I shall call for you at 11 in the morning.'

Murmuring her thanks, Anna wished him goodbye and, with a lighter heart than the one she had carried for the past week, fled upstairs to the sanctity of her room and wept.

Meanwhile Richard was talking to Ernest.

'Oh Martin, Martin,' cried the young fellow, searching his friend's face with flashing eyes.

'The forgiveness, she says,' enlightened Richard, 'is entirely on her part. She is to come here tomorrow, and told me to assure you that her heart is yours for ever.'

Ernest sank back in his chair.

'Thank you,' he said, 'thank you, Martin.'

CHAPTER 13

It was a sunny morning when Anna Mansall hurried up the stairs, to fall into the arms of her lover. It was still the same bright morn when Old Ledwhistle climbed the same steps and found his old partner's daughter in his son's arms. His eyes twinkled as they drew apart.

'My dear Anna,' he said. 'Can you forgive me?'

'Oh, yes, yes,' cried Anna, 'a thousand times.'

'What of your mother?' asked Andrew as he placed his stick by the door.

'I am afraid she is very much humbled by my father's disgrace,' Anna sighed, 'and I think papa is being punished. He is quite cast down.'

While this conversation was going on Robert Straffordson followed his father down through the city. His eyes were thoughtful as he saw the broad shoulders and weak head before him. He quickened his footsteps. He wondered what he should do. Would Victor Radenstone be pleased to own him? In a way he doubted it.

As he crossed the road he saw a cab bearing down on his father. He flung himself on the burly figure. There was a shout, a hoarse cry from the cabman, and Robert saw the shining blackness of the horses' hooves before the ground rushed with sickening force towards him.

CHAPTER 14

Robert lay on the bed, his brow furrowing as the June sun sought his eyes. He was in a large room with warm gold fittings. The boy heard the sound of cabs' wheels in the road below. He lay there languid and looked at his hands. They were thin and white and veined. A bell was on a small table by the side of him. He picked it up and shook it, while his wrist bent with the weight.

At once the door opened and a woman came into the room. She wore a white apron, and from her stringed cap peeped a fuzzy grey curl. She smiled at him and felt his pulse.

Robert said nothing, but watched her drowsily. He watched her move to the door and heard her footsteps on the stairs. Then he heard other footsteps, strong ones, slightly loping. The door opened and Robert saw his father.

'Robert,' cried Radenstone. 'Oh Robert.' He fell forward and kissed his son.

Straffordson felt suddenly tired and happy. His hand was once more in that well-loved big one.

As he slept, his father wept. 'Robert,' he said over and over again. As he felt the thin fingers tighten their grasp on his he thanked the good God for his mercy. Yet was it really mercy? His son would never walk again, for his legs had been amputated.

He stayed there all through the day and when finally Robert awoke supported him with his arm.

'Father,' said Straffordson, 'I'm frightened. I keep feeling for my legs but they're not there. There's only spaces, Father. Oh, what has happened?'

Briefly, his throat threatening to choke his words, Radenstone related the accident.

Robert nodded dumbly. He struggled a second, then lay back quite still.

'Don't leave me,' he said faintly. 'Don't ever leave me, Father.'

Then, as the shadows lengthened, they lay together, father and son, all barriers swept aside, and Robert slept.

CHAPTER 15

Fanny Ledwhistle stared dully up at the young man who was picking up the parcel that had slipped from her short fingers. Her mother smiled brightly and thanked him profusely. He was an immensely tall and thin young man, with huge, black-rimmed spectacles and nervous blinking eyes. His mouth hung open, while his wrists protruded well below his coat sleeves.

'The pleasure is entirely mine, Ma'm,' he returned, and he spoke with a pronounced American accent.

Fanny wondered absentmindedly if his voice had broken yet, or was just in the stages of doing so. One minute it was cracked and boyish, next it was lost in the depths of bass manhood.

'My name's James Coney,' he volunteered.

'Oh, indeed,' replied Mrs Ledwhistle. 'Well, thank you once again. Good morning.'

Stammering and blinking alternately, Mr James Coney was dismissed and Mrs Ledwhistle swept on majestically. 'Well,' she said to Fanny, 'I've heard these foreigners are forward, but Mr Coney is beyond himself.'

Fanny said nothing. She was already in the stages of a great romance, in which Mr Coney, whose voice was by this time broken, rescued her gallantly from drowning.

'Fanny,' cried Mrs Ledwhistle irritably, 'I've spoken to you 3 times, what is the matter?'

At their house, Jane was busily playing the piano, and Fanny was quite lost in admiration at the way in which her sister's sensitive fingers lingered over the mellow keys. Old Andrew was leaning back in his usual armchair, beating time with his foot. As his wife took off her shawl and bonnet, he chuckled.

'Andrew,' said Mary, 'what is making you laugh?'

'Young Andromikey invested £700 in a ship bound for the West Indies about 3 months ago,' replied Old Andrew happily, as he took his wife's hand in his. 'And furthermore our money has been doubled, for the trip proved highly successful.'

'I am glad,' cried Mary smiling, 'for I know your heart and soul is in the firm.'

'My heart and soul belongs to you, my dear,' replied Old Andrew huskily. 'You and our fine girls and sons.'

'As you know, Andrew,' related Mary, 'Fanny dropped her parcel and a most peculiar young American picked it up. He seemed very taken with Fanny – hardly took his eyes off her the whole time. But he was very forward.'

Jane giggled, and Charlotte tried to control herself also.

Fanny flamed an ugly red and Mrs Ledwhistle wished she wasn't so plain and stout. Still, that young fellow had seemed more than usually attracted. Now if it had been Jane, she mused. She looked hard at the girl at the piano, at the auburn hair and slight figure. Now that would be sensible, but Fanny!

Old Andrew smiled at his wife's expression. 'Wondering where Ernest is?' he asked.

Mrs Ledwhistle shook her head. 'No, I know where he is already. Rubin invited him for lunch.'

Charlotte put her head on one side. 'You know, Papa, Uncle Rubin has altered a great deal. Why, before 3 or 4 months ago he hardly ever came here, or invited us there.'

Old Andrew winked slyly at his wife. 'Yes,' he said slowly, 'Rubin's changed, but for the best. Have you finished your embroidery yet for your brother's wedding? You have not much time, you know.'

Charlotte sighed. 'It's very strange,' she said, 'but the threads seem to knot and break. Whatever I do, I doubt if Anna will ever use it.'

Mary Ledwhistle laughed in agreement. 'Come along, Fanny,' she called. 'Come and take your outdoor attire off.'

Fanny dutifully followed her mother out into the hall.

'Mary,' Old Andrew's voice floated up to them, 'don't forget that the Mansalls and Victor Radenstone and his son are coming tonight to dine.'

'Oh,' cried Mrs Ledwhistle incredulously, 'I'd quite forgotten. Where on earth did I put the key to the linen cupboard?'

Jane sat all through the afternoon at her beloved piano. Many a time Old Andrew would look in wonder at her, for the notes that she played seemed to hang clean in the air, till they dropped tinkling and sparkling into the mind.

'Father,' asked Jane suddenly, stopping her playing and laying her soft head on his knee. 'What do we say to poor Mr Straffordson?'

Old Andrew stroked her hair with gentle fingers as he puffed contentedly at his pipe. 'We just act as if nothing had happened,' he advised. 'You see, he is only young – little over 20 I should say – and like all young things he is very proud. Now do not worry your silky head, but play for me.'

As the dreamy melodies once more waved about his ears Old Andrew thought sagely, yes, like all young things, he is very proud. So's young Andromikey. I'm worried about him. He's so aloof, as if he resented any charity on our part. When he is 27, I shall most certainly give him his money. I warrant I'll have to convince him of its legality before he'll take it. He chuckled quietly, and Jane on her stool smiled.

Later that evening they all sat round the fire – Rubin, Radenstone and Old Andrew with glasses of good wine before them, and Robert and Ernest pulling rather self-consciously at their pipes. Robert was in a chair with a gay rug over his unsightly trunk. He was quite content with his lot. Later on, when he was stronger, he was to be fitted with two wooden legs. Mrs Mansall talked untiringly to her friend Mary Ledwhistle, while Jane sat quietly by her brother, her hands folded on her lap. Robert, whenever he looked at her, felt restful and tranquil. Once she looked at him, and found his eyes resting on her. She smiled, coloured and looked the other way. Radenstone kept close to him, for he did not wish ever to be away from his son again. Robert too liked him near, for Victor radiated protection and the love he craved.

Soon – ah, all too soon – the evening drew to its close, and the Radenstones and Mansalls bade them good-bye. Jane, as Robert bowed over her hands, felt more and more attracted to him. Then there was a slamming of doors, a crack of a whip, and he was gone.

CHAPTER 16

James Coney peered shortsightedly at the shop-window. He wondered if he could afford to buy that very important-looking hat. It would look so elegant, he mused. As he glanced up and down the street to see if anyone was watching him as he took out his wallet, he saw Fanny panting in his direction. He whistled softly, put his note-case hurriedly back, and bowed. Fanny was very taken aback when the very stranger who had been the central figure in her dreams for some time past accosted her. She blushed and gave a shy smile. James felt he had scored.

'Would you care to honour me by letting me walk a little way back with you?' he drawled.

'Well – I – er, that is –' gasped the flattered Fanny.

But her admirer had already taken her arm and was steering her across the street. 'You know, Miss, Miss –' Here James faltered affectedly.

'Ledwhistle,' interposed Fanny with more intelligence than was her wont.

'Miss Ledwhistle,' continued James, 'I couldn't get you out of my mind yesterday.'

Fanny felt as if she could cry, and nearly did when James added: 'I hope you don't think I am being a nuisance, but you see I got the instinctive feeling – I hope I do not presume – that you were drawn just the teeniest bit to me as well.' Here he cast a shy glance at Fanny, who stared at him stupidly, her mouth hanging open.

'Oh yes, yes indeed, Mr Coney,' she gasped. 'That is – oh dear, what have I said?'

'My dear Miss Ledwhistle,' cried James, 'let me say I much admire you.'

Fanny did not know what to say.

When she was bidding James Coney goodbye later on, she was both flustered and breathless. What would her mother say about her meeting a young man like that, and freely admitting her love for him? But Mrs Ledwhistle, when Fanny confusedly told her, just laughed and said it was about time one of her daughters got married.

That night Richard came to dine, and Old Andrew congratulated him on his successful venture. 'But of course, Martin,' Old Andrew told him, 'you must not repeat your action. It's too reckless, you know.'

Ernest spoke slowly, from his seat by the table. 'I don't agree, Father,' he said. 'You were very pleased when all this money came in now, were you not?'

'But Ernest,' choked his father. 'You can't put the same sums into unsteady gambles for the rest of your days. Why, it would mean ruin.'

His son waved his hand in an impatient gesture. 'But Papa, life is one gamble itself. Everyone takes risks. At your age, Father, there's nothing left for you but to take risks.'

Old Andrew shook his head heatedly. 'You're wrong, boy,' he stuttered. 'Where do you think the firm would be today if I had gambled in my time? No, no, it's too dangerous, too unsteady.'

He cleared his throat testily, and Ernest was wise enough to hold his silence.

Richard, however, was not to be subdued. 'Sir,' he said distinctly, 'does not this firm belong now to Ernest and me?'

Old Andrew could not but guess the intrusion behind this bald fact. He coloured, and Ernest sprang angrily to his feet.

'How dare you, Martin,' he thundered. 'I think you'd better go.'

'Now, now,' soothed Old Andrew. 'He's right, you know,

my boy – only my whole soul's wrapped up in the firm, and I can't quite realise I do not have a hand in its workings any longer.'

It was Richard's turn to colour. 'I'm sorry, Sir,' he said, quietly. 'You know best, but I do want to build up the name of the Ledwhistle and Andromikey.' And as he said this Richard felt more of a hypocrite than he should have done.

When the two young men had gone, Old Andrew sat awhile in his chair. Finally, he got up and crossed to the window. The larches surrounding the Moleson house swayed darkly, and all the street seemed shrouded in the dark and unending drift of sleep. The lamp-lighter had visited here long ago, and the yellow glow shone and swam in the gutter below. Up above, a crescent moon brightly rested among his blue-black train of clouds. A cruel wind was rising, and Old Andrew shivered slightly. Yes, he was getting old. His hand trembled as he turned away. Ah well, he couldn't complain. He'd lived his years, and if his maker saw fit to call him – why, he'd go willingly. He chuckled. He couldn't very well do anything else. He puffed at his pipe, and brought once more his diary out. He was glad the feud between him and Rubin had ended – better for all sides, he thought, as his pen scratched away. Ernest was to be married soon, and he and Mary were delighted. Anna was a good girl. Why, when Young Martin married he would give him his money and his blessing.

Old Andrew stopped writing and lifted his head. Martin . . . ah Martin, that impetuous young rascal, how his thoughts seemed to dwell continually on him. The boy was so proud and so distant. He never unbended. He'd seemed to keep a barrier between himself and them. Only with Ernest did he seem to relax. The sonorous notes of the old clock boomed out and he hurriedly finished his entry. It was a matter of seconds only before the candles were extinguished and the diary locked away.

CHAPTER 17

'Why hasn't Old Ledwhistle thrown Richard out of the firm yet?' worried Rupert Bigarstaff. 'That last venture must have lost them a small fortune. I wager Old Ledwhistle was pretty soured by it.'

'And rightly so,' said Gasper Liverwick. 'The young beggar narrowly missed bankrupting them.'

Rupert nodded. 'Hm,' he assented ungraciously, 'but it's a damned nuisance. We could use some money, Gasper, me lad.'

He got to his feet, shoved the table away from him and they walked out into the street. The pavements were thronged with people hurrying hither and thither. Gasper suddenly clutched Rupert's arm.

'Look,' he gasped. 'If it isn't young Master Francis himself.'

'Well, well now,' breathed Bigarstaff. 'Now isn't this going to be jolly! He's a proper young gent.'

Little Francis Ledwhistle at the age of nine was skipping gaily along the sidewalk clutching to himself a large ledger. His thick curls were free and his eyes were glowing like small boys' eyes will do when they are for the first time out in the great world of the city, on their own.

'Come, Gasper,' cried Bigarstaff in a pleasant voice, 'I'm quite sure our little friend would love us to keep an eye on him.'

Uneasily Liverwick followed, his ugly face in a worried frown.

'What's the game, Rupert?' he asked as they paced after young Francis.

'Really,' answered his crony, mockingly. 'You're very

crude. What possibly could be our game? Use your imagination,' he snapped curtly. 'Why on earth should the child be by himself in the city?'

The child passed down a dark alley and his hopping slowed into a subdued walk. For the first time he was a tiny bit frightened. It wasn't such fun after all slipping away from Fanny like that. He wondered tearfully why those two men were following him. He didn't like the way they gazed at him. Perhaps, perhaps . . . In a trice little Francis was running.

The footsteps behind him became quicker too, till Gasper and Bigarstaff were on his very heels. Francis felt his heart in his throat. Then it was in his mouth as the long arm of Rupert snaked out and held him by his collar. He stood there panting and gasping, his breath coming in great thudding bursts.

'Well,' said Bigarstaff, 'that's a nice thing to do, running from your friends, me little dear.'

He bent down swiftly and dived his hand into the boy's pocket.

'Huh,' said Gasper as a minute handkerchief was brought to light, finely edged with lace. 'Quite a toff, ain't we?' he murmured, as he sniffed daintily.

The two of them roared with laughter and Francis snivelled. Rupert dealt him a mild cuff on the ear and he stuffed a trinket into his trouser pocket.

Then everything happened at once. There was a sound of light shoes on the cobbles and the two rascals took to their heels. James Coney picked the child up and dabbed helpfully at the boy's stained cheeks with an equally stained piece of cloth. 'There, there, my little boyo,' he soothed. When Francis had calmed down somewhat he asked the child its name.

'My name,' said little Francis proudly, 'is Ledwhistle.'

'No, it can't be,' gasped his rescuer, frantically. 'Oh, this is fate.'

Francis found his hand seized in that of a large bony one, and found he was being trotted along at a great rate. His small legs went pattering after each other till, almost running, they reached his house.

'Oh, Master Francis,' squealed Connie, the parlour maid, 'how could you!'

They were ushered into the hall, and Francis was immediately enfolded to his mother's capacious bosom.

'Frankie, you wicked boy,' she sobbed and scolded.

James coughed.

'Good heavens,' cried Mrs Ledwhistle, 'is it — is it Mr Coney?'

'Yes, Ma'am,' replied that worthy modestly.

He was then swept into a large room, and here the family were assembled. Once more James was forgotten as in turn the returned one was petted and cooed over.

Then Andrew lurched to his feet. 'And to you, my dear young sir, I can but be ever indebted.'

He paused for words, and Francis began talking. 'But you don't know all, Papa,' he cried shrilly. 'Two wicked men accosted me and stole that lace handkerchief of mother's, beside that necklace I got when I was four.'

James waved his hand modestly. 'Oh, that was nothing, sonny,' he said wisely.

Old Andrew's eyes met those of his wife. They crinkled at the corners as he saw Fanny blushing a fearsome red. Charlotte bent suspiciously over her book.

Soon James was seated and accepted by all. His drawling voice, and blinking eyes, with his boyish hair on end, made him look rather pathetic. Fanny, as her eyes rested on his face, felt her heart give a silly leap.

In the fireside corner on the couch sat Anna. On her knee sat a little boy in petticoats, for two years Ernest and she had been happily married. But Old Andrew had aged. His hair was scantier than before, while the few locks were white and grizzled. His beard too was white, but here and there threaded a thick black hair. It was the firm that had aged him, for since Richard Soleway's unsuccessful investiture the business had dropped to its minimum.

'You will stay to lunch, won't you?' invited Mrs Ledwhistle.

'Oh well,' said James, '– that is, if everybody's willing.'

He looked pointedly at Fanny, whose plain face was quite intelligent with the love that glowed through her.

There were eager assents on all sides, and so James became a firm friend of the Ledwhistles.

CHAPTER 18

Phillip Hobart, Knight, sat ponderingly at his desk. His long fingers drummed in irritating rhythm on the polished surface. Before him sat Richard Soleway.

'Look here, young fellow,' he advised. 'Don't you think you'd better turn your hand to something you understand? The Exchange isn't a gambling den, Dick.'

'I know what I'm doing,' rapped Richard. 'I wish to invest £2,800 in cash, and £5,000 worth in bonds in the New Westworth Papers.'

'But it's the most surest thing that that will fall through,' gasped Hobart.

'I have the cash here in notes,' continued Richard. 'I wish you to manage it for me at once, understand?'

He left a scandalised but resigned Chairman.

CHAPTER 19

Jacob Steinhouse came into the outer office, in breathless haste.

'Martin,' he gasped, 'Master Martin, what does it mean?'

'What does what mean, Steinhouse,' asked Richard tersely.

He turned to Ernest, who was gazing open-mouthed at the paper the old man had thrust on his desk.

Martin leant over and took it from him quickly. His heart gave a great leap as he read:

Westworth Paper fails to sell. The well-known firm of lawyers, Ledwhistle and Andromikey, lose over £7,000.

He scanned the society gossip column and read:

For some time past it has been noticed that Young Andromikey has been making wild speculations. This, we have no doubt, will be his last venture.

Richard felt a wave of thankfulness sweep over him. He had accomplished his task: now he could go and lead his own life. The curse of Martin Andromikey had been fulfilled.

Ernest slumped forward. 'My God, Martin,' he screeched. 'You damn fool, you damn blasted fool!'

He got to his feet slobbering, while Old Jacob wrung his hands in agony. 'What will Old Mr Andrew say?' he moaned.

'It will break his heart. Oh, oh.' He sat down suddenly, and shakily mopped his brow.

Richard gave a weary smile. He got to his feet and swallowed.

Ernest grabbed his arm. 'No,' he cried shrilly. 'No, you're not going, you dirty crook. You'll get years for this.' He then lapsed into the boy he was again. 'Who's going to tell Father?' he groaned sickly. 'My God, who's going to tell him? He'll know now – and just think,' he said in a low voice. 'He's bound to see the papers.'

It was a rainy day in July, and the weather outside was roaring and whistling down the streets. Ernest looked out of the rain-blotted window and choked in a whisper: 'He's coming here!' He turned a white face to the group before him. 'We've got to stand by him,' he ordered tensely. He cast a withering glance at Richard. 'As for you,' he spat out. 'You mustn't leave till I tell you.'

There were footsteps on the stairs. Then the door was thrust open and Old Andrew came hurrying in.

'Papa,' cried Ernest.

The old man was in a dreadful state. His head was bare, and his white locks clung damply to his neck. He wore no coat or shoes, but was dressed in his house suit and thin slippers. His eyes were rolling wildly, and his mouth twitched uncontrollably. Andrew took no notice of his son but glanced past at Richard, who sat at his desk scrutinising him carefully. Martin had certainly got his craving, for Andrew Ledwhistle was indeed suffering. The old man lumbered forward and seized his arm in a weak grip.

'You, you swine,' he cried.

He started back, clutched his chest and swayed on his feet. Ernest sprang forward, and was just in time to catch him before he became unconscious.

CHAPTER 20

The doctor thrust his thumbs into the waistcoat pockets of
his suit. He moved backwards and forwards, first on toes,
then heels. The sun streamed through the window and
glided over the face of the man on the bed. Old Andrew
never moved. Only the bright look of burning intensity in
his eyes betrayed that he lived, and was human. Oh, how
that kindly face had altered in a night! The skin was a roll
of parchment, yellow and frayed. The mouth, devoid of
blood, hung open, and the hot tongue licked feverishly at
the cracked lips. He never moved, and the blankets lay
smooth as glass on his wasted body. The doctor's countenance was grave. He turned to Mary Ledwhistle, who knelt
by the bed.

'Can you procure a lawyer right away?' he said. 'I do
not think he will last the night.'

CHAPTER 21

It is night now, and the air is as rich and sparkling as the points of the many stars that twinkle in the velvet night. Round the bed kneel 7 people. Mrs Ledwhistle, her white cheeks sunken, clasps and unclasps the book in her hand. It is an old book, and was written when the world began. It has been shunned and sacrileged, loved and revered. It has been bound in silver and gold, cloth and paper, but the words inside hang clear and liquid like drops of blood of the one who died for us. Little Francis kneels beside his sisters, his little white face alone calm and serene. Death holds no terror for the very young, for they know not what it is. Ernest and Anna are together on their knees, while the figure on the bed speaks for the last time . . . in this world.

Old Andrew moves restlessly.

'Try hard, young Ernest,' he whispers. 'Try hard.'

He sinks back. There is a low moan from his wife.

'Andrew, Andrew.'

The name shivers in the air, and goes through the halls of memory, echoing hollowly. Let Richard Soleway hear that cry, and let him be haunted by it. 'Andrew, Andrew.' And Andrew Ledwhistle is dead.

CHAPTER 22

Rupert Bigarstaff rolled a wad of tobacco in his cheek, a habit he had gained from Gasper.

'It's no use,' he muttered. 'No use. It's true right enough.'

He watched the coffin lowered into the ground as the remains of Old Ledwhistle were put to rest. His eyes noted that Richard Soleway was not present.

It was a cold morning, yet early, and St Carthage's graveyard was in the open country. The sycamores waved softly, their maturing leaves tinged with a faint rusty gold. The scarlet poppies were waving in the tall grasses, and for once Bigarstaff felt at peace with other mortals. He thought that it would be nice to die in a place like this.

The tall-necked clergyman was plainly shivering. Silly devil, thought Bigarstaff, his blue eyes hard. He wanted to die when his body was tensed to the chill air, when the songs of the birds were clear and keen, when the blood was so red it hurt your flesh – not when the air was warm and sickly. He became aware that the last prayer had finished, and the mourners were alone. He'd wondered what they'd put on his headstone. One day he'd come back and see, but now, there was work to be done.

Meanwhile Richard was in his rooms. His head ached infernally, and his throat was dry. There was a knock at the door and a boy thrust his head round.

'Gent said as 'ow I was to give you this,' he said loudly. 'Name of Ledwhistle. He said you'd give me something no doubt.'

'Clear off,' cried Richard. 'Don't be a little liar.'

With a grin the boy went, and Richard was left alone.

He slowly opened the long buff-coloured envelope, and drew out the contents. He started and nearly let the paper slip through his fingers, as the meaning soaked into the wool of his muddled brain.

You were left at your grandfather's death the sum of £45,000, but on the condition that you would enter the firm and make good. Owing to the bankruptcy of the firm that money can never be paid to you, or never will, owing to the fact that you ruined the name of Ledwhistle and Andromikey that my grandfather and yours made and founded. I can assure you that all this is true.

Ernest Ledwhistle.

For hours Richard sat slumped in his chair, his mind a blank. Finally, he drew a large sheet of paper towards him and began to write. When he had finished he folded it in four and put it in another envelope. Then he began his small amount of packing. In a cloth bag he pushed a couple of shirts and necessities and was ready.

He paid a call to a small bank, and then went to the shipping office. Here he booked a passage for America. He did not know that Gasper Liverwick and Rupert Bigarstaff did the same thing . . . They were to cling to him for years to come.

CHAPTER 23

Robert Straffordson dragged himself wearily along the road, his wooden legs in monotonous rhythm clicking after him. His father, Radenstone, was in his house and Robert felt lost and tired. It was afternoon and warm. He wished he could do some work or try his hardest to be useful, but he was not strong enough yet to be this. In a fortnight's time he and his father were leaving for America, and this was what Straffordson was looking forward to.

He wondered as he walked along what Ernest Ledwhistle was going to do. He had met the boy many times and liked him. Mrs Ledwhistle was very poor now, and all the debts had not been paid. They were all too proud to accept aid or charity, and had been reduced to extenuating circumstances.

Straffordson wondered if he ought to go and see the family, when suddenly he caught sight of Fanny Ledwhistle and a young man he had come to know as James Coney. Fanny's hair hung in disordered array as usual, but the shapeless lips were parted a trifle and she gazed at James in a way that could not be mistaken.

Robert bowed as best he could, and the two smiled at him, while Coney bowed also.

'I hope your mother is in good health?' asked Robert.

Fanny sighed.

'Poor Mama is very dejected of late, for the house is to be sold, and we are to move into rooms. Mother is very much put about over good Jacob Steinhouse, for it was well known that Papa intended him to retire, and receive a considerable pension.' She sighed again as she continued. 'Martin Andromikey has not been seen of, and Jane says it is a good thing, for Ernest would surely set on him.'

James pressed her fingers in sympathy, which made that young lady conclude: 'Dear James has been so kind. Mama would have been quite lost without him, and as for me —'

She stopped, as if the very thought of such magnanimity was not to be dreamt of. Robert could not but repress a smile, for Fanny was so evidently adoring.

James said: 'Miss Ledwhistle was always a one for exaggeration.' This with a tender smile.

Fanny blushed and lowered her head modestly. Robert coughed, for laughter must surely be disguised.

'I hear,' said James pleasantly, 'that you are to leave for America soon, with your celebrated father.'

'Ah,' sighed he, 'America is a wonderful place. What part are you aiming to settle in?' (this was said with real interest).

Robert's reply was veiled. 'East,' he prevaricated. He did not want this boyish Coney to know where they were going. Radenstone and he wanted to leave behind all the old life and live together in Virginia.

He became aware that James was wishing him goodbye.

'We shall see you again before you go of course, Mr Straffordson,' simpered Fanny.

It was not long before they had disappeared out of sight and Robert was by himself again.

CHAPTER 24

Ernest waved his hand for the last time, and he and his sister moved away. On board the small sailing ship Radenstone turned to his son gladly.

'Last tie snapped, Rob,' he said quietly, 'and I for one feel better for it.'

In another part of the ship, leaning over the rough side, Richard Soleway watched England slip away on the horizon. He was not sorry. The land of his birth was nothing but a sordid incident, an incident which had cost an old man's life and his widow's happiness. He watched as the sullen green waters swirled gently against the sides, and heard behind him the shouts of the deck hands.

Down in the bowels of the same ship stood two men, Gasper and Rupert. They leant over the pens of some big brown cows and Rupert held his nose in the air pettishly.

'Devilishly airless hole,' he mumbled disdainfully.

Around them the livestock and cattle of the passengers were tethered. All were here, rending the air with their cries as the ship rolled under them. Gasper was silent. He could smell nothing, though the very air was foul. He slapped a big roan on its side, and laughed hoarsely as it quivered and flared its nostrils.

Bigarstaff retreated, and made for the passage. 'I'm going below,' he cried. 'Young Soleway isn't in the hold.'

Ah, miserable creatures of the hold! People who had not the room of their thin beasts! Men and women whose faces were glowing with anticipation of the land that awaited them! They huddled together in the narrow hold, and tried to quench their hunger by dreaming of the fruit and fish they honestly thought would be theirs. They did not look up as Rupert entered, but went on staring with unseeing eyes, while their children slept uneasily in their mothers' laps.

Bigarstaff sat down and noted that nearly all were Irish. Now revolution had overtaken their country, and they were glad to leave. Up above in their secluded cabin Straffordson and his father were, and Bigarstaff envied them their space, but not their privacy. Alone, one is left to one's thoughts, while when a group of people surround you and take your interest things are forgotten and submerged.

Richard Soleway found no truth in that statement. As when alone, so was he tormented when he was in a crowd, for they seemed to glare with accusing eyes into his past. He shook his head in frenzy and tried to stamp all memories out.

Richard became aware that someone was at his elbow, and found the midnight visitor that had come so long ago at his side. He started, but was not afraid.

'Trying to forget Master Dicky, Richard?' said Gasper in a low voice.

'For God's sake stop persecuting me,' cried his victim. 'Leave me.'

Gasper smiled and never moved. His bantering grin was in Richard's vision and it danced before his eyes. His willpower snapped and his fist swept out. Then the two were rolling on the deck blow for blow, curse for curse, oath for oath. There was a cry from a deckhand and Captain Trevelian came hurrying. He was a cruel man, immensely tall and powerful. He swung Richard to his feet and gave him a brutal cut on the temple. Without a groan, Soleway hit the deck with a creaking of boards. Gasper was done the same to, and as he hit the deck he could hear the coarse yells of the crew, as oblivion swept over him.

When Gasper Liverwick awoke it was with a heavy pain in his head and an ache in his shoulders. He tried to move to relieve himself, but in vain. There were heavy manacles on his feet, and a length of rope round his arms. This rope looped through chains on his wrists and connected to his feet. He was on his back and his head bumped mercilessly on the timbers. By his side lay Richard also in irons, but he was unconscious and lying on his face. Liverwick could not but wince as the boy's features cracked with even constancy on the floor. They were in comparative darkness, which was not surprising, there being no portholes. Gasper shrewdly guessed it was night-time, and turned quickly as Richard gave a groan. The boy was in agony, for he had cramp, owing to the fact that the rope from shoulders to feet was drawn taut, curving his back. Gasper moved his body with difficulty and inserted his feet below Richard's stomach. He gave a heave, and Richard was also on his back. This seemed to ease him, but as yet he could not speak.

After a while he whispered, 'What is your name?'

'Gasper,' replied Liverwick cheerfully. 'How d'you feel, Mr Dicky?'

Richard when he spoke again sounded stronger. 'My head throbs like an old clock, and my back hurts deucedly bad,' he replied.

There was silence for a space. Then Liverwick said: 'How long d'you suppose they'll keep us ironed, me lad?'

'A couple of days, no more,' answered his fellow captive with confidence.

'Well, you're wrong,' cried Gasper. 'We're here for the trip. 'Tain't the first time I've been like this. Oh no, oh no. 'Tain't the first time.'

He could feel the boy's reaction and said in a gruff voice, 'Cheer up, Laddie. I tell you I've been in this way before, and I'm here to tell the tale.'

There was no reply, for Richard did not trust himself to speak. Finally, he sank into a painful slumber.

Gasper brought his head up with a shout. He had been

awakened by the floor meeting his head with a thud, and he found himself rolling across the floor. In doing so he collided with Richard.

'Master Dick,' cried Liverwick loudly. 'Master Dick, what by all the saints is happening?'

He could hardly hear his own voice, for outside the wind was roaring and hissing, only equalled by the noise of the sea.

Richard came in contact with a bar of wood and clenched his hands. They were both in an intolerable position, for they were at the sea's mercy. Up above they could hear dimly the noises of the animals, and the shouts that came from the hold above them. Then Gasper gave a panic-stricken shriek as there was the sound of a pistol above.

'My God, Richard,' he yelled. 'They're shooting the beasts. We're sinking, we're sinking.'

His voice was partly lost, but the significance was there, and Richard Soleway paled. There was a sudden crack, a break. Then the ship lurched as the mainstay mast came crashing down. There were shouts on deck as every man struggled for a seat in the boats.

'Let us out,' screeched Gasper, 'you dirty cowards. Let us out, for God's sake. Let us out.'

His voice faded away and he choked.

There was a swelling sob from Richard. 'They can't leave us like rats,' he breathed. 'They can't. Help, help.' But his voice was only a pathetic whisper.

'Rupert, Rupert,' cried Gasper tearingly. 'Oh my God, let me out, let me out.' His last words hung in the air and shivered away. 'Oh God,' he groaned. 'Oh, oh aaa, ohm.'

Backwards and forwards they rolled, and they both tried frantically to release their bonds. There was a pain-laden scream from Richard as his back was nearly bent double by his struggles. His head came with a muffled thud on a metal case, and for the second time he was unconscious. When he stirred the boat was swaying gently.

'Gasper,' he said faintly.

Then came the reply: 'You're lucky, man. You slept through the storm. We are on some rocks, and if we don't get out of this soon it's be all up with us.'

Richard could hardly believe his ears. He began to struggle hard, but was bade be still by his 'friend'.

'Don't hurt yourself,' cried Liverwick. 'I'm lying on my face by a nail, and with luck it will fray this rope.'

'It will take hours,' said Richard in despair once more. 'The rope is thick and hard.'

'So's my faith,' came the answer, and Richard was silent.

And so, four hours later, Gasper broke the rope that kept his hands to his feet. He put his arms above his head and slowly got to his feet, only to collapse.

'Steady,' warned Richard. This time Gasper wormed his way along the floor and gripped the boy's bonds. It was a difficult job to untie the knots, for his hands were hand-cuffed together, but at last it was done, and they were both partly free.

'We can't walk,' cried Richard, 'for our feet are in chains, but we can hop.'

They felt in the dingy light for the door and put their shoulders to the wood. Many times they collapsed and lay prone, but they always tried again, and at last the lock burst and they stumbled over the threshold. The light streamed down to them and they were half blinded. Up the steps they painfully went, and saw the animals lying stiff and cold in their stalls.

At last they reached the deck, and Richard gave a great shout.

'Land,' he gasped. 'We're on a beach. We're saved. Land.'

He fell on his knees and Gasper gazed awkwardly at him.

'Oh dear God,' cried Richard joyfully. 'We thank Thee for deliverance. Amen.'

'Amen,' said Gasper gruffly and wiped his eyes.

CHAPTER 25

The beach was white and fine, and, as it stretched beneath some green and sparkling trees, turned a soft yellow. The sun shone on wild flowers and dense woods, while the water around, lapping on the shingle, was a clear and radiant green.

Gasper bit his lip at the scene.

Richard too was overcome, but finally he turned and said: 'Gasper, my friend, we must find some tools that will free us from these encumbrances.'

They hopped along, and by mid-day – or so they guessed it to be – they were unshackled and free. They ran shouting to the side of the wrecked boat and raced madly up the shingle. Richard threw himself down and drank and drank the cool water that was in abundance.

When they had drunk their fill they looked about them and measured up their surroundings. Before was a great mass of trees, and to the right were two big islands.

'Well, seeing as 'ow we're here,' said Gasper heartily, 'we might as well eat. Let's get back to the boat, for there's plenty of good meat.'

'Look,' cried Richard. 'First I will build a fire, while you bring a calf or pig.'

So Gasper made for the boat while Richard busied himself collecting wood.

Richard found his flint had gone, but on striking his ring against the heel of his shoe a flame was soon burning, and then a fire.

Gasper came back across the sand bearing on his shoulders a calf and holding under his arm a knife. Richard would have draped the calf over the fire, but Gasper stayed him, laughed his great rumbling laugh.

266

'First we must skin him,' he cried, and set about it.

When it had been cleaned, he laid it down and looked about him. On arriving on the island they had been amazed by the giant shells covering the ground. The smallest was the size of a tray. Gasper seized one in his arms and put two stones on either side of the fire. In these he placed the shell, the outside crust to the heat. In this way the calf was hung on a platter above the flames.

'If you put the meat on top of the fire,' shouted Gasper, 'you'll char it and put the fire out as well. Now those stones keep the shell from resting on the wood, and so the meat will be browned in no time.'

Richard did not know what to say. 'To be sure, Gasper, you're a treasure, and no mistake.'

The roasted beef was succulent and juicy, and both tucked in with a will. Then the fire was put out and they rolled into the shade of the trees to sleep. They slept till evening, and they found the air was chill.

'We must get some shot and ball from the ship,' advised Richard. 'There may be inhabitants, or wild animals. It's best to be prepared.'

Back to the boat they trudged and got some pistols.

'There is enough wood to make a small boat,' said Gasper.

They collected blankets and more food and found to their amazement that a cow was lustily bellowing. They hurriedly untethered her and watched her go lumberingly up the beach. Then they gathered knives, a cask of butter, salt and a barrel of ale – this Richard was loath to take, knowing what mischief it could do, but Gasper was equally loath to leave it behind – and a saw. A saw, as Gasper pointed out, was very important.

With these they staggered up the sand and set them down. A cool wind was blowing from the sea, and neither felt disposed to sleep. So they each armed themselves with a gun and set off. Judging by the height and colour of the sun, Gasper guessed the time to be about 9, and there hung over the island that refreshing keenness that belongs to night.

They plunged through the wood and gazed about them, at the beauteous flowers and vines. Little streams gushed by them, and brightly feathered birds flew chatteringly by. They were very wild and scared, and that made the two doubly sure the island was uninhabited. At the other side of the wood came the sea again and, branching to their right, they could see nestling in the translucent waters the other two islands. They came to the shore and, being tired, sat for a long while on a square piece of land that later became known as the Rum Cove. It grew dark but still they sat on, and a queer friendship sprang up between the two men.

Suddenly Richard gave a shout. 'Look,' he yelled, 'the sea's parting and there's a strip of land from this isle to the next.'

Richard was all for journeying across that night, but Gasper was older and wiser and would not hear of it.

That night they slept by the east shore, and for once Richard forgot his misery and was happy.

CHAPTER 26

When he awoke, the sun was very high, and he heard the clear notes of a bird by his head. Looking up, he saw a bright blue head, and a green body. Sticking up from his head was a brilliant tuft of feathers. His little yellow eyes glittered, and his throat visibly swelled as the lonely notes rang out.

Richard propped himself on one elbow and gave a sigh of contentment. Gasper was nowhere in sight as he scrabbled hastily to his feet. Through the trees he soon came and he carried a large shell. As he hailed Richard, the boy saw it was full of milk, and guessed the cow had supplied it.

'Dick,' cried Gasper, 'will you go and gather some fruit. There's plenty if you look.'

Richard did look and came back laden with some green kind of apples and also some very small potatoes or taros. These were cooked as before, and when they tried the apples they proved very sweet and nourishing.

After this repast they hurried to the NE of the island to Rum Cove. But they could not find that strip of sand and Gasper Liverwick reasoned that the tides were irregular.

'It will probably be uncovered tonight,' he supplied.

'When can we get out of here?' asked Richard as they sat down. 'We can't stay here for the rest of our lives.'

'I wonder what happened to the captain and the crew?' said the other. 'That crew, that captain — if this were England they'd be put in jail for what they did. We could build a boat, Dick, but we have no compass and do not know where we are. We can only hope a ship will pass by.'

'What do you think our chances are?' was Richard's next question.

Gasper did not reply at once. Instead he gazed far out at sea, and his whiskers fluffed dreamily.

'I don't know,' he said at length. 'I don't know.'

Then he got to his feet and stretched himself. 'Stir yourself, Dick. We must see what shape the old ship's in. We could make her seaworthy in a couple of months, if there be nothing really amiss.'

The boat lay on her side, in the fine sand, her deck strewn with wreckage, her bottom partly stove in. The two went below into the cabin of Radenstone and his son and searched around for some clue as to who had occupied it. In one of the drawers by the ruined bunk a pistol was brought to light, a bible such as mariners carry, and a dog-eared book. Richard opened this at once, while beneath him, Gasper Liverwick busied himself with the dead animals.

As he turned the pages a scrap of paper fluttered out, and quickly he bent to pick it up. It was a picture, and Richard felt a queer intake of breath go through his chest as he saw the figure of a man on a cross. Below, there were some words in French. He deciphered with difficulty: 'Father, forgive them, for they know not what they do.' He put it down swiftly and turned away. He swallowed, turned back and put the paper inside the Bible.

Then he sat down and opened the other book once more. The second page was blank except for a small square in the top right-hand corner and Richard frowned as he read: 'Solomon Pertwee, Yankskee Villa, Lower Yangtsee, China.' He turned over rapidly and found that the middle pages contained cuttings. The writing was not English, but plainly Chinese characters. Richard's brow wrinkled as he saw written in the margin in faded writing: 'Map on back of Crucifiction.' He grew interested and fumbled eagerly for the picture he had pushed into the Bible. Turning it over he saw the map.

'Gasper,' he shouted, 'Gasper, quick, quick!'

He brought his foot down on the wood and his very skin seemed to tremble with excitement.

Gasper burst through the door.

Before he could speak, Richard had thrust the map before his eyes. 'Don't you see?' he cried. 'It's the island, this island! There's the cove where the strip of land appeared, and there's the other islands to the North East.'

His friend peered at it unbelievingly.

'Where did you get it?' he asked incredulously.

'In this cabin,' Richard cried. 'Gasper, what could it mean?'

'See if there's a name in that Bible,' Gasper advised. But before his friend could do this, he had picked it up.

'Quick,' he cried. 'What does it say?'

'*Victor Radenstone 1826*. Why,' cried Richard, 'I've met this man. He was in China through the Opium War. What is the connection though between him and Solomon Pertwee?' He chaffed irritably. 'If only I could understand Chinese.'

'Isn't there any English in that diary?' cried Gasper in a great state.

'There is not,' was the answer. 'But look, there are some arrows between the second and third island.'

'There should be arrows from this island to the next,' cried Gasper, 'but not from the second to the third. Unless of course there's another sea-causeway. We'll soon know anyhow, for we'll cross that strip tonight if it appears.'

They waited in a fever of impatience till sundown and then made their way to the East side of the island. But the sea stretched away to the other two islands in an unbroken carpet.

At Gasper's suggestion they waited till the moon arose, and finally, when the first star had climbed to its appointed place, the stretch was parted and the firm ground once more was there. In silence the two men walked over, and placed their feet on the second island. This was the same as its brother, but very much smaller. As they neared the middle, the trees grew thicker and then ended suddenly. The moon shone on a piece of grass-waste and they did not halt but strode on. There was a sudden scream from Richard, and Gasper was in time to see him sinking into the ground.

'Marsh,' he groaned, then raced to one side.

With much difficulty a very shaken Richard was hauled out of the treacherous mud.

'It didn't look dangerous,' protested Richard as, coated with green slime, he followed Gasper.

They skirted the marsh and came to the end once more. But no strip of land confronted them, so they moved along to the North. After walking for a short space they came to a steep hill. On climbing it, they beheld the sea, and here they saw another causeway.

'W—ell.' Hesitatingly Gasper Liverwick looked across to the third island. The moon had gone behind a bank of clouds, and the island looked grey and sharp.

'Come on,' cried Richard. 'Let's cross at once.'

Gasper Liverwick followed reluctantly.

CHAPTER 27

Robert Straffordson lay in the bottom of the small boat, his useless legs flat out before him. Beside him sat his father, while, his hawk-like face set in a black scowl, Captain Trevelian crouched in the stern. Five members of the rough crew were rowing strongly, and over to their right the second boat could be seen. Robert wore a white-set expression, and his father was the same. Now and again the two cast contemptuous glances at the rascally captain. Trevelian was aware of these looks and inwardly he cursed savagely. Doubtless those men he had locked in the hold had drowned, but father and son were safe, weren't they? Blast them. What did they think he was, a cushy owner of a luxury ship? He was responsible for his boat, and dammit but he'd get it when they reached land again – if we ever do, he thought, grimly gazing at the bleak outline of the unknown coast they were drawing nigh to. He shivered a little as he thought of the two poor devils locked behind in the hold. He huffed his shoulders. It wasn't the first time men had disappeared at sea. He wasn't caring, or was he?

They passed a finger of rocky land, and drew into a small bay. Stiffly Trevelian climbed onto the shingle and issued his orders. Two more boatfuls of men rowed in, and they moved off in a solid body inland. Rupert Bigarstaff found himself marching by Radenstone and son. He looked upward at the heavens and thought 'Old Gasper's getting his due, Lord.' He chuckled, as Robert limped along beside him, his wooden peg stumps sinking into the white sand.

Trevelian called a halt shortly, and they made camp for the night. Once one of the deck hands tenderly enquired about food, but no one seemed disposed to wander about this grim, rocky little island. So, rolled on the sparse ground, they slept till morning.

When light invaded their slumber, Robert woke to see a barren rocky land about him. Unlike its brothers, this island was not covered in tall trees and vegetation. He saw Trevelian standing with a knot of his crew, talking and deliberating. Rupert Bigarstaff was not with them, but was sitting on a boulder staring with a fiendish grin on his face at the group.

His father was nowhere in sight and he struggled to get to his feet. Bigarstaff strolled over to him and stretched forth his hands, and with hesitation Robert took them. When he was half on his feet, Rupert let go suddenly and Robert fell sharply, to lie helplessly on his back. With a laugh Bigarstaff walked back to his old seat and seemed to forget everything immediately.

Foolishly, Robert scrambled gamely to his feet and walked away. He cursed himself for his disability, as he shambled on, and not for the first time fell to thinking on Jane Ledwhistle. Then he saw his father and he was carrying a flask of clear water and a bunch of carrots.

'Good heavens,' cried Robert. 'Where on earth did you get those vegetables, Father?'

Radenstone smiled. 'Over in a sandy patch in the North side,' he provided. 'You know, Rob, I can't help thinking that someone was wrecked on this island like we are. Otherwise how are these –' pointing to the large carrots, '– to be explained?'

'Well,' answered Robert, his eyes lighting, 'whoever planted them is not here now. That means there's hope for us.'

They had by this time reached a small cave and, sitting down, began their meal. Flat yet sharp land sloped before them to the sea, and Victor remarked thoughtfully, 'You know, Rob, I have a feeling that I know this island, or at least by sight.'

His son gaped stupidly. 'What?'

'In China, some years ago,' said Radenstone, 'I met a man named Pertwee, Solomon Pertwee.'

Robert listened with interest.

'You see,' continued his father, 'being a missionary I met all sorts of people, and it was at a local function of other men in the same calling as myself that I met this man. He was small, very bald, and he wore no wig of any sort. I became very friendly with him, and he with me. During our friendship he told me of his life, and when he died he left me a small map of a group of islands. He said that on the third island to the extreme north he made a valuable oil discovery. His greatest ambition, he said, was to return to the island and stake his claim, thereby giving him the money which would bring relief to the people he devoted himself to. He said he wished me one day to journey there in his place. Ah, he was a good man —' this with a wistful note creeping into his voice.

'But Father,' interposed Robert excitedly, 'if this is the island, where is the oil? Have you the map?'

'Steady on, my boy.' But Radenstone himself found he was being carried away. 'Unfortunately it was in my cabin when we took to the boats,' he cried, and his voice sank to a mere whisper. 'It's gone below with those other two poor devils.'

Before they could say more there was a sound of lusty bellowing, and turning they faced Trevelian and his crew. Of Bigarstaff there was no sign.

The captain strode up with a bloated and annoyed countenance, and cried angrily enough, 'Look here, Mr Radenstone, Sir, you can't be going and slipping away like this. Mebbe you're a gentleman of quality and all, but on an island, God knows where, we're all alike, and must act as such. Now see this, Mr Radenstone, I'm the captain, and you takes orders from me along with the rest o' them.'

He rounded this off with such a superior and brutal air that Radenstone flushed and could barely suppress striking the man.

Robert looked shrewdly at the bully seaman. He wondered just how much had been overheard. He looked past at the crew, and at one man in particular. He was an ordinary deckhand, an old man with clouded eyes, and crinkled lips. His round arms were bare to the elbow, a ruddy brown and freckled all over. The rough shirt displayed a broad expanse of chest, deep and muscular and covered in fine hair. There was a look of disdain on his face as he looked at his captain. With a final sneer on his countenance Trevelian turned. His crew followed him, but the sailor made no effort to move.

'Mr Radenstone, sir,' he said hoarsely, and he spoke with a rich Scottish accent.

Robert waited expectantly and he was not disappointed.

'I'm very much afraid that Trevelian plans to do you harm, sir,' said the deckhand.

Radenstone paled.

'I feared as much,' he answered. 'What is your name?'

'John Pearson, Sir.'

'Well, Mr Pearson, would you be so good as to tell me and my son what you know, for I do not think you also wish us ill.'

'Indeed I do not,' protested John Pearson, his honest face worried. 'You see, we were all listening when you were telling young Mr Radenstone about the map and the oil. Captain Trevelian plans to get your map and find the oil for himself and he's promised the lads a share if we help him.'

'But I haven't –'

Before he could continue, Robert cut into his father's sentence. 'He won't get it in a hurry, I can assure you, John Pearson. Father will keep a good hold on it. But how do they plan to get it?'

Pearson shrugged his shoulders and under his tan he whitened. 'I wouldna like to say, but he'll stick at nothing.'

There was a sudden roar from the other direction.

'Captain wants me, no doubt,' he said.

Father and son watched him walk briskly away.

'Why did you not want him to know about the map?' asked Radenstone, when the burly form was lost from sight.

'Listen, Papa,' Robert said. 'If they think we have the map they won't start pumping for the oil just yet. We can stave them off for the time being with words, and also begin looking for the stuff ourselves. Look, Father, you've got to use your memory. What spot was the oil marked at?'

'But Robert,' gasped Radenstone. 'Don't you see what will happen to us? Even if we did strike the oil, how could we get off the island? We've no ship, we don't know even where we are, and we're hopelessly outnumbered.'

'Think, Papa, think,' urged Robert. 'Where did the oil mark come on the island? You've got to think. We must find the oil before them. They'll want to get off the island as much as we, so they'll make provisions. Now think. Think.'

CHAPTER 28

Radenstone looked anxiously at Robert Straffordson.

'Robert,' he said in a whisper, 'I don't like the look of it at all. I don't like it at all.'

Captain Trevelian and his roughened crew were seated on one side of a roaring fire. The faces glowed blackly and the shadows flickered and leapt on their countenances. They muttered and talked to each other. Rupert Bigarstaff looked on, a queer smile on his fiendish face, and Straffordson and Radenstone felt very uneasy. They had been on the island two days and a night and the men had grown increasingly restless as the hours had passed.

Suddenly there was a fierce shout from a look-out, and a sound of shouts. Trevelian sprang to his feet and looked wildly round, brandishing his sword. Through the darkness and into the firelight blundered two men in the grip of three stalwart deckhands.

'Gasper, my lad,' said Rupert softly, without the slightest surprise in his voice.

'Martin Andromikey,' gasped Radenstone.

'God in Heaven,' swore Trevelian with an oath. 'You?'

Gasper looked round and his eyes fell on Rupert Bigarstaff. Something pulled at his mouth, and it twitched uncontrollably. His head seemed to jerk back on his spine, and he shuddered as he caught the smouldering carnal green light in those eyes.

Richard Soleway switched himself forward and stuck his head out. 'You devil,' he hissed, 'you devil.'

Trevelian fell back a pace. He flourished his sword and began his blustering. The three stalwarts gripped Richard's arms and twisted them behind his back brutally.

Richard did not wince, though his eyes grew pinched. 'You devilish swine,' he said between clenched teeth.

This time he had cause to scream, and fell prostrate.

Straffordson stumbled forward. 'Leave him alone,' he shouted.

At that moment of tenseness anything could have happened. Then Rupert Bigarstaff the orator stepped forward and nothing did.

'Now, now,' he said, his voice a sea of velvet, 'don't let's be hasty.'

On and on he droned, and soon everyone was sullenly quiet. For the life of them they could not think how this small man had the power to rule over their wills.

When he had finished, Rupert Bigarstaff strolled away, and watched the great black clouds swirl above him. Radenstone pressed Richard's arm eagerly, and tried to forget that this one boy had been the cause of Old Andrew Ledwhistle's death.

'How on earth,' he cried, 'did you cross to here?'

Gasper pulled a bedraggled paper from his pocket. ''Ere's how we got across,' he said. 'We found this map in your cabin, Sir.' Robert staggered inwardly. Too late. There was a savage cry from Trevelian and the crew as they fell onto them, with guttural oaths.

Desperately they fought, but to no avail. Ropes were knotted round them, and they lay helpless on the ground, while Captain Trevelian grasped the chart with trembling fingers.

'Ah,' he cried, 'at last. We must begin work at once. We will cross to the other islands, and see if there are any materials for making picks and swords.'

Trevelian led his men over the causeways, and finally landed on the first isle.

Here in due course the old ship was sighted.

'We must repair her at once,' cried Trevelian. 'Now make yourselves useful.'

So in the light of the moon they began their task.

By dawn the animals were all out of the ship, and rope, pistols and the like had been carefully sorted. The Captain straightened his back thankfully.

'We can go back now,' he said. 'Those four will be getting restless.'

Talking and laughing, he led the men over the land. But the sea was not obligingly parted as before.

'By Heaven,' thundered Trevelian, 'we're trapped.' He grew steadier. 'It must be the tides,' he said wildly. 'You, Carson, stand post, and call us if the strip appears.'

Moodily they were marched back, and the unrelenting Captain kept them hard at it all day. A young bullock was roasted and torn asunder in greedy haste.

'By heck,' ejaculated Trevelian, 'but these dead animals are useful. But we must salt them, for already the flesh is rotting.'

'It's no wonder, is it, lads,' cried one Timothy Birney, the thin first mate, 'that those two dogs didn't go hungry.'

'Look here, Captain,' said another. 'How are we to know the oil be there?'

'We won't, till we've dug up every bit of the island,' answered Trevelian curtly. 'And look here, me lads. If you'll stick by me, I'll stand by you.'

'Aye, we will, Cappen, we will,' assented his crew.

Aye, poor devils, they can hardly refuse.

'When do you think the boat'll be fit for the sea, me lads?' asked Trevelian shortly.

He turned round and looked at the tossed black-timbered hulk.

'I shouldn't be surprised if we could have it ready in little over a week,' said the second mate. 'There's lots of new boards needed, and a mast, as well as a sail. Reckon her stern be stove in, but there's plenty of timber about, so it can't be such a job.'

'What about the money from the oil, Cappen?'

'What about that, eh?' put in another, his eyes glittering. 'You're sure you'll go halves with us?'

'Sure. You heard me give me word before,' thundered Trevelian. 'Now be content, and stir yourselves there. Come on. There's work to be done.'

CHAPTER 29

It is a fortnight later. In a rudely constructed hut lie four men – our four unfortunates.

The air was very close and hot, and not a breath of wind stirred. Overhead black clouds were gathering, and all was still and hushed, as if waiting for something.

'If only they'd make their move,' cried Richard at last, his brow furrowed with the heat.

The others made no reply but sat moodily brooding over their captivity. There was rustling outside and Johnny Pearson crept in. The others started hopefully.

'Now listen carefully,' cried the deckhand. 'The oil has been struck down to the south of the island. The boat's finished, and they intend to leave tonight.'

'But what about us?' gasped Radenstone weakly.

'You are to be disposed of,' was the grim answer. 'But listen. When it is dark I will come and let you loose. No more canna do. You must board the ship if you can without their knowledge.'

'But where is the boat?' hissed Gasper. 'Tell us that, John Pearson.'

'It's moored in a bay on the southern coast on the first island. They reckon it'll be safer to start from there, for the rocks round here are pretty treacherous. But there's one thing – once I cut you free, you're on your own. It's more than I can risk to aid you farther.'

'Thank you, thank you,' cried Radenstone. 'I promise that if we get to England safely, you'll benefit by it.'

'I dinna want no riches,' was the rough answer. 'All I want is my neck. Ye understand.' He cast a scared glance behind him, and the next moment had gone.

'Do you think we'll manage it,' asked Robert eagerly. 'How can we get food?'

Thus they talked in excited whispers, and mostly about their chances and about the oil. Darkness increased and the four could hear the shouts of the captain and his crew on the shore. Through the gloom crept Pearson. In his hand he clasped a large knife, and it was the work of a moment for the ropes to be sliced.

As he cut, he whispered, 'I was sent to kill you. If Trevelian finds you on board, your throats and mine will surely be slit. For God's sake, be careful.'

Then, hurrying away, he left them to themselves.

'Follow me,' cried Richard, as he led the way. The white moon sailed supreme, and caught a bright metallic glitter in the water. The sea lay dangerously passive and gave hardly a ripple as they crept over the rocky ground.

They came to the causeway and padded over. Suddenly, a sound of curses broke the stillness, and looking back they glimpsed black silhouettes leaping over the beach. With dismay they began to run, but Robert Straffordson was a great handicap. Before they reached the other side of the sandy strip the figures were some 200 yards behind them. Panting, Gasper reached the side strip and helped the stumbling Robert. Over the causeway came the crew, led by Trevelian. Richard, grunting, his breath coming in great tearing gasps, raced along. The sharp thuds that came from his feet landing on the hard grass of the second island went in rhythm with the beats of his heart, which seemed to be swimming in a sea of red heat. There were more shouts, that rang out very clear in the tropical night, and their pursuers were very close.

'The bog,' screamed Gasper. 'Let them outrun you.'

For a split-second Richard just let his legs carry him. Then he realised what was meant by that statement. Catching the hobbling Robert and his father by the shoulders, he jerked to a stop. Past them went Trevelian and his men. Into that luscious green they went. Trevelian's guttural bass rose to a gurgling treble as he sank to his knees. Struggling, he began to scream. By his side fought John Pearson. With a savage shriek Trevelian brought his knife up and stabbed it into the breast of the deckhand. Richard felt his stomach lurch as the moon shone on the rich red blood that flowed like wine from the gash. With one last agonised curse, the rascally captain sank from sight. Richard had the impression of a quiet bubbling stretch of mud. Then he was running again. Behind four men strode, the only remnants of the crew to escape such a terrifying end. Through the trees the chase went on. Down a hill and over the second causeway. Far behind came the oaths of their pursuers.

'Look,' gasped Radenstone. 'The gap's closing. The tide's moving over it. Hurry, run.'

It was true. With desperate speed, their legs moving like pistons, they flew along. A 100 yards or so from the causeway came the last four of the crew. Then they were over, and the sea lay in a sheet over the lane of sand.

'We're safe,' screamed Robert.

'We've got to keep on running,' panted Gasper. 'Those sailors can swim. Look, the boat.'

Moored to a rocky cleft lay the ship.

'There's a wind coming,' cried Radenstone. 'Oh thank God, thank God.'

With fumbling fingers Gasper Liverwick untied the rope, while Richard and Radenstone, helped by Robert, hauled up the sail. A queer sail it was too – a sheet of animal hide – but as the first puff of wind caught it she billowed and the ship was putting out.

At the wheel Gasper sank his head on his arms. 'Oh Jesus,' he moaned. 'Thanks be.' He thought of the eyes of Rupert Bigarstaff and gave thanks again.

The dangerous calm of the hour before had justified its warning. Irritable flicks of wave stung the ship's sides, and a few spots of rain began to fall. From the shore came great shouts.

'Never mind them,' yelled Robert. 'There's plenty of food for them, so they shan't starve.'

'What a night, Andromikey,' gasped Radenstone. 'Poor Pearson, poor Pearson.'

'There's a storm arising,' shouted Gasper. 'Slacken the main sail.'

This was duly done, and it was just in time, for a great gust of wind struck the ship and sent her prancing through the waves. Drenched to the skin, their hearts alight with hope, they waited for the morn.

CHAPTER 30

For three days and nights the storm raged, but on the fourth morning they awoke from their stupor to calm skies and unruffled waters. Robert Straffordson rubbed his eyes hard, and moved his wooden pegs. On the horizon he glimpsed a fine sailing ship, and he let out a hoarse cry.

'A ship,' he cried. 'Father, Gasper, look, look – a ship!'

Stumbling up, he raced to Liverwick, who lay against the boat's side, straining his eyes.

'You're right, lad,' he said huskily. 'A French craft, by the look of things.'

By now Richard Soleway and Radenstone had joined them.

'Raise a flag or sign,' cried the frenzied Robert. 'They must see us.'

'They will. Never fear,' cried Radenstone. 'They'll draw near in an hour or two's time, see if they don't.'

Shortly after 10, or so they judged it to be, they were within earshot of the French ship. A thin boy in a ragged shirt stood by the bows.

'English,' he called, cupping his hands together.

The sound had no time to fade, before Gasper yelled, 'Yes, can you take us on board? Our craft's in bad trim.'

The boy turned to the cluster of sailors on board, and a peak-capped man who was evidently the captain.

There was a consultation which took so long that Richard yelled out, 'Where are we?'

'About 180 miles from Cape Verdi Islands,' answered the boy.

The captain raised his voice. 'Come across,' he said with difficulty. 'My ship will come by yours. Draw in.'

They did, and the slight handsome captain boarded their boat. They made a queer group of men. Robert, a rent in his trouser leg showing a stretch of wood; Gasper, his rascally face partly hid by a three-weeks growth of beard; Radenstone, his big brown hands twitching; and Richard, wearing a sullen dogged expression, because for the first time in a fortnight the memory of Andrew Ledwhistle had again risen in his mind.

'Tous Anglais?' asked the Frenchman, and they nodded, or Richard did.

'War has been declared between the Russians and our people and yours,' said the captain.

Radenstone clasped the hand-rail. The rest said nothing. The Crimean War had begun. Their men would fight the stocky, solid, dissipated Russians: the cold, stout foreigners against the awkward bull-complexioned Britishers.

The handsome captain looked at them curiously and shrugged his shoulders affectedly.

''Tis très sad,' he murmured. He swept a pair of coal-black eyes over them. 'You are in need of food,' he said softly. 'Yes?'

They nodded dumbly.

'One of my men shall stay here in charge.' He lapsed into French and called something out.

Stiffly the four climbed to the other boat and watched three slim sailors man their own. They were led below and food was set before them. The white-faced boy sat with them. They learnt that his name was Jim Racliff.

'I went to sea when I was 15,' he told them. 'Captain is a good man and kind.'

They in their turn told them their story, and summoned the French captain. The map was brought out and the captain grew greatly excited.

'A find indeed,' he stuttered. 'Good sirs, permit.' He turned to Jim and spoke hurriedly. 'The captain begs that he should take you back to England and set out with an expedition to stake the oil,' interpreted Jim slowly.

CHAPTER 31

It is the year 1857 in the month of January.

There was in the room of a certain building down Pentworth Street a great bustling and removing. Hammers hammered, screws screwed, nails nailed and the like, as well as a hundred other such things. Richard Soleway stood by the door, sleeves rolled up and his hair on end. With him stood Gasper Liverwick. If Old Andrew had been alive, his diary would have been well-stocked. Three years ago the Crimean War had begun. The papers had been full of Palmerston, a plain woman called Nightingale or some such name, Sidney Herbert and many more. Two years ago Victor Radenstone and Robert Straffordson had gone to live on the New Era Isle. Less than a year ago the French Captain Defause and Liverwick and Soleway had located the oil, and claims had been staked. Radenstone had divided the oil between Defause, Gasper and Soleway. He had himself given a sum of money to the Chinese Missionary Society, and Richard was now a very rich man.

Gasper turned to his friend. 'What name shall we put on the door, Dick?'

'No name whatever as yet,' answered Richard. 'In another ten years or so I may put something up.' He took his coat off his peg and struggled into it. 'Yes,' he said softly. 'Maybe I will in ten years or so.'

CHAPTER 32

Phillip Hobart turned round to his friend Henry Cordane and said reflectively: 'That unnamed firm in Pentworth Street is doing damned well. They handled Crewell Newbolt's case last week.'

Cordane shrugged his slim shoulders. 'Really?' he yawned. 'I say, old chappie, your date's wrong. It's June 11th 1862 not July 7th.'

The firm of Gladridges and Wilkinson held a board meeting in the year 1879. 'We are met,' said the Chairman, 'to decide what we are to do in this great crisis. What can we do to keep our name? The Pentworth lawyers must be equalled.'

CHAPTER 33

Richard Soleway pushed a greying lock of hair back from off his forehead. He looked his 55 years, and the old man by his side shook his head.

'You need a holiday, Dick.'

Old Gasper Liverwick sounded concerned. He was 72, with a head of black hair not lightened by even a rumour of whiteness. The hands of the one-time sea-dog were traced with heavy purple veins, but they did not shake.

Richard leaned back in his chair and looked around him. 'Yes,' he said. 'And I'm going to have it. In a month's time we can leave this place and settle down far away.'

'You mean the business is all ready for Ernest Ledwhistle and his son?' asked Gasper heavily. He knew he did not need an answer. The last 30 years had been spent in hard brain-work with hardly a break. It had all been done for Ernest Ledwhistle and his son James, and now the task had been accomplished and they could rest.

Ernest sat in an office too that afternoon, but he was sick at heart. He had for 11 years sat at this high desk totting up figures. His mother was still alive, a frail voluptuous senile old hag of nearly 80. The years and the poverty had not gone well with her. She would at this moment be with Anna in their poky little parlour, for she lived with them now. His son James would not be at home. He would be at least growing strong and healthy in Virginia along with Charles Coney, his sister's boy. His memory drifted back to the days when Francis had been but seven and James barely two. James Coney had come in and Old Andrew had thanked him profusely. He remembered with a sudden smile how Fanny had blushed and how Charlotte had

stuffed her sampler into her mouth. '30 years ago,' he
sighed. '30 years ago −' his face darkened − 30 years ago
Martin Andromikey had killed his father. He had brought
shame and suffering to his poor old mother, and caused her
mentality. But for Martin Andromikey, Francis would not
be an incurable drunkard. But for Martin Andromikey −

His hands fell forward onto the desk and he groaned
hopelessly. 30 years ago all his castles had been brought
crashing to the ground, by that same Martin Andromikey.
'And 30 years from now,' he whispered, 'please God I shall
be dead.' And Jane and Francis, Charlotte and James,
what were they going to be? 'Oh God,' he muttered. 'Oh
God.'

CHAPTER 34

London
October 18th

Dear James,
This letter will be a great surprise to you no doubt but a pleasant surprise. 3 weeks ago I was handed the Pentworth firm. The mysterious owners disappeared leaving a document that entitled me to the business. Come home at once, son, for I wish to set up. Charles is needed too. Your mother has written to your aunt. Will expect you as soon as possible.

                                        Yours affectionately, Father.

This extraordinary letter James Ledwhistle read out to his cousin Charles.

'What on earth do you make of that?' gasped he in amazement. 'It's incoherent. Come home at once.'

Charles broke out in a delighted laugh. 'Think of it, Jim,' he cried. 'Just think of it. I can leave Father's shop and join forces with you, as Uncle suggests. Come, I want to talk to Mama.'

He led the way out of the room and they found Fanny seated on a couch sorting out some bills. But can this be the perspiring Fanny Ledwhistle of old? Where is the flustered stoutness, the foolish gaze? Certainly not in this competent matronly woman with the grey hair.

Her son waved the letter in front of her and sat down beside her.

'Mother,' he cried. 'Mother, is it true? Am I to go to England with James? Tell me, am I?'

The busy figure said primly, 'Yes, Charles, you are. I

should hardly have expected you to show joy at leaving your home.'

Before her son could reply, James Coney came into the room.

'So you know about it at last, do you, lads?' he said.

James had not altered. The grey hair hung jaggedly over his eyes and his long wrists shunned his coat sleeves.

'Uncle James,' asked young Ledwhistle perplexedly. 'What does it all mean? Has Father been left this − this Pentworth firm? And if he has, why? What does anyone know about Papa, that they should let him inherit this business? He's only a clerk.'

'It's quite true though, boy,' replied Coney. 'From what I can gather from your father's somewhat incoherent and muddled letter, these lawyers have totally disappeared leaving only this deed proclaiming a transfer of ownership.'

He turned to Charles and said somewhat drily: 'It's your chance to get out of the shop and incidentally your social rut.'

Fanny's lips tightened. If she had been a coquette, with perhaps some reason for being one, she would have tossed her head. James Coney's humour never failed to shock her, though her very being sometimes struggled to enjoy it.

Charles was silent. Inwardly he was transported with joy. His father, he knew, would not resent this feeling. James Ledwhistle was still puzzled. For his own part he had no yearning to return to the squalid home he had left at the age of 14. How different he thought was England and its people from such as these Virginians. He thought of the injustice, the filth and the greed of England. Outside the jasmine stirred and there drifted on his senses a lingering perfume. Here it was different: the black-skinned natives with their silky hair and even teeth. It was growing dusky, and faintly on the evening air that was heavy with the scent of flowers came the sound of a voice uplifted in song. The voice was rich and throbbed with feeling.

'Oh, Masser lying on the hard brown cross,
Masser's a-dying and we canna help.

The sky is growing heavy, it is blackening with its loss,
And that dear head is drooping,
It's a-drooping on de cross.'

And then there swelled on the breeze a chorus of other throats:

'Jesus oh Jesus, his head is drooping now,
Jesus, oh Jesus, we canna let yer die.
Oh, Masa, can't you see us crying?
Youse are going upward, youse are lifting up de sky.'

The little room was in darkness now and the flowered curtains swayed gently. Outside there was gathering a little group. Charles caught the gleam of a polished tooth, the white of a glistening eye and a shiny patch on an ebony skin.

'Draw the curtains,' said Fanny sharply, and he did.

CHAPTER 35

Ernest Ledwhistle ushered his son and nephew Charles Coney into the office of the firm of Ledwhistle and Coney. James was aghast at the magnificence of the surroundings. The polished woodwork, the burnished scuttle, the sparkling blackness of the grate and the bubble-like clarity of the windows overlooking the busy street.

Ernest smiled proudly as he said, 'One day, boys, this firm will be as great as my father made his.'

'But sir,' cried Charles, 'did you know the Pentworth lawyers? Were you a relation or an acquaintance of long standing?'

'I have never met them in my life,' was the answer. 'They have completely disappeared too, but they're genuine enough.'

He looked round with a long-drawn-out sigh of expectancy, as if he half hoped to see the disapproving face of Old Jacob Steinhouse staring at him from behind the half-opened door.

Charles sat down at a desk whose top, gleamed and burnished, waited for him. James was not so willing to adapt himself to a desk. He had last night met his grandmother and the incident had both sickened and revolted him. Ernest had not moved into their new house yet, and she sat among her squalid surroundings. They shared their house with a family of 9: a father and 8 children. James remembered going into the back parlour. The dingy light that filtered sluggishly through the window curtains lighted on a cage above a chair. The stench was horrible, and as he gazed with hot eyes the green parrot squawked loudly. And then he had seen his grandmother, Mary Ledwhistle. With what horror he saw the hair-rimmed eyes, the red amber light in those bright pupils, which were sparkling with the very emptiness of their gaze. The lips were drawn up and yellow, her chin low and hanging. Her face was covered in brown freckles and there were large bags under the visionless eyes. Her white hair, grey with dirt, hung round her ears. A drab shawl covered her shoulders and a shapeless colourless sack adorned her body. A disgusting pair of slippers covered her old feet, and her fading hands waved uselessly around in the air.

She saw James but took not the slightest notice of him. 'Folly,' she cackled, her eyes taking on an expression that was truly frightening in their intensity. 'Why, what are you squawking for, you foolish bird? Foolish. Feathers aren't green but feathers are yellow – yellow and blue.' She lapsed into silence and then cried out, gasping, 'Blue, yellow, red, grey and black. Purple too. Foolish, foolish. Wise bird, Polly, Polly.'

Then she seemed to take her grandson in. James shrank back from that stare. Ah, the stare of rotting age. You should see that stare, Richard Soleway, and shrink from it also.

She stopped her restless moving, and her stillness was more terrifying than her motion had been the moment before.

'You're Martin?' she screeched. 'You're Martin, aren't you? Andrew,' she wailed, 'quick, here's Andromikey. Quick, Andrew get the irons. Brand it on his forehead. Brand him, burn him!' Then she cried feverishly, 'It's blue and green and yellow, Francis. How naughty, Polly.'

At that moment Ernest had come into the room and the old woman had stopped her rambling. The old head had gone to one side, and she looked not unlike the green parrot, thought James.

'This is James, Mother,' said Ernest gently.

The old woman became still again and her eyes seemed to glow like the coal in a watchman's shelter. 'Ernest,' she croaked. 'It's that young Andromikey. He's there, can't you see?'

'Come, James,' Ernest had said calmly. 'Her brain has dissolved, poor soul. We will send the servant round with a bottle of port.'

Now James tried to forget her, and settle down to work, for he wanted to make a success of the firm which had landed on their laps, but oh, it was hard to banish his rotting grandmother from his mind, or to forget her strange words.

CHAPTER 36

We are in another part of the land, in the quiet country lane which leads to the gentle graveyard of St Carthage's. A figure is tottering betwixt the hedgerows, his gnarled hand clutching a stout walking-stick. There is something familiar in his gait, something that we have seen before in those rheumy blue eyes that tremble in the breeze blowing in from the sea.

A child comes across a field from the pleasant pinewoods that grow near to the sandhills, running in his rude petticoats, a nosegay of flowers in his chubby fist. His rusticated feet stumble on a piece of broken bottle and he cries out piteously, then hops to the bank of the lane and sits with the blood of his gashed foot mingling with the petals of his apple-blossom sprays.

The old man stumbles towards him. Shudder, reader, for it is none other than Rupert Bigarstaff, and there is no one abroad in the lane but he and the little damaged lad.

'Come unto me, all ye that are heavy laden,' says Bigarstaff and, taking off his befluffed necktie he kneels on his cracking joints to help the boy.

He is not feigning concern. Those eyes brim with moisture and spill down his careworn cheeks.

'Verily,' he says, 'you are sore wounded.'

Comforted, the child skips off and vanishes.

Can this be the Rupert Bigarstaff we used to know and fear? What miracle has wrought the change in him? That child could have breathed his last in that lane. And why is Bigarstaff not dead, stuck fast in that swamp of quicksand so many years before? To understand such a reclamation we must return to the past, to that dreadful moment when the sucking quicksands gave beneath his pounding feet.

CHAPTER 37

He shouted out, a great bellow of fear, and tried to fly out of the bog. But the more he struggled the more he sank, and finally, just as his mouth was on a level with the green slime, his threshing feet touched something. He stood there, hardly daring to breathe, afraid that what was under his boots would shift and he would be utterly lost. He did not doubt that what he perched on was the dead shoulders of the rascally Captain Trevelian. Or perhaps it was wretched, stabbed John Pearson.

Rupert did not pray. It was not in him to do so. But he murmured a line of a hymn that came back to him from his childhood days, and was stilled by it – 'There is a happy land, far, far away.'

Over his head the clouds were black and heavy, and a few spots of rain began to fall, hitting the green surface of the swamp in front of his nose. He could hear shouts in the distance. He wondered if he would die standing up, the skin falling from his face and his skull bleaching under the fierce noonday sun that would continue to blaze in the heavens when he was no more but gone to that happy land. 'You are doomed to hell eternal,' whispered the wind in the trees. 'There is no happy land for the likes of you.'

It was growing dark now, and as he peered ahead wraiths appeared on the edge of the swamp, holding out mocking arms. There was the young girl he had pushed into the murky waters of the Thames, her locks still streaming water, her face contorted with hatred of him. There was the sunny-haired sailor whom he had consigned to a watery grave so long ago, his knuckles still bright with blood from the cruel stamping against the stone. 'Hell eternal,' they echoed, and their voices rose to an eerie scream as the wind gathered gale force. Mercifully, Rupert Bigarstaff lost consciousness.

He had no idea how long it was he had been in a faint, and when he came to for a moment he feared he was indeed in hell. Jagged lightning zipped across the black sky, illuminating the jagged trees and vegetation, and booms of thunder rolled round his head. The very swamp seemed to be bubbling with unrest, as the rain fell in curtains across the island. He felt moisture lilting against his face, filling his ears. He screamed over and over. And then, suddenly, he found himself floating on his back, looking up at a scarlet flash. He was being carried along by some flood. Again he fainted.

When he woke up the second time he was on dry land, firm land, though soggy from the storm, and already dawn was lighting up the area in which he lay. He realised it was the sea that had flooded in pushed by the violence of the storm to cover the swamp and thus free him in a miraculous manner. He knelt and gave thanks to God, a penitent after all the awful years of sin, his heart full of appreciation to the merciful Lord.

A flash of silver caught his eye, somewhere on his left shoulder. He touched it – and it was his own hair, turned snow white in one ghastly night.

CHAPTER 38

He did not find it easy to be good. It was not all plain sailing. Two weeks after his salvation from death, the bodies of four sailors were washed up on the beach, their faces contorted with dire horror. Obviously they had tried to get away on some makeshift raft and had drowned in the storm. When he saw them he felt no pity for them and would have left them where they lay to rot, but then he could not sleep that night and had fearful dreams. He imagined he was again in the swamp, being pulled down, down, and woke with the sweat running into his scared eyes.

In the morning he dug a big hole and buried the sailors and stuck a branch on top of the mound and whispered some rough words over their burial. 'Forgive me, Lord,' he said. 'I cannot turn over a new leaf in a few short weeks. Give me more time.'

Once, he saw a turtle struggling on its back in the heat, its short legs waving incompetently. After many hours it managed to right itself and begin to crawl away in a weakened condition. He was about to run forward and upturn it again when an inner voice warned him of his wrong thinking.

After about a year, or so he took it to be, for time went neither slow nor fast on the island and he had no Big Ben to toll the hours away with its booming notes, he was walking along the causeway when he heard a commotion in a thicket. When he went to investigate he saw a mongoose caught in a sort of trap made by an accidental creeper which had bound the beast to a tree. He was about to walk on and leave it to its long fate when he paused. Was this a test from the Lord? Carefully he unwound the thick creeper and released the mongoose which flapped off at once.

Afterwards, though he dared not admit it out loud, he felt he had been foolish. He should have killed it for fresh meat, if a bird is meat. Then two days later, when he was sitting by his lonely camp-fire, chewing the last of the tobacco which had remained in his pocket when he had first been shipwrecked, a shadow fell across the sand and he saw the mongoose sitting there, looking at him. He said nothing. He gave no sign that he saw the bird. When he lay down to sleep he knew that the thing was still there, eyeing him with bald eyes.

In the morning the bird had gone, and he felt sad. It returned that night and every night for years to come, and though they never spoke Rupert and he became friends, and it was a bad day when the mongoose finally died of old age and was buried under a banyan tree in the far corner of the island. Then he did weep, freely and without shame, and he sang a long hymn in memory of that faithful feathered comrade.

CHAPTER 39

Seven years passed before two brigs sailed towards the island. It was the oil men come to stake their claims and dig for the precious liquid. Fortunately all the oil was on one side of the island and Rupert Bigarstaff was able to avoid such unwanted company. He did not feel he was ready to join the land of the living and clung to his solitude.

Sometimes the oil men thought they glimpsed a shadowy figure watching them from a distance, but though they sent out search parties they never found anyone and the captains wrote in their logs that it was probably just a mirage they had seen.

Only once did Rupert Bigarstaff fall from grace. One night he heard the noise of roistering in the distance, and creeping forward on his belly spied the oil men round their camp-fire, drinking from brandy bottles. His mouth watered and his head swam. If only he could get hold of a drink. He waited till they had fallen into a stupor. Then, flitting like a bat, he swooped down and bore off a bottle in his nerveless fingers.

For two days and nights he drank, and his stomach revolted, for it was a long time since a drop had passed his lips. He was afraid he would shout out and caper in his drunkenness, and he bound his mouth with leaves, and tied himself by the foot to a tree when the bottle was empty. It was a ghastly time for him. He got the shudders and the wraiths of his past misdemeanours returned tenfold and danced round him jeering, pointing their skinny fingers and hinting of a devilish revenge.

When the drink had worn off he made a solemn vow,

kneeling on the sand and clasping his trembling hands. 'I will not touch the stuff again,' he said. 'By all that's holy I am now cured.' After twenty-one years he decided that the time had come for him to return to England. He wanted to die in the pleasant churchyard in which Old Andrew Ledwhistle had long been laid to rest. Accordingly, he gathered his belongings together and cleaned out the leafy bower which had been his home for so long, and lingering for one last moment at the graveside of the mongoose to murmur goodbye, he went across the island to the oil men.

They were very surprised to meet him, and at first thought he was mad because he spoke like the Bible, and had forgotten any other words. After a good wash and a haircut they put him on the next brig and despatched him homewards.

CHAPTER 40

Now, his long voyage was over and he was home. Secure in the knowledge that he had been kind to a fellow human being, even one so small and insignificant as the child with the bloody foot, Rupert Bigarstaff continued on his way down the lane towards the church.

The sun was declining, casting ruddy beams in long flakes on the slumbering graveyard. It was a Norman church, and he thought of those warring men who had come to foreign shores and vanquished the population. Along this quiet lane they had trod their marauding way, spears flashing in the moonlight, elk horns curved in their brutal helmets.

'How long, O Lord,' he murmured. 'How long until men will learn to love each other and forsake their foolish ways?' But answer came there none.

Old Andrew's grave was covered all over with ivy. There was a statue of an angel with a broken wing poised in mid-flight over the puny stretch of tomb.

Rupert Bigarstaff was very tired. He had come a long distance, and the ways of men exhausted him. How easy it would be if he could give up the ghost now on this spot and return to his Maker. He knelt in the grass, his old soul swooning. A little breeze rustled the pine-trees. 'Hell,' they sighed. 'Hell waits.'

'No,' he cried aloud. 'I have paid for my sins. I demand heaven.'

And then a fearful pain grabbed his breast. He turned white and then blue. Was it all a trick? Was he to die cheated of his just reward? Had he sacrificed a life of enjoyment to the outworn story of a man on a cross?

He pitched forward, and as he did so the scarlet flames roared towards his proud soul. God is not mocked, reader! He knows what true repentance is, and what is not.

CHAPTER 41

Richard Soleway walked briskly down the little country lane. He was a heavier, more self-satisfied Richard – or no, perhaps that is being too harsh. Enough to say he was 75 years of age. Side-whiskers did not adorn his face, neither a growth of beard. His eyebrows, far from being bushy, were flat and scanty. A lifting of his bowler would have disclosed as bald a dome as any.

The evening was drawing to a close, and it was a time when darkness wrestled with dusk for the upper hand. It was a time too when country places seem to grow fanciful. Yes, that is the word, fanciful. The dark pines rustled darkly and, in the long rank grass, leaves whispered among themselves. As Richard turned a bend he seemed to go slower, and it was as if a weight was on his legs. Tap, tap, tap went the sharp pointed stick on the gravel, and St Carthage's was before him. Rupert Bigarstaff had found the lonely graveyard vaguely beautiful, but now, as dark shadows played on the great stone walls, it gave an impression of age and faint terror. Through its trees Richard caught the glint of the sea, and the departing sun lying white and wan, after its golden splendour on the edge of it. Softly he trod the grass and entered the yard. He would have strode on but something seemed to arrest him. On he went to the porch and, scarcely breathing, lifted the iron ring on the church door. It swung open and Richard stepped inside. Oh, how desolate it was. The rows and rows of empty pews, the dark curtains drawn before the altar. The sun with its dying palpitation rested heavily on the edge of the window, but had not the strength to peep within. Clank, clank went Soleway's footsteps. No scent of incense was on the air. No jewelled robe, no costly silver candle-holder was there, but God was here for all that and like a child Richard felt hushed and at peace. When the hollow notes of the vicar ring out, and the rows of people in their Sunday best listen with shut hearts, when one looks around to see what Mr Clarkson's niece is wearing and when people walk with pompous steps into their family pew, then Soleway was a stranger to the Lord's house. But now, when the clergyman is absent and no one's chatter distracts him, when he can walk about and need not to his knees bend, then was Richard Soleway at home.

He gazed with clear eyes at the brass cross that swung above him, small and shining. Then, turning, he left and came into the burial ground. All among the ivy he wended his way. As he saw the blackened monument to Andrew Ledwhistle he became aware of the body of a man flung across it. He dropped to one knee as he feverishly turned the old man over. Somehow, even before he saw those eyes, Richard knew who it would be.

'God,' he whispered as he gazed at Rupert Bigarstaff. The white hair hung over the small ears in jagged sprays. The lips were bloodless and the eyes were wide open and oh so cold. Green and cold and dead. Dead and cold and green. With a shudder Richard let the lifeless old frame drop. Stumbling and cursing, he ran to the gate. Sobbing, he wrenched it open and ran down the road. Cold and Green and Dead. Dead . . . Cold. He reached the vicarage path.

When the Reverend Peter Whit opened his door, he was fallen upon almost savagely by Richard Soleway.

'My dear man,' cried Whit, as he was shaken by the lapels till the teeth shook in his head. He was a big man and he was a strong man, but he had to be a clever man to stem Soleway's hysteria.

When he had succeeded in doing so, Soleway was drawn

into the back parlour. Peter Whit was a bachelor, and he lived without any servants. Therefore his room was essentially mannish. A grate held a coal fire, which was crackling and spitting. A cover with a green border hung over the mantelpiece, while above it a three-cornered mirror was fixed. On either side of the grate, high up, was a shelf of books with curtains ready to draw. In front of this was an old armchair, and a desk stood in the corner. On the mantelpiece was a queerly carved group of tiny statues and several Toby jugs. A warm rug lay by the hearth edge, and worn lino covered the rest. Seated on the armchair was a large dog, with ponderous chops. She was evidently a bitch, for a litter of puppies rolled and squeaked over her.

'Now what exactly has startled you, my dear sir?' Whit asked, his keen eyes noting the old man's prosperous appearance. He wondered rather ashamedly if this gentleman could be persuaded to subscribe for the annual school treat for the village boys.

'Out there,' whispered Richard, 'out there.' His hands clutched his coat hem and he shook uncontrollably. 'There's Bigarstaff and his eyes are cold and green out there.'

'Out where, who's out there?'

'Rupert Bigarstaff, in the graveyard and he's dead.'

Whit shot to his feet. 'Where? Quick.'

But Soleway only moaned and cursed. Peter Whit ran out of the house. He did not wait to go round to the gate, but squeezed through the fence. His eyes caught a white face and he knew Richard Soleway had spoken the truth.

CHAPTER 42

Charles Coney held tight to the shoulder of his son Colin.

'This,' he said, 'this is Ernest, son.'

Colin Coney put out his hand.

'How do you do,' he said embarrassedly.

Ernest Ledwhistle, the great-grandson of Andrew Ledwhistle, was not so shy. He was a well-built boy some 13 years of age and free from timidness. 'Hallo,' he said.

'Well,' stammered Charles, 'take your cousin to his room, son.'

When the two had gone he turned to his wife. 'You know,' he said, 'it is a shame, Sally. That boy is hiding his real feelings very well.'

Sally pushed a strand of wavy hair from off her brow. 'I know,' she said softly. 'I only wish James could do the same. He's broken-hearted. Not that I blame him. Elsie was the best wife any man could have.'

Charles sat down and drew out a letter. 'I got a letter from Robert Straffordson this morning,' he said. Seeing his wife's disinterested attitude, he went on: 'You know, Sally, Victor Radenstone's son. Surely you've heard of the great Opium hero?'

Sally put down her knitting. 'What is this leading to, dear?'

Charles looked at her sharply. 'It seems the old man wants me to get in touch with old Jane Ledwhistle.'

'Whatever for?' cried Sally, her hands for once idle in her lap. 'How very comical. How's he getting on in that tropical island of his?'

Charles smiled that slow, slow smile of his. 'As far as I can make out, very well indeed. He's not alone, though, for the miners' families are with him. He was very cut up when Radenstone died. Must have been getting on for 89.'

Sally settled down to her work once more while her husband went outside to talk in the garden with James, his cousin, father of the young Ernest. The letter remained on the chair and Sally gently picked it up. Robert Straffordson, Jane Ledwhistle, Ernest, Old Andrew, Martin Andromikey – what a lot of suffering had been known in Charles's family. His uncle's partner's ruthless ruin of the firm, whose downfall had been the tragic death of Old Andrew. Robert Straffordson, the legless old man who had been the son of the man who had helped to reunite Anna Mansall with her loved one. Jane, the one-time music player, now a silent old woman, sister of Francis, that drunkard and destitute man who ever came to call on Charles for money. Strange that one man could cause such suffering and death!

James came into the room. About 50, he was floridly handsome, and very grey. His face was lined and white, for the death of his wife had shocked him greatly.

'Sorry, Sally,' he said with an effort, as Charles's wife jerked her head up in startled amazement. 'What were you thinking about?'

'About Martin Andromikey,' answered Sally. 'Think of him, James. Think what he did to your father – to Old Andrew and his wife.'

James sank wearily into a chair and pressed the tips of his fingers together. 'Yes,' he said heavily. 'Poor father. But you know, Sally, he's been rewarded now, hasn't he? Think of the firm. Think of it.'

'He paid dearly enough for it, though, didn't he?' put in Sally, her eyes pools of brown.

James passed a hand across his brow. 'Ah well,' he said slowly, 'it's all over now. All the worry and trouble I mean. Still, I'd like to know where Martin is.'

Martin Andromikey himself was still mouldering in a

watery grave, but the bogus Martin, alias Richard Soleway, was seated in an old armchair. He sat gazing into the dying embers that had been a fire and wondered. Now and then a more healthy coal would leap into sudden life and throw the watcher's face into sharp relief.

'Gasper Liverwick,' he murmured, 'Victor Radenstone, Rupert Bigarstaff – they've all gone. And it will be me next.' His head nodded as if stressing the remark.

A coal fell into the grate, dangerously near the carpet, but he paid no heed. His hand went to his pocket bringing forth a key. Slowly he got to his feet and made his way to a cabinet that lay set in the wall. Click, the lock released its steely grip, and the door was open. Putting his hand inside, Richard brought forth a small oblong box. This he also unlocked and drew out an envelope. It was addressed in yellowish writing to Ernest Ledwhistle. He stumbled once more to his chair clasping the confession to him. Once more he took to musing. And as he fell asleep there was a smell of smoke in his nostrils.

Neighbours of Richard Soleway's were rudely awakened that night by the shout of 'Fire'. Standing in their groups, unable to stop its course, they watched the flames spread. And when the morning came, and the charred ashes were blown softly in all directions the unrecognisable body of Richard was found. In his hand was a bundle of ashes. So Richard Soleway perished, and with him his confession.

CHAPTER 43

And now, dear readers, I have reached the end of my story, and all that remains is for me to put down my pen and first think of a suitable patching up. I will now gather the loose threads of my story together and ease your minds on a few things.

First, James Ledwhistle settled down happily secure in the knowledge that his son would enter the business. Jane Ledwhistle received vaguely poetical letters from Robert Straffordson and wondered. Young Ernest grew into a fine young man, and eventually married, later having 5 sturdy sons to his credit. So, to finish on a faintly sad note, let us journey to St Carthage's, where lie the graves of 4 men. The ivy rustles softly, and on the air steals the sound of an organ. And looking upward through the arch of trees, with the sea beyond, we find that there are no clouds in the sky.

The End

18th August 1946   Begun June 1st, 1946